THE POLSKI TRILOGY
A Story of War, Survival, Guilt and Redemption

By

LEON H. GILDIN

DORRANCE PUBLISHING CO
EST. 1920
PITTSBURGH, PENNSYLVANIA 15238

Westhampton Free Library
7 Library Avenue
Westhampton Beach, NY 11978

The contents of this work, including, but not limited to, the accuracy of events, people, and places depicted; opinions expressed; permission to use previously published materials included; and any advice given or actions advocated are solely the responsibility of the author, who assumes all liability for said work and indemnifies the publisher against any claims stemming from publication of the work.

All Rights Reserved
Copyright © 2017 by Leon H. Gildin

No part of this book may be reproduced or transmitted, downloaded, distributed, reverse engineered, or stored in or introduced into any information storage and retrieval system, in any form or by any means, including photocopying and recording, whether electronic or mechanical, now known or hereinafter invented without permission in writing from the publisher.

Dorrance Publishing Co
585 Alpha Drive
Suite 103
Pittsburgh, PA 15238
Visit our website at *www.dorrancebookstore.com*

ISBN: 978-1-4809-5040-5
eISBN: 978-1-4809-5017-7

OTHER BOOKS
BY
LEON H. GILDIN

You Can't Do Business (or Most Anything Else) Without Yiddish
Hippocrene Books, NY, 2000

The Poems of H. Leivick and Others: Yiddish Poetry in Translation
Finishing Line Press, Georgetown, KY, 2015

THE POLSKI TRILOGY

THE POLSKI AFFAIR
Winner of the 2010 INTERNATIONAL BOOK AWARD
for historical fiction
Page 1

THE FAMILY AFFAIR
Page 171

THE FINAL AFFAIR
Page 369

ACKNOWLEDGMENT

The author wishes to express his gratitude to his friend, and former client, Abraham Shulman, for the extensive research done by Mr. Shulman as set forth in his book, THE CASE OF HOTEL POLSKI, written in 1982, published by Holocaust Publications, Inc., and distributed by Schocken Books, Inc.

The novel, THE POLSKI AFFAIR, confirms the existence and location of the Hotel Polski by the picture and map included therein, however, the characters, the dialogue and the situations contained herein are fictitious, but have as their basis the research and the narratives contained in Mr. Shulman's book.

The author is pleased to say that THE POLSKI AFFAIR was well received and well reviewed, translated into Hebrew and sold in Israel and resulted in the author being called upon to speak at book signings, book clubs and other organizational functions.

The audience's request to learn about the future of the characters and their new life caused the author to respond by saying he simply didn't know, but promised that a sequel would follow. And some two years later the second book of the Trilogy was published, THE FAMILY AFFAIR, which was also well received and well reviewed. So just as Mr. Shulman is acknowledged as the inspiration for the first book of the Trilogy, I must acknowledge the inquisitiveness and interest of the readers of the first book as the inspiration for the sequel.

Years went by and the lack of resolution of the issues caused the author to question whether the entire story had been told. So I guess I must acknowledge my own curiosity as to how the story would end that became the basis for the third book, *THE FINAL AFFAIR*.

Leon H. Gildin

DEDICATION

I dedicate this book to my beloved wife, Gloria, who was the first one to read all three in their very rough and primitive form. When she said to me, "You tell one helluva story", I know that no matter how long it would take, I would find an editor, I would find a publisher, and the story would be told. I thank her for her faith, her patience, and her encouragement.

Leon H. Gildin

THE POLSKI AFFAIR

Hotel Polski

CHAPTER I

When World War II ended in 1945, my home was in Tel Aviv. After the partition of Palestine in 1948, I was proud to become a citizen of Israel. Tel Aviv is a beautiful city, especially in the spring. What can be nicer than sitting on your terrace in the warm sun, overlooking the Mediterranean, drinking strong coffee, and reading the newspaper?

When I arrived in Palestine from Warsaw, Poland, I knew no Hebrew other than that contained in a prayer book. I spoke Yiddish, Polish, German, and a little Russian, but no conversational Hebrew. Since this was going to be my new home, my husband and I studied at an Ulpan, an intensive language course, and now, more than 25 years later, we both can read newspapers, novels and magazines in Hebrew.

It is true, as time passes, a life you could never have envisioned, a life you never thought you would have, can help ease the pain of the past. It doesn't go away; it never goes away. You never forget, but you do find a way to live with it, and even this is something you never thought possible.

The Warsaw ghetto was destroyed in 1943, and although Warsaw was officially cleared of its Jewish inhabitants, many thousands of Jews continued to live in Warsaw. They were hidden in the local cemetery, and in basements and attics on the 'Aryan' side. Some gambled with their lives because they possessed "Aryan" looks, and carried false papers, or no papers at all. These people lived in constant terror of being caught by Polish blackmailers called *"shmaltzovniks"*. If they were discovered, they were stripped of all remaining possessions and turned over to the Germans. Their fate was instant death.

My husband, Peter, my first husband, that is, and my two boys did not survive; they were murdered by the Nazis. Believe me, you don't forget. I escaped and lived in the woods with the partisans, but that is a later story. When I returned to Warsaw in 1944, the partisan leader decided that I should go to live in the Jewish cemetery in order to learn, if I could, about the goings on at the Hotel Polski.

Those of us who existed in the cemetery never understood why the Nazis let us live. I guess the dead Jews buried a hundred years before frightened the Nazis more than the living ones. It still defies explanation, even today.

But just surviving in those days defied explanation. How could a person try to understand the way animals think? That's what they were, animals. I don't dignify them by calling them Germans, or "people of culture." They were animals and may their children know the guilt of their parents to the tenth generation.

I never believed I could harbor such hatred. But enough of this bitterness. It's a beautiful day. Let me get back to my newspaper.

When I read an announcement I never expect to read; when I see a name that I never expect to see, and my heart races, and my mind fills with forgotten images, I know it is a special day.

"Chaim, Chaim, come here; look what is in the paper. You will never believe it."

Chaim is the man I have lived with since I arrived in Palestine. We have two children, Sholom and Tamar, both proud citizens of Israel. I call Chaim my husband, though we are not legally married. To us it makes no difference. Chaim's name used to be Itzik. Don't laugh. My name is Anna; it used to be Rosa.

"Chaim, this instant! Stop what you are doing and come see what is in the paper."

Chaim, a good man, had been my neighbor in the cemetery. His wife and four children were packed into cattle cars and taken God-knows-where, may they be with God. He survived because he was outside of the ghetto the day they rounded up his family. Because he still had his strength, he was chosen to do forced labor for the Nazi animals. When he returned, his family was gone. That's what you call luck; good and bad luck at the same time. Isn't that some kind of a joke?

When the ghetto was destroyed, Chaim escaped and found his way into the cemetery. When we met there, we found our way into each other's hearts. We had lost so many loved ones that each of us longed to find someone to whom we could relate, to whom we could cling, someone we understood, and who understood us. I know, every day, how fortunate I am to have found him.

Before the war, Chaim, whose name was Itzik Grynshpan, was a manager of a large men's clothing store. He was in charge of the buying and selling, with five salesmen under him. He was so well liked that many of the customers, the old-timers, insisted that only Chaim fit them and oversee their alterations. When he told me about his work and the name of the store, I laughed and told him that my Peter had bought his clothes there for many years. When I told him Peter's name, he too, laughed. He knew Peter, told me his size, described him, and said that he, personally, had fitted him the last time he'd come in. Then we held each other and cried like children.

When we first arrived in Palestine, Itzik, who was now Chaim Adler, went to work for a British clothing importer, a chain that owned stores in a number of British protectorates. After the UN resolution, we became the State of Israel and the owners of the store wanted out. Chaim fought in the War of Independence, and when, thank God, he came home safely, the store owners made him an offer he could not refuse. He became the owner of the Tel Aviv store.

The business has thrived, and life has been good to us here in Israel. Our children both served in the Army, and, thank God, they both came home safely. Sholom is a university professor and so reminds me of my Peter, not in looks, but in character. He is to be married soon to a beautiful girl, and Chaim and I are overjoyed.

Tamar is married to Avram and Feygl's son, Moshe, and lives on a kibbutz. She has two daughters. Yes, I am a grandmother. I wish they lived closer so we could see them more often, but we are always together on the holidays. Life has truly been good to us here in Israel.

"Nu, Anna, what is the news? Why all the excitement?" asked Chaim, coming onto the terrace.

"Chaim, it's the Hotel Polski. I don't know who is sponsoring it, but there is a reunion of all of the surviving "guests" who stayed there," I told him excitedly.

Chaim sat down, read the announcement and laughed. "Guests! Whoever put that announcement in the paper has a strange sense of humor. Why would we go back there? Who would we know?"

"We would know each other," I replied. "That is where our life began. Who knows who we might meet? Who knows who is still alive? Please, I want so much to go."

"Corpses!" Chaim exploded. "That's what the ad should have said. How dare they call us 'guests'? We were dead people who didn't have the sense to lie down. We lived in a cemetery, and that's where we belonged. That's where you and I met, not at the Hotel Polski. Why should I want to go back there? I don't need the ghetto to remember my wife and children, and I don't need the Hotel Polski..."

He never finished the sentence. His eyes filled with tears, and I rose from my chair taking his face in my hands, quietly kissing his forehead. "It is months away," I said softly. "Let us just think about it."

"In his own way, Chaim is right," I thought to myself.

There is an old expression in Yiddish. "Two corpses are going to dance." That is what we were...corpses who wouldn't lie down. I would not let Chaim see my eyes were welling up with tears

I never knew his family, but I know Chaim's wife and children must have been wonderful. Peter and my boys, they are gone, and I am here. I have Chaim; I have a new family; I have a new life. What did I do to deserve all this? Sometimes even I cannot believe what I did.

"Stop it, Anna," I said to myself with gritted teeth. Then, I wondered, whether the announcement would appear in any newspapers in Germany? Would Googy have the nerve to show up? My God, what am I thinking?

But think about it, I did.

When we arrived in Palestine before the war ended, we were nine "couples," some with children. After we arrived and had gotten settled, we would meet at various gatherings for newly arrived immigrants. We would hug and kiss one another, ask about the children, and promise each other that we would always stay in touch. But promises like that are short lived. Some of the couples broke up; others emigrated to the United States and Canada. Every now and then we would get a card from one of them, but just as our life went on, their lives went on, and before long, they were a memory.

Some of us did stay together, however, and some five years later we were introduced to a newly arrived couple with two boys who had come from a Displaced Persons camp in Europe. Their names were Avram and Feygl. Avram was about Chaim's age and Feygl was a few years younger than I. She had a kind of bubbly personality, liked to chatter, and in conversation mentioned the Hotel Polski.

It turned out that they had both been at the Hotel Polski for no more than a week or two while Chaim and I were there. At that time they were Shloime and Rivka, but now they had new names. Just like Chaim and I. How they got to the Polski and what happened to them after they left is a story for another time. But we became fast friends, and even became family.

Feygl is my daughter's mother-in-law. Sweet Feygl, she is the only one who knows my secrets. I must call her and ask her if she saw the announcement about the reunion.

"Yes, I saw it", Feygl replied.

"I want so much to go", I told her. "If the men won't go, will you come with me?"

"But why are you so anxious to go? " asked Feygl. "Who do you think you will see there? And if you run into someone you know, what will you do, compare horror stories? Anna, I was there, too. Didn't you have enough of that place? Whoever arranged this is sick to think any of us would have any interest in going back."

"But that is where your life began," I protested. "I want to take the children and the grandchildren. Let them know; let them learn who we are, where we came from."

"I'll ask the Prime Minister if he will let Eitan resign his commission and get out of the army so I can take him to a reunion," she laughed. "Don't forget, my boys were there," Feygl replied. "Take it easy and think about it, Anna. Talk to Chaim; I will speak to Avram. I don't know. I just don't know."

I had told Chaim that we should think about it. Now, Feygl tells me that I should think about it. Among the other burdens I carry with me, the Hotel Polski lies like a stone upon my heart. What others think they know they never speak of and what I know I certainly never speak of. But think about it, that I do.

CHAPTER II

My maiden name was Rosa Herzog and I lived a good life in a Jewish suburb of Warsaw. My marriage to Peter Feurmann, a college professor, was a happy one, and our children, who were good students, brought us much pride. I don't mean to boast, but I was considered quite good looking at the time, and on more than one occasion received invitations I would never accept from men I thought were our friends.

But since everything in life is fortuitous, I am thankful for my good looks, yet ashamed of some of my choices. The things you are forced to do that end up saving your live can be unimaginable.

In September, 1940, after the Germans had occupied Warsaw for a little more than a month, they outlined an area that would later become "the ghetto." The Polish residents of the area were told to move out, a high wall was built, and in November 1940, the ghetto was sealed. Shortly thereafter, my husband, my children and I were forced to move there.

Peter had lost his position at the university immediately after the Germans occupied Poland, but he continued to tutor some of his students. However, it had to be done quietly, and with as few people knowing about it as possible. In time, Peter became very depressed, and after we entered the ghetto, he tried to earn a living doing odd jobs.

At about the same time that our family was pushed into the ghetto, our good friends Yossi, Clara and their boys were forced out of their large, impressive home on the outskirts of Warsaw. Yossi had been a well-respected lawyer, but his license to practice had been revoked almost immediately after the Nazis invasion. Their children were close in age to ours, and when the families got together, it was guaranteed that both the children and the adults would have a good time.

I ran into Yossi on the street shortly after our internment and learned that he had been given a custodian's apartment in the basement of a large apartment house some two blocks away from where Peter, the children and I were living. We visited him on one occasion and told him how lucky he was. The apartment had a tiny kitchen and two other small rooms. The children took one room and the adults took the other. They were lucky because they, at least, lived alone, as a family, with no outsiders.

A couple of months after getting settled in the ghetto, I again ran into Yossi, I thought by chance. He said to me, "Rosa, I have been looking for you. I would like you and Peter to come to my apartment this evening at about eight. There is somebody who wants to meet you."

"Meet me?" I questioned. "Why would anyone want to meet me?'

"Don't ask," replied Yossi. "Just come. We still have enough hot water to make a glass of tea. Eight o'clock, don't be late."

At this point, Peter was more fearful than I. He had been a scholar, and his loss of scholarship left him with nothing. When I told him about meeting Yossi and the invitation to his place, Peter did not want to go. He was frightened and suspicious. "Nothing good can come of this," was his reply. "Why would anyone want to meet you? I am sure it is a trap."

"Come on, Peter," I said. "Would Yossi do such a thing to us? He said we would have a glass of tea with him. I wish I had a piece of cake to bring. Don't be so worried."

When I told the children where we were going, they wanted to come and play with Yossi's children, but I told them it was too late and the meeting was for adults only. We kissed the children good night, and at that moment wondered if perhaps Peter was right. Why would anyone want to meet me? We rarely went out at night. My God, if I were arrested, I might never see the children again. What would become of them? Who would care for them?

Peter brought me out of this haze by asking if I was ready. At eight o'clock, we were at Yossi's door.

We received big hugs and kisses from Yossi and Clara, and from the children who came out of their room to greet us. Sitting quietly in the corner of the front room was a little man, poorly dressed, with a big cap on his head, who was smiling and obviously enjoying the expressions of love and good feeling. When the children went back to their room and closed their door, Yossi took Peter and me over to his guest, who rose and was introduced to us as Dovid HaMelech.

"David the King, King David," said Peter. "I never thought I would meet you here in the Warsaw ghetto."

"Why not?" replied Dovid. "It is at times like this that we hope for the Messiah. And when he comes, will not King David be with him?"

At that point, I said, "We could certainly use the Messiah at this time, and King David could certainly accompany him. But the question is, why would the Messiah or King David want to meet Rosa Feurmann?'

There was silence. Clara was pouring tea, and there were some crackers and jam on the table. She invited everyone to sit. When Dovid sat down, he lit a cigarette and shook his head.

"I see that Rosa Feurmann is a no-nonsense lady. I like that. Now let me tell you not only what I know, but why I wanted to meet you. Am I correct in saying that you were a chemistry teacher in the Gymnasium and have a degree in chemistry?'

"If I were not in Yossi and Clara's home, and if I did not believe that you heard that information from them, I would assume you were a Gestapo agent. What does my background matter to you, a complete stranger?" I replied suspiciously.

"To the point," responded Dovid with a smile. "One thing you may be sure of, a Gestapo agent I am not. May name is Dovid, and I am the king because I am the leader of the largest partisan unit that operates in the woods outside of Warsaw. We, the Jews who have survived, the Jews who will not die, need your knowledge and your expertise. We want you to teach us how to make bombs so that we can destroy the rail lines out of Warsaw, and hopefully slow down the coming deportation. Yes, deportation to the death camps. They, the Germans tell us we are being taken to labor camps. But that is a lie. It will start slowly but swell like a flood. The ghetto was only the first step in rounding up the Jews. We need your specific knowledge. Will you help us?"

At this point, Peter stood up. His face was flushed, and his hands were shaking. "She will not help you. How can you have the nerve to ask a mother to endanger not only her own life, but that of her children? If she is captured, we will all be killed. If someone makes a mistake, she could blow herself up. And where do you think she can find the necessary ingredients to make a bomb? Go to Gestapo headquarters and ask for them? You may be Dovid HaMelech, but you are asking too much."

I had to calm Peter down, so I took him by the hand, made him sit down, and said, "Peter, darling Peter, you raise some excellent issues. Let us hear how Dovid responds."

"Peter," said Dovid, "I will be brutally honest with you. I want nothing more than that you and your family survives. But I can all but guarantee that will not happen if we don't have the cooperation of people like Rosa. Yossi will teach her how to get out of Warsaw by use of the sewers and other tunnels under the city. He, or someone from our group, will always accompany her. She will never be in possession of any chemicals or explosives. They will be at what we call our "lab", and if after two or three visits she has taught us well, she will have our thanks and our gratitude, and be done."

Turning to me, he went on. "Yossi will be your contact here in the ghetto. Please talk it over among yourselves and let me have your answer by tomorrow. Yossi knows how to reach me. I must leave now. There are others I must see."

Peter rose and grudgingly shook Dovid's hand. Yossi and Clara gave Dovid a big hug, and he then turned to me saying, "I hope you are with us." Taking a raggedy coat that hung on a rack near the door, Dovid draped it over his shoulders like a cape, turned, waved, and was gone.

We all took our seats and looked at one another. No one spoke. Finally, Peter said, "Rosa, I will not let you do this. You must listen to me."

I did not answer. I looked at Yossi and shrugged as if to say "What should I do?"

Speaking quietly, Yossi said, "I do not like to get in between a husband and wife, and especially not between two of my best and oldest friends. But times have changed. Things are not as they used to be. We are talking about survival. How can anyone refuse to help when people like Dovid and those close to him survive only from day to day? One false step and they are gone. Rosa, they need your knowledge and expertise. I will be with you every step of the way. Peter, trust me. I can promise you that on occasion, there will be an extra loaf of bread, some sugar or some marmalade. Maybe even a chicken. Trust me, Peter, I will try not to let anything happen to Rosa."

And so it was that I became a member of the partisans. Yossi taught me all about the sewers and the tunnels under the city. These were passageways that no one but city workers knew. They were smelly and filthy, but I got out and back to the ghetto every time I was called upon. I had never made a bomb, but I knew enough about the chemical composition that I could teach others to assemble one. I don't know where they got the materials I requested, but they always appeared. I never asked and, truth be told, I never really wanted to know.

Life in the ghetto was not only sad, it was frightening. The life of a Jew meant nothing to the Germans. You could be shot for what they deemed to be an infraction of the rules, or dragged away to Gestapo headquarters and never heard from again.

I, on the other hand, was able to move about with somewhat greater freedom. My contacts on the outside gave me some hope, and as Yossi had promised an extra loaf of bread, on occasion. The chicken I never saw. The children went to whatever school there was in the ghetto and tried to make new friends. It was difficult to explain what became of their friends when, suddenly, one or another might disappear. Although the times were difficult, we tried to maintain some atmosphere of normalcy and family togetherness.

From Yossi I learned that at least two of my bombs had been successful. The resulting toll upon the Jews in the ghetto, however, was horrendous. Upon the repair of the tracks, the deportations increased and I actually heard from others who did not know that I was in any way involved, that they wished the partisans would stop their activities. Life in the ghetto was preferable to death by deportation.

Conditions continued to deteriorate; deportation and death were constant. I was fortunate never to be caught on my trips out of the ghetto, but after one of those trips I returned to find that Peter and the children had been put aboard a transport to the East. At that point, all my hopes and good fortune dissolved, and I was overcome by despair.

I rushed around to friends and neighbors. Perhaps it had been a mistake? Perhaps they were just visiting? I ran to Yossi's apartment. It was vacant. I learned from others in the building that he was arrested by the Gestapo, but no one knew what became of Clara and the children. I was hysterical.

"My Peter, my babies, where are you? I should have been with you." I never got over the feelings of desperation and guilt, wondering why I survived and they didn't.

I refuse to believe that my work with the partisans could have been responsible for the roundup in which Peter and my boys were taken to a death camp. But in all honesty, the idea gnaws away at me. Was I responsible for the murder of my own family?

But survive I did, and I knew I must leave the ghetto at once, never to return. I escaped through the sewers and the tunnels and lived in the woods outside of Warsaw with the partisans until the ghetto was destroyed.

CHAPTER III

The final battle for the Warsaw ghetto started in April, 1943. The Jewish defenders fought heroically but were ultimately no match for the German army. The battle ended and the ghetto was destroyed by the end of April of that year.

Some months later, the partisans, who still operated out of the woods on the outskirts of Warsaw, heard rumors of strange goings-on at the Hotel Polski. The hotel was located at Dluga 29, just outside the ghetto. The hotel's location turned out to be fortuitous in that it was an insignificant hotel with an undistinguished dining room. Had it been located just a few blocks over, it would have been destroyed with the rest of the ghetto. Because it was on the Aryan side, it became a house of death for some, and a house of life for others.

The rumors that reached the partisans were unbelievable and made no sense. It was decided that I should go back to Warsaw to learn what I could. Since there was no place I could present myself openly, Dovid decided that the Jewish cemetery, on the other side of the ghetto from the Hotel Polski, would be the safest place for me to live and to avoid capture. The Jews living in the cemetery with whom the partisans had contact would become my contact.

Before the ghetto was destroyed, the Germans knew the partisans used the sewers and the tunnels as a way to get in and out of the city.

So not only did the partisans have to be careful about the direction they were taking, because the sewers and the tunnels were terribly confusing, but they also had to be on the look-out for the German patrols who were constantly trying to flush them out of the sewers. Once the ghetto was destroyed, there were still occasional German patrols sent to try and find any Jews who might have survived, however, by virtue of the destruction, many of the sewers and tunnels had also been destroyed by the bombing and shelling of the ghetto.

So, back I went through the sewers and tunnels under the city. To me, this time was different. The cemetery was on the opposite side of the ghetto from where I had been forced to live. The partisans supplied me with a new map, went over the details with me on two separate occasions, and showed me which tunnels and which passageways were open and which were closed. The difference was that now I had to navigate my way through by myself.

One of Dovid's men took me to the edge of town, went over the map with me for the third time, and wished me the best of luck. I knew who to contact in the cemetery once I got there, but now I was on my own. About half way through on my way to the cemetery, I heard voices and other noises. I had been assured that the Germans no longer patrolled the sewers, so I had no idea what I was hearing. I was frightened and my heart was pounding. Was I going to be captured and killed in the sewers of Warsaw after having survived this long?

I had no alternative. I had to go the way the map was drawn. I knew of no alternate route, so, I continued on in the direction of the sounds. According to the map, I was getting close to the boundary of where the ghetto had been. The cemetery could not be far.

Moving slowly through the stink of the sewer, I saw what looked like flickering firelight, and getting even closer, in the shadow of the flickering light, I saw four people huddled in blankets, talking Yiddish. My God, Jews were now living in the sewer.

Needless to say, they were startled when I called to them out of the darkness. I reassured them that I was a Jew and was trying to find my way out of the sewer into the cemetery. They were hesitant and distrustful at first, but I sat and talked with them, told of the family I had lost in the ghetto, and they were ultimately convinced that I meant them no harm. It was from these people that I learned that when the weather became too wet or too cold, the people from the cemetery had nowhere else to go other than the sewer. One tragedy heaped upon another.

Living outdoors with the partisans and eating meagerly had caused me to lose weight, but I could hardly believe the sight before me when I finally arrived at the cemetery. The people were completely emaciated – living corpses. But they were Jews, and they were alive. And, as Jews before them had done for two thousand years, they would do what was necessary to stay alive.

I met Itzik on my first night in the cemetery. A group of us huddled around a small fire, shared whatever food there was and talked of our earlier life of those who were no longer here, and people who had not known one another before held each other and wept.

As others drifted off to sleep, Itzik and I stayed together. We talked and cried. We too, ultimately, drifted off to sleep and we became inseparable for the next two weeks.

The rumor heard by the partisans was that if Jews presented themselves at the gates of the Hotel Polski, they would be allowed in, fed, housed, and given a number of as yet unknown benefits. At the same time, if the very same Jew was to appear in the street, he would be shot on sight. Not only was it absurd, it was absolutely unbelievable. Jews from all over Warsaw were being driven through the gates in the false backs of wardrobes or hidden in pickle barrels. Even caskets were suddenly appearing in the yard of the hotel with a live Jew inside. Despite their modes of transport, they brought with them whatever cash or jewelry they possessed, anticipating that funds would be needed to pay for the hotel stay or for other possible necessaries.

I was shocked to learn that when I got to the cemetery these rumors had already spread like wildfire among those living in the cemetery. This made things more complicated. I would now need a plan not only to get out of the cemetery over to the Hotel Polski, but one getting me back with the information I learned as a result of my having been there.

Rather than pretend to be a Jew seeking asylum, I decided to pretend to be a Polish maid who worked at the hotel. Although I was not blonde, I had blue eyes and I could pass as a Gentile. I spoke perfect Polish, and if I could succeed in my efforts to gain admission, I could then move around and learn more about what was actually happening. I also felt that, as a Polish maid, I would be freer to leave and return to the cemetery. Itzik and some others agreed that if I did not return in four days, it would mean that it would be safe for them to come to the hotel. The idea of a warm bed and a hot meal was enough of an incentive. Getting out of the cemetery and being treated, if only for one day, like a human being, was worth the risk.

Those willing to take the risk would have to work out how to get to the hotel without being caught in the streets. Of course, my not returning in four days could also have meant that I was dead or in prison, but the others had begun to look to me as some kind of leader. If after four days it was safe, then that was the plan and they agreed to follow it.

I had enough on my conscience as it was. If I was going to be the cause of someone else's death, I hoped I would be dead first and never know what I had done. I just couldn't bear it.

I listened to all the rumors and discussed my plan with Itzik and some of the others. Although I had little faith in what I was doing, I knew it was time for me to go. Itzik and I held each other in a long embrace, knowing that we might never see each other again should I be caught. We refused to express it and spoke with confidence to one another as I headed out of the cemetery.

I was given a maid's uniform by one of the other women in the cemetery; however, the uniform was small and quite tight across my bosom, so I decided that two open buttons might speed my entrance into the hotel. But this time it was not going to be through the sewers. The German patrols had stopped.

The ghetto was a ghost town. The devastation was unbelievable. Not a single building had been left standing. The streets were covered with rubble from the shelling. There were no Jews to be seen, although every few blocks someone would appear to fly across the street and vanish into the destruction. Where were they going? Who was still alive? But since there were no Jews other than the ghosts that would appear and vanish, there were no Germans. Nevertheless, I crossed the ghetto behind walls and over rubble in an attempt to keep hidden. It took a good half hour, and during that time I thought about the risk I was taking. After all, someone must know who the maids are. What would happen if the Germans questioned me? I had no papers. I could be arrested within five minutes after arriving. I realized that it wasn't much of a plan, but others were depending on me, and it was all we had.

My confidence returned as I made my way out of the ghetto. I found Dluga 29 and waited for the moment when no one appeared to be entering or leaving. The Polish guard out front looked me over pretty well, but when I spoke to him in Polish and told him I was reporting for work, he gave me a big wink and didn't ask for my papers. To my relief, he appeared to be more interested in the two open buttons at the top of my uniform. He let me in without a moment's hesitation. It was almost too easy, and I began to think, "What do I do now?"

The lobby of the hotel was small and extremely busy. I heard laughter and shouting, and saw a Jew arguing with a Gestapo officer who was sitting at a table in the lobby with papers in front of him. How could a Jew have the nerve to argue with a Gestapo officer, I wondered? Wasn't the Jew risking his life?

But, no, the officer answered him in a civil manner, and the Jew, obviously satisfied, simply walked away as the next group of people approached. At times it was a single man or woman who would enter into discussion with the Gestapo officer. At other times it was a group of two or even four people, and in some instances they even had children with them.

People sat on the steps leading up to the rooms. People were going up and some were coming down, some carried valises and others were dressed in their very best; some even dared to wear jewelry.

To my amazement, Jews were being served a meal in the dining room; by their dress, they appeared to be orthodox. I later learned that the kitchen was kosher. My head was spinning - this was madness! I could not believe what I was seeing, nor did I have a plan how I could get word to anyone on the outside about what was taking place here. And if I could get word to them, what would I tell them? I certainly didn't understand it.

I decided to made myself as invisible as possible and just observe, hoping an opportunity would appear so I could get a message to the cemetery, and they, in turn, to the Resistance leaders who had sent me to this madhouse.

I found a broom and a dust pan and walked around as if I were sweeping up after the guests. During the first two days, various Nazi officers appeared and called out people's names. Some groups looked overjoyed that they had been called; others screamed with fright. Nothing made sense. What was going on?

Then the one thing I never expected happened. I looked up and saw George and Krista, one of the few Gentile couples who had been my neighbors in the old neighborhood. They were lovely people, but what were they doing here? Why were they talking to the Gestapo officer? Suddenly, the couple turned from the table where they were standing and looked directly at me. I put my finger to my lips as if to say, "Don't say a word, don't even recognize me." I walked away, but they caught up to me as I was heading for the kitchen.

"Rosa, is it you? Why are you here dressed as a maid?" Krista asked. "Is Peter here, and the children?" The question had never been put to me so directly.

"Peter and the children are dead," I replied. "I am trying to stay alive. Having you recognize me and speak to me does not increase my chances."

These people had been good neighbors. Perhaps they had brought in some people they'd hidden in their basement? I wondered what they were doing here. Dare I ask?

Summoning up my courage, I decided to speak honestly. "Why are you here?" I asked. "Did you bring some Jews you were hiding? Otherwise, why do you not run from this place?"

"I cannot live in this city any longer," George answered. "This is not my Warsaw. If I tell them we are Jews, they will provide us with exit visas to South America. I have money and I will pay them whatever they ask."

The words "exit visas" suddenly made sense. Everybody, George and Krista, all the other guests are trying to buy their way out. That is what they are negotiating.

"I cannot believe what I am hearing," I answered. "At this time in your life, in the life of Poland, in the life of Warsaw, now you want to pretend to be Jewish? How can you trust the Nazis? How do you know they won't take your money and kill you, as they have all the other Jews? You, at least, can live in the Aryan section and survive."

"Oh, Rosa, I know what they have done," Krista responded. "But, do you know who is here? I understand that the head of a Jewish agency is here and is working with the Nazis distributing the visas. The Red Cross knows of this plan, and we have heard that they, too, are helping. This is a real chance for us to get out. One cannot give up hope."

"May God bless both of you," I replied. "I hope you know what you are doing. This is a dangerous game you are playing." I embraced them and walked away. I saw them once more, but we never spoke again. They hung around the hotel for two more days, but from what I learned, they never did get their visas, despite whatever payment they might have made. It was simply too late for them to change their story and claim to be Gentiles.

They had come in claiming to be Jews without papers, and, as such, they were rounded up with all the others who had no papers. When their names were called, I saw the fear on their faces. I later learned that they were taken to Pawiak prison, the only building left standing in the center of the ghetto and a short ride from the Hotel, and were executed as people of no value to the Third Reich.

During my stay at the Hotel Polski, I learned of many Gentile families who came to the hotel to attempt to buy their way out of Poland by pretending to be Jewish. To the best of my knowledge, none were successful. This was not the time to decide that being a Jew was the way to survive.

CHAPTER IV

Four days passed, then five days, and there was no sign of Itzik. Others who had been in the cemetery came to the hotel. How they got there, I do not know, but I recognized them. They did not know me, and I chose not to speak to them. I still felt that the fewer people I talked to, the safer I was, so I never asked about Itzik.

I understood that trying to negotiate for a visa or an exit permit was vital if one wanted to save themselves and their family. Since Jews presented no particular danger to the Germans, they could be shot or deported just as easily as issued an exit permit. It continued to make no sense. What were the Germans accomplishing by selling visas? Was it about the money or was this, in reality, simply another way of rounding up those Jews who were still alive in Warsaw?

There was, however, one Jew at the hotel who seemed to be knowledgeable about what was going on and who was constantly in touch with the Gestapo. He must be the Jewish organizational representative my neighbor had described. Because his wife and two children were with him, I decided to reveal myself to him and see what he could tell me about what was going on.

The opportunity presented itself on my sixth day at the Hotel Polski. I watched as the Jew walked out the back entrance of the hotel, sat on the steps alone, and put his head despairingly in his hands. At that moment, no one else was close enough to hear us. Nevertheless, I spoke softly because I did not want to frighten him, telling him my name, and explaining why I was at the hotel. I then asked him, assuming he was someone who clearly knew what was going on, if he could explain to me what was happening at the hotel.

His answer shocked me. "Firstly, my name is Berel Rabinowitz and I am here because this entire operation was thrown out of the Hotel Royal. Do you know the Hotel Royal?" he asked bitterly.

"Of course," I replied. "It is one of the better hotels in Warsaw. But what were you doing there?"

"The Nazis told Jewish collaborators, of whom there are many, to spread the word that the Gestapo had obtained visas from foreign consulates for entry into neutral countries. For a price, one could get out of Warsaw. The Hotel Royal had no guards and was open to whoever wished to enter. The first to arrive were Jewish citizens of other countries, with their passports. They were promised safe passage out of Poland to a transfer camp for foreign internees in Vittel, in the south of France. Their passage did take place, but not exactly as promised."

I was fascinated. "What happened?" I asked, fearing the worst.

Soon the word got out that a trainload of Jews had been taken in first class style to France. That brought a flood of Jews out of hiding. They flocked to the Royal, and what happened next was inevitable. The hotel was an upper-class hotel for foreign visitors and German officials. Do you think they would tolerate being under the same roof with Jews?"

"No," I agreed. "So what happened then?"

"The entire operation was ordered by the Nazis to move to the Hotel Polski, and that is why I am here."

I sat quietly looking down at the steps and slowly shaking my head, trying to digest what I had just learned and when I looked up, I saw a truck drive into the yard where we were sitting. The driver emerged, unloaded some crates onto the ground, and started to open one of the crates. I wondered why he opened it so cautiously, and was amazed to see, as the crate was dismantled, that it contained human cargo. Men emerged from the crate, and I realized, to my amazement, that the first was a man whom I recognized from the cemetery, and the second to step out of the crate was Itzik! My heart leaped and I wanted to rush to greet him, but I forced myself to hold my feelings in check.

When Itzik saw me, he gave a big smile and walked toward me. As soon as he was within whispering distance, I told him to find a place to rest in the lobby and we would speak later. He just nodded and went in. I was so excited to know that he was safe and, if not safe, at least alive.

"How much does the underground know about all of this?" I asked Berel, my newfound source of information.

"I don't know," he replied, "nor do I know if they wish to be involved or how they can help. I have no idea as to how you can inform them, and I would not leave the hotel if I were you. If you are caught and the Germans discover you are a member of the underground, you will jeopardize the lives of everyone in the hotel."

His works were prophetic. I was never able to get back to the cemetery; I was never able to report on what was going on at the Hotel Polski, and I was literally a prisoner there for the next number of months.

"I gather that the gentleman who just arrived is a friend?" Berel continued.

"Yes," I replied. "We met in the cemetery, and I have become very fond of him. He is a good man, and anything that I can do to help him, I will. But tell me", I continued, "Why are the Nazis engaged in this entire process? There is no logic to it."

He thought this over and then replied, "You ask for logic from people who confine us to a ghetto, shoot us for no reason, bury us in mass graves, and deport us to gas chambers? In truth, the logic escapes me. I have no answers. I don't even know what I am doing here." He stood up, offered his hand to help me up and said, "I think we should go inside. We have been talking long enough."

When I walked in, I saw Itzik sitting on one of the two shabby couches in the lobby. He sat with his head back and his eyes closed, clearly grateful to have found a seat. The couches only accommodated three people each and were separated by an old table with a lamp and an ashtray. Directly across from the couches was the check-in desk, and the Gestapo officer had set up a card table in front of the desk where he and Berel sat when interviewing people. The lobby was in its usual state of confusion, in that there were people who were talking to the German officer while others were talking privately with Berel. Others were sitting on the steps waiting to be assigned a room, and had to keep getting up while others passed them to walk up and down the stairs. There was no way I could sit beside Itzik and have a quiet conversation. So I went to him, knelt before him, and touched his hand. He jerked upright, but when he saw it was me, he smiled and said, "I'm so glad to see you. I have been very worried about you."

"I, too, was worried when you didn't show up. There are others from the cemetery here. I recognized them but didn't ask about you. I didn't know who to trust," I admitted. "But now that you are here, let us find a place where we can talk so I can tell you what I know."

Itzik got up from the couch and followed me as I went around to the rear of the lobby where there was a small telephone room with two booths that could provide a caller some privacy. The room was empty, so we went in, gave each other a quick hug, and sat down on the two hardback chairs.

"What is going on?" Itzik asked. "I see you are still wearing your maid's uniform. Since you never returned to the cemetery, I assume you have never left the hotel, nor ever made contact with the partisans."

"As to what is going on," I replied, "It defies description." I then told him what I had learned while I was at the hotel. "As far as the maid's uniform goes, no one has bothered me while I have been here, but I have done very little maid's work. I still do not understand this business about selling the visas and exit permits. I see people come and go, but I have no idea where they are headed.

Shaking my head, I continued, "And no, I have never left the hotel, nor have I made contact with anyone. I don't know what I would tell them if I did speak with them. Now let me tell you what you must do. Do you have your false papers?"

"Of course," he replied, unsure where I was going with this.

"Then you must go to the desk and register as a hotel guest." I instructed him. "That will give you more status. Whatever will happen from that point on, at least we will be together. Now, we had better get out of this room. I do not want the Gestapo to see us sitting in here too long, or they will suspect we are plotting something."

I turned to him, finally unable to stop myself. "Oh, Itzik," I said, hugging him again, "I am so happy to see you."

We left the telephone room and went to the desk. By this time it was not crowded, and Itzik did not have to wait long to register. The authorities examined his papers, registered him as a guest of the hotel, and told him he would be sharing a room with three other men. I stood nearby and pretended I was dusting the end of the desk, thrilled that Itzik would finally have a real bed to sleep in.

CHAPTER V

When one hungers for a shred of hope, the one thing that can satisfy that hunger is a good rumor. "Did you hear the latest?" "Do you think it can be true?" "Oh, my God, if that is so…"

This particular rumor was that the endlessly benevolent United States of America had passed a law proclaiming that every Polish Jew was, from this day forward, an American citizen and should thus be afforded protection.

"If this is true, then we are saved." If only Dvoira could have lived to see it, Shloime Katz thought to himself.

Shloime had survived the destruction of the Warsaw ghetto by living with his wife, in hiding, on the Aryan side of Warsaw. He was a fine craftsman and worked for a boss who was willing to risk hiding him and his wife in the basement of the shop where they both worked.

On more than one occasion, Shloime had hidden behind a false wall in the basement when Nazi officers came into the shop for gifts to send back to their wives and girlfriends. He got a kick out of the thought that these aristocratic ladies, may they roast in hell, would be wearing a piece of jewelry crafted by a first-class Jewish artist,.

Dvoira's parents were imprisoned in the ghetto. At the beginning of the Occupation, she was able, with false papers, to go back and forth and bring them food and other delicacies she could buy on the Aryan side. Shloime's boss paid him a fair wage for his work, but nowhere near what he would have earned if he had owned his own shop. At least with his salary, he could live better than those in the ghetto.

Their children, two boys, were also in hiding in the Aryan section of Warsaw. Although the parents saw the children on occasion, the fact that the children were getting no schooling and could not visit with other children made life difficult for both the children and the parents.

Dvoira and Shloime would visit the children separately because the people hiding them did not want more than one person to visit at a time. Too many visitors might attract unwanted attention. The children looked forward to their parents' visits. They knew that the visits often included gifts of books, games and even new clothes, and there was always a little slice of cake or chocolates to add sweetness to their difficult life.

Dvoira and Shloime often worried that the children might become ill. It was impossible to get medicine without a prescription, and one could not get a prescription without a doctor's visit — a rare occurrence. Too many people would have to know too many things, and that would endanger not only the children but those who cared for them. The people who chose to hide a Jewish child were considered "blessed," since they were in as much danger as the child.

One day, during a trip to the ghetto to visit her parents, Dvoira was arrested and failed to return to her husband. Shloime never knew what happened and was unable to make any inquiries. Finally, after a month, a postcard was delivered to the shop where Shloime worked. It was from Shloime's mother-in-law, but was addressed to his boss. It was written in Polish but had a German postmark, Bergen-Belsen.

It said that Dvoira was with her parents, and Shloime knew the truth. In his heart, he had said goodbye to Dvoira after her arrest. He and the children cried when he told them that their mama had been arrested. Now, after receiving the postcard, he was sure she was gone for good, but he would never tell the children. He wanted to let them hope they would, someday, when this horror was over, see their mama again.

On occasion, another Jew in hiding on the Aryan side of town would suddenly appear in the shop. Shloime's boss would look the other way, and after a brief conversation, the visitor would leave. It was in this way that Shloime learned of the Hotel Royal and the ability of Jews to purchase visas, exit permits, or other documents that might save their lives.

Since there was little upon which Shloime could spend the money he earned at the shop, he had accumulated many zlotys. Through bribery or other means, he felt he could use this money to buy salvation for himself and his children. And so, with one pocket stuffed with zlotys and another with gold and silver trinkets saved from years of working in the shop (they were imperfect and not saleable – Shloime would never have taken anything from his boss without permission), he dressed in his best Shabbos suit, took false papers describing him as a Polish citizen from a distant city, and headed for the Royal.

No one stopped Shloime in the street, and he arrived at the Hotel Royal without incident. At the door, he was greeted by a uniformed doorman who opened the door for him as if he were an invited guest. Upon entering the lobby, Shloime knew immediately that something was wrong. When Jews were willing to sacrifice their lives to come out of hiding to negotiate for exit permits, the lobby should be full of people. There should be noise; there should be shouting, pushing, and God knows what else.

But the lobby of the Hotel Royal was quiet and sedate; guests were having tea served to them; Nazi officers in shiny black boots were sitting and smoking and Shloime felt bewildered, frightened and desolate. "Is it too late?" He wondered. "Are my children and I doomed to spend our lives in hiding? Will this nightmare ever end?"

While standing and taking all of this in, a bellboy approached Shloime and asked if he could be of help. With fear in his voice, Shloime replied, "This is not what I expected."

"You are a Jew?" the bellboy asked.

Shloime, not knowing how to respond, simply nodded.

"Go to the Hotel Polski on Dluga Street," the bellboy whispered and turned away.

Relived not to have been arrested, Shloime left the Royal quickly and headed for the Hotel Polski. Boarding a streetcar would be safer, because in the street he could be stopped, but the Germans rarely rode the streetcars. Besides, this would give him a chance to rest and to think about what might lie ahead. Traveling through Warsaw, the Warsaw that Shloime loved, he could not believe that this part of the city was still so beautiful, with parks and cafes. At the same time, a large portion of the city served as a death camp for many of its citizens.

He jumped off the street car a block from the hotel. At the front gate, a doorman Shloime thought might have been a Jew asked, "Can I help you?"

"I am a guest," Shloime answered. The doorman nodded and silently opened the door for him.

As quiet and sedate as the Hotel Royal had been, the Hotel Polski was the exact opposite. The lobby was noisy and tumultuous, with people rushing around, and many who were obviously Jews were standing, sitting, sleeping, and arguing amongst themselves, and one Gestapo officer who listened made notes and accepted money.

Shloime decided to watch the passing scene for a while, paying attention to who, amongst the Jews, he should approach. It did not take long for Shloime to make up his mind. When he saw the Gestapo officers call over a particular man, obviously a Jew, on more than one occasion for a brief meeting, or to act as an interpreter when a Jew could not speak German, Shloime decided that he was the person who could be of most help.

A group of Jews now surrounded this man and kept him engaged for what, to Shloime, seemed like an eternity. When the meeting broke up, Shloime went over to him and came right to the point. "You appear to me to be a person who is in charge here."

The gentleman replied, "The Gestapo is in charge here."

Feeling that perhaps he had come on too strong, Shloime said, "Yes, I understand that, but I was hoping that you could help me."

"What can I do for you?" asked the gentleman.

"I have zlotys, gold, and silver. I wish to buy necessary documents, a visa perhaps, to a country that would admit me as a refugee."

"Go register as a guest of the hotel and then come back and see me. I will then see what I can do for you."

"My wife is dead, but I have two boys who are in hiding on the Aryan side," Shloime whispered. "Shall I send for them?"

"All decisions will be made after I see what I can do for you and how much it will cost. Now go do as you were instructed." the man told him.

"Thank you, sir. You have saved my life."

"Not so fast," cautioned his potential savior. "Don't call me 'Sir.' My name is Berel Rabinowitz, and I am just a Jew trying to stay alive, as are you. And don't thank me yet. If you are out of here and alive a year from now, then you can thank me," Berel said gently.

Shloime ran to the desk, waited in line, registered as a guest, and was given a bed in which he knew he would never sleep. He then sought out his newfound friend, engaged in a second whispered conversation, and finally left the hotel to return to the jewelry shop.

The trip back was also, fortunately, without incident. Shloime's boss was glad to see him, but told him how worried he had been when he had not heard from him all day. Faced with the problem of how much to reveal to his boss, Shloime made a sudden decision. He knew his boss was a righteous person and would not betray him, so Shloime took a risk and told him the entire story of the day's events.

To his relief, his response was just as Shloime had expected. "May you and the boys be safe, and may God look after you. And remember, you are always welcome here."

Shloime embraced his boss, and with tears in his eyes said, "When I leave here, I will never return. Either I will make it, or I will be dead."

Mournfully shaking his head, his boss replied, "What a crazy world we live in."

CHAPTER VI

As instructed, Shloime went back to the Hotel Polski in two days and met with Berel.

"I have arranged for you and your boys to get visas to Uruguay. However, there will be a woman traveling with you who will be your 'wife' and the boys' 'mother'", said Berel.

"How can that be?" asked Shloime. "I assume that my wife is dead. The boys don't know that, but..."

"Don't ask," Berel interrupted. "These are the arrangements that have been made and that must be adhered to. I would also suggest that you do not leave the hotel. Can you get word to your boys and have them join you here?"

Shloime indicated such a thing would be impossible. He would have to go back, pick up the boys, and return to the hotel.

"That presents a problem," said Berel. "You must pay me now for the arrangements I have made, but if you do not return in time, it will all be for nothing. You must be here when the next roundup is called, and I don't know when that will be."

"I will be back," said Shloime. "I promise you. I will be back with the boys by this evening." After the financial arrangements were seen to, Shloime was left with only a few zlotys, but he still had the gold and silver which he hoped to convert if needed.

Shloime went to see his boss and told him that the arrangements had been made. His boss embraced Shloime with great warmth and each shed a tear. Shloime then packed a valise with as many clothes as he could squeeze into it and went to pick up his boys. Ernst, the eldest, was eight years old and was thrilled to see his father for an unexpected visit. Shloime told the people who had cared for Ernst that he was taking him away but chose not to provide any further details. He helped his son pack a small valise. The people who cared for Ernst hugged and kissed him and wished him well. As nervous as Shloime was about being in the street with Ernst, that is how excited Ernst was about going somewhere new with his father.

The next stop was some five blocks away where Moishele, who was four years old, was being cared for by a lovely couple. They were surprised by Shloime's visit in that it was unexpected, and particularly surprised to see him accompanied by Ernst. They knew that Moishele had an older brother, but had never met him. The couple was even more surprised and shocked to learn that Shloime was taking both boys with him. Ernst and Moishele were happy to see each other. They had not played together for almost a year. As overjoyed as the children were to be together again and with their papa, that is how nervous and tense Shloime was.

The people who had cared for Moishele gave each of the boys a piece of cake while Shloime packed Moishele's things. He then sat down with the boys and told them they were going to ride on the street car and that if they should have to say anything to one another, they should speak only in Polish. "If anyone speaks to you, do not answer; let papa answer for you," Shloime cautioned them.

Shloime kissed Moishele's caretakers and thanked them again and again. They wished him the best. "Take care of the boys; be careful in the street, and God bless all of you."

As they went out into the street with their valises, the boys were excited by the adventure, while Shloime's heart pounded in his chest. They got on the street car which fortunately was quite crowded with people going home from work, got off a few blocks away from the hotel, and walked the last few blocks. Shloime was sweating from nervousness and from having to carry all the valises, but they arrived at the hotel without incident. By early evening, Shloime was back with the two boys, as he had promised Berel.

The room that Berel had arranged for Shloime had two beds, but one was occupied by another man. Shloime gave the boys his bed to sleep in and napped on the couch in the lobby. The very presence of German soldiers and Gestapo officers in the same lobby made him crazy. He worried that at any minute he would be arrested, and when the boys came down the next morning, their papa would be gone.

"What have I done?" he agonized. He spent the night weeping and eventually dropped off to sleep out of sheer exhaustion.

For the first time in more than a year, Shloime had breakfast with his sons. Fear tightened their faces, for sitting at the next table was a Gestapo officer. To quell their panic, Shloime spoke quietly to his sons, trying to reassure them that they had nothing to fear. He himself did not believe it, but he had to let them know that he had the situation under control.

At first Ernst said nothing, but when he spoke it was with anger and resentment. "Papa, we were safe where we were," he said. "Why did you have to bring us here?"

Without mentioning the woman they would soon meet who would play a vital role in their survival, Shloime tried to explain that he had purchased visas for all of them to Uruguay, and they would soon be leaving this terrifying place.

"Don't be afraid," he told them. "The man with whom I have made these arrangements assured me that no harm will come to us as long as we are here. Don't you trust your papa? Would I let anything happen to you? Eat your breakfast and give thanks; we are together for the first time in over a year. This is a celebration for us."

At this point, Moishele started to cry. "What is wrong, Moishele?" asked Shloime.

"If this is a celebration, then mama should be here," said the little one.

At that very moment, Berel, accompanied by a pleasant-looking younger woman entered the dining room and came to the table where Shloime and the boys were sitting. He pulled up two empty chairs from an adjoining table, and said without ceremony, "Shloime, this is Rivka Bronstein. She will be accompanying you on your trip as your wife and as the mother of the boys.

He then took out exit permits and travel documents from his pocket along with a photo showing a husband and wife with two boys. The photo bore little resemblance to those at the table, but no one said a word. "These are the travel documents. They are valid and will do the job. No questions are to be asked," instructed Berel.

"The most important part of this game that you will be playing," he went on, "is that you are no longer Shloime and Rivka; you are now Avram and Feygl. Those are your new names and the names you must all remember. They correspond to your visa and exit permits, and no mistakes will be tolerated."

"Boys", he said, addressing the children, "your names are the same, the documents simply say 'two children, male', but you must remember that your mother and father are now Avram and Feygl."

Turning back to Shloime, Berel said, "Forget Katz and Bronstein. Learn your new last name, Grossman, and remember it as if your life depended on it, because it does. You will stay in the hotel until your names are called, and you will then be taken to Vittel in France. This is a resort area. You will be well treated there. You will then be transported to a port city for the trip to Uruguay. I wish you all the best of luck."

He rose from the table, shook hands with Shloime and Rivka and left the dining room. No one said a word. Finally, Moishele began to sob quietly.

"Rivka, no, I mean Feygl, these are my boys. The older one is Ernst and the little one is Moishele. And I guess I am Avram."

Feygl smiled. "I am so happy to meet all of you. But, Moishele, why are you crying?" she asked gently.

"You are not my mama," said Moishele. "Papa, where is mama? I want my real mama," he cried.

"I do, too," said Avram, "And as soon as we get settled, we will try to find her. I promise you. But for now, Feygl will be traveling with us and we must be nice to her. Then you will see that only good things will happen from now on."

Feygl went around the table and picked up Moishele. The boy was so in need of comfort that he held on to her for dear life. She reached over and took Ernst by the had and said, "Come, let us get out of the dining room and see where we will be staying."

As they were leaving, Berel returned with a key in his hand. "I have gotten you a new room with two beds. The children will sleep in one and the two of you in the other. Go gather your things and stay close to the lobby until you hear your names called." Quietly, under his breath, he looked at them and said, "May God be with you."

For two days, the children played quietly in their room. Avram and Feygl sat and talked about their lives before the coming of the Nazis. For as quiet and controlled as Feygl seemed to be, she would have had reason to be a raving lunatic considering what she and her family had gone through. The story she told was brutal.

Rivka, now Feygl, had come from a large family. She was twenty-four and unmarried. She had two older brothers, two sisters-in-law, two younger sisters, and the baby was a boy. The family was orthodox, and her father's beard, his pride, ultimately caused his death. When brought to the ghetto, her family was put in two rooms in a larger apartment, which already had three other families living in it. Against the wishes of the father, Rivka and her brothers became active in the Resistance, attempting to make contact with sources who would supply them with small arms. Each day when they went out, no one knew with any certainty who would come back. They did know that, if caught, it would mean death.

It was never anticipated, however, that the first to die would be her father, a quiet and saintly man.

"On his way to synagogue one morning" Feygl said, "He was surrounded by a group of young German soldiers."

"Rabbi, Rabbi," they taunted him. "Show us how a Rabbi dances."

"I am not a Rabbi and I will show you nothing", replied the old man with a defiance no one knew he possessed. "I am on my way to the synagogue, and I will even pray for your miserable souls." Papa spoke German, and the soldiers laughed at his response."

"By this time a crowd had gathered, but the soldiers were without shame or fear. Taking out his bayonet, one of the soldiers grabbed the old man's beard and said, "If you are not a Rabbi, then why do you need this beard? Only Rabbis need a beard."

"With a strength that must have come only from God," Feygl continued, "Papa raised his knee and kicked the German soldier in the groin. The soldier fell back, dropped the bayonet, grabbed himself by the groin with one hand, and with the other took out his pistol and shouted, "You dirty Jew bastard!" He shot Papa dead right there in the street. We learned all of this a few minutes later when someone in the crowd who knew us came to our apartment and told us what had happened."

"The reaction to Papa's death was strange. "Mama screamed when she heard the news, and then sat down and wept. My brothers rushed out into the street to try and retrieve the body, but it was already gone. Dead bodies in the ghetto were no novelty. The Germans picked them up in wagons, and God knows where they were dumped. We could not even give Papa a decent Jewish burial. So, I suppose, you can say that the reaction to Papa's death by my brothers and myself was, obviously, sadness, but even greater was the bitterness and the hatred."

"Within a week, the destruction of the ghetto began. My brothers and I took our assigned places, and for two weeks we were successful in our efforts. By the third week, the Germans had brought in the heavy artillery, and we were no match for their weapons. We saw our family whenever we could, but one night when I went back to them, I found that the house had been blown to bits. My mother, my baby sister and brother, my brothers' wives, all were dead. I thought I knew where I could find my brothers, but when I went to their station I learned from the person in charge that they had both been killed that night."

"I still had my weapon with me and I made up my mind that I was not going to die. In one night, I had lost my entire family to these animals. I knew my way in and out of the ghetto, but because of the destruction, I was not sure of anything. I decided to hide for the rest of the night, and I would get out once I could see where I was going. So, I curled up in the basement of one of the buildings that had been destroyed, did what I could to shut out the world around me, and swore to myself that if I got out of this war alive, I would marry and have lots of children and name them after my parents and my brothers and sisters. That is how I would honor those whom I lost, all in one night. They deserved that honor."

"The next morning I made my way to the cemetery. The ghetto fight lasted for another few days, and then it was over. More people came to the cemetery, and I remained there for two months until I was told about the Hotel Polski. I was starving and I heard you could get a free meal. I was determined to get here; I knew nothing else about this place."

"I had no papers, I had no money, and if it weren't for Berel, I would never have met you. In the two weeks I have been here, I stuffed myself and gained more than five pounds."

"Avram, what will become of us?"

By the third day, the children were growing restless; Avram and Feygl did what they could to entertain them. They let them play with some other children on the same floor of the hotel, and then tried to get some books for them to read. They even started a little school for the children.

After about a week, Avram went to seek out Berel to see if he had any news about what was happening. To his surprise, he learned that Berel and his family had left a day or so earlier for an unknown destination.

He also learned that the commandant was no longer there and a new Gestapo officer had been put in charge. Avram's heart sank... this did not bode well for him and his family. His deal had been made with Berel and the commandant who was then in charge. Would a new officer honor the commitment?

Avram told Feygl of his concerns, but hid his worries from the children. He insisted that all was well and that they would soon be leaving.

The newly formed Grossman family seemed to be as close-knit as one could expect under the circumstances. After waiting for two nerve-racking weeks, their names were called, and they were told, along with others, to be ready at three the next morning. Their journey to freedom was to begin.

At three A.M. the following day, German soldiers lined up the Grossmans, twenty-five other couples, and some ten children in the lobby. The doors to the hotel were opened and the "guests" were ushered into a convoy of army trucks. Avram said nothing because he did not want to frighten the children, but this was not the way he imagined they would be taken to Vittel. Perhaps the trucks were taking them to the railway station or to a bus depot where they would travel to France by bus or by train.

The trucks were loaded and the convoy started to move. A canvas flap had been tied down at the back of the truck so the passengers could see little. As a result, silence blanketed the convoy during the short trip.

When the trucks stopped and the canvas was removed, Avram could see that the trucks were surrounded by German soldiers with rifles at the ready. They were told to disembark, and it was only then that the adults all realized they had been taken to Pawiak prison.

CHAPTER VII

I never signed up to obtain an exit permit. I continued to play the role of the Polish maid which gave me the opportunity to spend quiet time with Itzik. Although there was always nervous excitement in the lobby of the Hotel Polski, the buying, the selling, the transporting, the calling of names, all slowed down. Since neither Itzik nor I understood the real reason for why all of this was taking place, we also failed to understand why it had slowed down.

The one fear I had was that Itzik would be called and would have to leave without either of us knowing where he was going or why. He had false papers, but no money, so he had no way of buying one of the more expensive visas. No one really knew what happened to those people who could neither pay for, nor bribe the authorities, for an exit permit.

Itzik and I had grown close emotionally, and we told each other how we wished we could be together, alone for a night, or at least for a couple of hours. Itzik's room was never without someone in it and I had no room. A number of the men who had originally been in Itzik's room had already left and been replaced by others. I was sleeping in the maid's quarters, and there certainly was no privacy there.

Constantly on my mind was the need to get information to the underground and find out what they knew or understood about what was taking place at the Hotel Polski. More importantly, why were the

Germans doing this and why was a Jewish organizational representative participating. I finally decided that I would pretend to go home, leave the hotel, and report back to my contacts in the cemetery. Just as I was fearful of Itzik being called away, so Itzik was fearful that if I left the hotel he would never see me again. We finally made peace with the idea that I would leave the following evening and try to return by morning.

When that evening came, I said goodbye to Itzik, made him promise that he would not worry, and reassured him that I would be back in the morning. He stood in the rear of the lobby as I headed towards the door, when the Gestapo colonel in charge of the operations at the hotel, approached me and asked, "Where are you going, Fraulein?" Although I understood him perfectly I continued my role playing and replied in Polish, "I do not speak German. I am a Polish maid." The colonel smiled, took me by the arm, and led me back into the lobby, to the desk where Berel was sitting. Berel stood up as a sign of respect to the colonel and said, "What can I do for you, sir?"

"This woman claims she speaks no German. Ask her where she is going." Berel, knowing full well that I understood German perfectly, nevertheless spoke Polish to me. "The colonel would like to know where you are going."

"I am a Polish maid. My shift is over and I am going home," I replied in Polish, which Berel then translated into German.

"Then ask her why she has been here for a number of weeks and has never left the hotel before?" Berel translated and I responded, "Because it has been very busy, I had been asked to stay, and now things appear to be a bit quieter, so, I thought I could go home."

"Isn't it wonderful to have an answer for everything," said the colonel, sarcastically. Speaking to both Berel and me he went on to say, "Well I think she is Jewish, pretending to be a maid, and I think she is a spy for the underground. Since it is my opinion that counts," he said, addressing me directly, "you can either follow my instructions, or I can have you and your gentleman friend who is lurking in the shadows arrested, taken to Pawiak and shot. Which shall it be?"

Left with no alternative, and speaking in German, I said, "I shall be happy to follow your instructions, colonel."

Turning to Berel, the colonel said, "I thank you for your translation services even though they weren't necessary. You knew that, didn't you?" He inquired of Berel.

Shifting from one foot to the other and failing to look at the colonel, Berel said nothing hoping the colonel would let it go. But it was not to be.

"Do not attempt to deceive me again, Mr. Rabinowitz", said the colonel in a stern voice, as he turned to speak to Rosa, but in obviously growing anger, turned back to Berel. "Remember, you and your wife are here under special dispensation of the German government." And with a sneer, he went on, "Perhaps you are really a spy as well, or a member of the OSS acting as a social worker. Your behavior makes me believe that. Trying to deceive me makes me think that possibly you are the one who should be sent to Pawiak along with your co-conspirator and her gentlemen friend."

"Please sir", said Berel, and before he could say another word, the colonel interrupted him, and shaking his head as if he knew he had frightened Berel enough, said in a sarcastic tone, "You may now return to whatever you were doing", as he turned to Rosa.

Taking me by the arm, the colonel walked over to the main desk in the lobby and asked me, "Since you pretend to be a maid, do you have a pass key to the rooms?"

"No," I replied.

Turning to the clerk he said, "Give this woman a key to my suite," which the clerk did at once. Again taking me by the arm, he walked me to the elevator, past Itzik, who stood as if chiseled in marble. At the elevator, the colonel said, "I am Colonel Peter Hauptmann, and I am in charge of the operations in this place. Go to my suite, the number is on the key. Shower and clean yourself up. You will find some make up in the medicine cabinet, and in one of the closets you will find both men's and women's clothes. Take off the silly, ill fitting thing you are wearing and find a dress that fits you. If it has holes in it, you will find a needle and thread in one of the drawers. Fix it and meet me in the dining room in one hour for dinner. From this point on, you will be my personal servant and companion. Do not worry. No harm will befall your gentleman friend."

I looked at him without saying a word. The elevator door opened and the colonel turned on his heel and walked away. I entered the elevator, and went to the fourth floor, and found the colonel's suite. It was not luxurious; nothing in the hotel was. It consisted of a living room with a couch, two overstuffed chairs, and tables at either end of the couch with lamps, a coffee table, and in the corner a large armoire. The bedroom had a double bed, end tables and lamps, a dresser, and in one of the corners another large armoire. Both rooms had old, worn rugs. The bathroom was small but adequate, and quite clean. There were fresh towels and soap. The chambermaids did their best for the colonel, I thought.

Needless to say, I knew who the colonel was. A tall, athletic looking man, quite handsome, he could be a poster boy for the S.S. in his dress uniform and boots. Although he was in charge, his orders were given quietly, in an almost bored manner. I think this quiet approach to his duties frightened people more than if he had shouted and acted like those officers who were in charge of troops. He had never been heard to threaten anyone; his orders were obeyed. Threats were unnecessary.

My thoughts were racing. I have been here for weeks. Why has he chosen me now? He never even spoke to me before tonight. How did he know I was about to leave? He stopped me at the door. Perhaps if I had left when he was in his office, he would not have seen me. This is crazy. I have only an hour to get ready. Is this good luck or bad? Where will this lead? What will become of me, and what will become of Itzik? Will we be separated and never see each other again? The colonel's name is Peter. My beautiful Peter is gone and the colonel is trying to take his place. What are my duties as his servant and companion? My God, will he try to make love to me? What will I do?

Stop it, stop it, Rosa. Get a hold of yourself. You must be ready to meet him in one hour. Rosa Feurmann is going on a date with Gestapo colonel, Peter Hauptmann. If I survive this, I will be crazy. Poor Itzik, how can he live his life with a crazy woman after all he has been through? It is not fair to him. I must make an opportunity to talk to him and to explain what is happening. But now, I must pick out a dress.

Going to the armoire in the bedroom, I found it to contain nothing but uniforms, shirts and belts that belonged to the colonel. In the living room armoire, I found the clothes he had spoken of and I chose a dress. There was a hole in it, and in the dresser in the bedroom I found a needle and thread. While repairing the damage I realized that this dress must have been worn by a woman who was executed. They saved the clothing of the wealthier victims and gave them to the officers. First nothing was happening, and now everything is happening. My head was spinning! The label in this dress was from a French atelier. I will wear a dead woman's dress with a French designer label and have dinner with a Gestapo colonel. I am already crazy and dinner has not yet been served. My Peter is gone; my boys are gone. I should have let them execute me and then I would be with my family.

I finished sewing, stripped off all my clothes, washed my underclothes and hung them to dry, and stepped into a hot shower. I washed my hair and soaped my body. By my estimate, I had no more than another thirty minutes to get ready. After rinsing myself off, I got out of the shower, towel dried my hair, found lipstick and blush in the medicine cabinet, put on my underclothes which were still damp but I knew they would dry by the heat of my body, put on my new designer dress, combed my hair, and was ready. Crazy or not, I looked at myself in the mirror - I was still a terribly attractive woman.

I took the elevator to the lobby and saw Itzik waiting on one of the couches. I walked by mouthing to him, "Not now," and walked into the dining room. When I appeared at the entrance, all conversation stopped. The colonel was at the bar at the far end of the room with a drink in his had. The bartender nodded in the direction of the door, and the colonel turned. Upon seeing me, even he was overwhelmed. He came to the entrance, took me by the arm and steered me to his especially reserved table. He held the chair for me, and as we sat, a new life began for Rosa Feurmann.

CHAPTER VIII

"You are a very beautiful woman," said the colonel. "I see you followed my instructions and I am pleased. Now, may I know your name?"

"Rosa Feurmann," I replied. "My husband was Peter Feurmann, professor of European history."

"Was?" inquired the colonel. "Is he not with you? The gentleman with whom you spend so much time is not your husband?" Without waiting for an answer, he went on, "How interesting, both your husband and I are named Peter."

"My Peter," I replied bitterly, "is hopefully with God, as are my children, courtesy of the German government. The gentleman to whom you refer," I went on, "lost his wife and his children in the same way, and we have naturally become close. We spend our time speaking of atrocities, and we find comfort in each other. I am very fond of him, as he is of me."

Nodding his head in understanding, and about to speak, the colonel remained silent as the waiter approached the table. The colonel ordered for us both and asked that a bottle of wine be brought to the table. I immediately became fearful. Would the wine make me drunk? I had not had any alcohol in well over a year. What if the colonel became inebriated and tried to take advantage of me?

"Thank you, colonel, but I do not drink," I said firmly.

"Come, now," said the colonel. "I know there are many holidays and festivals at which Jewish people consume wine. I am sure you are not a stranger to these celebrations. Let us make believe that our being together this evening is something to celebrate." His voice softened. "I am sorry for your loss, Rosa. It would be inappropriate for me to lecture you on the evils of war. But orders must be obeyed, no matter how distasteful they may be. Let us try and enjoy our time together and not speak of this again. Ah, here is the wine. Let the waiter pour a glass for you."

"My God, what is going on?" I asked myself. How can I get away from this man and save both myself and Itzik? Perhaps I can appeal to him; he seems like a reasonable person. But if I anger him, I might be killed and this is only my first night with him. I had better play it out and try to learn more. After all, not every woman, and certainly not every Jewish woman, can have dinner with a Gestapo colonel. There is no question in my mind; I am going crazy, but oh, this wine is good.

I found the dinner merely adequate, and the colonel seemed to agree, complaining often about what a second-rate dining experience this was. He even seemed to resent having to eat here so often. Despite his annoyance, he kept trying to make conversation with me, but the wine was making me feel disoriented. I realized even then that I wasn't sure how relevant my answers were to the colonel's questions.

Somehow, I got through the dinner without making a complete fool of myself. After the dishes were removed from the table, the colonel leaned over and offered me a cigarette. I accepted.

At one point during dinner, I saw Itzik and some other men come into the dining room and sit down for a meal. As a registered guest of the hotel, they were entitled to eat with the others, but throughout the meal Itzik never took his eyes off me. I tried not to make eye contact with Itzik because I feared it would anger the colonel. If he wasn't already aware of it, the colonel didn't have to know that both he and I were being closely observed.

When he had finished the bottle of wine and his cigarette, the colonel whispered, "Now go to my suite and wait for me." I felt my cheeks flame, but I dutifully rose from the table, walked past Itzik, shrugging my shoulders as if to say, "Don't ask me what's going on!"

Taking the elevator up to the fourth floor, I got off and walked the length of the corridor. As I turned the corner, I saw one of the chambermaids coming out of what appeared to be the colonel's suite. She glared at me with such hatred that I literally was stopped in my tracks.

"Whore!" the chambermaid hissed in Polish. Apparently, word about my new relationship had already leaked out.

"My God," I thought. So this is what it feels like to be branded a collaborator. I did not ask for this. Why is this happening to me? All I want to do is to stay alive. Itzik, what should I do? I will tell the colonel, that's what I'll do. How low am I sinking if a Polish chambermaid can call me a whore? If the colonel has any humanity, he will release me from this burden. A Jewish woman simply cannot be the companion of a Gestapo colonel.

Yes she can if she is a whore. The dresses in the armoire; the makeup in the medicine cabinet. I have seen women come in and go up in the elevator. Now I realize who they were. Whores going to the colonel's suite. He rewards them with a new dress or some makeup. They sew up the holes. To the chambermaid I am another one of those women. I am a whore. But then they leave with their dresses and their makeup. Will I be allowed to leave? Will he really protect Itzik?

I stopped, realizing that I was living in a new world. If I offended or resisted this man, he could send me to Pawiak for execution and Itzik as well. Trembling now, I walked shakily into the suite and collapsed to my knees in the living room. "Oh, Peter, my Peter, tell me what to do," I cried in despair.

"When you call out to Peter and ask him what to do, I assume you are not calling out to me," a voice said softly. The colonel had quietly entered the suite without my hearing him, and I felt trapped as never before.

"Come now, Rosa, do not be so frightened," he soothed, offering his hand to help me from my knees. "Do you think I am such a terrible person?"

It was the humanity in his voice that pushed me over the edge. I broke down completely, trying to talk through my tears. "No, colonel, you are not a terrible person," I assured him, trying to remain calm. "But I can never call you 'Peter'."

The commandant was watching me carefully, and said nothing.

I could no longer restrain myself. "That man was my husband, the father of my children, and you and your people murdered them all."

Still he said nothing. I began to collect my wits, and turned to him with a trace of a smile. "Is there no other name I can call you?"

Laughing, relieved, he embraced me and asked, "May I tell you a secret?"

I remembered my manners and agreed, "Of course."

He led me to the couch, where we both sat down, and then he took both of my hands in his. "I had a nickname, my family called me 'Googy'."

"Googy?" That is a funny nickname. Why did they call you that?" I asked.

"Apparently, when I was a baby that was the word I used for everything. The name stuck until this day. When I go home, my parents still call me Googy." Now, he turned to me with a warm smile. I felt myself begin to relax, and he reached over and kissed me on the cheek. "It will be our little secret," he said. "You may call me 'Googy' when we are together, but never in the presence of others. You must promise me."

"I promise, Googy," I said, and couldn't help but smile. Googy! What an unexpected name for a Nazi! Feeling a bit more confident,

I blurted out, "But now you must tell me, what are we doing? Why have you chosen me? What are my duties?"

To my surprise, the colonel's demeanor instantly changed, and suddenly: 'Googy' was gone. "Your duties are to do what I tell you to do. I have chosen you because I need a personal servant and companion. You are an attractive woman and your looks appeal to me. From our short time together, I know that you are bright and can follow orders. I am sure you will do just fine."

"But why did you not choose a German female soldier, a person with whom you would have and more in common?" I asked.

"Because I chose you, and now I choose not to answer any more questions," he replied. "These are my instructions. You will sleep on the couch tonight. There are linens in the armoire. During the day, if I am busy, you may spend time with your friend or do whatever else you wish. However, you will remain in the hotel and be available when I need you. Is that clear? Now I have business downstairs and will return later. I assume you will be asleep when I return."

"May I ask one more question before you go?" I asked with false bravado.

"And what is that?" replied the colonel, a bit impatiently.

"Will I always be sleeping on the couch?" The colonel looked at me for a long minute before replying.

"I'll tell you what you need to know when you need to know it." Shaking his head with a smile on his face, the colonel went on, "Don't worry, you will do just fine." Rising from the couch, he brushed my cheek and quickly left the suite.

I sat stunned. "What a fool I am," I thought to myself. How could I ask such a question? I am behaving like a school girl. He'll take me to bed and treat me like a whore. I'll deserve it. Rosa, Rosa, what did you do?

I was asleep when the colonel returned to the suite. I did not hear him come in, and he made no attempt to wake me.

Nothing more was said the following morning when a waiter from the dining room brought coffee and a roll to the suite. There was only a serving for one. I was awake and dressed before the colonel, and answered the door when the waiter knocked. He simply set the tray on the coffee table in the living room and left.

The knocking awoke the colonel, and he emerged from the bedroom in his robe. "I am sorry," he said, "I did not tell them to bring you any coffee. You may go down to the dining room and have breakfast. You know where my office is. You will meet me there after you have finished. I will have some errands for you. Did you sleep well?"

Without waiting for an answer, he went on, "I am sure it will be more comfortable for you when you are in my bed. Now, you may go."

I left the suite, my head spinning, and I shivered with fear and anticipation. He had said the words: "In my bed." I felt as if he were treating me like a whore. I could not let this happen.

I took the elevator down to the lobby and, to my surprise, found Itzik waiting for me. He embraced me for all to see and said, "Come, let us have breakfast."

The restaurant had not filled up yet, and we easily found a table for two. We were both quiet until the waiter took our order. "Before you say anything," I began, "I don't know what is going on. You saw him stop me before I could leave. He calls me his 'companion' and his 'assistant', and promised me that nothing would happen to you. He knows of our relationship; I told him at once. He has been pleasant, but very strict."

I watched Itzik's face. I could see he didn't fully comprehend what this new relationship might imply. My confidence began to crumple. "Itzik, I think I'm going crazy. I am having dinner with a Gestapo colonel, but he says that during the day, if he does not need me, I can spend the time with you. Now you tell me - what is this all about?"

Before he could answer, I continued chattering away nervously, "And his name is Peter. My husband's name was Peter. He asked me to call him Peter. I said I would not, and I accused him of murdering my Peter and my children. Do you see why I am going crazy?"

Itzik, the sweet man that he was, looked at me with a smile and said, "You are not going crazy. Maybe this is all for the best. I never thought we would be so important that we would come under the protection of a Gestapo colonel. I thank you for that. But always remember that I am here for you. I am waiting for you, so just play it out, even if it gives us just a few more days together."

Breakfast was served, and I began to calm down. Being with Itzik relaxed me, if only for a moment. "After breakfast, I must go to his office," I told Itzik, stroking his hand. "He said he may have some errands for me, but I am not to leave the hotel." I rose, kissed him on the forehead, and told him, "I will see you later."

Five more days went by in almost the same way. Itzik and I would have breakfast, and then I would do some menial chores for the colonel. There was no further talk of sleeping in the colonel's bed, and I began to hope he would forget. Most afternoons I'd spend with Itzik.

On one occasion, Berel approached me. He didn't quite understand what was going on and asked if I had anything I wanted to share with him. I related what I had told Itzik, and Berel then shook his head in bewilderment. He also said, "Just play it out. Perhaps some good will come of all this."

I found the evenings the most nerve-wracking. First, I would have dinner with the colonel, and then precede him up to the suite where I would read some magazines while he spoke on the phone, or sew up holes in some of the other dresses.

At other times, we just sat and talked to one another, about what I cannot recall. If he had business to attend to, he went down to his office for an hour or so. I found myself becoming more and more confused. I realized that I had feelings toward him I hadn't wanted to recognize or admit.

The offers I had received from other men while I was married to Peter Feurmann came back to me, and I knew that when the time came, my next encounter would not be an offer, but a command.

"What will I tell Itzik?" I thought. "Maybe I won't tell him anything. He cannot be that naive, can he? He never once asked about our sleeping arrangements. What a wonderful, tolerant person he is."

Finally, on the sixth night, I found the colonel feeling very relaxed after dinner. We had consumed a bottle of wine - by now I was sharing it with the colonel with slightly more enthusiasm.

Back in the suite, the colonel teased me by saying that I had almost called him "Googy" at dinner in front of one of the other officers. I had to laugh remembering that moment, and said, "But I didn't. You know I always follow your orders."

At this point, the colonel had taken off his jacket and hung it in his armoire, removed his tie, and was taking off his shirt. He looked at me oddly, and then said, "Yes, you do follow orders well, but I would prefer this not be an order. I hope it will be a simple request, Rosa. I would like you to join me in bed this evening."

I flushed with fear, with lust; with emotions I had never felt shooting through me. "It's finally happened," I told myself. "How should I handle this? What should I say? What should I do?"

Stalling for time, I put a demure smile on my face and replied, "I was under the impression that it was a crime for a German officer to have relations with a Jewish woman. Isn't it a violation of the Nuremberg Laws?"

"You are absolutely right," said the colonel as he approached me. He took me in his arms. "Are you a Jewish woman? I thought you were a Polish maid," he said, laughing as he kissed me full on the mouth.

I gasped. No one had kissed me like that for years! My blood was boiling from desire, from insanity, from God knows what. He took me by the hand and we slowly walked into the bedroom.

As soon as I sat on the bed, I knew instinctively that Colonel Peter Hauptmann was a magnificent lover. He undressed me gently and kissed by body everywhere, over and over again. There was no place that his lips, his tongue did not go. He went wild over my breasts, and I found myself actually resenting the ten seconds in which he stopped to undress himself.

Once we were both naked in bed, I threw myself into the act with as much desire and enthusiasm as he. My body seemed to be on fire, and I kissed him, bit him, sucked him, and when he could no longer hold out, I let him enter me. Then, I matched him thrust for thrust until we both came.

Afterward, we lay together, trying to catch our breath. We spoke quietly while smoking a single cigarette. "You were magnificent, my darling Rosa," beamed the colonel.

"As were you, Googy," I replied, matching his smile. "Will you spend the night here with me?" he asked, "Or are you more comfortable on the couch?"

"If I spend the night here with you, I doubt whether either of us will get much rest," I said, running my hand down his body. Feeling him partially erect, I looked at him, licked my lips, and said, "I don't think I'm quite ready for sleep."

The ritual began, this time much slower, but with even greater passion. It ended with me on my knees as the colonel entered me from behind, firmly holding onto my breasts. Afterwards, I know that there was more than one animal in this room. The experience was exhilarating.

When it was over and we lay next to each other, we kissed one another as if we were lovers. Finally, I offered, "Let me get a towel for you," as I slid out of bed and went into the bathroom. Bringing the wet towel back to the bed, I found the colonel fast asleep. Looking down at him I thought, "He looks like a little boy. No uniform, no boots, no orders delivered in sharp tones." Closing my eyes, I looked up to heaven and said quietly, "Rosa, you are quite mad."

Going back into the bathroom, I turned on the shower as hot as I could stand it and felt the tears begin. Soon, I was hysterical. "The chambermaid was right," I kept repeating. "I am a whore."

"For all I know, he was the officer who ordered that Peter and the boys be taken away - and yet, I can't get enough of him in bed. Meanwhile, my beloved Itzik waits for me downstairs. I wonder what he imagines we are doing, but he continues to ask nothing and say nothing."

There is, in fact, nothing to ask or to say. The colonel and I are not 'making love.' The word is never mentioned. How can there be love between us? There is nothing but animal lust. Who am I? What have I become? The deaths of Peter and my boys have made me a crazy woman. That is why I behave as I do; I am insane. There can be no other explanation.

I turned off the shower, dried myself, put on a nightgown, made up the couch, and within minutes, I was asleep. Perhaps tomorrow would bring me more answers.

For the next three to four weeks, the routine was about the same. I did notice, though, that Itzik was becoming more nervous and more high-strung. He had little to do to pass the time and only waited for me to come to him. He read the newspapers that were brought into the hotel and started playing cards with some of the men, but quickly got up to leave as soon as I appeared.

He had heard remarks from more than one person about me and the colonel. Staunchly, Itzik defended me as best he could. People came and went, and some of the men with whom he played cards were called and taken away. Itzik heard rumors that they had been executed, and other rumors that they had been freed. Of course, he could confirm neither.

Although some of the men told him they had received exit permits and visas to other countries, once they were gone, no one could confirm whether the papers they had purchased had given them a new life, or ended the old one.

On one now-typical evening, an unusual incident occurred. Over the past few weeks I had found new dresses in the living room armoire and assumed they had been hung there by the maids for my use. I sometimes wondered exactly where they had come from, but something stopped me from asking the colonel.

One evening, after dinner, we came back to the suite and found a rather large package on the coffee table. Looking inquiringly at him, I asked, "What is this?"

The colonel smiled with satisfaction and told me that a package of clothing had been received from Pawiak and he had it sent up to the suite so I could pick out anything I liked. He also told me there were men's clothing in the package that my friend might like.

Eagerly, I tore open the package and found a rather attractive dress on the top. Taking it out and holding it up, I felt a chill run through me. Looking at the colonel, I said, "Some two days ago, a woman left the hotel wearing this dress."

The colonel blanched, realizing he had said too much. With a laugh, he replied, "Come on, Rosa, there must be more than one such dress in all of Poland."

But I couldn't let it go. "No, I'm sure this was the dress she had worn," I insisted. The colonel replied angrily, "Rosa, you are the best cared for Jewish woman in Poland. Let it go."

And so I did. I dropped the dress back on the pile and told the colonel that both 'my friend' and I had enough clothes and did not need any more.

The colonel spun on his heel and angrily called down to the desk. "Get someone up here to pick up a package," he snapped, and then slammed down the phone.

Little else was said between us that evening or for the next few days. I began to worry about having made the colonel angry. The fear that he could turn on me and Itzik was always on my mind. The colonel, too, seemed to regret the incident, and his anger slowly dissipated. Both of us wanted to reestablish the old routine. By now he was inviting me to his bed two to three times a week, which was considerably more than before.

I was anxious for his embrace and wanted to please him, but I could never be the one to initiate the encounter. The invitation had to come from him. I was just glad to again have returned to his favor.

By the end of the month, I had missed my period. At first I had not noticed it in that this was not the first time it had happened. I recalled that the stress of having to move into the ghetto caused me to be late as did the fear and nervousness of learning my way through the sewers. When a few more days went by, I knew it was not from fear or nervousness. I was pregnant.

Realizing this monumental truth and knowing I could never tell the colonel or Itzik, I went into an emotional tailspin. What I did to stay alive was my business, but to bring a child into this world, at this time - a Jewish child with a Gestapo colonel as the father - would be madness. I knew I had experienced morning sickness with the boys. How could I explain my nausea if it should happen again.

Worst of all, I had betrayed the memory of my Peter, and I had betrayed the boys. I simply did not know what to do. Years ago, I had a miscarriage. Perhaps it would happen again. That is the best I could hope for. Any other alternative was too horrible to consider. But, than again, I would be with my boys and with my Peter. As for my life, everyone had said, "Play it out." What other choice did I have?

Then I remembered Itzik. Did I have the right to abandon him after all he has been through? With no one I could confide in, I realized I must make this decision on my own. I would play it out.

CHAPTER IX

Pawiak prison was built by the Russian Tsar in the middle of the nineteenth century when Poland was part of Russia. It stood right in the middle of the ghetto, and all of its prisoners, previously confined for the commission of crimes, were taken elsewhere. It was now used by the Nazis as a place of confinement and a slaughterhouse for Jews. It was gray and depressing in appearance, and, if one looked carefully, one could not only see gallows, but blood on the walls of the yard where prisoners had been executed. Originally, the prison housed men only, but it was now occupied by men, women, and children.

There were two truckloads that arrived this day from the Hotel Polski. When the soldiers lowered the tailgate of the trucks, they helped the people off with a certain degree of civility. However, as soon as the people had disembarked, the soldiers separated the men from the women and children, leading each group off in different directions.

Moishele screamed, "Papa", but Feygl took him in her arms and led him and Ernst away following the other women and children. Ernst held Feygl's hand but angrily and fearfully did not say a word.

The soldiers took the women and children to cells on the first floor of the prison. They were given threadbare blankets but allowed to keep whatever luggage they had with them. The cell to which Feygl and the boys were assigned was no more then ten feet square and had two bunks that hung from opposite walls on chains. The bunks were made of wood that looked as if it had come from the days of the Tsar and were covered with thin straw mattresses. Feygl gave each of the boys a bunk and opened the valises taking out sweaters for the three of them, then folded up her blanket and lay down between the bunks on the hard, cold floor. Moishele wept without stopping, but not a sound from Ernst. Weeping could be heard from the other cells, but no words of comfort could overcome the fear of the unknown. "Is this how it will end?" thought Feygl.

※

The men were led by a German officer to the office of the prison commandant. Each one was taken into the commandant's office separately by the commandant's aide.

As Avram entered the office, the aide requested his identification papers and travel documents, which were handed to the commandant. Examining them carefully, the commandant did not say a word to Avram. He took the papers, put them into a big folder and said to the aide, "Next".

"But my travel documents," Avram said.

"They will be returned when you leave this place," the commandant replied. In his mind, Avram doubted he would ever leave Pawiak alive.

Taking Avram by the arm, the aide escorted him from the office where he waited with the other men until all of the men had their papers taken from them. The men were instructed not to speak with each other, so they stood in silence.

When the inspection process was completed, the commandant's aide lined them up and marched them to the second story of the prison. Avram and three other men were assigned to a cell and each given their own threadbare blanket. Avram still had his own valise with him which contained not only his clothing but some of

Feygl's, as well. How he would get the clothes to Feygl he did not know.

The cells were the same cold, lifeless quarters that the women and children occupied. Since there were four men and only two bunks, it was decided that they would sleep in shifts so that all four men could make use of the bunks.

There was little to do during the day. The cells were open, and the men wandered back and forth, speaking to one another about the war. It was late summer of 1944, and they all had heard of the Allied invasion. Rumors were that the Germans were losing the war, but no one could say whether this would be good for the prisoners or would hasten their death.

Rosh Hashanah and Yom Kippur came and went. Chanting could be heard; weeping could be heard, but no one was quite sure what sins they had committed or for what they had to atone. Three times a week, the men were led out into the exercise yard when executions were not taking place. Again, no one knew who was being executed, why they were being executed, or who would be next.

The initial fear turned to boredom. There was no place that they could go, but since they were not really confined, they were not really prisoners. No one was physically mistreated, and the one thing everyone looked forward to was the possibility that the women and children would be allowed out into the yard with the men.

This happened for the first time some two weeks after the Grossmans arrived at Pawiak. When the men saw the women and children come out, they cheered and ran to find one another. They were separated by barbed wire, but at least they now knew that no harm had befallen any of them. This first reunion lasted about an hour.

Avram and Feygl held hands as if they were a long married couple. "Oh, thank you, thank you, for caring for the children," said Avram repeatedly. "What would I have done without you?" he cried with joy.

"Do not thank me," replied Feygl. "You know I will take care of them," she went on. "But you must speak to Ernst. He is so angry with you that he will barely speak to me."

Moishele jumped up and down with happiness to see his papa. He would have gone through the barbed wire had Feygl not restrained him. Ernst refused to speak.

"Ernst, tatele, why will you not speak to your papa?" asked Avram. "Do not be angry with me. You may be sure, this will soon be over and we will be out of here. Think of the good times we will have." Ernst glared but would not say a word.

※

The rations were meager, and the men with families always tried to put aside a little extra for when they would see their children. On the other hand, the children, although always hungry, were the best at adapting to prison life. Previously, when concealed, they had no one to play with. Suddenly, there were other children around. Some of the women were teachers and classes were organized for the children. Contained in the luggage were books and games. The women and children were not confined during the day; they, too, could wander from cell to cell. Under the circumstances, a certain social atmosphere developed, and, to a degree, eased the months of confinement.

Some ten weeks after arriving at Pawiak, the group that came with Avram and Feygl was, without warning, told to be ready the following morning to leave for Vittel. Some of the prisoners, knowing how deceitful the Germans were, assumed that they were really going to Bergen-Belsen. Everyone knew someone who had been sent there and never heard from again. Others felt encouraged and dared to hope that this was the beginning of their trip to freedom. Nevertheless, fear was stamped on every face and in every heart.

The next morning, dressed warmly and with their luggage in hand, the families were reunited, their exit permits and visas returned, and the group was loaded onto trucks and taken to the railway station. To everyone's surprise, there, at the station, was a first-class train with comfortable seats. After their papers were again checked, the group boarded the train. German soldiers stood guard at the front and back of each car, but the atmosphere was otherwise relaxed; the families were together, and there were enough empty seats so that the children could lie down and sleep.

Although no one announced their destination, there was no question that the train was heading west out of Poland and in the direction of Vittel, France. They had no idea what would await them in Vittel, but at least now there was hope. The trip took two days. Food, by concessionaires, was supplied at various stops along the way. It was far better than the prison rations. The children were given fresh milk with bread and cheese. The adults would not eat the meat that was offered knowing it was not kosher, but they were pleased with the dairy selection and, on occasion, some vegetables. The German soldiers started to mingle with the group, and there was actually a feeling that maybe they would survive.

Best known as an exclusive resort and spa, Vittel was a small town in southern France that boasted a number of beautiful hotels, gourmet restaurants, a casino, and an opera house. The Nazis had originally chosen this posh location as an internment camp for British and American citizens, hoping that both countries would treat any Germans they might intern in a similar fashion.

When the Grossmans and the rest of their group arrived, they were overwhelmed by what seemed to be their good fortune. Yes, there was barbed wire between the hotels, and German soldiers appeared everywhere, but the sun shone and both Jews and non-Jews walked the grounds of the hotel as if they were free.

The newly arrived 'guests' were registered in one of the luxurious hotels and given a small suite. The boys had their own room and the adults had theirs. For the first time in their lives, Avram and Feygl were alone, behind closed doors. In all the time they had been together, they had never actually seen each other undressed. Avram's body was rigid. He just didn't know what to do. He had never been with a woman other than his wife. The most he was able to do was take off his shoes. Twelve years younger than Avram, Feygl's experience was limited, but she knew instinctively what Avram was feeling and what she must do to put him at ease.

"My darling Avram," she said tenderly. "We are alone. There is nothing to fear. Let me help you." And with that, she embraced him warmly and reduced him to tears.

"My Feygl" he sobbed. "Where would I be without you? I am indebted to you; my boys are indebted to you. You have become their mama. They love you so. I love you so."

And slowly, enveloped by the strength of their love for each other, they undressed, got under the covers, made love and slept together as Mr. and Mrs. Grossman.

The next morning, the Grossman family went down to breakfast together. As they were shown to a table in the dining room, Ernst turned to his father, his eyes filled with tears. As his father sat down, Ernst went to him and hugged him for the first time since Avram had taken him out of hiding in Warsaw. "Thank you, Papa," Ernst whispered to Avram. "You kept your promise."

It did not take long for the newcomers to start to mingle with some of the internees who had been in Vittel for many months - some close to a year. Some of them were foreign nationals with legitimate citizenship papers from other countries who had no idea why they were never called or permitted to leave.

Those who had been there for months argued that the place was a sham. They related incidents of German Foreign Office officials coming to the camp, offering false encouragement to the internees, and then leaving with nothing having happened and no one having been released. On the other hand, it was true that a year or so before, after a visit from the German Foreign Office, a group of American and British citizens who had been caught in Poland at the time of the Nazi invasion were finally permitted to exit the country.

Apparently, some Red Cross Volunteers revealed, those internees had been taken by train through Spain to Portugal. In Lisbon, the English and the Americans each boarded ships for home. For them the horror was at an end.

As beautiful as the surroundings were, the circumstances caused the newcomers to become increasingly depressed. Rations were inadequate, and it was only thanks to Red Cross supplements of food that the residents didn't starve. Again, everyone shared and saw that the children received whatever little extra there might have been.

The town of Vittel was small and had originally been composed primarily of non-Jews. Many of the townspeople worked in the hotels and objected to serving and catering to the Jews. On more than one occasion they asked the German commandant to get the Jews out of Vittel so it could again become a European resort. The commandant promised that this would happen, but could not say when.

There were a few Gentile internees, amongst them nuns, who were housed in a separate hotel. No one was quite sure why they had been interned. They were kind, compassionate women, and although they were segregated from the Jewish prisoners, Avram did have the opportunity to speak with them through the barbed wire fence that separated the hotels.

The nuns told Avram that several months ago; a group of Jews with South American "citizenship" was told to prepare to leave. They had been in Vittel for many months. Some were overjoyed and others took it as a sign that the end was near, but the transport left Vittel with great fanfare. Later, the nuns learned that the transport had taken its occupants to Drancy, from which it was inferred that they would be shipped back to Poland. Three Jews committed suicide. They could foresee their future with great clarity.

After hearing that story, the Grossmans understood that if this had happened to one group with South American "citizenship", it could happen again. They decided to shield the children from this information, consoled by the nuns' promise that they would not allow the Germans to take the children. If it came to that, they would see that they were hidden in a nearby convent.

But what could these well-meaning women really do? After all, they, too, were internees. On the other hand, they did have contact with the outside world; priests and nuns came to visit them from time to time. Maybe the children could be saved. Things were so crazy that no one knew what to believe.

This life of hope and despair went on for weeks, which turned into months. A group from the Hotel Polski with South American visas had arrived two months earlier. They did leave, but no one knew where they went, and their ultimate fate remained a mystery.

Conditions at the hotel deteriorated; the Germans cut rations even further, and the only positive piece of news to emerge from this was the clear message that the Germans were losing the war.

Some four or more months had passed when German Foreign Office officials appeared. The loudspeakers blared; Avram and those in the group that had arrived with him were told to be ready to leave by six that evening.

This was the word everyone had been waiting for but in no way was it greeted with enthusiasm. Again, the fear of the unknown. Did this mean their long awaited freedom, or did this mean death?

CHAPTER X

The group assembled, as ordered. There was no sense of joy or excitement. Fear radiated from every face, becoming even more pronounced when everyone was, again, crammed into army trucks.

The rear canvases were tightly tied to deny the passengers any sense of where the trucks might be headed. To everyone's surprise, the trip was short, taking less than ten minutes from the hotel to the railway station. When the trucks were unloaded, the families stood together and, for the first time, breathed a sigh of relief. The railway cars were first class, Wagon-Lits.

As their names were called, the internees boarded the train. Hope rose in their hearts, as they told themselves that such a luxury would not be offered to internees who were being shipped to their deaths.

The train consisted of an engine, a coal tender, and three passenger cars. Two passenger cars were more than enough to hold the group; the third was for the soldiers who guarded them. It was not until the train got underway and the soldiers entered the car that the internees realized these were different soldiers than had surrounded them when they left the hotel. These were young boys and older men. That, too, was reassuring. The regular soldiers were probably needed to fight, while these men could be spared for this type of duty.

Despite the fact the windows were covered with blankets which the group was told not to remove, a sense of optimism began to emerge. Perhaps the long months of waiting and sacrifice were really coming to an end.

After the children went to sleep, the adults sat around wondering out loud about how they would fare in Uruguay when none of them spoke Spanish - - or was it Portuguese? This made them all laugh. No one quite knew the language of the country of which they were allegedly citizens. Then, little by little, the adults drifted off as the train rocked them to sleep. No guards were present. This had to be a good sign.

Morning came, and with it, hunger. No one had eaten since the night before, and the train showed no signs of slowing down. The guards came in from the rear car, and, when asked about coffee or milk for the children, simply shrugged their shoulders and said nothing.

After this, the attitude of the passengers began to change to doubt and uncertainty. Children awoke and cried when they were told that there was nothing for breakfast. The hoped-for road to freedom of last night suddenly appeared to be exactly the opposite this morning. "Where are we going? Where are they taking us?" everyone began to murmur.

There was only one way to find out, and to hell with their instructions not to remove the blankets. "If we're going to be free," someone offered, "then let's see where we are headed. After all, if we're going to be killed, what difference does it make if we see where we're going?"

Against the advice of the many that still feared what the soldiers would do if they found a window uncovered, Avram ripped off the blanket. He gasped. While the train should have been heading west, away from the rising sun, the angle of the morning sun revealed that they were actually heading northeast.

A chill went down his spine as he realized they were probably in or near Germany, either headed towards Bergen-Belsen or going back, via Poland, to Auschwitz.

Now nothing made sense. Has this whole affair been a sham? But why? Avram asked himself. They could have taken us to the camps without this entire pretense. In the history of the world, why had they been victims of this elaborate, outlandish plan to kill Jews?

The men started to murmur among themselves and the women insisted on knowing what the men were saying. When told, "We are not headed in the right direction," the women began to sob. When the children saw the women crying, they started to weep even louder. Men walked up and down the aisle of the train saying, "How could they do this to us? Haven't we suffered enough?" Feygl sat with the two boys in her arms and just rocked back and forth, saying nothing.

Now, knowing which direction was east, the orthodox Jews amongst them took out their prayer shawls and began their morning prayers, facing in the direction the train was heading. The others watched the men who rocked back and forth and asked themselves, "To whom were they praying?" They and their families would soon be with God. They didn't have to ask Him to hurry the process. The Germans were taking care of that.

"Maybe we are headed to Bremerhaven?" someone speculated hopefully. "We're heading in that direction, and it is a port of embarkation. Perhaps we are misjudging the situation and being too pessimistic. But why won't they stop so we can get something to eat? The children are hungry. It just doesn't make sense." The others said nothing.

Unexpectedly, in mid-morning, the train slowed, crossed the French border and came to a halt in a small town in Germany. The engine needed water and the soldiers needed to stretch their legs. Seeing that it was a first-class train, townspeople appeared with sandwiches, cheese, and coffee. The passengers tore the covering off the windows, opened them, and bought whatever was for sale. For many this was the last of the money that they had brought with them to the Hotel Polski.

Because many of the group spoke excellent German, the townspeople were unaware that this was a trainload of Jews, and when asked to get milk for the children, they ran to do so.

Some of the group had no money, but it made no difference. Everyone chipped in with whatever they had and made sure the children were fed and the adults had enough to satisfy them for the time being. The soldiers did not interfere. On the contrary, they handed the food and coffee to the adults through the windows.

Now, the emotions of the group were on a roller-coaster. With the hot coffee and sandwiches, their optimism returned. Yes, they thought, we are probably headed for Bremerhaven. After all, that's the only thing that makes sense.

A half hour later, the train continued on its journey into the unknown. The passengers were quiet; the children slept or played games. The adults sat and looked out the windows. No one had bothered to put the blankets back up, and now no one cared. When the soldiers walked through, it was if the windows had never been covered.

The afternoon wore on, and as the sun began to set, some of the passengers started to weep. The fantasy of Bremerhaven had dissolved, and they knew that this would be their final journey.

At about five in the evening, the train stopped in the middle of a field. Night had not yet fallen, and it was clear to all that they were nowhere. A coldness settled over the group. Now, they imagined, they would be taken off the train, lined up, and shot. What else could they expect?

Outside, they could see the soldiers running up to the engine. Suddenly, there was a jolt, and the engine freed itself from the passenger cars. The soldiers jumped on the engine and the coal car as they pulled away, leaving the passenger cars standing alone on the tracks, waiting. Waiting, for what? For several minutes no one said a word.

Could this be? Were they suddenly free? True, they were unguarded, but how could a group of Jews be free in the middle of a German field? This was unbelievable - no, this was truly insanity.

The men tentatively started to disembark and look around in an attempt to get their bearings, but it was impossible to tell where they were. Within the next fifteen minutes, it would be completely dark.

The field was surrounded by a forest, and as it became darker, they could see lights through the trees. This meant that there was a town within walking distance.

But a town could mean German soldiers, so two of the men who spoke fluent German, against the protestations of the women with whom they were traveling, volunteered to go through the woods and act as scouts. They estimated it would take about fifteen minutes for them to reach the town, some ten minutes to look around, and another fifteen minutes to get back. Everyone was to stay on or near the train for the next forty-five or fifty minutes until the scouts returned.

It actually took close to an hour for the men to return, and by the time they did, the rest of the group was bordering on hysteria. They assumed that German soldiers would be coming through the trees any minute, and were immensely relieved that not only did no Germans appear, but when the men returned, they brought two loaves of bread with them. The men had found an inn in the small town on the other side of the forest. Because the men were respectably dressed and spoke perfect German, the question of identity was not an issue. In fact, when they explained that they were passengers on a train that had gotten stuck in a field, the innkeeper agreed to feed the families with children first, and the other passengers later. They also learned that all the German soldiers had left the town two days prior and had not been seen since.

Abandoning the train in the field suddenly made perfect sense. Now it was a certainty: the Germans were losing the war. All soldiers, young and old, were being pulled to the front, wherever the front might be.

Grateful for the opportunity to have a meal, the problem arose as to how they would pay for food for the group. Whatever zlotys they had from Poland, or francs from Vittel, had been all but used up at the station that morning. No one had deutschmarks.

At this point, Avram spoke up and said, "I lived on the Aryan side and worked for a jeweler before coming to the Hotel Polski.

When he learned that I was planning to buy travel documents to get out of Poland, he allowed me to take some gold and silver with me. I'm sure the innkeeper will accept gold as payment for our meals. Now let us go. We don't know if the soldiers will be coming back, and we must make our plans."

The men and women hugged and kissed Avram, and from the depths of despair, hope rose once again.

One of the two men who had gone ahead as a scout led Avram and Feygl, the women and all the children into town, A half hour or so later, the rest of the men came led by the other scout. This was the first real meal that many of them had eaten in a long time; by ten in the evening, they were all back on the train.

No longer hungry and not quite sure of what was happening, the women put the children to sleep. Feeling somewhat safe, no one minded that there was simply no place to go. It was night, it was dark, it was frightening, but yet they all agreed that, for the moment, they felt somewhat safe. If the solders failed to return with the first sunrise, the group would consider what the day might bring and where they might go from here.

CHAPTER XI

On the morning after I discovered I was pregnant, the colonel spoke to me clearly and with military precision.

"This evening, General Seidl will be coming from Berlin to meet with me. He will be wearing civilian clothes and will arrive at 6 P.M. I have ordered dinner, brandy, and cigars, all to be served here in the suite. You will find a maid's uniform that fits properly. See to it that there is whiskey and soda before dinner. I will wait for him in the lobby and bring him up. Dinner will be brought up at 7:45 and you will serve. Before dinner you will see to it that we have drinks. When dinner is over, you will stack the dishes on the serving table and wheel it out into the hall. You will serve brandy and cigars and then go into the bedroom, close the door and read a magazine. I will call you if there is anything that the general requires. Otherwise, you will not appear again until he leaves. This meeting is very important to me and I do not want anything to upset the general. Do you understand me? Do you have any questions?"

When the colonel spoke in this manner, I responded in kind. "No, colonel, I have no questions; I understand you completely."

Now his tone softened. "You are a good girl, Rosa. You make my life bearable in this awful job. For that I am grateful."

Although thankful for the change in tone, I thought better of continuing this conversation. "If you will excuse me," I said, "I must go down to the kitchen and see if I can borrow a maid's uniform that will be appropriate."

The colonel nodded and I left the suite.

"Now what is this all about?" I thought to myself as I took the elevator down to the kitchen. Any change, no matter how small, caused me to be fearful. "Who is this general? Why is he coming to see the colonel? Will it have an effect on me and Itzik?" What difference does it make? I suppose I am really nothing more than a maid and a bed companion. I am lucky to have stayed alive this long.

All the arrangements were made just as the colonel requested. When I asked for something, the hotel employees understood that it was really the colonel asking, and it was done at once. Although he had not requested it, I had flowers brought to the suite and hoped that the general was not allergic to them. A mistake like that and I could end up in Pawiak. The whiskey, soda, and ice were on the table in the living room, and the brandy and cigars were in the bedroom to be brought out later.

On one trip downstairs, I took a few minutes to tell Itzik that I would not see him that evening. The colonel had a guest and I had to be in attendance. Itzik just shook his head and asked, "When will this all end?"

With the accuracy and precision of the Nazi war machine, General Seidl arrived at precisely 6 P.M. and was shown up to the suite. He was fat and squat, and had both the looks and the manners of a pig. Since I greeted him in German, he knew I spoke the language, but it did not deter him from talking about me as if I were not in the room.

When I took his coat and hat, he slowly looked me up and down and said to the colonel, "So, are you fucking her?"

"Of course not," the colonel reassured him. "She's just my servant, and a Jew. Why would I lower myself? Besides, it would be against the law."

The general laughed and said, "The hell with the law. If I had more time, I would fuck her myself."

I refused to react to the general's obscene remarks, but I noticed that the colonel shot me a look that was almost apologetic. I served the whiskey and soda and went into the bedroom to await the dinner, which was delivered punctually at 7:45.

I opened the door when the waiter knocked, and all conversation stopped while he wheeled in the dinner cart. I helped him set the food out on the coffee table, and then the waiter left and I moved the cart out into the hallway.

Looking into the living room, I saw that the two men were deep in conversation, and went into the bedroom. Frankly, I had no intention of reading a magazine. Why would I when I might hear something that would be of benefit to Itzik and me? I closed the door most of the way, but left it open just a crack so I could hear their voices.

Unfortunately, I heard nothing of consequence during dinner, and, finally, the colonel called for me to take away the dishes and serve the coffee, brandy and cigars.

No one spoke a word while I was in the room, but after dinner, the general said he had to use the bathroom. Winking at me, he asked me if I would like to join him. Needless to say, I ignored him and saw to it that I was in the bedroom with the door almost closed by the time he came out of the bathroom. I stood at the door, hoping I could hear what they were saying.

The two men settled down with brandy and cigars, and I heard the general ask, "So, Peter how goes it here?"

"To be honest," the colonel replied, "I don't know what the hell I am doing. I am a military commander, not a Jewish social worker. I have visas, I have passports, I have exit permits and I spend my time trying to match people to the documents with no idea as to where any of them end up. If we are sincere in what we are doing, using Jews in exchange for Germans interned in foreign countries, then perhaps we are justified. If, on the other had, this is just another way of rounding up those Jews left in Warsaw and sending them for resettlement, we are going to a lot of trouble for nothing. What will all this bring us except condemnation for our deceit?"

"I'll tell you what it will bring us," said the general. "As you correctly put it, this will bring us the release of German nationals interned in foreign countries around the world. The Jews are our tradeoff. When the ghetto was destroyed, we found countless documents from foreign countries. Many of the ghetto dwellers were visitors who had come to Poland years ago, stayed in Warsaw, and still had their old immigration papers. We took these papers to the consulates and the embassies in Berlin, they contacted their governments, and, at our request, re-issued new documents based upon the old."

"But half of these countries are our allies, have no German internees, and certainly don't want the Jews," responded the colonel. "And if this project is shown to have been nothing more than a way of getting rid of those Jews who survived, then, when the time comes," he said, shaking his head knowingly, "we will be looked upon as the worst war criminals."

"Peter, Peter, don't be such a pessimist," soothed the general. "You continue putting together the new families that correspond to the visas, for which they pay dearly, and when we ship them out of here, we will be through with them. You're doing a wonderful job. Where they go and who sends them there is not our concern. It is a masterful plan; visas issued to dead Jews will bring us back a boatload of live Germans."

"I wish I could share your enthusiasm," the colonel replied, still unconvinced. "When I first heard of the plan, I thought it was the craziest idea Berlin had ever come up with! I couldn't believe there was anything we could offer that would induce Jews to come out of hiding."

"But now you realize that is where the Poles come in," the general replied. "They are our biggest ally. They hate the Jews more than we do and they were pleased when we destroyed the ghetto. We have gotten rid of the Jews at no cost to them, and they are the first ones to turn over a Jew if they find him hiding on the 'Aryan' side. The Jews know this, so when they learned there was a chance to survive, that there was still hope to stay alive, they appeared in droves. Look at the success of the plan at the Royal and now here at the Polski!"

"General Seidl," said the colonel, very seriously, "I am not asking where these people go after they leave the hotel, but I am still left with one very serious problem. I have Jews here without a zloty to their name, and I have others who are buying up the visas with cash, gold and jewelry. My problem is knowing what to do with the group with no funds."

Raising his had to hold off any response from the general; he went on, "Please don't say anything." Getting up, he went to the door and through the closed door called, "Rosa, take the dishes down to the kitchen and do not return until the general leaves. I will call for you."

As he turned and went back into the living room, I opened the door, left the bedroom, and exited the suite. I wheeled the cart with the dishes to the kitchen and then went to look for Itzik. I found him in the card room off the lobby where he was sitting reading a newspaper. He was both surprised and delighted to see me. He embraced me warmly, and we sat and talked for an hour or more. I told him everything that I had heard of the conversation between the colonel and the general, explaining that I was not quite sure why I had been sent out at that point in the conversation.

Itzik suggested one possibility. "Since we are the ones with no money to buy the expensive visas, maybe he didn't want you to hear what they plan for us. Didn't you tell me about your neighbors who pretended to be Jews, and even with money, they ended up in Pawiak? Maybe that will be our fate as well. Ah, Rosa," he sighed, "I hope I'm wrong about this."

Suddenly all conversation and card playing stopped. The colonel entered the room and nodded to me. I squeezed Itzik's hand and got up. I could feel the color rush to my face because I knew that everyone was looking at me. The colonel turned and walked out and I followed like a well trained puppy.

For two days afterwards, the colonel was very moody, almost depressed. He did tell me that he thought the flowers were a nice touch. On the second night following the general's visit, the colonel invited me into his bed. He was excited, he was driven, and the wilder he became, the more I responded. After all, I was pregnant; that was for sure. Nothing more could happen to me now.

Lying side by side and smoking a cigarette, I said, "Googy, you were a wild man tonight, but you have been moody for the past two days." And for the first time in my many months of being the colonel's "companion", I asked him a personal question, showing my concern. "Is there something troubling you that you can tell me about?"

Raising himself up on his elbow, and looking into my eyes, he said sadly, "Rosa, my love, this is goodbye. I am being transferred and will be leaving the Polski within the next few days. I have arranged for you and Itzik, as well as a number of other couples, to go to Palestine. The Turks are holding a large group of German nationals, and we will trade them for you and the others. Please bring me my briefcase from the dresser and I will give you your exit papers and your visas."

I was dumbstruck. He called me "my love". He was leaving. We will be leaving. My head beat like a trip-hammer. "But, Googy," I said, "we have no money. We have nothing; we have no way to paying for these visas."

"Rosa", he replied, "being the commandant does have certain privileges. Now do as I say. Bring me my briefcase." I got out of bed and brought him the briefcase; he pulled a folder from it, and took out a set of official-looking documents. "From tomorrow, and probably for the rest of your life, you and Itzik will be known as Anna and Chaim Adler. This is the name that appears on your exit permit and your visa. Tomorrow, after breakfast, the group will be called. They will get their papers, and you must be ready to leave by noon. You will be taken from Warsaw by train to Leghorn in Italy. There you will be transferred to a Turkish freighter which will take you to

Haifa. After you disembark in Haifa, you are on your own. You will be safe, and I hope you will have a good life that will make up for all the suffering you have lived through. You have been a good friend, Rosa, and I will not forget you."

I threw my arms around the colonel's neck and wept like a baby. "Oh, Googy", I said. "I thank you and I will never forget you. You have been kind to both me and Itzik. Please take care of yourself, and perhaps, after the war…"

He kissed me gently on the lips and said, "My imagination does not carry me that far. Let us both get out of this alive." Holding each other as tightly as we could, he then asked, "Will you sleep here with me tonight?"

The nest morning, it was business as usual. The group was assembled, and at noon, with their new identities in their pockets, they boarded trucks that would take them to the railway station. From there, things proceeded exactly as the colonel had described. Some ten days later, Anna and Chaim Adler arrived in Palestine. They received financial help from various Jewish relief agencies and settled in Tel Aviv. The Hotel Polski was a thing of the past.

The very first time that Chaim and I had an hour to ourselves, we made love. Although Chaim was not quite as experienced as the colonel, I held on to him and would not let go. We finally got into our apartment in Tel Aviv. We had been in Palestine for a month living in temporary quarters, and it was only then that I broke the news.

"Chaim, I have something to tell you."

"And what is that, my Annichke?" inquired Chaim.

"We are going to be parents", I said, with a big smile. "I am pregnant. I am so happy. We will have our own family." My eyes filled with tears as I thought about those whom I had lost.

Chaim embraced me and kissed me with deep feeling. "I could not be happier", he replied. "But now we have to plan for a larger apartment with a nursery. We must find a doctor to care for you. We must see to it that nothing goes wrong. Oh, Annichke, I am so happy for us."

Chaim said he was happy, but I wondered whether he was really surprised. I was aware that I was getting a bit thick in the waist. Was he aware that the child that I was carrying was not his?

But he never said a word. We celebrated the birth of our first child, Sholom, some seven and a half months after arriving in Palestine. He was a full term baby.

Things went well for us. Some two years later, we moved to a bigger apartment, I gave birth to Tamar, and a year after that, the State of Israel was born.

It was of no real importance to either of us that we marry. Based on our visas, we were Chaim and Anna Adler, citizens of Israel. No one questioned our marital status, and to go back over the past and try and explain where the names came from was no one's business.

In my eyes, as I watched Sholom grow, I saw his resemblance to the colonel becoming more pronounced. But nothing made me feel better than when we were with friends who said, when looking at Sholom, "He looks just like Chaim!"

CHAPTER XII

"What does it look like to you, sarge?' asked the lieutenant.

"Beats the shit out of me, sir", replied the sergeant. "They look like they're dressed for church. Who the hell would abandon a first-class passenger train in the middle of a field?"

Some fifteen hundred yards to the south and west of the stalled train, an American infantry unit was trying to understand what they were seeing as the sun came up. It was a cool spring morning. The people they were observing were mostly men, middle aged men dressed in warm coats, slowly coming out of the first two cars of the train. No one came out of the third car. Suddenly, children appeared, followed by women who were hollering at them.

"This is a hell of a time and place for a family outing", said the sergeant. "Do you think it could be a booby trap? Krauts in the woods? Will they open fire as we approach the train?"

"Why use women and children?" replied the lieutenant. "It just doesn't make sense. Listen, sarge. Take two jeeps and a platoon of men. Approach the train from the front and the back. See if you draw any fire. For some reason, I don't think you will. But if one shot is fired, we will storm the woods. Stay on the phone and let me know what is happening."

The lieutenant continued to observe the progress of his troops. The two jeeps approached from either end of the train, and as soon as the people saw the jeeps coming toward them, the women gathered the children to them and the men put up their hands, as if to surrender. The soldiers got out of the jeeps, and suddenly the people started to holler and jump up and down. They grabbed the soldiers, both the men and women, and started to hug and kiss them.

"Sarge, what the hell is going on down there?" the lieutenant shouted into his phone. "Who are those people?"

"Send down the boychik from Brooklyn" answered the sergeant. "He speaks their language. These are Jews who were being taken, God knows where. I guess the Krauts just abandoned them here when they learned we were in the area. I don't know what the hell we'll do with them, but now they're ours."

"Goldstein, get your ass over here," shouted the lieutenant. Corporal Goldstein, the boychik from Brooklyn, came right over. He was a giant of a man and was the one everyone wanted on their side, simply because of his size and his strength. He was a strong defender of his faith, and anyone foolish enough to make any remark that he took to be remotely anti-Semitic would usually end up with a broken jaw or a crooked nose.

Goldstein had risen to the rank of Staff Sergeant, but had been court martialed so many times for fighting that he'd dropped in rank to corporal. His other peculiarity was that he liked to speak as if he were a Negro. Since the Army was not integrated and there were no Negroes in the unit, he always gave the others a laugh with his mimicry.

"Listen to me, sergeant," said the lieutenant.

"Ah ain't no sagint," said Goldstein. "Ah's a copral."

"For Christ sakes, Goldstein, have you been busted again?" asked the lieutenant. "The sleeves of your uniform must be ragged with your stripes comin' off and on. Are you up on your Yiddish?" asked the lieutenant, thinking here I'm asking him about Yiddish and he's answering me in Negro dialect.

"Ah sutt'nly is, sir", responded Goldstein, who still corresponded with his parents in Yiddish, even though it delayed his mail because of censorship. He refused to stop despite his C.O.'s orders to do so. He claimed that his parents would be insulted if he wrote in any other language.

"Stop with the nigger talk and listen to me," said the lieutenant. "Those people down there are Jews who were being shipped to what was probably a death camp. The Germans abandoned them, but luckily for them, we came along. Go down and see how you can help them. They only speak Yiddish. Debrief their leader, if they have one. If all is well, we'll send two trucks down and pick them up. Report to the Sergeant and he'll call me."

And so, Corporal Goldstein, this giant of a man, this class clown, this devout Yiddishist, was the first American soldier to learn about the Hotel Polski, Pawiak prison, Vittel and all the other trials and tribulations that the group had experienced.

He accompanied the group behind the lines where their testimony was recorded by American Army Intelligence. Since his knowledge of Yiddish was badly needed, Goldstein was transferred to the Intelligence unit, where he continued to be of service, particularly with those Jews who were being liberated from the concentration and the death camps.

Avram, Feygl and the boys, along with the rest of the group from the train, were placed in one of the first Displaced Persons camps established in Germany. Although they were well fed, given new warm clothing for winter and light clothing for the summer, the situation did not temper their resentment. The war ended in the next few months, but the Jews were back in the camps.

Administrators were plagued with the problem. Where could these people go? Although they continued to call themselves by the names on their visas, it was obvious that they were not citizens of the countries that had issued the visas.

None of them wanted to return to Poland; their homes were destroyed and their families were gone. And so, the Grossmans, and some of the others who had no family in America or elsewhere to vouch for them, remained in the DP camp until the beginning of 1949.

During those years in the camp, Ernst became known as Ernie; he had his Bar Mitzvah in the shul that was established on the camp grounds. The GI's taught him English, and his favorite sport became baseball. Moishele was called Moe. As he grew older, he never mentioned his mother. Feygl became the only mother that he knew. He was smart in school and his teachers really liked him. In spite of their situation, the Grossmans were finally a real family.

Avram worked in the nearby city for a jeweler who was, of course, a German who knew that Avram was a Jew. They never spoke of it; they never spoke of politics; they never spoke of the war. As a matter of fact, they spoke very little. The jeweler acknowledged that Avram was a good craftsman, and most of the pieces that he created were purchased by GI's or Department of the Army civilians. Neither the jeweler nor Avram had much to complain about.

Feygl went to work in the kindergarten the Americans established at the camp. As the years went on, there were many people, other than Jews, that were brought into the camp. Poles, and even some Germans whose towns and cities were destroyed, were also displaced persons.

Feygl loved the little children and they loved her. But two questions hung over all of their heads: When will we get out of the camp and where will we go?

After the establishment of the State of Israel and the War of Independence, Avram and Feygl decided that Israel was the only place to raise a Jewish family. They made applications to emigrate. Their acceptance to Israel was quick; and in May of 1949, they left Europe for good to make Israel their home. There, Ernie became Eitan and Moe went back to Moshe. He was too old to be called Moishele.

Although expensive jewelry was beyond the price range of many people in those years in Israel, Avram had no trouble getting a job at the best jewelry house in Tel Aviv. There were two such houses, one in Tel Aviv and one in Jerusalem; both did a good business. When, at a meeting of Holocaust survivors, Feygl and Avram met with Anna and Chaim and started to talk, the conversation got around to the Hotel Polski. "When were you there?" "When were you there?", and "Do you remember this one and do you remember that one?" From then on, they became inseparable. The horror of life in Europe was now a story to be told and an evil to guard against.

A new life had begun and Anna and Fegyl became best of friends. But even best of friends do not reveal everything to one another.

CHAPTER XIII

Although both we and the Grossmans were happy in Israel, the early years were difficult. There was little food available in the markets, gasoline was very expensive, and when getting together for a social evening, the most one could afford to serve were nuts and olives.

Still, we were free and we were together like family. Eitan and Moshe treated Sholom and Tamar as their little cousins. Tamar was growing up; she was four years of age and a pretty child. We used to kid each other saying that if one of the boys chose to marry Tamar, then we really would be family. (Little did we know it would really happen.)

When we got together, the adults spoke of their early lives in Poland, the families we'd lost, how we survived, the Hotel Polski, Pawiak prison, Vittel, the months of endless waiting, the deception.... As time passed, though we told and retold the stories as tears were shed, it became time to let those days go. Of all of them, I spoke the least. I could find no way to talk about my life in the Hotel Polski.

As the days turned to months and a sense of normalcy and everyday life overtook us, our conversations turned to Israeli politics, what was going on in the world, the Mercedes taxis that had come from Germany, the children's schools, learning Hebrew, and all things relevant to our new lives. In fact, it did not take long before we began to speak Hebrew to each other using Yiddish or Polish only if we could not find the right Hebrew word or expression. In our hearts and minds, our old lives were over, and we were, without a doubt, citizens of Israel.

It was the spring of 1950; I was trying my best to read the Hebrew paper when my doorbell rang. Without questioning who was at the door, I opened it. Standing there to my surprise was an American Army captain.

"Can I help you?" I asked.

"Are you Anna Adler?" asked the captain.

"Yes, I am." I answered. "What can I do for you?"

"The International Military Tribunal needs your help, and I would like to speak with you," replied the captain. "May I come in?"

"Of course," I said, allowing the captain to enter.

As the captain was seating himself, I said, "I cannot imagine how I can be of help to the International Military Tribunal since I don't really know what it is. Before you begin, though, can I offer you a coffee? I was having one; it is already made."

"I would love it," said the captain, "black, no sugar, please."

I went into the kitchen and carried out a tray with my cup, a cup for the captain and a plate of cookies. "Home baked; the children love them," I said.

"It is amazing," said the captain with a big smile. "I have never visited a Jewish home where I was not treated with kindness and good cookies or cake."

"It is a cultural phenomenon," I laughed. "That's the word, isn't it? But please excuse my English. I never studied it. For me it was a pick-up language from magazines, newspapers, the movies, T.V., and some of the tourists who are starting to come to Israel."

"You are doing wonderfully," replied the captain. "It never occurred to me that I might need a translator." Biting into a cookie, he went on, "You are right, the cookies are delicious, and the coffee is good and strong."

"Now that we have so much in common," I said. "Tell me how I can be of help. What is the International Military Tribunal?"

"Before I answer your question", the Captain said, "There is one question I must ask you.

"Of course," I replied.

"Were you ever known as Rosa Feurmann?"

I was dumbstruck. A million thoughts ran through my head and a shiver ran down my spine. It had been years since I thought of Rosa Feurmann. A strange look came over my face and as my eyes filled with tears, I answered, "Yes, in another life I was Rosa Feurmann. What does she have to do with your visit to the home of Anna Adler?"

Seeing how upset and emotional I had become, the captain, in a most unexpected move, came to me, knelt on one knee, took my hand in his and said, "I am so sorry to have upset you but I beg you to understand that I had to be sure I was talking to the right Anna Adler. My question was only for the purpose of verifying your identity. What I have to tell you and what I have to ask is only for the Anna Adler who had been Rosa Feurmann. Again, please forgive me and let me tell you why I am here."

In that my reaction had been so sudden and the captain's apology had been so sincere, I immediately regained my composure, and said, "I apologize for my behavior. I had not heard or thought of Rosa Feurmann in many years and you took me by surprise. Please, tell me why you are here?"

Going back to his chair and taking a sip of coffee, the captain spoke seriously. "I am sure you recall that after the war ended, it took less than six months for the Nuremberg trials to be convened. By this time, many of the major war criminals had been apprehended; however, the search goes on. Upon the apprehensions, the trials themselves are conducted by the International Military Tribunal, in many cases in the countries where the offenses took place.'

"Please be advised that I am here to inform you that, just recently, a Colonel Peter Hauptmann was apprehended. For reasons that are unknown to me, he is to be tried in Heidelberg."

I held up my hand to stop the captain from continuing. I took a sip of coffee and said, "May I ask you a question?"

"Of course," replied the captain.

With a look of amazement upon my face, I asked, "How on earth did you find me? When I knew Colonel Hauptmann my name was Rosa Feurmann, as you know. But from the day I left the Hotel Polski, I never used that name again."

Smiling and taking a bite out of his cookie, the captain replied, "The Germans, in many cases, made their own prosecution easier by virtue of the meticulous records that they kept. When American Intelligence learned of the Hotel Polski, they confiscated all of the records that had been left there. That is how they learned that Rosa Feurmann became Anna Adler who emigrated to Palestine. It meant nothing to us until Colonel Hauptmann was captured. In order to prosecute him, we now had the job of gathering the witnesses, and this is why I am here."

Continuing to nibble on his cookie and sip his coffee, the captain went on. "Please understand that I am merely the messenger. I know very little about your circumstances or your involvement. I am only here to serve you with papers that require your attendance at the trial of Colonel Peter Hauptmann, to be held in Heidelberg some three months from now. There are instructions as to how to get there, where you will stay, and whom you may bring with you. Does any of this present a problem for you?"

I was dumbfounded, but I did not say a word. It had taken years for me to stop thinking of Peter Hauptmann, Colonel Peter Hauptmann, Googy. Now I would have to face him again. My God, will this never be over?

The captain waited an appropriate time for a response, and getting none, he asked, "Are you all right, Mrs. Adler? Is there anything I can get you?"

"Suppose I choose not to go? I asked, ignoring the captain's concern.

Taken aback by the question, the captain replied, "No one has ever asked me that question before. Why would you not want to go? Everyone to whom I have spoken in the past has always been pleased to learn that these people were caught. The survivors are grateful to tell their stories and to have their say regarding the atrocities that were committed. I understand that it may be emotionally difficult, but no one has ever refused. This is a way of bringing closure to a terrible time in your life."

"Suppose I choose not to go?" I repeated. "And why do you think I have not brought closure to that terrible time in my life?" I asked, not really expecting an answer. "I have young children at home. My husband works, and I just can't take off for I don't know how long."

"Is there no one with whom you can leave the children?" Asked the captain. "It would be only a few days."

"My family was wiped out by the Nazis." I said with great emotion. "Who do you think I have here that would look after my children?"

Seeing that Anna was getting worked up, the captain said, "Mrs. Adler, we cannot force you to come. I am sure the Tribunal would not be calling you as a witness if they did not feel you had something of importance to add. These people must be held accountable for their acts, for their crimes, and for their inhumanity to man. Only survivors such as yourself can do that. I will leave the papers with you. Talk to your husband, and when you decide, there is a number to call. I am sorry that I upset you, Mrs. Adler. At any rate, thank you for the coffee and cookies."

As he got up to leave, I stopped him, "No, I thank you for coming, captain. I will discuss it with my husband, and when I make a decision, I will call the number on the papers you have left me." With that I opened the door and the captain left, leaving the papers on the coffee table.

When Chaim came home, I told him about the captain's visit. His response was, "Just as I could not tell you what to do when we were in the Hotel Polski, I cannot tell you what to do now. They have asked you to appear. They have not asked me to appear. If you wish to go, I suggest that you take Feygl with you. I will look after the children. You need not worry about that."

"But if I take Feygl, then I must tell her about what took place at the Hotel." I replied. "I have never told anyone, not even you."

"That's because I never asked you," said Chaim, tenderly. "When and if you have something to tell me, you will tell me."

"My God, Chaim" I replied. "I thought this was all behind me."

We said nothing more that evening.

We said nothing more for two weeks. Then one morning, I called Feygl. "Feygl, can we have lunch today? I will come to you. I will pick up some hummus and pita and...."

Before I could finish, Feygl interrupted, "Since when have you had to bring food when we have lunch in my house? You sound very upset. What is wrong, Anna?"

"Nothing is wrong," I responded. "Every one is O.K. I won't bring my hummus. How about a piece of kugel?"

"That you can bring," Feygl said. "I'll see you at noon. You're sure you're O.K.?"

"We'll talk when I get there" I said hanging up the phone.

At twelve noon, kugel in hand, I appeared at Feygl's. After a kiss and a lot of how are you's, how is this one and how is that one, Feygl said, "You know, Anna, we have not talked in two weeks. That's not like you. What is happening?"

"So why didn't you call me if you didn't hear from me in two weeks?" I replied. "The phone doesn't work in two directions?"

"All of a sudden you are feeling better. I can tell. You're making jokes," said Feygl with a smile.

"No, I'm not making jokes," I said, embracing Feygl. "But just being with you makes me feel better. I have something on my mind that has been troubling me, and we must talk."

"Please, let us sit and have a coffee," responded Feygl. "You talk and I will listen."

I sat down at the table, took a piece of pita, and started to nibble. "Let me start from the beginning," I said.

"Some two weeks ago an American Officer, a captain, came to my house and served me with papers, ordering me to come to Heidelberg to testify at the war crimes trial of Colonel Peter Hauptmann. When I asked him what would happen if I didn't come, he said something very strange to me. He said I was the first person who had ever asked that question."

"Well, why wouldn't you go?" asked Feygl.

"I told the captain that I had no one to look after the children. But Chaim said that he would look after them and that I should take you. If I decide to go, will you come with me?"

"Of course I will " answered Feygl. "But why are you so troubled by this? Was not Colonel Hauptmann the commanding officer at the Polski? I don't even remember him. When I arrived he was still there, but he left in just a few days or a week. I didn't even know you in those days."

"Yes, I know," I said shaking my head in recall. "If the truth be known, I would like to go and I would like to take you with me. But there are things that I must tell you first. You are my dearest friend, Feygl, but there are things about me that you just don't know and you must never repeat them. Promise me, not to Avram, not to Chaim, not to anyone. You must promise me."

Feygl sat speechless for a few seconds, trying to digest Anna's request. Then she responded, "Anna, would I ever betray you? What you tell me remains here in this kitchen. Because of what we have both been through, for the families we both lost, we are soul mates. Tell me whatever you wish and it will be our secret."

And so I began the story that started in the ghetto and ended with our arrival in Palestine. I did not leave out any details. We laughed together and wept together. The hours passed, coffee was drunk, another pot was made, the kugel was eaten, and the afternoon ended in hugs and kisses and the promise to go to Heidelberg together.

That night I told Chaim that I had made up my mind. Feygl and I were going to Heidelberg.

The next day I called the number on the American captain's paperwork, told the operator who I was, why I was calling, and with whom I would be traveling. An officer got on the line and I was given instructions when to arrive, who would pick us up at the airport, where we would be staying, and who would pick us up for my appearance in court. The deed was done. Googy was back in my life.

CHAPTER XIV

Heidelberg is a beautiful city. For reasons no one seems to know, it remained untouched by the war. Once the war ended, the office of the High Commissioner of Germany chose Heidelberg as its headquarters. Both the American military and the Department of the Army civilians who worked under contract to the military all lived very well in property confiscated for their use. Castles on the Neckar River and Gothic mansions were taken over for use as offices and residences. It was to just such a mansion that Feygl and I were taken upon our arrival after checking into our hotel and eating lunch.

Feygl was asked to wait in the outer room while I was shown into an inner office. The room was magnificent; it must have originally been a ballroom. It was huge with shiny parquet inlaid with intricate borders of darker wood. Three enormous crystal chandeliers hung from a painted ceiling. The walls were paneled in dark wood and one wall of bookcases had what appeared to be hundreds of volumes of legal books. The colonel who used this room as his office did not sit at a desk but at a beautiful antique writing table. His chair was a high-backed judge's chair which looked somehow out of place among all of the ornate furnishings.

I had never been in such a room. The chair in which I sat was one of a dozen or so brocade chairs with gilt wooden arms and legs placed throughout the room. The fact that this had, at one time, been the home of a German aristocrat made me angry, but I said nothing until the colonel spoke.

"Mrs. Adler" said the colonel, after greeting me, "You are the last witness in the case against Colonel Hauptmann. We are aware of the fact that you knew him well, and all we ask of you is that you tell your story honestly and to the best of your recollection. Please do not say things you think the court wants to hear. These are war crime trials. People tend to get very emotional and, in some instances, say things that are not quite accurate in their desire to convict. Colonel Hauptmann's role as commandant of the Hotel Polski is strange and still not fully understood. It is hoped that by virtue of your closeness to the colonel, you will be able to shed some light on this enigma. By the way, I never asked you if you felt you would need an interpreter. One can be made available, should you so desire."

I did not respond to the question. Running through my mind were the remarks, the innuendo, of what the colonel had said, "You knew him well by virtue of your closeness?" This clearly was not the time to inquire what he had meant by these remarks. Finally, looking around the room and then back at the colonel, I asked, "Whose home was this before the war?"

"I really don't know," replied the colonel. "The Judge Advocate was assigned to this building. We are very fortunate to have such beautiful offices."

Getting around to answering the last question, I finally said, "No, I won't need an interpreter. If I have any question about the meaning of a word or expression, I will inquire. An interpreter will not be necessary. By the way, will you be doing the questioning? Are you the one I will see in court?"

"Oh, no," said the colonel. "The trial is being conducted by Major Stanley Lefkowitz, a very good prosecutor. It is held before three judges, one Russian, one French, and the presiding judge is an

Englishman. The Russian and the French judges will wear head phones for immediate translation, as will the defendant and his lawyer. The courthouse is a little ways out of town. You and your companion will be picked up at 0900 hours. At ten hundred hours, you will be called to testify. I thank you for coming. We want the world to know how important these trials are. When people from all over the world come to testify, it shows that what we are doing has significance. Do you have any questions?"

"Yes," I replied, "I have two questions. The first is, where was Colonel Hauptmann apprehended? The second is, why is this trial not being held in Poland? The officer who came to my home in Tel-Aviv said that these trials were often held in the country where the offenses occurred."

"As to the first question," the colonel replied, "Colonel Hauptmann, from what we have learned, lived on a farm on the outskirts of Munich. It was not easy to find him since his name was rather common. We did not know whether he had changed it to avoid being apprehended, but he was, in fact, caught due to a mistake, a rather silly mistake on his part. He continued to use the name Peter Hauptmann and purchased airline tickets to Israel on El Al, leaving from the Munich airport. The Israelis checked his passport and found his name on a list of known war criminals, and grabbed him right then and there."

"Oh, my God," I thought, turning white as a sheet. "He must have remembered my name," I said to myself. "He was coming to see me. What if he had opened the door and seen Sholom? He would have known. Thank God he was apprehended."

"Are you O.K.?" asked the colonel. "You suddenly turned pale; can I get you a glass of water?"

"I'll be fine," I replied, as the color returned to my face. "Did anyone ask him why he was going to Israel?"

"No," responded the colonel. "Many German tourists have been visiting Israel, of late. If the Israelis asked him, they never told us."

"And in answer to your second question, we know that all the people who were sheltered in the Hotel Polski were Poles, but the places they were sent and the many visas and passports that were found gave the prosecution of Colonel Hauptmann a more international implication. It is for this reason that he is being tried here, in Heidelberg."

Pausing to see if I had any more questions, he went on, "If you have no further questions, I suppose we are through. I really hope that your testimony will not be too upsetting to you." Coming out from behind the writing table, the colonel shook hands warmly with me and repeated, "Again, I thank you for coming."

I rose from my chair and nodded to the colonel without saying a word. He escorted me to the door. Feygl and I left the building and were driven back to our hotel. We said nothing to each other in the car, except to admire the beauty of the building that we had just left.

Once back in the hotel, we decided to have our meals in the room. Neither one of us had any desire to see the city, despite its beauty. We both resented being back in Germany, and although I still spoke an almost perfect German, we did not care to walk around Heidelberg or go into a restaurant speaking Hebrew to each other. It would have made us very uncomfortable.

It was now some five years since Feygl had been rescued from the train in the middle of the field by the Americans. Seeming to read my mind, she said at just that moment, "My life was saved. I have no doubt that train was headed for a death camp. If it weren't for our friendship, Germany is not a place I would ever have returned to voluntarily." Neither of us could help but see every German man as a Nazi. So, without any further discussion, we silently agreed that staying in the hotel would make our stay in Germany as bearable as possible.

We each undressed and put on robes. I ordered dinner from room service, and while we ate, I told Feygl everything that had taken place in the colonel's office. I was still stunned by the fact that Googy had been on his way to Israel when he was apprehended. When I told that to Feygl, she was shocked. "Do you think he was trying to find you?" she asked. "I immediately wondered the same thing," I replied. "Thank God they caught him in Munich."

I then related the schedule for the following days and we both agreed that, assuming I was through in one day, we would leave for home the following morning. There was certainly nothing to keep us in Germany.

After dinner we read some magazines that we'd brought from home, and since it had been a long day, we both decided we would try and get a good night's sleep. Feygl dropped off almost immediately. I lay there and sobbed quietly. Peter and the boys. How would they look today if they had the chance to grow up? My sweet Itzik, Oh, my God, I haven't called him that in years. Sholom, I know who your father is; beautiful Tamar. How I love you both. Feygl lost her whole family, yet she can sleep. Why can't I? My life is new, just like hers. I am happy in Israel with my new family. Oh, Googy, what have you done to me? Why must I come back and face you? I remember saying, "Maybe after the war...", and you said you could not imagine it. This is not what I meant. I don't know what I meant, but this is not it. I was insane at the Hotel Polski. The things that were happening to me ... the way I behaved. I cannot wait for tomorrow to be over. Another day and I will go back to my good life. I deserve a good life after what I have been through. I do not deserve this. Googy, why weren't you killed on the Russian front? Then I wouldn't be here. I wouldn't have to see you or look into your eyes.

Out of sheer exhaustion, both physical and emotional, I finally dropped off to sleep.

CHAPTER XV

Breakfast was served in our room, and at nine o'clock a staff car pulled up in front of the hotel and took us to a small building on the outskirts of the city. I assumed the building must have been a rural police station at one time since a number of the windows on the first floor were barred. The courtroom on the second floor was a good size, but I believed it must have been made by knocking out three or four walls and converting it into one room. It was new, and modern, but very plain. There was a raised bench for the judges, a reporter's table and chair next to the witness box, which was located to the right of the judge's bench. Two tables, some fifteen feet back, stood in front of the judge's bench for use by the prosecution and the defendant. A major and a lieutenant sat on plain wooden chairs at one of the tables. When Feygl and I were shown into the room, Feygl was asked to sit in the visitor's section. There was one other woman sitting there.

Upon seeing us enter the room and Feygl take a seat in the visitor's section, the major walked over to me and said, "I assume you are Anna Adler. My name is Major Stanley Lefkowitz. I will be conducting the case for the prosecution. I want to express my heartfelt thanks to you for willingly appearing and testifying in this matter."

I replied, "The colonel, whose name I do not recall, the one I met yesterday, told me I would be meeting you." And to myself I said, "Willingly appearing? I wonder."

"May I ask you a question?" I inquired.

"Certainly," replied the major.

"Who is the other woman sitting in the visitor's section?"

"Oh, that is Colonel Hauptmann's wife," said the major.

"His wife? I asked. "I didn't know he was married. He never mentioned a wife to me when I knew him."

"According to the record," answered the major, "his first wife was killed in a bombing raid. He married this woman after the war. Is this of concern to you?"

"Oh, no," I replied. "I just wondered. By the way, when the colonel was apprehended by the Israelis, was his wife with him?"

"To my knowledge", said the major, "he was traveling alone."

I'm sure he was coming to see me, I thought to myself. I wonder if he was married when he called me "my love"? Turning to the major, I said, "I am ready whenever you are."

The major replied, "As soon as the judges take their places, the MP's will bring in the prisoner and you will be called. Please take a seat for the time being."

"Thank you," I said as I sat down next to Feygl in the visitor's section. I whispered to Feygl, "They refer to him as 'the prisoner'. My, how things have changed."

Before Feygl could reply, the door behind the judge's bench opened and the three judges came out. Everyone rose as the court was called to order. The Presiding judge, the Englishman, sat between the other two, who immediately put on their headsets. The M.P. on duty was then instructed to bring in the prisoner. From a side door, the prisoner was escorted to a seat at the defendant's table by two military policemen. He was in shackles. Prior to actually sitting down, he looked over at his wife and nodded to her. Then he looked at me and seemed to knit his browns for a few seconds in shock and recognition. He quickly regained his composure and turned, shook hands with his lawyer, and took his seat. Both the colonel and his counsel put on their headphones.

The presiding judge then asked Major Lefkowitz, "I understand that you have one more witness in this matter. Is that so?"

The major replied, "Yes, your honor, we are ready to proceed."

The judge nodded and the major called, "Anna Adler, to the witness box, please."

I rose from my seat and walked slowly to the witness box, but never took my eyes off Peter Hauptmann. It had been some six years since I had last seen him. The man I now saw before me looked smaller, and twenty years older. He appeared to have shrunken into himself and bore no resemblance to my Googy. "Oh, my God, don't let me call him Googy when I testify," I thought.

Standing in the witness box, I was sworn in, I sat down and the questioning began:

Q: What is your name and where do you reside?
A: My name is Anna Adler, and I reside in Tel Aviv in the State of Israel.
Q: Were you ever known by the name Rosa Feurmann?
A: I was.
Q: Why did you change your name?
A: I did not change my name. It was changed for me.
Q: Can you explain that for the court?
A: I was confined to the Hotel Polski in Warsaw after the destruction of the Warsaw ghetto. For some reason, which I still do not understand, Colonel Hauptmann, who was in charge of operations at the hotel, chose me to be his companion and his servant. A number of months after this relationship began; the colonel informed me that I and a dear friend who was also confined at the Hotel Polski, along with a number of others, were to be traded for a number of

German nationals who were interned in Turkey. In furtherance of our release to Palestine, and as part of the trade, my friend Itzik Grynshpan and I were to travel as husband and wife under the names Chaim and Anna Adler. This was the way the exit documents were written, and this is the way our visas were issued by the Turkish government. I assume that these documents came from a family that had been killed by the Nazis. The same procedure took place for about twenty other people who also were part of the trade. From that time on, and until this day, I call myself Anna Adler. Rosa Feurmann lived another life in another time. She had another family, and they no longer exist. I, fortunately or unfortunately, was out of the ghetto at the time they were picked up and sent to a death camp.

A momentary silence hung over the court. Colonel Hauptmann's head was down, and when I looked over at him, it almost appeared as if he were crying.

Major Lefkowitz continued, "I am sorry for your suffering and for your loss. You must be a very strong woman. Are you prepared to continue?" I nodded affirmatively.

> **Q:** What were your duties as Colonel Hauptmann's companion and servant?
> **A:** I did whatever he asked of me. I had no say in the matter.
> **Q:** Describe for the court some of the things that he asked of you.
> **A:** He asked me to do chores in his office and to keep it clean. He asked me to dine with him. He asked me to serve him in his suite when he had guests.
> **Q:** Did you sleep with him in his suite?
> **A:** He slept in the bedroom, and I slept on the couch in the living room. That is as far as it went.
> **Q:** Mrs. Adler, please understand that before you were called as a

witness in this matter, you were fully investigated. I must therefore tell you that it has been reported that when you left for Palestine, you were pregnant, and, some seven-and-a-half months later, you gave birth to your son. Is that correct?

A: When I left for Palestine, I was not aware that I was pregnant. My son's father is Chaim Adler. And, in any case, what does any of this have to do with the prosecution of Colonel Hauptmann for the war crimes?

Turning to the presiding judge, Major Lefkowitz asked, "May I have the court's permission to respond to the witness? Her question deserves an answer."

The presiding judge replied, "It is a good question. I am somewhat interested in the answer as well, but I feel you are going a bit far afield." He looked at the other judges and smiled as they nodded in agreement.

Major Lefkowitz continued, "If it pleases the court, it must be understood that the nature of the witness' relationship with the accused plays a vital role in the testimony we are about to hear. If she had a romantic relationship with the accused, then..."

Interrupting the major mid-sentence, I asked, "May I respond before the major goes any further, Your Honor?"

The Court: "Yes, you may, Mrs. Adler."

Speaking slowly and quietly, and with anger in my eyes and my voice, I said,

"Regardless of what my relationship was with the accused, I barely recognize the person sitting at the defendant's table now. He bears no resemblance to the Colonel Hauptmann I knew six or more years ago. You are therefore asking me to testify about someone who, to me, is not even in this courtroom. You used the word 'romantic' to describe my relationship with Colonel Hauptmann after I told you that my husband, Professor Peter Feurmann, and my two sons died in the ovens. Colonel Hauptmann was a Gestapo colonel, perhaps the one responsible for the death of my family, and you want to know if I had a 'romantic' relationship with him? You are a Jew, Major Lefkowitz. But for the grace of God, you could have lived in Warsaw. Perhaps that is where your family comes from. Could you have had a 'romantic relationship'...? "

The Court: "I see where this is going, and I am obligated to tell you, Mrs. Adler, that Major Lefkowitz is neither a witness nor a defendant in this matter. He is therefore not required to answer your hypothetical questions. Furthermore, your relationship with the defendant is a relevant matter, and the major has a right to inquire into it."

I sat dumbfounded. I felt that I could scream. It was some ten years since I had left the Hotel Polski and I had kept the story of my life there to myself, with the exception of Feygl. Now I was being forced to reveal it to these people, to these strangers. "What if I were to leave the witness box and walk out?" I said to myself. "To hell with them and their trial. Let him go free. He gave me my freedom, and now I can repay the favor." Suddenly the voice of Major Lefkowitz interrupted my thoughts.

Major Lefkowitz: "I am sorry I upset you, Mrs. Adler. If you would permit, me, I have just a few more questions about your relationship with the colonel."

I shook my head knowing I had no choice.

Q   Did you have a physical relationship with the colonel?
A: Yes.
Q: How often?
A: Whenever he would require it.
Q: Do you feel that he raped you?
A: If you mean that he forced himself upon me, the answer is no. But to the best of my knowledge, rape has more than one definition.
Q: What do you mean by that?

Looking squarely at the judge, I replied, "This is not hypothetical." Turning back to look at Major Lefkowitz, I continued.

> A: If a Jewish woman and the man with whom she is involved have come out of hiding in Warsaw after the destruction of the Ghetto and find themselves under the protection of a Gestapo colonel, who, under any pretext, can send them both to Pawiak prison to be executed, and the colonel requests sex from the woman, would that not come under the definition of rape? I am sorry, I forgot. I am not permitted to ask any questions. Let me state it as a fact.

Major Lefkowitz stood silently, shaking his head in agreement. No one said a word.

The Court: "Do you have anything further, major?"

Major Lefkowitz: "Yes I do, with the court's permission."

> Q: Were you in the service of Colonel Hauptmann when General Seidl came for a visit to the Hotel Polski?
> A: Yes, I was.
> Q: Did you meet the general?
> A: I was never introduced formally, but he did inquire of the colonel whether he was fucking me and expressed an interest in doing so himself. I was present when he made those comments, and those were his exact words.

Major Lefkowitz looked up, sighed, and shook his head in disbelief. "Again, my apologies for putting you through this," said the major. "May I continue?" I nodded.

> Q: Did you hear any of their conversation?
> A: When I was present in the room, they spoke of nothing of consequence that I can recall. I was told to wait in the

bedroom after dinner had been served so that I would be available if they should need anything else. It was then that I heard through the door I had left open just a bit, just a crack, so that I could hear. They were discussing the things that were taking place at the hotel.

Q: Can you tell us what you heard, to the best of your recollection?

A: Colonel Hauptmann complained that he was not a Jewish social service worker and did not understand what he was doing or why he was chosen to be at the Polski. General Seidl responded by telling him what a diabolical plan it was. How the visas and the passports of dead Jews would bring them a boatload of live Germans. Matching up families, matching people to visas and exit permits. I know for a fact, that is just what Colonel Hautpmann was doing.

Q: How do you know this?

A: A few days later, after General Seidl's visit, Colonel Hauptmann revealed to me that he was leaving the Hotel Polski. He had received another assignment, and as I stated earlier, he had arranged for me and my friend Itzik, the father of my son Sholom, which means peace, to be traded for a number of Germans interned in Turkey. He did this for some twenty other individuals and families as well, by giving them new identities and arranging for our transport out of Poland and, ultimately, to Palestine. I do not know what testimony you may have heard from others, nor do I know which war crimes Colonel Hauptmann is charged with. I do know that he saved my life, the life of my friend Itzik, who is now my husband, Chaim Adler, and the lives of all the others who left Poland for Palestine.

Q: Do you know a person by the name of Shimon Cohen, who was formerly known as Berel Rabinowitz?

A: Of course. He and his family were on the transport to

Palestine with Itzik, myself and others.

Q: Do you know if he had any sort of special job during the time you were both at the Hotel Polski?

A: He dealt with Colonel Hauptmann, I believe, on behalf of a Jewish organization that was trying to save the last of the Jews that still lived in Warsaw. He negotiated with Colonel Hauptmann for the sale of visas and exit permits to those countries that would accept the Jews as refugees.

Q: Are you aware that most of the South American countries that offered a safe haven to the Jews were on the side of the Nazis and never interned any Germans?

A: No, I knew nothing of that. If that was the case, then what was the point of the entire operation? My apologies. No questions.

Q: Are you aware that Mr. Cohen testified that he argued repeatedly with Colonel Hauptmann that selling visas to these countries and allegedly sending the people from the Hotel Polski to these countries was, in fact, sending them to their death?

Before I could answer, Colonel Hauptmann's lawyer rose and objected to the question. "This witness just testified that she knew nothing of this matter. Asking these questions is simply allowing counsel to rehash the earlier witness' testimony."

The Court: "Objection sustained. Do you have anything else to ask this witness?"

Major Lefkowitz replied, "Another few questions, if I may?"

Q: Do you know what became of the cash, gold, and silver that was used to purchase these visas?

A: I assume it all went to the German government, but I have no direct knowledge of this.

Q: Did Colonel Hauptmann and General Seidl speak of the money or the gold?

A: I do not recall any such conversation, but I do recall Colonel Hauptmann telling General Seidl that if his actions were nothing but a sham or a fraud, then there would come a day that both he and General Seidl would be held accountable.

Q: Is it your opinion that what was taking place at the Hotel Polski, what Colonel Hauptmann was doing, was a sham or a fraud?

A: I don't know. I just don't know. It was strange. My friend, Feygl, who is here with me in the courtroom ... her husband paid dearly for their visas to Uruguay. This was just a week or so before Colonel Hauptmann left the Hotel Polski. Feygl's group was taken from the hotel to Pawiak Prison and from there to Vittel in France. I am sure the court has heard testimony from other witnesses about these places. From there, they were taken to God knows where, when they were abandoned by the Germans in the middle of a field and rescued by the Americans. She and her husband assumed they were on their way to a death camp. Yet, those of us who had no money and nothing with which to buy visas were saved and sent to Palestine. To this day, after having lived through it, I still don't understand it. I don't think I will ever understand it. The colonel to whom I spoke yesterday used the word 'enigma'. I believe that means mystery. What were the Germans trying to accomplish? Was it a sham or a fraud? For what, for a few zlotys? They could have just killed the Jews and taken their gold without the entire pretense. I don't know what I think. It is still a mystery."

Major Lefkowitz nodded, "I thank you Mrs. Adler." Turning to the bench he said, "I have no further questions. The prosecution rests."

"May I make one other statement before I leave the witness box?" I asked.

"Of course," responded Major Lefkowitz.

"In the months I spent at the Hotel Polski," I said directly to the judges, "I never heard Colonel Hauptmann order anyone to Pawiak or to Bergen-Belsen. Whether he knew where these transports were going, I do not know. If he knew, he never said."

The Court: "Counsel, do you wish to cross examine?" he asked of the Colonel's attorney.

Counsel: "I do not, your Honor. The defense rests, and I wish to thank the last witness for her honesty," he said, nodding to Anna.

The Court: "I, too, wish to thank the witness for speaking her mind so honestly and forthrightly. This case is now closed. The prisoner will be remanded until sentencing."

As the M.P. walked toward Colonel Hauptmann to take him back into custody, he arose and addressed the court as the judges were about to leave the bench. Removing his headphones, he said in German, "May I have the court's permission to speak privately with the witness?" The presiding judge, not understanding German, turned to me as I walked from the witness box toward Feygl and asked what the prisoner had said.

I stood still as if I were frozen in place. I slowly turned to the judge and said, "The prisoner wishes to speak privately with me. Is he permitted to do that?"

The three judges huddled together. All spoke enough English that they could converse about this matter. The colonel's wife stood rigid at the bar separating the visitors from the courtroom and shook her head as if she feared that nothing good would come of this. The judge turned to me and said, "Do you wish to speak with him? This is a most unusual request."

I hesitated for a minute and said to myself, "Googy, you made me Anna Adler. You will never be able to take that away from me." Looking at the judge, I replied, "If the prisoner wishes to speak with me, I am willing to do so."

Turning to the MP, the judge said, "Take the prisoner and escort Mrs Adler to the small conference room, off the courtroom. Stand guard and watch through the window in the door. They are not to touch each other or give anything to one another. Is this understood, Mrs. Adler? You have five minutes."

One MP took the colonel while another escorted me to the conference room as the presiding judge had instructed.

It had nothing but a table and four chairs. The colonel sat down on one side and I sat on the other. He was still manacled.

Speaking in English, the colonel said to me, "You called me 'the prisoner'? I may not look the same as I did years ago. Have you forgotten my name?"

"It would have been inappropriate for me to call you 'Googy' in the courtroom, but I see you have learned English. What is it that you wish to talk about after all these years?" I asked.

"I always knew some English, even when we were together at the Hotel Polski," said the colonel. "Being a prisoner of the Americans has improved my knowledge, but my language skills are not important now." He reached across the table, as of to take my hands in his. I drew back, but the colonel went on, "We have a son, Rosa. Please do not deny it. Tell me about him."

"My name is Anna. That is the name you gave me. And you had a wife when you were ordering me into your bed," I said angrily.

"I never ordered you," said the colonel. "I remember saying I did not want it to be an order. I had hoped that we had developed some kind of understanding, some kind of relationship. I wanted you to come to me on your own, and you did. You know you did. Was I not kind to you? Did I not protect you and your gentleman friend? My wife had died more than a year before I came to the Hotel Polski. Please, Rosa ... or Anna, as you wish.... you know I was not a monster. I had come to love you, and from that love we produced a child. I beg you, tell me about him."

Never expecting that I would again be talking to Colonel Peter Hauptmann, I was momentarily taken aback.

"We have no son," I replied slowly and with exactness. "And there is nothing to talk about. You are again a married man. Whatever the future holds for you, I wish you the best. Even though you know where I live, never try to contact me again. Our months at the Hotel Polski are a dim memory to me and can never be resurrected. I thanked you in the courtroom for giving me my freedom, and I hope that my testimony will be of benefit to you. I thank you again here in this room. I understand you were apprehended at the airport heading for Israel. I don't know what that was all about. If you were coming to find me, I say now and forever, you have no right to re-enter my life. And now, I believe our five minutes are up."

I rose from my chair without giving the colonel any opportunity to respond, and the MP opened the door for me. The colonel sat, dejected and not moving. I went back into the courtroom where Feygl was waiting for me, as was the colonel's wife. As I came through the door, the colonel's wife approached, "How is Peter? Did he speak of me?" she asked in English.

I looked at her with pity and replied in German, "Oh, yes. He spoke of you and said he loved you very much."

"Oh, thank you, thank you so much," she replied in German. "And thank you for your testimony on behalf of Peter. You were very kind, and I know it will be of help to him."

"I hope so," I said, as I walked away and took Feygl by the arm. Our car was waiting to take us back to over hotel. By the next day we were back in Israel.

Upon my return, Chaim and the children ran to me and I hugged them as if I had been away for a year. Finally, when the children were in bed and Chaim and I had time for us, he asked me, "Nu, how was it?"

"Oh, Heidelberg is a beautiful city," I replied. "And the lawyer's offices were in the most spectacular building I have ever seen. It was like a castle."

Smiling and shaking his head, Chaim said, "Anna, you'll describe the architecture later. That's not what I'm asking you. How was the trial, and how are you?"

I thought for a moment before speaking. "It was difficult," I said. "Colonel Hauptmann looked like a little old man to me. He married after the war, and his wife was in court." Suddenly, with tears in my eyes, I reached out to Chaim and said, "Oh, Chaim, I have so much to tell you."

Chaim took my hands in his and said softly, "Are you going to tell me things that I don't already know? I doubt it. I am sure you have told those things, those secrets that you have kept bottled up all these years, to Feygl, and I imagine that you may have had to testify about those things in the court. That must have been very painful for you. You don't have to tell me anything, my darling Anna. And do you know why?"

By this time the tears were running down my cheeks. "Why, Chaim? Tell me why."

"Because I am in your debt, Anna, or should I call you Rosa?" He said with a smile, "and I will always be in your debt."

"My debt?" I sniffed. "What have I done that you are in by debt, Itzik?" I asked as I threw my arms around him.

"You saved my life, just as you saved yours," he replied. "You got us to Palestine. You gave us two wonderful children. How you were ever able to accomplish these miracles, I will never question. One does not question a miracle. Perhaps it was even the hand of God."

I stepped back and took Chaim's face in my hands and said, "It must have been through the hand of God that I found you. That is the biggest miracle of all."

CHAPTER XVI

Some six months after returning from Germany, I received an envelope bearing the insignia of the International Military Tribunal. When I opened it, I saw that it contained the decision and the opinion of the court in the matter of the War Crimes Trial of Colonel Peter Hauptmann.

Before reading it, I decided to call Feygl. "Feygl, you'll never guess what I received in the mail."

"You won the Irish Sweepstakes," said Feygl, "and since I am your best friend, you are prepared to share the proceeds with me."

Completely ignoring Feygl, I replied, "I received the decision of the court in the case against Peter Hauptmann."

"Nu," said Feygl, "What does it say?"

"I haven't read it. I decided to call you first because I don't know if I want to read it. You tell me what to do."

"Make coffee and I'll come over. We'll read it together," responded Feygl. "Is that all right with you?"

"Yes, please come over. I promise you I won't read it until you get here."

I put the pages back into the envelope and was almost wooden as I went about making coffee. I set the table and put out cake as if I were preparing for a party. Suddenly, I sat down and started to cry. "I have never testified in court before, let alone in a war crimes trial," I said to myself. "And now I might be responsible for sending a man to his death. How could I be responsible for the death of the person who saved my life? Yes, Googy, for a moment when we were making love, and that is what we were doing, I loved you, too. And we had a son. Sholom is your son. He even looks like you. I lied to you. I had to lie to you to preserve my sanity. And now I feel as if I am again as insane as I was when we were together. When will this end?"

Some ten minutes later, Feygl let herself in with the key I'd given her long ago and walked into the kitchen where she found me weeping hysterically.

"Anna, darling," she said, putting her arms around me. "What is it? Why are you crying so? Have you read the opinion?"

"Feygl, what happens if they have sentenced him to death?" I asked hysterically. "He saved my life. He is Sholom's father. I didn't have to go; I didn't have to testify. I would never have known the outcome."

"Stop it, Anna," said Feygl sternly. "Just stop it. Of course you would have known. Once they asked you to come, you knew he was being tried. How could you not have gone? It is your testimony that probably saved him." Holding me at arm's length and picking up a napkin from the table, Feygl wiped the tears from my eyes. "You serve the coffee and I will read the opinion to you. Is that what you want?"

Hugging Feygl, I said, "I don't know what I would do without you. Yes, that will be good." I poured the coffee and put the pot back on the stove, handing Feygl the envelope as we both sat down.

Feygl pulled the pages from the envelope, unfolded them and read the caption and the names of the three judges. She then went on to read, "This was one of the most difficult and confusing cases to come before this court. The determination of the guilt or innocence of the accused is dependent upon those events that took place at the Hotel Polski during the period when the accused was the commandant of the hotel. This court grants that the idea of recovering documents from Jews who were killed and using them to assign new identities to surviving Jews who came first to the Hotel Royal and then to the Hotel Polski seeking salvation was a disgraceful concept that originated in Berlin. The fact that the operation lasted as long as it did under the jurisdiction of at least three different commandants leads this court to believe that those who were in charge had to have known the end results of the implementation of this scheme."

Feygl looked at Anna, took a sip of her coffee, and continued reading. "It has been confirmed that certain foreign nationals with legitimate passports were, after an extended period of confinement, returned to their native lands. It has also been confirmed that certain people, even after having paid the ransom demanded by the implementers of this nefarious scheme, were, for reasons that defy explanation, taken to Pawiak prison or elsewhere and executed."

"In that no one, not even the accused, can give a rational explanation for what the German government was attempting to accomplish by selling visas issued by countries which had no German internees and which had no interest in accepting Jewish refugees, this court has no choice but to deem all activities that took place under the direction and command of the accused to have been a sham and a fraud of the most despicable nature."

Feygl glanced at me, but I implored her with my eyes to keep reading. I was so nervous - but I needed to know what they had decided to do to Googy.

"Despite the foregoing, and despite the deaths of the many people who sought salvation for themselves and their families by paying for exit documents and being offered in exchange for German nationals, there has been no direct testimony linking the accused to that which took place after those people left the Hotel Polski. Who ordered the convoys to Pawiak and who directed the convoys to Vittel are questions for which no answers have been provided. Nevertheless, this court finds it impossible to believe that the accused had no knowledge of the consequences of his actions when he literally robbed the survivors of their gold, their jewelry, and their money. This behavior was unconscionable, and one can only assume that when these people were called and told that they were leaving the Hotel Polski, the accused knew where they were going. It is therefore the decision of this court that the accused is guilty as charged and sentenced to ten years at hard labor to be served in Spandau Prison in Berlin."

I sat shaking as if I was praying. My eyes were closed, but Feygl could see the tears running down my cheeks.

"Anna," said Feygl, quietly, after a long silence, "no more crying. It is over. You have closure."

"But they didn't even mention the people he saved, "I replied.

"Yes they did, my darling Anna," said Feygl, folding me in her arms. "If you had not been there to testify that he saved your life, they would have ordered his execution. You must read between the lines, Anna, darling. It is over. You will never see him again. We will live our lives here; we are Israelis. The Hotel Polski is in the past. You must forget it. Never let Chaim see you like this. It would be an insult to the love he has for you. Come, let me see you smile. A new life really begins today. We have had so many new lives, but today is the best one."

I took the pages from Feygl, put them back in the envelope, and put them in a drawer in my dresser in the bedroom. I came back into the kitchen as Feygl was putting the dishes into the sink. I waited 'till Feygl's hands were free and I hugged her with all my strength. "Feygl, I love you so. Without you I would never have gotten through this. You are right," I went on, "Chaim must never see me like this. But I will let him read the decision. He is entitled to that, and then I will say to him the matter is closed."

"But you must believe it," Feygl said. "Otherwise you, too, will be guilty of a sham and a fraud."

"Yes, I do believe it," I said. "The matter is closed."

On occasion, I would see the name of Shimon Cohen in the newspaper or in a magazine. Since we both arrived in Palestine at the same time, we would run into each other at various social or political functions. Since Shimon had been an organizational representative at the Polski under his original name of Berel Rabinowitz, when he came to Palestine, he went right back into the same profession. With the birth of the State and the huge influx of refugees from all over the world, Shimon became a high-ranking government official whose job it was to sort out who was a Jew and who was entitled to come to Israel under the Law of Return.

At a social function held not long after I received the opinion of the Tribunal, I ran into Shimon and we had a few minutes to chat.

"Did you know that I was called to testify against Colonel Hauptmann at the trial?" I asked, "They told me you had already testified."

"Yes, I did," replied Shimon. "I saw your name on a witness list when I was there. I didn't know whether you would appear."

"It was not easy for me, but I went," I answered. "And I assume you received a copy of the decision?"

"I did," said Shimon. "I thought it was a rather logical and fair decision."

"I did as well," I replied. "But did you know that he was apprehended by Israeli authorities at the airport in Munich? He was on the way to Israel when he was caught."

"My God, why?" questioned Shimon. "I had not heard that. Why would be come to Israel?"

"For as great a mystery as the Hotel Polski was," I replied. "The reason Colonel Hauptmann would come to Israel is an even greater one."

We both embraced one another and said our goodbyes. We each knew the other was lying. Every time I looked at Sholom, I saw Googy.

CHAPTER XVII

The warm spring turned into a hot summer. After the first time I saw the announcement of the reunion at the Hotel Polski and spoke to both Chaim and Feygl about going, the announcement appeared on the third week of each month thereafter in the same newspaper. The reunion was scheduled for October, after the Jewish holidays, and was being sponsored by a group that called itself The Survivors of the Hotel Polski. I was sure that both Chaim and Feygl saw the repeated announcement of the reunion, but no mention was made of the matter, and I never spoke of it again.

Shimon Cohen was now a member of the Prime Minister's cabinet, but was always gracious when he would run into Chaim and me at an event, or if one of us ever called him.

When I saw the second or third announcement, I decided I would call Shimon to see what he knew about the reunion. I was put through to him immediately.

"Have you seen the announcement in the paper about the reunion at the Hotel Polski?" I inquired. "Do you know anything about it or the group that is sponsoring it?"

"Yes, I have seen it," replied Shimon, "but I know nothing about it. I have no idea what this group is. At first I thought I would inquire, but then I said to myself, why bother? I can think of no good reason to go back there."

"After all, you were the one who probably saved most of their lives," I said. "Wouldn't it have made sense for them to contact you?"

"I thought the same thing," said Shimon, "but then I realized that in order to find you or me, they would have had to know our new names. If we were to indicate a desire to go, then all this information would come out. Who needs it? And if these people came to the Polski after we left for Palestine, they wouldn't know us at all. Anna, it's over. It's yesterday's news. We are alive and well; we know what we lived through and we know what we lost. That's enough for me."

"It is interesting that you, who were so important to everyone at the hotel, say the things you do and feel the way you do," I responded. "I don't know why I am so obsessed with the idea of returning. Chaim and my friends, Avram and Feygl, you remember them, don't you ... all feel as you do."

"Of course, I remember them. I matched them up just a few days before we left," he replied. "They are the ones who were saved by the Americans. That was an unbelievable story. But as far as your obsession to return and attend this reunion, all I can say is that you are driven by the devil inside you. It would be a greater tragedy if you went and you knew nobody. What if you barely recognize the place and came home with a completely empty feeling? Then you would say to yourself. 'Why did I go? I should have listened to Shimon.' Anna, I have another call. I must run. It is your decision. Give my best to Chaim."

"Thank you, Shimon," I replied. "It is always good to talk with you."

Both of our families belonged to a beach club in Herzliya. Every weekend during the summer, if we were not visiting our children and grandchildren, or taking a trip, we would go to the beach to get out of the heat.

I kept my figure during all the years that passed, and Chaim was very proud of the way I looked. When some young kid, who could have been my son, gave me one of those looks, Chaim would laugh and call me his Beach Beauty Bubba.

And so, one day following my conversation with Shimon, in the middle of summer, on the beach, I told them all that I had an announcement to make.

"Please don't tell us you're pregnant," said Feygl.

"What would be so bad about that?" I asked. "I could get one of these young guys. You see how they look at me?"

"All right," interrupted Chaim, "enough of this nonsense. What is your announcement?"

Standing up from my sand chair, I turned to the others and said, "I am aware that none of you has mentioned the reunion, as it is called, at the Hotel Polski, and I assume that you have done so purposely in the hope that I will forget about it. Well, I spoke to Shimon Cohen, and he felt exactly the way you feel. He has no interest in going and knows nothing about the group that is sponsoring the event. With all due respect to the three of you ... you are my dearest and my closest family ... I have to say that I do not understand ... your lack of curiosity. By the same token, there is so much that I do not understand. This place played such a vital role in our lives, but I am not saying this to try and convince you. Quite simply, I am going. I am compelled to go."

At this point, Feygl started to get up from her chair, but I went on and Feygl sat down. "No, Feygl, I am not asking you to come with me. I know I asked you originally, but knowing how you feel, I do not wish to obligate you. I will go by myself. It will be for only three days. After all, I know my way around Warsaw, even if I have not been there for some twenty-five or more years. When I come home, we will all have dinner together and I promise that I will be honest with you. We will see then whether it was a waste of time or not."

This time, Feygl did get up from her chair and said, "Anna, I cannot believe you. What has …?"

Interrupting her, Avram said, "Feygl, for once in your life, stop talking. Anna has made her decision and it is not your business. It is between Anna and Chaim. There is nothing more for you to say, so come swimming with me." With that, he took her by the arm down the beach and into the water.

Chaim sat spread out on his beach chair and, with a smile, shook his head at me. "Nu, Mr. Sphinx," I asked. "What do you have to say? Can you understand me?"

"Anna, my love," replied Chaim. "I understand you so well, it frightens me. My only question is: are you a little crazy or are you a lot crazy? You have some sort of obsession with those years, with the Hotel Polski. If this will be the way to cure that obsession, then go enjoy your trip. And as you say, when you return, we will see whether it was a waste of time or not. I have never stood in your way and I will not do so now."

Dropping to my knees in the sand, I embraced Chaim and said to him, "I could not live without you. You ask nothing but you know everything. You are the best. You are my love."

Following the instructions set forth in the announcement, I contacted the reunion sponsors and was told I would be picked up at the airport in Warsaw and taken to the hotel. The dates were fixed. I called Feygl and told her when I would be leaving and when I would be returning. She promised that on the day I came home, she would have everyone, including the children and the grandchildren, over for dinner. They would all be there to welcome me.

The tickets were fairly reasonable, so I made the arrangements, and not another word was said.

Chaim drove me to the airport. I thanked him over and over for being so understanding, and he kidded me for being so "meshuggah," He dropped me off at the terminal, and I was on my way. Twenty-seven years ago I had left Warsaw. Now I was returning. Who knew what I would find when I got there?

CHAPTER XVIII

Traveling on the same plane to the reunion were two of the couples who had come to Israel with Chaim and me some twenty-seven years ago. I had seen them on occasion at meetings of Holocaust survivors, but had not remained friendly with them. Nevertheless, we greeted each other warmly and they asked after Chaim. When I told them he was not making the trip, they indicated they were glad he was well, but then they sat and talked among themselves, leaving me to read my newspaper.

I always had the feeling that my relationship with Colonel Hauptmann, a situation over which I really had no control, had created a barrier between the other survivors and me. Could I still be considered a collaborator? The Polish maid had called me a whore. That was something I would never forget. I must admit that these things were on my mind as I made my plans to attend the reunion. Perhaps others considered these things as well and would have been embarrassed to go with me. "Cut it out, Anna. You're talking about Chaim and Feygl and Avram." I shook my head to clear these thoughts from my mind.

Although the flight was without incident, the thoughts that flooded my brain would not let me rest. Would I be able to see the suite where I lived with Googy? I thought of the bed we'd shared and

I know I blushed with excitement. How could I ever forget the dinners, the wine, and the shared cigarette ... the passion that ensued? I was crazy then and I am still crazy. The Hotel must have been refurbished after all these years. Nothing will be the same. I will probably recognize no one, and no one will know me. The others were right. There really was no point in going. This is a waste of time and money. And so, round and round I went until the plane landed. It was then that I got my first shock.

Disembarking, I had no luggage to claim since my small valise had fit into the overhead compartment. I was to be picked up at the luggage carousel, and it was there that I saw a driver holding up a sign with the name "Rosa Feurmann." Anna Adler meant nothing to the sponsors of the reunion. When I registered, Rosa Feurmann was the name I had given them. Even that had created a problem because I had never been registered as a guest of the Hotel, so my name was not on the survivors' list. When I told them that I had been at the hotel as a maid on behalf of the partisans, they were more than happy to accept me. Seeing my name held up like that on the sign gave me a chill. Rosa Feurmann was a name from another life. It turned out they could have held up a sign that said Hotel Polski. I was the only one going to the hotel from the airport. The others who had flown with me were renting a car and planning to stay in Warsaw for a week. Although they offered to drive me to the hotel, I told them I had already arranged transportation and thanked them for their offer.

Rosa Feurmann was back in Warsaw. I was driven to the hotel and found that when called upon to speak Polish to the driver, it was not as easy as I had anticipated. So many years had passed since I had occasion to use Polish, that words were forgotten. I even used a Hebrew word instead of a Polish word once, laughing at my mistake and thinking to myself that I would never have believed my tongue would be so thick when it came to what had been my native language.

Arriving at the hotel, I realized that I must have passed through the ghetto, but it had been unrecognizable. It had been completely rebuilt with apartment houses, shops and hotels. But the Hotel Polski looked the same. Perhaps a bit cleaner, but the same four-story, hundred-year-old, mid-European hotel. We drove through the arch into the courtyard where I exited the car and walked into the lobby.

There was a registration desk set up where I checked in. I received a schedule of events. There were others at the registration desk, but I recognized no one. Was this going to be a waste of time? I was assigned a room with a private bath on the second floor where I unpacked the few things I had brought with me, lay down on the bed to rest, and looked over the schedule. A pre-dinner cocktail party and reception was being held in the lobby at six. Dinner would be at seven. I was not sure whether there were other guests staying at the hotel, or if the reunion had taken over the entire premises. Questions, questions.

The next morning, after breakfast, there would be a city tour. I was looking forward to that. I hoped it might take me back to where I had lived before the war. Just thinking about it brought back Peter and my babies. My eyes filled with tears. They would be grown men now, with families of their own. Peter would have been retired from the university, and we would be living a good life. The tears flowed. But then, I wouldn't have Chaim and Sholom and Tamar, and the girls. How could I be without the little ones? Chaim, why did you not stop me from coming? What am I doing here? What am I looking for? Why do others see things so clearly while I am so hung up on the past that I can't let go? I should not have come.

I remembered what Chaim had said when the colonel chose me as his companion. I could not understand what was happening, and he said, "Play it out." That's what I will do now ... I will play it out. In three days I'll be home. I can leave earlier if I choose. I don't have to stay for three days. Stop it, Anna, you just arrived. You wanted to come. You insisted upon it. Were you hoping Googy would be here? You can't be that naive. And if he was here, what would you do? Take him to bed with you? Try and rekindle the old romance, knowing that Itzik is waiting for you in the lobby? Get over it; you're not Rosa Feurmann anymore. You're Anna Adler, with a family, with children and grandchildren. Your son is to be married soon, and, if all goes well, by this time next year you may be a grandmother again. Grow up. These thoughts should have been out of your head years ago. Try and get some rest before the cocktail party.

Putting down the schedule of events, I put my arm over my eyes to shield them from the light. I rolled over on my side, weeping copiously, and dropped off to sleep.

It was six o'clock when I awoke. Although I was not interested in the cocktails, I did want to see if I knew any of the other guests who had come to the reunion. After a quick shower, I slipped on the dressiest dress I had brought with me and was out the door by a quarter of seven. On my way downstairs, I laughed to myself as I thought it was lucky I didn't have to sew up any bullet holes in my dress.

At quick count, there were some thirty or thirty-five people at the cocktail party. Other than the four people who came with me from Israel, I recognized no one and wondered where the others were from and when had they been at the Hotel. Out of obsessive curiosity, I went to the registration desk and inquired of the clerk whether there were still suites on the fourth floor. I was told that the suites were still there, but that they had all been refurbished. Some had been broken through to form larger suites, and everything was quite different. For as ridiculous as it might have been, I was momentarily disappointed. But then again, everyone's life had changed in the last quarter century. Why not the Hotel Polski?

Thanking the clerk and walking away from the desk, I took a glass of wine from a passing waiter and decided to try and mingle with the other guest. I was looking about the lobby, trying to remember where the old furniture had been, where the card room was, where the telephone room was, where I had first spoken to Itzik upon his arrival from the cemetery, when suddenly, a distinguished white-haired gentleman approached me.

"I beg your pardon," he said. "I don't know if you remember me. My name is Seymour Schwartz. When I left here for Palestine, I was Simcha Shvartz. My name before that is not important, but my wife Itka and I left with you and Itzik, Berel Rabinowitz and his family, and others. Two of the couples here recognized you and pointed you out. You have hardly changed. Believe it or not, I even remember you from the cemetery. I also recall that at that time your name was Rosa. Your friends tell me that you are now Anna."

I was dumbfounded, as I had no recollection of who this man was. Since he was so polite and so complimentary, I could not let on so, I said, "Simcha, yes, of course, I remember you. I gather that you did not remain in Israel for long because I do not recall having seen you there. By the way, thank you for the compliment. Itzik, whose name is now Chaim and I are grandparents, so it is good to know that the years have been kind to me. And Itka? She is not with you?"

"Oh, no," he replied. "Itka died a few years ago. We only stayed in Israel for a year and then went to the United States. Life was good to us as far as our business went. We, too, have children and grandchildren, but then Itka developed cancer. She died rather quickly. I would not have wanted to see her suffer."

"How sad for you," I said. "But tell me, why are you here?"

"I have never forgotten this place," replied Seymour. "Not because it was so unforgettable, but because it was such a puzzle to me. What was it all about? I do not mean to embarrass you, but I also recall that in the time that we were all here, you had a special relationship with Commandant Hauptmann. I often wondered about that."

My God, I thought. This man remembers everything. How come I cannot place him? He even remembers me from the cemetery.

"Yes, you are right. You have an excellent memory," I responded. "As you can imagine, my relationship with the colonel was not of my doing. I protested to him at the time. And now that you speak of it, I recall a conversation I had with him when I asked him why he had not chosen a German female soldier, someone with whom he would have had more in common. He became belligerent when I asked the question, telling me that he had chosen me, and that was the end of the conversation. I always feared that if I angered him, both Itzik and I would end up in Pawiak, which, as you know, would not have been a good thing."

At this point dinner was announced. Seymour asked me if he could escort me in to dinner so we could continue our conversation. I was not sure I wanted this man to accompany me, but in that I was alone, I graciously accepted his invitation. I took his arm and we went into the dining room where we were seated at a table with six other people.

Dinner was pleasant, the conversation light. Everyone seemed somewhat restrained. During the conversation, we learned that the six others at the table had been 'guests' of the hotel when the Russians drove the Germans out of Warsaw. None of them had been at the hotel for more than a few weeks, and although they had heard about the purchase of visas and exit permits, they had not experienced it first hand. Most of the conversation revolved around the schedule for the next two days.

I wondered to myself why these people had even chosen to come. Who did they wish to see? Who would they know? When I expressed these thoughts quietly to Seymour, he laughed and said he had been thinking the same thing. "These people may have found their way to the Hotel Polski twenty-five or more years ago," Seymour said, "but they really had no feel for what the place was. They didn't witness the murder of those who came seeking salvation or the new life given to those who didn't really know why they were saved. It was a puzzle then, and it remains a puzzle today."

The next morning, after breakfast, a modern bus awaited the reunion guests of the hotel. Our tour of Warsaw turned into a memoriam. As the bus drove through the different neighborhoods, we could hear sobbing from both the men and the women as they saw the places where they had lived, remembered how they had been forced out, relived the death of their loved ones, and thought of families who were no more. The deep, gut-wrenching pain over why we had survived and the others had not, never left us.

Lunch back at the hotel was quiet, and then the first session of the reunion started in the afternoon. It was obvious that there were no other guests at the hotel. Once lunch was over, our group was asked to remain in the dining room as fresh tea and coffee was served. Each individual or couple was asked to give their name and tell a little bit about their stay at the Hotel Polski. It was in this way that I learned that two of the couples had been on the train with Avram and Feygl. After the session ended, I had occasion to speak with them. They remembered Avram with kindness, so I took their addresses and promised that Feygl would be in touch with them.

A number of the others were rescued from the death camps by the Russians. These were people who had gone from the Polski to Vittel, and from Vittel back into Germany or Poland. Others were in Vittel when the war ended. I concluded, as a result, that very few of the guests had known Colonel Peter Hauptmann. For this I was grateful.

When it came my turn to speak, I introduced myself, spoke of Peter and my boys, the partisans, the cemetery, and my stay at the Hotel Polski. I then went on to tell of my life in Israel, and how I got there. I became the hero of the afternoon when I told the group that I had testified at the War Crimes Trial of Colonel Peter Hauptmann, the commandant of the Hotel Polski when I was there. When I finished with the fact that the colonel had received a ten year sentence in Spandau Prison, the crowd applauded. They saw me as a woman who had done something to protest the indignities, the horror, and the tragedy they had all lived through. I was to be commended.

I had dinner that night with Seymour, but now everybody wanted to talk to me. I was the local celebrity and, as a result, I was up until almost midnight chatting with this group and that. When the evening wound down, I said goodnight to Seymour and went back to my room.

The conversations with the other guests stayed with me, and as elated as I had felt about being the center of attention, that was how depressed I now felt because I thought of myself as a fraud. I got undressed, removed my makeup, washed my face, and stared at myself in the mirror. I was an iceberg ... one-tenth above water and nine-tenths below.

Everyone knew of the Nuremberg trials and the war crime trials that followed, but all they knew was what they read in the newspapers. That was not what I knew. Why had I been called as a witness? Calling Shimon made sense; he had played an important role in the operations of the Hotel Polski. What role had I played? Could I even dare to admit to those people who had showered me with congratulations that I had survived because I'd been Colonel Hauptmann's mistress? Even Seymour had alluded to it in a backhanded way. Thank God he did not mention my relationship with the colonel to the others.

That which is hidden must remain hidden. This is my life, and that is the way it must be. "Anna Adler," I said to myself, "turn off the light and go to sleep. Tomorrow will be a full day, and as others have said, I will 'play it out'."

The next morning, after breakfast, I told Seymour that I did not wish to follow the schedule but preferred to walk about the streets that had been the ghetto and into the cemetery. He was more than pleased to accompany me. We left the hotel and wandered the streets whose names we knew so well but whose buildings were now totally new and unrecognizable. Slowly, we made our way across the ghetto until we reached the cemetery. Here we wandered in silence. The cemetery was familiar, yet strange. Thankfully, no one had lived there for quite some time. It was finally occupied only by ghosts.

Not wanting to go back to the Hotel for lunch, we sought out a restaurant we both remembered from before the war. The neighborhood was still upscale and the restaurant was still there. It was as if thirty years had vanished. A leisurely lunch and a walk back to the hotel ended our tour, but not before we stopped at a beautiful gift shop. Looking at each other, we laughed in unison and said, "The grandchildren." In we went.

Seymour bought what he thought was appropriate, and I bought two beautifully costumed dolls for the girls, knowing they would love them.

When we reached the hotel, we each went to our respective rooms to rest, saying we were looking forward to dinner that evening. Dinner was a farewell banquet because the reunion would be over the following day.

The next morning, goodbyes were said all around. Strangers had become, friends and addresses were exchanged, even though each of us knew we would never hear from the other. A large number of people were heading to the airport, so this time I did not travel alone. Seymour was with me, as were the two couples who had known Avram, Feygl, as well as others. There were more goodbyes at the airport. Seymour embraced me and thanked me for making the reunion more pleasant than he could ever have expected. He extended his best wishes to Itzik, and then we each went our own way.

When I got off the plane at Lod, Chaim was waiting for me with a big bouquet of flowers. He stopped me from telling my stories about the reunion because he knew I would have to tell them all over again that evening. The whole family would be at Feygl's, so I should rest now and he would listen to all the stories when we had dinner with the children. I insisted that there was one thing I had to tell him. Finally, giving in he said, "Nu?"

"It wasn't a waste of time," I said.

CHAPTER XIX

No one got in to see Shimon Cohen without an appointment. Dealing with the emotional questions of immigration, whose heritage made one a Jew, who they'd lost in the Holocaust, and other issues such as these, made Shimon a sounding board for tears, for shouting and screaming, for table-pounding, and for every other expression of why the protagonist was right and Shimon was wrong. So, out of self-preservation, Shimon ordered that no one, other than the Prime Minister, could visit his office without an appointment.

But for every rule, there is an exception. On the day Anna's plane landed in Warsaw, Shimon's secretary came into his office with an interesting tale. "There is a well dressed gentleman in the waiting room who says he knew you many years ago, and that you were one of the few who saved his life. He identifies himself as Peter Hauptmann, and he would like fifteen minutes of your time." Leaning over in a confidential manner, she went on to say, quietly, "He started to speak English to me, but I heard a thick German accent, so I asked him if he would be more comfortable speaking German. He nodded his head and thanked me. Frankly, to me, he smells like an old Nazi. Do you know him?"

"Oh, yes," said Shimon. "I know him very well. It has been close to twenty years since I have seen him, but I certainly do know him. He is an old Nazi. Show him in, but after fifteen minutes, buzz me and remind me of my next appointment."

※

Peter Hauptmann looked better than he had at his trial. A quick tally made him close to seventy years of age, but he had regained a certain strength in his walk and had good color in his cheeks. The sallow old man who had been on trial was gone. A shirt, tie and jacket were in direct contrast with Shimon's informal, open-shirt look.

"Colonel Peter Hauptmann," said Shimon, rising and extending his hand. "I must admit that on the list of people I never expected to see today, you may be number one. What brings you to Israel, and why to see me?"

"Oh, please," responded Hauptmann. "Do not call me colonel. That is a thing of the past. I am a gentleman farmer and a tourist in your country. I am here with my wife; she is out shopping with a group of women. I told her I had some business to attend to, and being a dutiful wife, she asked no further questions."

"And I gather that coming to visit me is the business of which you spoke?"

"Berel Rabinowitz was the name by which I knew you," responded Hauptmann.

"Shimon Cohen is the name I must have given you, although, in all truth, I really don't recall. But I have seen your name in the newspapers in Germany. I realized from your position that you must have been Berel Rabinowitz, and I come to you now on a matter of personal privilege. I ask that what we say in this office remains in this office."

"I am listening," replied Shimon. "You have my word."

"The last witness at my trial some seventeen years ago," Hauptmann went on, "was Rosa Feurmann, now known as Anna Adler, through my good grace. When I learned that she'd been pregnant when she left the Hotel Polski and that she'd had a son, I asked to speak privately with her, and the judges permitted it. She refused to acknowledge that the boy was my son and warned me never to interfere in her life again. I do not wish to interfere in her life ... that is the reason I am coming to you. I have no knowledge of the boy's whereabouts. He should be in his twenties at this time, a mature young man. I would like to meet him just a few minutes without his mother knowing of my visit. Is this something that you would do for me?"

It took a moment for Shimon to respond. "Why should I?" asked Shimon. "Why should I betray my friends, Chaim and Anna Adler, for the likes of you? Have Anna and I not done enough for you by saving you from the hangman's noose?"

Twisting uncomfortably in his chair, Hauptmann clenched his hands in his lap, and shaking his head in acknowledgment, he said, "You are making this very difficult for me. I had not intended to tell you what I am going to tell you, but now, after so many years, it makes little difference. I needed you, Herr Cohen, at the Hotel Polski, to help keep order and discipline among the so-called guests. Your presence was vital. But I also kept my eye on the other people around you. I had been watching Rosa, and noticed that despite her maid's uniform; she really rendered no service and spoke with you far too frequently to be a Polish maid. I recall telling you when I stopped her at the door of the Hotel that I thought she was a spy for the underground, but in all the time that she and I were together, I never asked her and she never told me. It was because I came to care for her that I did not want to know. Yes, I may have been a Gestapo colonel, but I was still a person with a certain amount of decency and a great amount of bitterness. My wife had been killed in an Allied air raid, and here I was shuffling papers like a clerk. What happened between Rosa and me was real, but has remained unspoken for obvious reasons. So when I learned, in later life, that I had a child about whom I knew nothing, my natural inclination was to want to meet him, or at least see him. Do you understand that?"

"Herr Cohen," he went on, "I served my time for my war crimes. I thanked you then and I thank you now for your honest testimony.

However, I am speaking not only as a father, but as a person who can say to you, you owe me. Herr Cohen, I saved your life, the lives of your wife and your children. Just tell me where I can find the young man. If he chooses to tell his mother about my visit, then that is between them. Is what I am asking so outlandish?"

Shimon was troubled. What Peter Hauptmann asked and said was neither outlandish nor basically untrue. Shimon knew that Sholom Adler was a professor at Tel-Aviv University. His specialty was history, and, among other things, he was researching the role of the Hotel Polski in the overall tragedy of the Holocaust. "This would be an opportunity for Sholom to speak to someone with first hand knowledge of the subject from the German point of view," Shimon thought to himself. "The decision should be his, but I cannot let Anna or Chaim know that I am responsible for facilitating this meeting. Perhaps at a later time, but not now. I just don't know if I am doing the right thing. Do I, in fact, owe this Nazi bastard anything? Shimon, you decide the fate of others all day long. Make a decision."

There was a long silence. "Are you a gentleman?" Shimon asked.

"You know that I am," replied Hauptmann. "Any conditions you set, I will adhere to them strictly. You have my word."

"There are two things we must agree on, so much so that without such an agreement, I will tell you nothing," said Shimon.

"Please let me have your terms," replied Hauptmann.

"If I tell you where you can find Sholom Adler, you must promise me that my name will never come up in the discussion. He must never know that I gave you his address," Shimon said forcefully.

"Done," said Hauptmann. "And what is the second term?"

Heaving a sigh, Shimon went on. "If I should learn, in the future, and you may be sure that I will, that you discussed his mother's relationship with you or your insistence that he is your child, I will seek you out, no matter where you are, and I will kill you. I may have saved your life once, but not this time. Are we in agreement?"

"On my honor as a gentleman," Hauptmann replied. "It had never occurred to me to mention your name, and I would never do anything to displease Rosa. My relationship with her meant too much to me. I just want to meet the young man, speak with him, and wish him a good life. I promise I will not upset him in any way. Again, I promise this on my honor and on the threat to my life. I take you seriously, Herr Cohen. It is good to know that people have such good friends in this world."

"Herr Hauptmann, the information I am about to give you I offer not for you, but for Sholom. He is a professor of history at Tel-Aviv University and is doing research on the Hotel Polski. What better person, with first hand knowledge, is there than Colonel Peter Hauptmann, the commandant of the Hotel? Tell him that you learned of his research and that you thought that you could be of help. Make up any excuse that you wish. I am sure you will be well received. By the way, one thing that I am sure you are not aware of is, that this very day, there is a reunion at the Hotel Polski for those people who spent time there and survived the war. I know that Mrs. Adler wanted to go. Whether she went or not, I do not know."

Getting up, smiling, and with an outstretched hand, Herr Hauptmann said, "One thing I know for sure is that I survived the war, but I would not be welcome at the reunion. Herr Cohen, I thank you for your time and courtesy. My fifteen minutes are up. I promise to abide by our agreement, and I am grateful for your understanding. I doubt if we will ever see each other again."

They shook hands, and with that he turned on his heel and marched out.

CHAPTER XX

When Chaim and I arrived at Feygl's house, there was such hugging and kissing and carrying on that you would have thought I had been gone for a year. Moshe, Tamar, and the girls were there, and although Tamar and I usually spoke at least twice a week, and sometimes more, we had not seen each other for some two months. I took one look at Tamar and said, "You're pregnant." When Tamar nodded her head in acknowledgment, the hugging and kissing started all over again. The questions flew. "When are you due?" "Is it a boy or a girl?" "Why didn't you tell me?" and on and on, to the point that everyone forgot that I had been away.

No one was happier to see their grandparents than the girls. They knew that whenever Grandma went on a trip, there would be something for them. When they saw the dolls, there were more hugs and kisses, followed by squeals of delight.

Sholom and Chava were there, as well. The fact that they were living together, unmarried did not thrill me or Chaim, but these are today's young people. Besides, we loved Chava, so there was nothing more to be said. She was one of the family, and who were we to talk about living together without being married? Chava also brought a little something for the girls, and besides, to them, she was their aunt.

Avram served wine to the adults and soda to the children. As everyone finally settled down, Feygl called the family to the table.

Like me, there were two times when Feygl didn't lock her door. The first was when the family was coming. Rather than get up each time someone arrived, it was easier to leave the door open and holler, "come in," whenever anyone knocked. The other time was at the Passover Seder. Since Elijah, the prophet, was expected, the door was to remain open. So, that evening when everyone came into the dining room and were about to take their places at the table, Feygl heard the door open without anyone knocking. "Who could it be?" she asked as she walked out into the foyer. The next thing we heard was a scream of joy. In came Feygl with Eitan, in beret and full uniform, and again the screaming, the shouting, the hugging, and the kissing. Eitan might be a major in IDF intelligence, but here he was, a son, a brother, an uncle, a beloved member of a beloved family. "So why isn't he married?" Feygl asked Avram privately.

There was no one in the world more proud of Eitan than Avram. Through all the years he never forgot the days when Eitan, then Ernst, was so angry with him that he wouldn't speak to him. And when they were at Pawiak prison and would meet at the fence, had it not been for Feygl's insistence, Ernst wouldn't even look at him. "How lucky I was to have had Feygl in those days," thought Avram, as he rushed to hug and kiss his son.

Moishele had taken to Feygl instantly. She became his Eema[1] from the day he met her. At this time, his recollection of his mother was, at best, vague and unclear. Not so, for Eitan. He was older, and he remembered his mother quite clearly. For as much as he loved Feygl ... and he did love her with all his heart ... he still called her Feygl and not Eema.

Strangely, but for as happy and content as Feygl always seemed to be, there also existed in her anger and jealously that she never expressed, but which I could feel. Over the years, having lunch,

---
[1] Mother

sitting on the beach during the week when the men were at work, she would talk. Remembering the promise she'd made to herself on the night she discovered that her entire family had been killed, she could never make peace with the fact that she wanted her own children desperately, but it never came to pass. She loved Avram dearly, and she loved the two boys with all her heart. But they weren't hers. She and Avram had tried to have children of their own, but for some reason she never became pregnant. They sought medical advice, but to no avail. Could what she had lived through have caused her to become sterile? Avram was OK, according to the doctors, so it must be her. Honor your family. She just could not do it. And for this reason, I felt, she was always jealous of me. I lived through tragedy. I lost my husband and two boys. I lost my children; not my brother and sisters. Yet, I became pregnant again, not once, but twice. My figure was still attractive in a bathing suit, but Feygl had let herself go. "Be thankful that Avram loves you and still wants you. We all have things that we have to make peace with," I told her when she was in one of her moods.

"What a wonderful surprise," Avram said to Eitan. "What are you doing here?"

"Did Feygl not tell you that I spoke to her a few days ago? She told me all about the family getting together," replied Eitan. "So I hopped on a military transport and will spend a few days, if you haven't rented out my room."

At which point Moshe said laughingly, "They'll have to throw out the tenant and make room for you. That is the least they can do."

"Right you are," said Eitan, with his arms around Moshe and Tamar. "I see the two of you have been pretty busy," he quipped, looking at Tamar's belly. "I thought you were supposed to work on the kibbutz?"

"We get an hour off each day," said Tamar, kissing Eitan on the cheek, "for rest and relaxation. You ought to come and visit us some day. We might find someone with whom you can rest and relax."

"That is sounding better and better." replied Eitan, as he kneeled and took hugs and kisses from his nieces.

Another place was set at the table, more wine was poured, and we all drank a toast to Tamar and Moshe on the addition to their family and to me on my return from Warsaw.

"So," said Avram, from the head of the table, 'tell us, Anna, how was Warsaw? It has been so many years for all of us."

"Before I tell you about Warsaw and the reunion," I said, as I took out a sheet of paper from my pocket, "I met two couples who were on the train with you when you were rescued by the Americans. They remembered you, Avram, with great warmth. They said you saved their lives. That's a story you have never told us. They live in the United States, and I told them you would be in touch with them." Handing the paper to Avram, I said to the children, "Can you believe that after all these years, there are still stories that we have not heard and things that we don't know about each other?"

Avram looked at the paper, showed the names to Feygl, and asked if she remembered either of the couples. Feygl said she had no idea who these people were; maybe they had changed their names in America.

I laughed and said, "Now, it's up to you to choose whether to get in touch with them, but I know just what you mean. I'll tell you a story about not remembering someone that is even more embarrassing."

Feygl served dinner and I started my story from the beginning. I told them about the two couples from Israel on the plane with me, my reaction upon seeing the sign with the name Rosa Feurmann, and the fact that the Hotel Polski looked almost exactly as it had a quarter of a century ago. I got a good laugh when I told them about Seymour Schwartz, who had remembered me from the cemetery and who came to Israel with us, although I still could not recall him at all. "But I couldn't admit it," I went on, "especially when he told me how little I had changed."

"Eema, he was probably trying to hit on you," Sholom interjected, "a good looking grandma, traveling by herself. Was his wife there?"

"Don't be such a smart alec, Professor," I responded. "No, his wife had died of cancer, and he was the perfect gentleman at all times."

I then went on to describe our trip around Warsaw and how sad it was. It was strange. Everyone had looked forward to it, but when we got underway and went into some of the residential neighborhoods, you could hear sighs and weeping - so much sadness and many, many memories.

"Then in the afternoon," I said with a smile, "everyone told a little bit about themselves and the Hotel Polski, and I became the star of the show."

"How did that happen?" asked Chaim. "What did you do?"

"I told them some of my experiences," I replied. "But when I told them that I had testified at the trial of Colonel Hauptmann, and the ten years he served in prison, they all applauded. That evening, at dinner, people kept coming to the table. I was up until close to midnight talking about the Hotel, Pawiak, and what happened while we were there. You must realize that many of these people were not at the hotel during our stay. Most of them were liberated later on by the Russians, and none of them understood the business of selling exit permits or matching families to the visas of those who had been killed. I was very hard pressed to explain it logically. I don't think that I did a very good job."

My family sat in rapt attention as I continued. I went on to tell them about my choice not to follow the schedule the next day. I described my walk with Seymour through the streets that had once been the ghetto; how unrecognizable they were, and how silent was the cemetery. I concluded my story by saying that the trip had been most worthwhile. I did not, in the final analysis, regret having taken it, and above all, it was certainly not a waste of time.

Different questions were asked as the coffee and dessert were served. The girls had long since left the room to watch television, and as the discussion seemed to quiet down, Sholom spoke up and announced, "Now, I have a story to tell you which is, I guess you could say, a perfect ending to what we have heard this evening. I am glad you went, Eema, because for my research there are a lot of questions I would like to ask you. You see things and you evaluate things differently twenty-five years later."

"I suppose you are right," I smiled at my son. "I would be happy to be debriefed by you." Turning to Eitan I said, "Is that the right word, my handsome intelligence officer?"

"You know what," said Eitan. "I think Sholom is right. Seymour was probably trying to hit on you."

As everyone laughed, I responded, "How can I leave the defense of our country to a wise guy like you?" I got up and went around the table to give him a big hug and a kiss. Going back to my seat, I looked at Sholom and inquired, "So, what is your story?"

"Before we get to your story, Sholom," Eitan interrupted, "please let me comment, seriously, on what your mother has just told us. I would like to have gone to that reunion. Remember, Moshe and I were there. In those years we called him Moishele," he said with a smile. "I remember everything, to the extent that I would have liked to retrace our lives from the Polski to when we were rescued."

"What did I say?" I turned to Feygl. "I wanted to take the children, even the little ones, but no one would listen to me."

"I don't know if I could have gotten away," replied Eitan with a wave of his hand, "but those days are very clear in my mind." Looking to his brother, he went on. "I don't know what you remember of those times. We never spoke of it, which I suppose is somewhat strange, but ..."

"I'll tell you what I remember," said Moshe quietly. "I remember the first breakfast we had with Abba at the Polski, and he said we were together and it was like a party. And I started to cry and said if this was a party, then Mama should be there with us." With this, Moshe's eyes filled with tears.

Seeing her husband so upset, Tamar rose from her chair, took one step and sat down in her husband's lap, pulling him to her in a fierce embrace, saying, "Oh Moishi, Moishi, I never knew."

No one said a word for a full minute or more. This was the first time in close to thirty years that Moshe had spoken of his mother.

Freeing himself from Tamar's embrace, Moshe dried his eyes and said, "It's OK, honey, I'm OK. But there is one other story that stays with me, to this day. I don't remember whether it was that morning or a few days later when we first met Eema. From that day on, I never said a word, but I knew in my heart that we would never see Mama again. So I started to cry, and Eema came and picked me up, and I hung on to her for dear life."

Hearing this, Feygl burst into tears, rushed around the table to Moshe and Tamar, embraced them both, saying "Oh, how I remember; I remember knowing I would never let you go, my little Moishele."

As the moments passed, the silence was broken only by sobs. Feygl returned to her chair next to Avram, and Eitan said, "Those were sad times, hard times."

"And they were bitter times, added Avram. "Eitan wouldn't talk to me. Then, we called him Ernst. I didn't know what I had done wrong, but if there was anyone who saved us and made us a family again, it was Feygl. Here is a good one," he went on. "When Berel came to the table and introduced us to the lady who would be traveling with us, he told us her name was Rivka, but I should get used to calling her Feygl because that is what the travel documents said." Avram reached out to take Feygl's hand, picked it up, and put it to his lips. "I never knew her as Rivka. To me, she has always been Feygl, the one who kept my family together," and with that he, too, started to weep. "The mother to my children." We were all sobbing.

"Enough," said Eitan. "I started this, but this was not what I intended. Tell me, Abba[2], when we left Vittel and headed back into Germany, do you remember the name of the town we saw through the woods? Some of the other men went into town and brought back bread for us, and then we all went into town to an inn to eat."

"I know I have it marked down somewhere in my records," Avram replied, as he dried his tears. "But I don't recall it." Turning to Chaim

---

[2] Father

and Anna, he went on. "You must realize, we had no idea where we were. We assumed we were back in Germany, getting close to Bergen-Belsen, because the one time the train stopped, it was at a border crossing between France and Germany." Turning back to Eitan, he said, "Do you remember that giant of an American who spoke Yiddish? We all hugged and kissed him."

At which point, Chaim interrupted Avram and said, "Since we are all in the reunion mode, how about telling us the story of why the people Anna met consider you such a hero. Let your children know what a hero you are."

"I'll bet you I know," said Eitan with a big smile. "But let Abba tell it."

Everyone turned to Avram. He bit his lip in a pensive manner and said, "I guess they are talking about what happened when the Germans abandoned us, thank God, in the field. To tell you the truth, I don't remember whether we were more scared with them gone, or when they were with us. When they left, we didn't know what would happen next. Would they come back? We were in Germany? Would other soldiers come, find a trainload of Jews and kill us on the spot? Where were the Russians? Where were the Americans? We had so many questions and no answers. Since we had no alternative, we had to make do for ourselves. It started to get dark, and from the train we saw lights through the woods ... a town, and another question with no answer. A town could mean soldiers. Should we try and get food, at least for the children, or would we be endangering all of us? I know I told you most of this story before, but the one thing I didn't tell you was when the decision was made to go into town, the question came up as to who had any money with which to buy anything. Most of us had used the last of it at the previous stop. Feygl was the only one who knew that before leaving Warsaw, my boss had given me some scrap gold and silver to be used when I decided it was necessary. I chose that time to tell the others that I still had the gold and silver, and I was sure it would be good for buying food. Everyone was thankful, and when things went as they did, my having the gold and silver made me the hero of the moment. Consider the chances we took. Had we sat quietly for the night, eaten nothing, and just waited, we would have been rescued the next morning, just as we were. My having the gold and silver endangered everyone. It gave us the wherewithal to go into town, which could have been a bigger danger than sitting and waiting. Thank God, it all worked out, and now you know the story."

"That's it," said Eitan. "That's the exact story that I knew you would tell, Abba." Turning to Moshe, "Do you remember any of it?"

"Not a word," replied Moshe. "I was probably asleep on the train, but I do recall being left in the field and seeing the Americans the next morning. Enough of this," Moshe went on. "We have one more story to hear. What's up, Sholom?"

Getting right to the point, Sholom said, "Two days ago I met Colonel Hauptmann." You could have heard a pin drop, and I nearly choked on my coffee. "How so?" asked Moshe.

"He was vague about it, but said he had heard about my research on the role of the Hotel Polski and thought I might like to interview someone who could speak of it from the German point of view. I think we must have spent three hours together, and the funny thing is, Eema, I get the feeling that even he never fully understood what was taking place. It was strange talking to him. I felt like I knew him from somewhere. He looked familiar to me. It was as if I was having a reunion with someone I had known in the past. But he was very nice, he was very polite, and he responded to all of my questions."

"Did he say anything about your mother or me?" asked Chaim.

"Yes, he remembered you, and, of course, he remembered Eema because she testified against him. He said she saved his life, and he was very thankful. He said he was a Gestapo colonel, but he was so gentlemanly that it was hard to picture him in that role."

Turning to Avram and Feygl, Sholom said, "I told him about your story; going to Pawiak and then to Vittel and how you were rescued. He told me he'd known that the people headed to Vittel were very often taken to Pawiak and held there until space was available for them at Vittel. However, he insisted that he had no knowledge of what happened to those people after they arrived at Vittel. He had no explanation for the sale of visas to those countries who were not at war with Germany and who had no German internees. It was his feeling that was the very act that resulted in his being deemed a war criminal, and he expressed this to his commanding officer when he visited him at the Hotel Polski.

"Eema, it was fascinating. I could never have gotten this information or the slant from anyone other than Colonel Hauptmann. I am grateful that he came to see me. Do you see how it ties in with your visit to Warsaw?"

No one at the table said a word. I was so angry I could have exploded and Chaim held my hand tightly. Someone had to say something. The young people had nothing to add, and Chaim realized that he could not let me loose at this moment. So he spoke up.

"Your mother is very angry; not at you, but at Colonel Hauptmann. She worked as a clerk for the colonel and it was her good work that saved our lives. I suppose I owe the colonel that. The authorities hoped that since she worked as a clerk, perhaps she might have heard or overheard things, or perhaps seen some documents that would have been of value in the prosecution of the colonel. This was the reason she was called to testify. She had the opportunity to speak privately with the colonel for a few minutes at the end of the trial, and she told him never to interfere in her life again. They were even. He saved our lives, and she saved his. Her anger stems from the fact that he did not do as she asked. By coming to see you, she feels he interfered. Do you understand?"

"Not really," replied Sholom. "I certainly understand your desire to be rid of Colonel Hauptmann for who he was and what he represented, but I do not understand your anger, Eema. He did not interfere with your life. He came to me to aid in my research, for which I am thankful. Are you afraid that you now owe him something, or is there more to this story that I do not know?"

"Sholom," said Chaim.

"No," I said, interrupting Chaim. "Let me answer. It is my anger which Sholom is questioning, and it's my duty to respond. No, Sholom, there is nothing more that you should know. But let me tell you the difference between life and research. You know that before I met your father, who is God's gift to me, I was married to Peter Feurmann, a professor at the university in Warsaw. You have heard the story more than once. When I first met the colonel, he was respectful to me but did not permit me to ask any questions. I was his clerk and he gave me orders. On occasion he asked me to dine with him, and on one such occasion, he suggested that I call him, in private only, by his first name. As you now know, his first name is Peter. I became hysterical and accused him of having given the order to take my Peter and my two boys into the transport. My husband's name was Peter and I could never call the colonel by that name. At that moment, I hated him, and despite the fact that he saved our lives, your father's and mine, I continued to hate him, not for what he was, but for what he might have been. My testimony was true. I knew nothing about his sending people to Pawiak to be executed or taken to the death camps. Was he responsible? I don't know. But, Sholom, as you said, he was a Gestapo colonel; handsome in his black boots. Did he save our lives? Yes, but it must come to an end. Your father had a wife and four children - gone; while he was out on a work detail for the Nazis ... those animals. It is almost thirty years; a half of a lifetime and this bastard is still in my life. He comes to visit my son. For you, it is research. For me, it is the Holocaust. It is my husband and my children, it is your father's wife and his four children; it is Avram's wife and it is Feygl's entire family. You have heard all of these stories. Put them into context, and perhaps you will understand my anger."

Again there was silence, until Avram spoke up. "There are few enough occasions that the entire family is together. Let us celebrate our lives here in Israel, Anna, my beloved, my sweet Anna. To hell with Colonel Hauptmann. He is gone from our lives. We will never hear from him or see him again. If Sholom is content with the colonel's visit from a research point of view, then some good has come of it. We cannot waste our lives being angry. We have things to live for. We are going to a wedding soon. Let us drink all'chaim to Anna's safe return, to Sholom's research, to Sholom and Chava's wedding, to Moshe and Tamar's baby, to Eitan being here with us. We have so much to be thankful for." And so saying, he went around the table with an after dinner wine and refilled all the glasses.

I shook my head and smiled. "You are right, Avram, we have so much to be thankful for." Chaim and I clinked glasses, and he said, "Welcome home, Anna."

On the way home Chaim said, "Interesting evening. I love when the whole family is together."

CHAPTER XXI

"An interesting evening, indeed," thought Chaim. Anna was silent. Chaim never assumed that Sholom was his child, but never questioned Anna or accused her of anything. His debt to her was too great.

Chaim was aware of Anna's passion. He had enjoyed it many times over the years and he assumed that Colonel Hauptmann had enjoyed it as well. But how could he accuse her? How could he condemn her? She might have been a victim, but of what? Had her passion turned to love? Perhaps. But that was not for him to ask or for him to know. "She is now my Anna, and who she was before is over and done with. But I must say," Chaim thought to himself, "Her answer and her analysis of her anger were superb. For that I give her credit. I do not know if I could have responded to Sholom as well as she did. But then again, her motivation was different."

CHAPTER XXII

"I cannot let go," I thought to myself. "I wonder how he found out where Sholom worked." I spoke to no one about what was on my mind, but I kept mulling it over and kept questioning myself since I did not know who I could ask. Interestingly enough, I no longer thought of him as Googy. I felt betrayed. I had told him never to interfere in my life again, and then he showed up to meet Sholom." Not to see me but to see Sholom.

On the other hand, he is Sholom's father. But does that give him the right to appear out of nowhere? Was Avram right when he said that now we will never see him again? He met his son; he spoke to him, he saw what a bright, intelligent young man he is, but will that be the end? Sholom benefitted from the visit, it was even an asset to his research. He might use this research in getting his doctorate. I wonder if Sholom took his address so that he could send him a copy of the work, if it is ever published." Anna, you're getting a little ridiculous - enough of Colonel Hauptmann.

Some three to four weeks later, there was an organizational dinner being held at the Tel-Aviv Hilton which we attended with Feygl and Avram, primarily because Shimon Cohen was the principal speaker and he was receiving an award. Arriving early and mingling with the crowd, many of whom we knew, we spotted Shimon. When we waved to him, he broke away from the circle of people around him and came over to greet us.

"Shimon," said Feygl, "you look so handsome in your tuxedo. If you were the head waiter, I would give you a tip."

"The way the government is cutting funds to my agency," replied Shimon, "I could use a tip. A little extra never hurt."

We shared a couple of more minutes of conversation, and then the ballroom was open for dinner. Before parting, Shimon said, "If you can spare the time, after the evening is over, meet me in the coffee shop. I want to talk to all of you. Is that OK?" When we all agreed, we said our goodbyes, I wished him congratulations, and told him that we would see him later.

"I wonder what that's all about?" asked Chaim.

"I can't imagine," said Feygl, "but since he was the matchmaker that put me together with Avram, anything that he has to say, I'll listen to." And with that we went in to the awards dinner.

The evening was well run, and the food was better than one could expect at this kind of affair. The speeches were kept mercifully short. Shimon was gracious in accepting his award, and spoke for about twenty minutes. He is an excellent speaker who always has something of interest to say. This evening was no exception.

Once the formal part of the evening was over and while Shimon was shaking hands and accepting congratulations, we decided to head for the coffee shop and await Shimon's arrival. He showed up about fifteen minutes later, apologized for keeping us waiting, and sat down to order coffee and a rich dessert. The rest of us were already drinking coffee and eating babka.

He then turned to me and asked, "Did you attend the reunion at the Polski? I meant to call you and ask you, but I have been so busy, it slipped my mind. When I saw all of you this evening, I decided we should have a few minutes together."

"Yes, I did go," I replied, "and as I told everybody, it was quite an interesting trip. I don't know what I expected, but I am not sorry I went. It was not a waste of time or money."

"I'm glad," said Shimon. "I would like to talk to you about it at greater length sometime, but I have something to tell you that has been on my mind. I also assume that when I speak to the four of you about the old days, I am not speaking out of turn. As I recall, your children are married to one another and we are all, and I include myself when I say, 'mishpocha?'"

My heart started to pound. I knew where this discussion was going. Staying calm, I replied to Shimon, "Whatever you have to discuss, you can say to the four of us. There is no one in the world with whom I am closer."

"Well, then," said Shimon, "Let me tell you about a reunion I attended, quite unexpectedly. On the day that you went to Warsaw, I received a visit from everyone's favorite Gestapo Colonel, Peter Hauptmann."

"I knew it," I said. "I knew it had to be someone. He couldn't have gotten to Sholom …"

"Stop it," said Chaim. "Let Shimon finish."

"Please, Anna, be calm," said Shimon. "He came to me with one request. He wanted to meet Sholom, and he presented a pretty plausible argument," Shimon went on. "I was hard pressed to say yes, but I couldn't come up with a good enough argument to say no. So I set two conditions. The first was that he was not to tell Sholom that I sent him, and the second … the second, and I put it delicately, was a threat on his life if he said things that were, shall we say, uncalled for."

"You threatened his life?" asked Avram incredulously. "You really said that?"

"Yes," said Shimon, "and I meant it. But frankly, from Sholom's point of view, I could not think of anyone who was better source material for his research on the Hotel Polski than Hauptmann. It is no secret that Sholom has spoken at length to me about his work, and

I tried to use my influence in the government to get German records about the operation at the Polski for him. I don't know if any of you are aware of it, but the Hotel Polski was mentioned at the Nuremberg Trials, but no in-depth discussion was ever had. Well, the German Government was unable to supply me with any information from their wartime files. It was as if the project never existed."

"But how can that be? I interrupted. "We were all there. We know the place existed and functioned. At Hauptmann's trial, I testified about the visit of General Seidl from Berlin."

"Well that is the interesting thing about the Hotel Polski," replied Shimon. "In that it was not a death camp or a work camp, it fit into no particular category. As an Israeli government official, I discussed this at length with the Judge Advocate when I went to testify. Hauptmann was the first and only commandant of the Hotel, of record. They didn't even know who preceded him or who took over after he left because the place lasted only a few more months before the Russians came. It was really because of people like us that Hauptmann was deemed a war criminal and subject to arrest and trial."

"I don't quite follow that," Feygl said."

"Anna, Chaim, I'm sure you recall that when we arrived in Palestine, our stories were told to both Jewish and British intelligence. I was asked to repeat my story on more than one occasion. When I first met you, Avram and Feygl, you told me that you had been questioned at length by American intelligence. So, in our own way, we and people like us, other survivors, backed Hauptmann into a corner, and his indictment followed. For as much as I know, the entire concept of the Hotel Polski was some Nazi official's idea; if it worked, he would be a hero; if not, there would be no records to indicate that the idea had ever existed."

"But since we all know that it did exist, how could I not let Sholom have access to a piece of research that no one else in the world would have? I started my discussion with Hauptmann by asking him if he was an honorable person. He assured me that he was, and although he had been a Nazi colonel, I believed him. It was only then that I set forth my conditions, and upon his solemn handshake, gave him the information he sought. I gather, Anna, from your reaction that Sholom told you of Hauptmann's visit?"

Shaking my head but not replying at once, I finally said, "Yes, Shimon, he told us all about the visit when I returned from Warsaw." After asking the waiter to refill everyone's coffee cup, I went on. "How strange our lives have become. You, Shimon, are the only one I know who was lucky enough to keep his entire family intact, to have them all survive. Between us, I would say we have lost between twelve to fifteen members of our immediate families, not including uncles and aunts, but husbands, children, parents, brothers and sisters, immediate family. If it was not Peter Hauptmann who ordered their deaths, it was a reasonable facsimile. And now," as tears welled up in my eyes, "you shake hands and tell us you relied upon his word as a gentleman, a man of honor."

At this point, Chaim could no longer sit quietly by. "Anna" he said, "I have never interfered with your decisions, nor have I ever criticized you for anything you have done. How could I, when you saved our lives? But I will not allow you to criticize Shimon for making a decision that, in the last analysis, worked out for the best. No one has been hurt by what Shimon did. Do not let your pride blind you."

"No," interrupted Shimon. "This must be talked out. If Anna feels I had no right to do what I did, then she has the right to say so." Looking directly at me, he asked, "Was I wrong? What would you have done? He told me that you had warned him never to interfere in your life again, and that is why he did not want to see or speak to you. He simply wanted to meet Sholom. Tell me what I should have done."

I did not answer at once. I could not. Everyone was watching me, and I looked back at them. Drying my eyes with my napkin, I smiled and said, "No, I will not be blinded by my pride or my tears." Getting up from my chair, I went over to Shimon. As I approached, he stood up, not knowing what to expect. I threw my arms around him and said, "Shimon. Next to Chaim, you are my oldest friend from the Hotel Polski. I remember sitting on the back steps with you when we saw Itzik come out of the crate. I remember the colonel telling you never to try and fool him again when you translated for him. I pretended not to understand German, but you knew that I did. I remember you telling me to just play it out when I told you that I did not understand what was happening. As you have always done, you did what you thought was best for me and for my family. I thank you for that and I love you for that. Yes, Shimon, in your position I would have done just what you did."

Hugging me and kissing me on the cheek, Shimon replied, "I remember it all so clearly, and I thank you, Anna. It weighed upon me, and I knew I had to tell you. I thank you for understanding. But now, I have an admission to make. In our days at the Hotel Polski, I saw us as a triangle: you, the colonel and me. And although I cannot trace it with any precision, I sincerely believe that it was your relationship with the colonel that saved my life and the life of my wife and my children. You brought out his humanity, and that humanity saved those of us who had nothing, could not buy visas, and could only be sent to Palestine to be traded for Germans interned by the Turks. We, as were many of the others at the hotel, were people of no value to the Third Reich. We could have ended up in Pawiak, as so many did. But you, not even knowing that you were doing it, did not let that happen. So I, too, owe you a great debt that I can never repay. It may all be in my mind, but that is the way I see it." And with that, he again embraced me as the tears rolled down my cheeks.

"Oh, Shimon, Shimon", I said, not knowing what else to say, as I went back to my chair.

It was strange. We sat together for another few minutes, finishing our coffee, but no one said a word. Was there anything else to be said?

Shimon called for the check, paid and left a tip. We all stood up and Shimon embraced each one of us. I was the last one, and when he came to me, he had tears in his eyes. We again held each other with great feeling and emotion.

We then said good night to Shimon, and he walked away. We sauntered out of the restaurant, still not speaking to each other. When we reached the lobby of the hotel, I turned to the others, extended my arms as if to embrace them all, and said, "You know what? The reunion is over." And with a sigh, knowing that a burden had been lifted from my shoulders, I shook my head in silent agreement with myself and said, "All the reunions are over."

THE END

THE
FAMILY AFFAIR

Spring 1972
Tel Aviv

Anna

Chapter I

Everyone knows my secret, even though they pretend they don't and never speak of it.

Feygl, my best friend, has never said a word and my husband Chaim, dear sweet Chaim; he knows but has never questioned nor accused me. And Shimon? Shimon knows. When he told us he threatened to kill the Colonel if he said anything out of line to my son Sholom, the threat meant that he knew.

Shimon Cohen and his wife are really our oldest friends here in Israel. After all, they came over with us from the Hotel Polski. Even though he rose to become a member of the Prime Minister's cabinet, Shimon has never been too busy to talk with us. We do not see him that often, but when we do, it is as if we were old friends.

Actually, Chaim sees him more than I do. Shimon buys his suits, shirts, and accessories from Chaim's store, and once in a while, Chaim tells me, if Shimon is in Tel Aviv, he will drop in for lunch.

When the weather gets warm, I sit out on the terrace overlooking the Mediterranean. It is my favorite thing to do. I bring my coffee and my newspaper, but the most important thing I bring is the telephone with its long cord. Sitting on the terrace, I can read the paper or do the puzzle or talk to Feygl. Even when we have nothing to say, we talk, we schmooze about the grandchildren and the next trip to the kibbutz to see Moshe and Tamar. It was such a joke. Years ago when the children were little we said, "If your Moshe married my Tamar, not only would we be friends, but we would be *mischpocha*."[3] And that's just what happened.

When each of Tamar's girls was born, she and Moshe named them after Feygl's sisters who were killed in the Warsaw ghetto. I knew that Avram, Moshe's father, wanted one of the girls to be named for his wife, Dvoira, Moshe's mother. After all, she deserved to be remembered. But he bit his lip and said nothing.

I was honored when they had the baby and told me that they were naming him Pinchas, in memory of my husband Peter who was killed by the Nazis. He's such a cute little one that we call him Pinky. Avram and Feygl are such dear people, but unfortunately, they never had any children of their own. Still we all love being grandparents; it is such fun. If Eitan, Moshe's older brother, ever gets married perhaps he will have children and can name one of them after his mother. After all, he still remembers her. Avram would be so happy.

All of this came to mind just because I came out to the terrace with my coffee, the newspaper and the telephone. Sitting down and taking a sip of the coffee, it occurred to me that it was just about two years ago when the announcement about the reunion at the Hotel Polski appeared in the paper. I will never forget how Chaim's eyes filled with tears when I mentioned wanting to attend the reunion. "I don't need the Hotel Polski to remember my wife and children," he said. But I was adamant. I had to go.

Feygl had no interest in going and told me to think about it before making a decision. I asked Chaim to think about it, but no one saw it my way. When I came home, I learned that Googy, Colonel Hauptmann had come to visit Sholom at the university while I was in Warsaw at the reunion. Hearing of his visit frightened me. What did they talk about? What did Sholom gather from their conversation? I was livid with anger. I had told Googy years earlier

---

[3] Family

never to interfere in my life again and now I learned that he had come to Israel.

My eyes fill with tears and my hands shake as I recall the fear and anger that I felt at that time. How ironic, I went to a reunion at the Hotel Polski in Warsaw while the Nazi commandment of the Hotel Polski had a reunion with his son in Tel Aviv. Well, not exactly a reunion. He had never met Sholom before, but he knew.

Oh, God, it is more than twenty-five…almost thirty years since we left the Polski, still I cannot get it out of my head. I think of the Polski and I think of my Peter and Yossi and little Natan. The boys would be grown men and have families of their own. But I was a partisan and was out of the ghetto when Peter and my babies were taken from me. *Peter, are you looking down on me? Did you try to protect the children? Please forgive me for not being with you.*

And, as the tears roll down my cheeks, I worry about the need for counseling. There are counselors who deal with the issue of survival… the guilt of survival. To whom can I talk about what I feel?

Wiping my tears away with a napkin, I ask myself, with fierce determination and pride, "Of what am I guilty?" I did what was asked of me in the ghetto. I helped destroy the railroad tracks. Here, in Israel, I raised a family, which fought in two wars. My children and my grandchildren love me as I love them, and my husband is as devoted to me as I am to him. I must emerge from this fog that envelops me and…as the phone rings, I smile as I say out loud to no one in particular, "And I must answer the phone, maybe it's Feygl."

"Do you remember that you have an appointment at the florist this afternoon?" It is Chaim and I laugh in response. "Would I forget such an appointment? Sholom and Chava are getting married in two weeks and we are responsible for the flowers. Do you think I would forget? And, after the florist, Chava's mother is meeting me at the dressmaker. I have a full schedule today. Have the boys all come in for their tuxedos? Is Eitan going to be in uniform?"

"I just wanted to give you a little *kibbitz*,"[4] replied Chaim with a chuckle. "I knew you wouldn't forget. But as to Eitan, I don't know. Please call Feygl and ask her, or ask her to have Eitan call me and tell me what he will be wearing. If he needs a tuxedo, he must come in for a fitting."

"Just tell me," I say seductively, "are you going to be as handsome as the groom?"

"That I don't know," replies Chaim, "but I do know that my Anna will be as beautiful as the bride."

"I can see that you're looking for trouble," I laugh, "so I better get a move on. I will call Feygl and I'll see you at home for dinner."

Sweet Chaim, I think to myself as I hang up the phone. Chaim might look as handsome as Sholom, but Sholom is, in my eyes, looking more and more like... I remember Sholom saying that the Colonel, when he visited him, looked familiar, as if he had seen him before. Colonel Hauptmann…"Googy"… Sholom. As long as I have Sholom, I will always have Googy's face in front of me. Enough, I say to myself. I came out here with the paper, which I didn't read, with my coffee, which I didn't drink, and with the telephone. At least Chaim called and we talked. At least I did something. I am glad Chava's parents are so nice. A little too orthodox for us, but I know we will see them after the wedding. Pull yourself together, Anna. It is time to move on.

And move on we did. The wedding was everything we anticipated. Chava looked beautiful in her gown and her parents beamed when she walked around Sholom seven times as the *chazzan*[5] intoned the blessings. They had lived together before the wedding for a couple of years, and we never knew why they decided to get married now.

---

[4] To josh, or comment.

[5] Cantor

After Sholom had broken the glass and everyone wished them a *mazel-tov*[6], I said to Chaim, "I know why they decided to get married."

"Nu?" said he.

"I think she's pregnant."

A month later, when we welcomed them back from their honeymoon, we went to Chava's parents' house for dinner and her mother was glowing with happiness. "*Mazel-tov*,"[4] she said as she embraced both Chaim and myself. "We're going to be grandparents."

When I looked at Chaim with a big smile on my face, he leaned over and said to me, "I think you're a witch."

Chava had an easy delivery. She gave birth to a son whom they named Ari, after Chava's grandfather, whose Yiddish name was Leib and who had died a number of years ago. Sholom continued to teach and do his research for his doctorate. I knew that his subject was the Hotel Polski, a little-known piece of the Holocaust, but he never spoke of his work to me and I never asked him about his progress. The last time we spoke of it was upon my return from Warsaw some two years ago. I recall I was left with an uncomfortable feeling when I learned that Colonel Hauptmann had visited him.

Shortly after Ari's birth Sholom and Chava visited our apartment so that I could play with the baby, and Sholom told us he was leaving the university. He intended to take a leave of absence from his doctoral studies and go to work for the government agency, which our friend, Shimon headed. Immigrants were pouring into Israel, and Shimon approached Sholom, offering to make him deputy head of the agency researching the history and Jewish background, of the immigrants. Since the salary was greater than he was receiving as an assistant professor, and with the baby, and Chava being unable to work, both Sholom and Chava were happy that Shimon had offered such a prestigious position. Sholom was honored to accept. We congratulated him but were somewhat saddened to learn that his new office would be located in Jerusalem and they would have to move.

---

[6] Congratulations. Good Luck

During the next month, Chava's mother and I helped get the family settled in their new home, and although we had all driven from Tel Aviv to Jerusalem on many occasions, when we said goodbye, we suddenly felt that the distance between the two cities had become greater.

"It is not any longer than the trip to the *kibbutz*,"[7] I said to Chaim, trying to convince myself. "So now we have two children who are no longer next door to us. Let them live and be well."

And that's just how it was. We were all well and happy, and even I felt that the fog was lifting. The children were healthy; the grandchildren were healthy and Chaim's business was good. Feygl told us that Eitan was going with a very nice lady by the name of Miriam who had a higher rank in the army than his, but to avoid any conflict with military directives, they never wore their uniforms when they were off duty.

We were all delighted when Rosh Hashonah came, and the whole family was together. Shimon and his wife were there and he told us how pleased he was with Sholom's work. With the kids and the grandkids, we made quite a crowd. Even Eitan came with Miriam, both needless to say, out of uniform. She was lovely and fitted right in with the family. Her parents were abroad for the holidays and she expected them back for Yom Kippur. It could not have been a happier new year for all.

The eight days passed and then on the eve of Yom Kippur, war broke out. No one expected it, and we were certainly not ready for it on the holiest day of the year. We knew nothing of Eitan's or Miriam's whereabouts. As farmers, living on a *kibbutz* Moshe and Tamar were exempt from reporting for military duty since he was needed for food production and she to care for the children. Despite their new baby, both Sholom and Chava were called up. The question arose, who would care for Ari, who was now almost a year old. Tamar came to the rescue. With the girls and little Pinchas, another child

---

[7] Israeli Settlement

would be no problem, since she was in charge of the *kibbutz* children and had others to help her. Ari knew her, and she reassured us that both she and the children would be happy to have him. That is what was decided.

Tamar came down to Jerusalem from the *kibbutz* and we drove over from Tel Aviv with Chava's parents. Both Sholom and Chava were beside themselves when it came time to say goodbye to Ari. The baby thought it was a party with both sets of grandparents and his aunt Tamar there. Taking Ari with his car seat, his clothes, and his toys, Tamar left first since she had the longest drive home. The rest of us sat, talked, and hugged one another until it was time for Sholom and Chava to go. We again reassured them that we would look after the baby and their apartment and begged them to stay in touch with us as much as possible. We tried not to cry when we said goodbye, but it was war. Who knew what the future would bring.

It took the Israeli forces a few days to recover from the surprise attack and get organized, but when they did, the tide turned quickly. We did not know anyone's whereabouts until, some ten days later, as we were preparing for bed, the doorbell rang. We could not imagine who would be calling at this hour. We opened the door to Chava's parents who fell in upon us weeping hysterically. Chava had been killed.

Chapter II

Chava was buried with full military honors and Sholom was released from active duty to attend the funeral. Moshe and Tamar came with their three children and Ari. When Ari saw his *abba*[8], he stretched out his arms to him as Sholom ran to him, scooped him up in his arms and held him tight. Whether in his little mind he asked for his mother, we will never know.

Only God knows how word of a tragedy gets around. Feygl and Avram, of course, were there; Eitan and Miriam, both in full uniform, were there; as was Shimon and his wife, along with people from Sholom's office. Students and teachers from the university were there, as was all of Chava's family who were not serving in the military.

After services, many went to the home of Chava's parents where *shiva*[9] was to be sat for the next seven days. The mirrors and pictures were covered and little benches were brought in for the mourners to sit on. Everyone, even those in uniform, pinned a small black piece of cloth to their clothes commemorating the loss. Tamar's girls were old enough to understand the tragedy, but Ari and little Pinky were put down to nap in one of the bedrooms.

As the mourners departed, leaving mostly family, Sholom announced that he had to report back in seven days. With hugs, kisses,

---

[8] Father
[9] Period of mourning

and much weeping, he informed us and Chava's parents that he would be going back to the *kibbutz* with Moshe and Tamar because he wanted to spend all of his remaining free time with Ari. I know that Chava's parents assumed that he would be spending the *shiva* period with them, but they accepted his decision and said that they understood. When they left, my heart was breaking for Sholom and for Chava's parents. How could such tragedy befall us? But we weren't alone. We knew that the same tragedy was befalling other families throughout Israel.

The Yom Kippur War lasted some twenty days. During the last week of the war, we were grateful and relieved to hear from Sholom, and, thankfully, Feygl heard from Eitan.

When the war ended, the reservists were sent home and Sholom told us he was returning to his apartment in Jerusalem for a while, and then going up to the *kibbutz* to see Ari and spend some time with Tamar and Moshe. There was nothing that either Chaim or I could say. Our son had suffered a tragedy, an irreparable loss, and we knew he had to deal with it as he saw fit. We also told him that we understood and asked him to please come back and spend some time with us when he was ready. He agreed, and with tears in our eyes, we again said goodbye to our son.

After he left, I said to Chaim, "What about his job? I assume that Shimon is waiting for him to come back to work. Maybe I'll call Shimon."

"Please," said Chaim. "Don't mix in. He's a grown man. He knows his responsibilities. He doesn't need Mama to look after him."

"I know you're right, but I just want things to get back to normal. How can I say that?" I said shaking my head. "How can anything be normal after we just buried Chava?" as I let the tears flow.

We did not hear from Sholom for some two weeks, but we heard from Tamar and knew that Sholom was with her. When I asked how he was and what they talked about, she said that he and Ari were having a great time together but avoided telling me what they discussed or whether he spoke of Chava. I comforted myself by saying we would know it all when he was ready to tell us.

Without warning, Sholom came home. He looked well rested and seemed pleased to be back in his old room. We did not press him about anything but the baby, and he told us, with a big grin, how in just a matter of a few weeks, he was already steady on his feet. His cousins loved him and he fit right in with all the other kids on the *kibbutz*. And then, for the first time, speaking her name, he said, "Chava would have been so proud."

No one said a word. If I had said anything, I would have started to cry, and I didn't want to do that.

Finally, Chaim broke the silence and said, "Yes, she would. She would have been proud." But not wanting to leave it there, he went on, "And how about you? When do you expect to go back to work? Have you spoken with Shimon?"

Sholom paused, kind of bit his lip, and said, "Let me tell you what I am going to do. I have spoken with Shimon and I told him that I would not be returning to my job at the agency." An announcement like this frightened me, but, for the moment, I didn't know why. "Why wouldn't you go back to such a prestigious job?" I asked.

"*Eema*,[10] don't get nervous," he replied with a smile. "All is well; I've given this a lot of thought. Moshe and Tamar are going to keep Ari for the next three to six months. They are happy to do so. I am going back to my doctoral studies. If I am going to advance, either academically or in the government, I need my doctorate. I learned much when I worked for Shimon. I was amazed at how many people who came from Poland, many from Warsaw, never heard of the Hotel Polski. As a result, I realized even more than before, that this is a very unique subject. The professors who will question me at the time I have to defend my dissertation will know far less than I. I will have become the *maven*[11] of the Hotel Polski," he said with a smile.

---

[10] Mother

[11] A trusted expert in a particular field

My heart skipped a beat. It has been so many years and I thought the fog had lifted, and I would never again be burdened with my recollections. "How do you intend to go about it?" I asked casually, fearful of the answer.

"I intend to go to Europe, starting with Warsaw…to actually stay at the Polski. I then want to go into the German archives to see if there is any mention of the hotel and what went on there. So far, I have found nothing in my research here in Israel," he went on. "And I imagine this should be the last bit of research I'll have to do to complete my studies."

I was dumbfounded and could not speak.

"And when would you be leaving?" Chaim asked.

"I can't leave before the *shloshim*[12]," he replied. "You know that within thirty days after the funeral the Army sets the stone for Chava. I'll then have about two more weeks of work before I leave. I hope I can impose on your generosity and that you won't charge me too much rent while I stay here," he said with a big smile.

"What do you think *eema?*" Chaim said, looking at me. "Should we let him stay rent free?"

"Will you two stop it?" I said. I was nervous enough to begin with and jokes were not my thing, especially when we were talking about Chava's unveiling. "Of course you will stay here, but what will you do with the apartment?"

"That is one of the things I must take care of before I leave," he answered. "I must move out, and Moshe said that he can use our furniture on the *kibbutz*. He will meet me with a truck and some men. Because of Chava's death, the landlord said he would release me from my lease. Then I must go back, speak to some of my professors, and arrange my research leave from the university. Working for the government was one thing, but this is something else entirely. I am hoping once I earn my doctorate, they will offer me a full professorship. But there is a lot of politics involved, which

---

[12] Thirty

is why I need the time. And I must go back to the *kibbutz* to say goodbye to Ari."

"Can you work that out on a day that *abba*[13] is not in the store?" I asked. "Then we will go with you."

"That would be wonderful," replied Sholom. "You tell me the day that is good for you, and I'll work around it."

Exactly to the day, the Army notified Sholom of the setting of the stone for Chava. It was on a warm and beautiful Sunday at the end of November. Moshe, Tamar, their girls and Ari were there, and I ran to hold the baby. The ceremony was sad and dignified. A military cemetery is a sea of green with white stones, all the same in remembrance of the young men and women who died for their country. Rich or poor, educated or uneducated; in the cemetery all were equal.

Chava's parents stood with Chaim and me as we all wept. The only one that we envied, in a way, was Ari, who was surrounded by a family who loved him and had no idea we were saying goodbye to his mother.

The next two weeks passed quickly. Sholom went back and forth to Jerusalem, and I went with him when Moshe came down with the truck and the men. I helped with the packing. We gave Chava's clothes and personal things to charity. Sholom was grateful that I was there because he was unable to look at her things without his eyes filling with tears. I felt the same way, but someone had to do it.

Although he never told us the details, we assumed he worked out the politics at the university. We spent a day at the *kibbutz*. We visited the children and the grandchildren, had lunch with everyone, got lots of hugs and kisses, and then drove back to the city.

Two days later, Sholom came home with a plane ticket in his hand and told us that he was leaving the next day. He didn't know when he

---

[13] Father

would be returning, so he had purchased an open ticket. He would call us when his research was finished.

Like the good mother that I am, I again helped him pack, making sure he had warm clothes since central Europe is very cold in the winter. The following morning, Chaim and I drove him to Lod Airport. We wished him well, told him to stay in touch and to have much success in his research. Under my breath, I said, "Give my regards to the Hotel Polski."

Winter 1973

Sholom

Chapter III

Smiling at no one in particular, I thought to myself: I'm a very unusual Israeli. I'm almost thirty years old and this is the first time I've ever left Israel other than for my honeymoon. Most students take a year off and travel, but not me. Looking out the plane window, I saw the coastline disappear as the plane headed west over the Mediterranean.

The flight was uneventful, and when I reached Warsaw, I realized how unprepared I was to be in Poland. Other than a few words of Polish, I knew nothing of the language. My parents spoke it when they didn't want Tamar or me to understand what they were saying. However, my German was pretty good, since much of research necessitated my having to read German-language documents. Above all, I hoped I would find people who spoke English, a language in which I was reasonably fluent. Fortunately, the signs in the airport had little drawings next to them, and I found my way to the luggage carousel and from there to the taxi stand.

"Hotel Polski, Dluga 29," I said to the cab driver.

"You no speak Polish?" the driver asked me in broken English, obviously recognizing that I was not a native. "Where you come from?"

"Israel," I replied.

"Oh, Israel," he said with an air of respect. "You make shit out of Arab in the war," he went on. "So why you stay in such old, cheap hotel?" he asked.

"I'm here to do some research at the Hotel Polski," I answered.

"Research at Polski?" he said with a chuckle. "Is old, cheap hotel. You find no research there," he said shaking his head knowingly. "How long you stay here in Warsaw? I pick you up and take you back to airport. No research at Polski."

"You're probably right," I said. "How come you speak English so well?"

"Thirty years ago, I fight Nazis. I am captured and put into POW camp with Americans and British soldiers. They teach me. I old man now, but I remember, and I talk a lot with tourists. How many languages you speak?"

"Not too many," I replied. "I speak Hebrew, a little Yiddish, a little German, and a little English."

"Hebrew, that tough language. You read backwards, you talk backwards," he said with a laugh.

There was no more conversation until we pulled into the courtyard of the hotel. He was right. It was an old hotel. How cheap, I didn't know, but I would find out soon enough. "How much do I owe you?" I asked.

"You have *zlotys*[14], or better still, you have American dollars?" he asked.

"I have some *zlotys*, have some Deutschmark, and I have some dollars," I replied.

"What you do tomorrow?" he asked. "No research here. I pick you up in morning and take you around city. I show you where ghetto was, and when ready, I take you back to airport. We settle up then."

Not knowing if I was falling into the hands of someone who would try to swindle me, I decided to take a chance. He spoke English, he knew the city, and perhaps I could use him in my research. He was

---

[14] Polish money

old enough to remember the war years. "Okay," I said, "You have a deal. Tomorrow morning at ten." As I got out of the cab, he said to me, "What your name?"

"Sholom," I responded. "That means, 'peace,' in Hebrew."

"Peace is a good thing," he replied, shaking his head in agreement. "Tomorrow at ten."

"What is your name?" I asked.

"Tomas," he replied as he drove off.

As I entered the hotel, my mind went back to the stories that *eema* had told us on so many different occasions. Yes, the hotel was old, but it looked quite clean and presentable. I checked in with little difficulty despite the fact that the clerk spoke less English than Tomas. He treated me, I felt, with great respect when he saw my Israeli passport.

More than anything, I wanted to absorb the sense and feel of the hotel. Without Colonel Hauptmann, without Itzik and Berel, as *eema* told me they were called in those days, it would obviously not be the same. But this is where Itzik became Chaim and Berel became Shimon. This is where they were granted their freedom. And above all, this is where *eema*, who was known as Rosa then, became Anna. Even though Tomas said, "No research in Polski," the sense of history that I was feeling was research to me.

My room was small, but more than adequate. I unpacked, washed my hands and face, and went down to the hotel restaurant for lunch. As I was shown to a table, I thought to myself: This is where *eema* and Colonel Hauptmann had their first dinner, and many dinners thereafter.

The menu was in Polish and German, so I was able to order with some actual sense of what I was going to eat. It turned out to be rather tasty. I signed my room number to the bill with a fifteen percent tip in *zlotys*, not knowing if this was enough. The waiter seemed satisfied, and I walked out of the dining room and decided to do a little exploring of the hotel. At the end of the check-in counter was a booth with the word "Concierge" over it. (I wondered what that word would be in Polish.) I walked around and located the telephone room that *eema* had described; the only change I noticed was a small store selling maps of Warsaw, newspapers, chewing gum and candy, and some other necessities. Maybe this was where *abba* played cards? I decided that if anyone spoke English or German for that matter, it would have to be the concierge. So, I went over to him, introduced myself, and asked him if he knew any of the hotel's history during the war years. He claimed to know nothing about the hotel prior to coming to work there two years ago, but suggested that I go out the door and down the block to Dluga 6, where, I would find a building devoted to the National Polish Archives. He was sure that was where I might find the information I was seeking.

It was only 2:30 in the afternoon, and although I was somewhat tired, I decided to take a walk. I had picked up some time flying from East to West, and I wanted to take as much advantage of it as I could. If I found nothing of interest to keep me here, I thought I might leave Warsaw by tomorrow evening. But checkout time was noon and Tomas was picking me up for a tour of the city at 10 o'clock, so I guess I would stay another day.

Dluga 6 was an impressive building; here the signs were all in Polish, with no little pictures to guide me. I had no choice but to ask the guard at the door if he spoke English, to which he shook his head and pointed me to a door, which I figured must be the administrative office. I went to the desk where an attractive young woman of about my age asked me, in Polish, if she could help me. (I assumed that is what she asked.) I asked her if she spoke English or German and she said she spoke both, but would prefer to speak English. I told her about my research and asked her if she could help me to find any records, particularly German records, if they existed, of events that took place at the Hotel Polski during the war and after the destruction of the ghetto.

She escorted me to a small conference room and told me to wait. I stood and looked out the window for about ten minutes before she returned with some folders. Placing them on the table, she said that she could find nothing in German but did find some Polish references to the Hotel Polski, which she would be happy to translate for me. I thanked her and asked her for one more favor. I had completely neglected to bring pen or paper with me, and I did want to make notes if there was anything relevant in those records. I asked her if she would get me a pad of paper and a pen while apologizing for my stupidity. She was back in a minute, and she began reading aloud in Polish from the folders. I understood nothing.

"Excuse me," I interrupted her, "but what is your name?"

"Angela," she replied. "And your name is…?"

"Sholom, Sholom Adler," I responded. "Angela, I thank you for all your help, but reading to me in Polish isn't really very helpful. Is there anything in these folders that is relevant to the Hotel Polski? Why is the hotel even mentioned? What role did it play that it should be recorded in these archives?"

"I apologize," said Angela, with an embarrassed smile. "Of course, you do not speak Polish. How silly of me. However, in scanning these folders, I see that they speak of the hotel as a place of rescue for Jews who wished to purchase their way out of Poland during the time of the Nazi occupation."

"Yes," I answered. "That is exactly what I'm looking for. Does it describe the source of this information or mention the years the hotel was used as you describe? What I'm specifically looking for is the reason why the Germans engaged in this activity. Do your records speak of any of that?"

"Unfortunately, I cannot answer any of those questions," she responded. "Until you asked for information about the Hotel Polski, I had never heard of the place, other than the fact that almost every city in Poland has a Hotel Polski and there is one down the block. To answer your questions, I would have to read over this material carefully and that will take me a bit of time. May I suggest that you go up to the cafeteria on the second floor and have a coffee? Meet me here in half an hour and I'll see what I can find."

"Angela, you're being wonderful, and I thank you. I'll do just as you suggest and see you back here in half an hour," I stood, opened the door for Angela and followed her out of the room. She went to her office as I walked to the elevator.

The cake and coffee were delicious and I was back in the room in twenty minutes only to find Angela was already there with a doubtful look on her face.

"What I told you before is just about all there is," she related. "It is interesting that they don't even describe this as a program that the Germans instituted, but it is obvious since the Germans occupied Poland in 1939 and the ghetto was destroyed in 1943. It had to be their idea, but whoever wrote this archive just left that hanging, as if it were to be assumed. No mention whatsoever of the German concept or what they were attempting to accomplish. I am sorry, Sholom, but that is the best I can do." Closing the folders, she went on. "Where are you going from here?"

"The German commandant of the hotel was tried many years ago by the International War Crimes Tribunal, and the transcript is in Ludwigsburg, Germany. I am headed there when I leave Warsaw," I responded.

"Before you leave the city, may I make one other suggestion?" she asked.

"Of course," I replied.

"I suggest that you visit St. Jacek's church. They have plaques commemorating the resistance fighters and leaders of the movement during World War II, and it is possible that they might have some information that you can use."

"Please write down the name and the address for me. I have a taxi picking me up tomorrow morning and I'll have him take me there."

Tearing a page off the pad she had given me, Angela wrote down the information, folded the sheet and handed it to me. She then asked, "I am assuming you are alone here in Warsaw and I thought that you might like to have company this evening? There is even an Israeli restaurant we can go to."

Putting the paper into my pocket, I looked at Angela, and a great sadness overcame me. "I thank you, Angela, for the invitation. I'm just not ready yet to go on a date," I replied. "You see, I have just become a widower. My wife and I were soldiers, and she was killed in the war in Israel some two months ago. My son is with my sister while I'm here. It's sweet of you to be concerned, but it would not be right."

"Oh, Sholom," she responded. "I am so sorry. I didn't mean to be so forward. Please forgive me."

"There is nothing to forgive," I said, taking her hand in mine. "There was no way that you could have known. You have really been most helpful and most gracious. Had things been different, perhaps...?" And with that, I held open the door. As Angela walked out, she turned to wave and I did the same as I headed to the building exit.

Back at the hotel, I went to the concierge desk; the same man was still on duty. "Did you visit the archives?" he asked.

"I did, but it was of no real help to me," I responded. "Can you do one other thing for me?" I asked. "I am sure you have a map of the city. Can you mark off certain things for me?" Taking a map from under the counter and unfolding it, the concierge inquired, "What would you like to know?"

"Please show me where we are now and show me where the ghetto was." Circling the location of the hotel, he said to my amazement. "I really don't know where the ghetto was. I do know it was somewhere nearby. I have been told there is a memorial not too far from here. But I was born after the war ended."

"Do you know where the Jewish cemetery is?" I asked.

"Oh, yes, sir," he replied. Taking his pen, he circled the area that was marked Cmentacz Zydowski.

Once I knew where the hotel was and the location of the cemetery, I had a pretty good idea of where the ghetto had been, since my mother had described the area in such detail, and had told of her having gone from the cemetery through the ghetto to the hotel.

"One other thing," I asked. Taking the folded paper from my packet, I read "St. Jacek's Church. Frita 8 /10."

It took a few moments, but he found it, circled it, and folded up the map. I took the map from him, thanked him, and went up to my room to rest.

Chapter IV

By ten the next morning, I had eaten breakfast and was out in the courtyard of the hotel waiting for Tomas. I was sure he would come because I had not paid him for yesterday's ride, and within a minute or two, there he was.

As I got into the cab, he said to me, "So, how goes the research?"

"Nothing exciting yet," I responded. Taking out my map, I said, "Let me tell you what I would like to see."

"I tour guide," Tomas replied. "I tell you what you want to see."

Ignoring him, I went on. "Drive me through what used to be the ghetto, let me see the memorial and then take me to the Jewish cemetery on the other side of the ghetto. I then want to go to St. Jacek's. Do you know where that is?"

Pulling out of the courtyard, he said, "The ghetto and the cemetery are on my list. But St. Jacek's? Why you want go there?"

"I'll tell you later," I said. "Now tell me about the ghetto. I know it must be close by."

We drove just a few blocks and then started to go up and down the streets that had been completely rebuilt with new apartments, stores, and a huge commemorative square with a beautiful sculpture. This had been the ghetto, Tomas told me, and I recognized some of the streets by the names that *eema* had mentioned when she described her ordeal. It was truly impossible to believe that hundreds of thousands of people were imprisoned in this area, only to be taken out and murdered.

As we zigzagged our way across the ghetto, we came to the cemetery. We drove in and I asked Tomas to stop. I got out of the taxi and walked about, trying to recollect some of the stories about how Itzik met Rosa more than a quarter of a century ago. That people actually *lived* here and hid from the Germans was unbelievable. It simply defied understanding.

Back in the taxi, I told Tomas to sit with me while I asked him if he knew anything about the Hotel Polski during the war years. He said no and asked why I was interested in the Polski. In that he had nothing to add, I asked him to head toward St. Jacek's. I told him a little bit about what had happened at the Polski after the destruction of the ghetto, how my parents met, and about the change of names. I then told him; at St. Jacek's there were plaques commemorating the resistance fighters and I hoped that perhaps someone at the church would have some knowledge that might be useful to me. Tomas doubted it, but on the way to St. Jacek's, he gave me a tour of the city. When we arrived at the church, I told him to wait as I got out of the taxi.

The church was very old. Tomas told me that it had been built in the 17th century. To the right of the entrance, something caught my eye. A large framed information board, such as are seen in front of most houses of worship, gave the hours of the services and other things written in Polish, which I did not understand. But the name of the priest, Rev. Josef Feurmann, gave me pause to think. That was the name of *eema's* oldest son who was killed by the Nazis. Feurmann is not necessarily a Jewish name. It must be a coincidence. I shrugged, got out of the taxi, stared for another moment at the plaque and went into the church.

The interior was dark, cool, and quite beautiful. On the walls on either side of the entry were the plaques that Angela had told me about. They were illuminated with picture lights. I found the names of some Polish-Jewish members of the resistance, but most of the names were unfamiliar to me. As I went from one to another, a young priest approached me and asked in Polish, "Is there anything I can do for you?"

"Do you speak English?" I inquired.

"Yes I do," he responded, "Rather poorly."

"Are you Father Feurmann?" I asked.

"Oh, no," replied the young priest. "Father Feurmann is away today on church business but will return tomorrow. Are you a friend of his? Do you know him?"

"No," I answered. "But I would like to meet him and have a word with him. Do you think that would be possible?"

"You are not a member of this parish, are you?" asked the young priest. "I do not recall ever having seen you before."

"The answer is no to all of your questions, Father," I said with a smile. "Not only am I not a member of this parish, I'm not even a Catholic. I'm an Israeli and I have interest in the plaques that hang on the church wall. Does Father Feurmann know anything about them?"

"Oh, yes, he is quite knowledgeable about resistance fighters. I am sure he would be most happy to discuss with you. If you write down your number for me, I'll leave a note on his desk and he will call in morning. What time would be right for you? Father is up quite early for six o'clock Mass."

Reaching into my pocket, I took out the folded piece of paper with the name and address of St. Jacek's, tore off the bottom half, and wrote my name and the name and address of the hotel. "I am sorry," I said, "I don't know the phone number, but I marked down my room and I will wait for the Father's call at about eight. Would that be convenient?"

"Certainly," said the young priest. "I will see he gets message and he will reach you tomorrow morning." Looking at the message, he went on. "I see your name is Sholom. In Hebrew that means peace, does it not?"

"And peace to you, Father," I said as we shook hands. "But before I go, Father, I have one other question. Father Feurmann's first name is Josef, is it not?"

"Yes it is," replied the young priest.

"Is it possible?" I said to myself, as I left the church.

Getting back into the taxi, I asked Tomas. "Where shall we go for lunch?"

"There is Israeli restaurant here in Warsaw," replied Tomas. "Hummus very good." And without a word from me, we were off.

The hummus was, in fact, very good, and with a Jerusalem salad and fresh pita, I learned there was quite a community of Israeli expatriots in Warsaw. It was good to speak Hebrew again. Tomas enjoyed his lunch, as well, and sat and grinned as I spoke Hebrew to the waiters and he repeated what he had said before. "You write backwards and you speak backwards."

I had much on my mind that I didn't care to share with Tomas, although I really had no one else to talk to. As we finished our coffee and Tomas lit a cigarette, I said to him, "Tomas, you have been a good friend, but I think the time is coming when we must say goodbye to each other."

"Why?" he responded. "You no like my taxi? When you leave Warsaw? I take you to airport."

"I'm not leaving Warsaw," I said. "I have to meet someone tomorrow and I might then have to stay for a few more days. I can't expect you to keep driving me around. You have to make a living and sitting and waiting for me does not put *zlotys* in your pocket."

"What time you have appointment tomorrow?" asked Tomas.

"I expect a call at eight in the morning. I will not know until then."

"I wait for you at Polski at eight o'clock. If you need me, I there. If no, we settle up and say goodbye. Okay with you?" he asked.

"Fair enough," I said. "Take me back to the hotel now, and I will see you tomorrow morning.

We both sat quietly on the ride back. I was lucky to have gotten into Tomas' taxi. He was a good guy. When we got to the hotel, we waved to each other without saying a word. I knew he would be there tomorrow, but that was all I was sure of.

It was still the middle of the afternoon, and although I had nothing else to do, my head was spinning. I went up to my room, called down to the bar, and asked them to send up a bottle of red wine and a bottle of club soda with ice. I wasn't a big drinker, but I needed something to relax me, and perhaps help me sleep for an hour or two.

"Suppose he is *eema's* son," I thought to myself. "Is Josef Feurmann such a common name? But he is a Catholic priest. There is no way that we can be talking about the same person," I concluded.

The wine and club soda arrived. The waiter opened the wine bottle and poured a glass for me while I opened the club soda and poured it over the ice. From my briefcase, I took out a pad of paper, and while I was drinking, I started writing down questions I would ask Father Feurmann. I didn't have to write the answers. If he gave them to me, I wondered how I could ever tell *eema*. By the time I finished half the bottle, I was so tired I couldn't keep my eyes open. I lay down and dropped off to sleep. When I awoke, it was dark out and I had a headache from the wine. I realized I was hungry and ready for dinner, but remained anxious for tomorrow. Taking two aspirin, I washed my face, combed my hair, and went down to dinner in the hotel restaurant. After dinner, I went back up to my room, turned on the television, and finally got an English language news program. While surfing the channels, I found "Hawaii 5-0" in English with Polish subtitles. I got a kick out of it because it was the same way in Israel, English but with Hebrew subtitles. I turned off the television, read for a while, and decided that the fastest way for eight o'clock to come was to go to sleep.

By eight the next morning, I was showered, shaved and dressed, and had ordered coffee and toast brought up to my room. Although I expected the call, I was somewhat startled when the phone rang. Picking up the receiver, I said, "Father Feurmann?"

To which he replied, "You are expecting my call?"

"Frankly," I said with a laugh, "I know no one else in Warsaw, so it had to be you."

"Then I gather I am speaking to Sholom Adler," he said with a laugh, "and I understand that you have some interest in the plaques that hang in my church." Without replying to his question, I said, "I am here in Warsaw to do some research, and I was hoping that I might have an opportunity to speak with you."

"It would be my pleasure," responded Father Feurmann, "but I can't imagine what help I could be to you. Nevertheless, if you are free this morning, I would be happy to see you in my office at nine. Is that too early for you?"

"Oh, no," I responded. "That will be perfect. See you at nine."

"Calm yourself, Sholom," I said to myself. "He seemed like a perfectly nice fellow. Don't let your imagination get the best of you.

When I got downstairs, at 8:15, Tomas was waiting in the yard. "Good morning, Tomas," I said. "Please take me back to St. Jacek's. I have a meeting with the priest. If I'll be delayed, I will come and tell you so you don't have to wait. Then I'll let you know when to pick me up."

"A meeting with priest?" asked Tomas with surprise. "What you doing, becoming Catholic? The next thing, you be an anti-Semite. Is good joke, an Israeli anti-Semite."

"That's a good joke, but it's not funny," I replied. "No, I just have to talk with him and get some information. That is what research is all about."

"Okay, if you say so, Mr. Sholom," said Tomas. "You do research, I make jokes.

By 8:45, we were at St. Jacek's. I decided to go in and spend the next fifteen minutes looking at the plaques. If the young priest approached me, I would tell him I am a few minutes early for my appointment with Father Feurmann. I told Tomas to wait and went into the church. But instead of the young priest, I was met by an older priest who said, "Sholom Adler, I am Father Feurmann."

Chapter V

Josef Fuermann was a man about ten years older than I. That fit with what I knew. His hair was dark but graying at the temples and his moustache was salt and pepper. He must have been close to six feet tall and had a calm and kindly look about him. He bore no resemblance to *eema*, and although she had saved some pictures of her first husband, Peter, I had no recollection of what he looked like.

"I understand you were here yesterday to examine the plaques," Father Feurmann said to me. "Is there something of particular interest that I may be of help?"

My stomach was churning; my head was spinning. Let me get right to it, I decided. "Yes," I replied. "There is something of particular interest I would like to talk to you about. May we go into your office?"

"Certainly, Mr. Adler," said the priest. "You intrigue me. Is this a mystery we are trying to unravel?" He said this while we walked down the length of the church. At the altar, he knelt briefly and crossed himself, and then took me into his office at the far end of the church. It was quite large, with an overflowing bookcase, a huge desk covered with books and papers, an ornate high-backed chair behind the desk, and two rather comfortable-looking visitor's chairs in front of the desk.

Seating himself behind the desk and offering me one of the visitor's chairs, he asked me, "Would you care for coffee?"

"No, thank you," I responded. "I've already had my breakfast, but, please, have coffee if you wish."

Speaking into an intercom on his desk, Father Feurmann said, "May I please have my morning coffee?" Then turning to me, he went on. "Now, Mr. Adler, as to your mystery."

"It's not really a mystery, more of an inquiry," I responded.

But before I could say another word, the door opened and in came a nun carrying a tray with coffee, milk, sugar, and some sweet rolls. Looking up at the nun, he said with a smile, "Thank you, Sister Agnes." And turning to me, he again asked, "Are you sure you won't have some? Sister Agnes would be happy to bring you a tray."

"Thank you, Father," I said. "I'll pass this time," and turning to Sister Agnes, I said, "and thank you, Sister." With a nod to me and a smile to Father Feurmann, she left the office.

Nothing more was said while the priest poured his coffee, added milk and sugar and took a bite out of his sweet roll. "Okay, Mr. Adler, what's on your mind?"

"I understand that your first name is Josef. Is that so?" I inquired.

"Not only is it so," responded Father Feurmann, "but it is also the source of some amusement among my brethren."

"Amusement?" I inquired. "What can be amusing about the name Josef?"

"When I first was assigned to this church," the priest explained, "the Bishop could not recall my name but remembered that it started with the letter J. Since the church was St. Jacek's he started to call me Jacek and the name stuck. Now, with good humor, my brethren also call me Jacek."

Realizing that I was not amused by the story, Father Feurmann sipped his coffee and said, "Sorry, Mr. Adler, I didn't mean to interrupt you."

With no break in tempo, and speaking softly, I asked, "Does the name Rosa Feurmann mean anything you?" I cannot begin to describe the priest's reaction. He put down his cup, continued to chew his sweet roll, and when he swallowed, which seemed like an eternity to me, he responded, "That was the name of my mother." I was literally shaking as I went on. "How about Professor Peter Feurmann? Was he your father?"

"Yes, he was," replied the priest with a growing sense of anger. "And my little brother was Natan. But I assume you know that. Who are you, Mr. Adler, and how do you know these names?" he asked with his voice rising.

Not knowing quite how to answer, I stood up from my chair and looked directly at Father Josef Feurmann and said, "I believe we are half-brothers. Rosa Feurmann is also my mother, except now, she is known as Anna Adler. You also have a half-sister by the name of Tamar, as well as nieces and nephews."

Not a word was said for the longest time. Finally, the priest stood up from behind his desk, wiped his mouth with his napkin and said, "I cannot believe this. We have much to talk about." Coming out from behind the desk, with a big smile on his face, he extended his arms and said, "May I have a hug, my brother?" And with that, we embraced as long lost relatives, and when we stepped away, both of us had tears running down our cheeks.

"I trust you can spend the better part of the day with me?"

"Yes, I can," I responded. "I have a driver outside. I will tell him to pick me up at two. I hope that we can have lunch together?"

"That would be perfect," the priest said. "While you speak to your driver, I will tell Sister Agnes to cancel my morning appointments. You can find your way out and back?"

"Yes, of course," I responded. "Just give me a few minutes." And out I went to Tomas who was waiting and smoking and told him to pick me up at two.

He on the other hand, looked at me and said, "You know, you don't look like a Catholic." I waved goodbye and went back to Father Feurmann's, rather my brother's, office.

As I entered the office, Josef was finishing his coffee and I said to him, "Now that my stomach is no longer churning, could Sister Agnes bring me a coffee? I could really use one."

"And you'll love the sweet rolls," said Josef with a grin as he asked Sister Agnes for a tray for me and a refill for himself. Turning to me, he said, "The biggest mystery of all is, how did you find me?"

"Strictly by chance," I answered. "But let me start from the beginning, and then I have a question to ask you. No, let me ask the question first. We have time for stories. I may need some priestly advice. How do you suggest that I tell our mother about this? I can't just call and say 'Guess who I found in Warsaw?'"

"To notify our mother would truly be a Christian act," said Josef with a big laugh. "But, seriously, you are right. Such news cannot simply be sprung upon her. Can you reach your father at his place of business? I would tell him and let him break the news to mother."

"I thought the same, but I'm also going to insist they come here to meet you. I assume that will be the first thing she will want to do."

"Before we start to tell our stories, then, please feel free to use the telephone on my desk and call your father. If you wish privacy, I will excuse myself."

"Oh, no," I responded. "You are the story. I'm sure you'll enjoy the reaction.

Handing the phone to me at my side of the desk, I dialed the store. The phone was immediately answered by Rochl, the cashier. Speaking in Hebrew, I asked her if my father was there, and she immediately put him on the phone.

"Sholom, are you all right?" he asked. "You've only been gone three days. Is everything all right?"

"*Abba*," I said, "*ha-kol b'seder*[15], everything is just fine. But I suggest you sit down because I have some unbelievable news for you." And without waiting for a response, I went on. "Does the name Josef Feurmann mean anything to you?"

---

[15] Everything is in order

There was dead silence. I looked at Josef who was sitting across from me with a big grin on his face.

"If my memory serves me," my father ultimately responded, "that was the name of *eema's* oldest son who was taken from the ghetto. Am I right?"

"You are right, *abba*," I said. "But Josef is alive. I have found him by the most fortuitous of circumstances. He is handsome and well, and one more thing, *abba*, that you will not believe."

"I don't believe any of this," my father replied, "So tell me the one more thing. He is married and has children?"

Taking a deep breath, I answered, "Just the opposite. He is a Catholic priest."

It was not distinct, but I could swear I heard *abba* say, "Oh, Jesus." After what seemed like a long pause, he went on. "I am not busy today. I will go home right now and tell this to your mother. Give me the number where you are now, and we will call you. I am certain that we will be in Warsaw by tomorrow. Sholom, the world is full of wonders."

"Yes, it is wonderful, *abba*," I agreed. "I'll wait for your call here in Josef's office." I gave him the number and said, "We have much to talk about and we'll be here for another couple of hours." Hanging up the phone, I looked at my long lost brother and said, "Well, the deed is done. Now we can talk." And with that, I started my story about the Hotel Polski, Colonel Hauptmann, the travel documents, the change of names, and even the story of Aviam and Feygl since they were now part of the family.

During this time, the phone rang on a couple of occasions, but it was church business, which Josef took care of quickly. At about noon, the phone rang again and Josef answered it, saying "Father Feurmann." I don't know what he heard on the other end, but his eyes filled with tears as he said, "Yes, mama, it is me." I then heard him say, "Good. I look forward to it. It has been a long time.

"Here is Sholom," he said, handing the phone to me.

As soon as I heard my mother's voice, I knew she had been crying. "*Abba* is on the other line and he has confirmed a flight to Warsaw in three hours," she said. "Will you meet us at the airport? I do not want to stay at the Polski. Get out of there and get us two rooms at the Warsaw Hilton. And ask Josef if he can spend the day with us tomorrow."

"Yes, *eema*, I have a car and driver and will be waiting for you at the airport," I promised. "I'll check out of the Polski and have rooms for us at the Hilton. It is a lovely hotel, and I'll ask Josef to be with us tomorrow."

I now had much to do. Josef promised to spend the day with us. I suggested that we meet at the Hilton, rather than bring the folks to the church. I didn't think they'd be very comfortable there. He understood, and we arranged to have breakfast at nine the next morning at the hotel. I then told Josef I was holding back on his story because I knew our mother would want all the details and, in that way, he would only have to tell it once. He understood and agreed. With that, we again embraced, promised to see each other the next morning, and I left, hoping that Tomas would be waiting for me.

It was only one o'clock, and I had told Tomas to pick me up at two, but he was already in front of the church. "No jokes," I warned him. "We have a busy afternoon and evening. Please take me back to the Polski and wait while I check out then go to the Hilton, and this evening we will go to the airport to meet my parents. Then you'll take us back to the Hilton, and you and I will settle up and say goodbye. Is that okay with you?"

"Oh, I understand," said Tomas. "Once you become Catholic, you become rich man. Go from Polski to Hilton. You good boy, Sholom," he said with a laugh. "You make good research at St. Jacek's."

Arriving at the Polski, I told the desk clerk I was checking out. It was after twelve, and he tried to hold me up for another day, but I refused, and we settled for the three nights I had been there. I went upstairs, packed quickly, came down, paid the bill with a credit card, climbed into the taxi, and was off to the Hilton where I took a room and reserved a room for my parents. I went up to my room and by the time I unpacked, it was time to go to the airport. It was a good forty-five minute drive. Tomas parked the car and went in with me to help with the luggage. We had to wait for close to half an hour, but the plane from Israel finally arrived and there were *abba* and *eema*. With hugs and kisses, we went to get their luggage, which was only one bag. Tomas ran to get the taxi after reassuring my parents in Polish that I was a good boy and did good research. Then we were off to the Hilton.

When we arrived at the hotel, my parents picked up their reservation while I settled up with Tomas. He asked me for American dollars, which I gave him. We embraced like old friends, and I thanked him for his help and his loyalty. I then caught up with my parents, waited while they went up to their room to freshen up, and we then went to dinner in the hotel restaurant. It was there that I told them the whole story of how I came to meet Josef. The fact that he was a Catholic priest weighed heavily on *eema's* mind but was never mentioned. That was something that she would have to resolve with Josef when she met him.

It had been a long, exciting and emotionally challenging day for all of us. Who knew what tomorrow would bring? We all agreed that a good night's sleep was in order, and we went to our separate rooms knowing that Josef would be meeting us at nine the next morning.

Chapter VI

I cannot speak for my parents, but I know that I had a good night's sleep and was up, showered, shaved, and dressed by 8:45. I went down to the lobby and found my parents waiting.

"Did you sleep well?" I asked.

"I think I was up every hour on the hour to look at the clock," *eema* replied. "Need I say more? A good night's sleep we did not have," said *abba*.

"Take it easy," I said, trying to calm them down. "He will be on time."

And with that, in walked Josef. For some reason, the cross hanging from his neck seemed more obvious today than it did yesterday.

"There he is," I said as I stood up and went to greet him.

My parents stood up, my mother took one step forward then stood frozen in place. The look on her face was indescribable. "He looks just like Peter," she whispered under her breath. Taking another step forward, she said, "Yossi?"

Approaching her with caution, Josef replied, "Yes, mama, it is me."

With a scream I thought would bring down the Hilton, *eema* repeated, "Yossi!" She burst into tears and threw her arms around him, then took his face in her hands, and they both started kissing each other. I am sure the people in the lobby thought it strange to see a Catholic priest engaged in such behavior with a woman in public, but, then again, what did they know? Josef was laughing and crying at the same time. They seemed to hold on to each other forever. But when both *abba* and I walked up to them, they parted and *eema* introduced Josef to Chaim. They embraced each other with great emotion, and we decided we could talk in the coffee shop while having breakfast.

As we approached the coffee shop, the hostess, a very pretty young lady with a cross hanging down in her ample bosom, appeared to be entranced as the handsome Father Feurmann asked her to seat us at a quiet table and indicated that we might stay for a couple of hours. She promised that we could stay as long as we wished, and that our coffee cups would be refilled. *Eema* sat next to Josef and continued to hold his hand and caress his arm. During breakfast there was little said. *Abba* asked me whether, other than finding Josef, I had discovered anything else in Warsaw. *Eema* asked me how the Polski looked, and I described it to her as best I could. And when the dishes were removed and a pot of coffee was set before us on the table, *eema* looked at Josef and said, "Tell me, my little Yossi, tell me how you survived."

Starting slowly, Josef took our mother's hands in his and said, "You were out of the ghetto when the Germans swept the neighborhood and took us all to the train station. Papa held Natan in his arms and held me by the hand. When we got to the station, I remember seeing your friend, Clara with Max and Zisha, but we could not get close enough to speak to them. I don't know how many of us were forced into the rickety old cattle cars. It took over an hour to get the train loaded. It was so crowded, we couldn't sit down. I just held on to papa's leg. Natan was crying, and so were a lot of the other children. We stood like this and traveled until the sun went down. Suddenly, there was a loud explosion, and the train stopped. We looked through the slats of our car and saw the soldiers run toward the front of the train. The men said that the partisans had blown up the tracks. When all the soldiers had run up to the front of the train, some of the stronger men started kicking out the slats of the car. When the opening was big enough, some of the men and some children jumped off and ran. Papa said I should go. I didn't want to, but he insisted, and some of the other men also said I should go. Natan wanted to go with me but Papa said he was too little. I think I was about nine years old at the time, and I jumped out and ran. In a few minutes, I was in the woods. It was dark and I was so scared. I heard other people, but I did not want to call out. I was afraid to be alone and I was afraid to be with others. I don't know how long I kept running, but soon, the woods ended and I found myself in a field. The moon came up and I could see a farm ahead. I wanted to reach the barn and hoped no one would come along until the morning. At least I could sleep for a few hours and then I would keep running. Where to, I didn't know. And don't forget, I was still wearing a Jewish star sewn to my shirt. I thought I should get rid of it. When I got to the barn, there were cows and sheep, but there was also a place where the fresh hay was stored. I lay down there, took off my shirt, ripped off the Jewish star, hid it under the hay, and fell asleep.

At this point, *eema* refilled everyone's cup, and *abba* said to Josef, "The ways of the world defy understanding."

"What do you mean by that?" asked Josef.

"For as strange as it may seem to you, and as unbelievable as it may be, your mother saved your life," replied *abba*.

"That is both unbelievable and not understandable," replied Josef with a questioning grin taking *eema's* hand. "How so?"

Do you remember when your mother used to leave the house with Max and Zisha's father and be gone for many hours?" And without waiting for an answer, he went on. "They went to the woods where the partisans were hiding, and your mother, who had been a chemistry teacher, taught them how to make bombs to blow up the tracks. It was her teaching and their action that enabled you to escape. Is that not truly unbelievable? Is it fate? I cannot explain it."

On more than one occasion I had heard the story of how *eema* had been recruited by the partisans to teach them to make bombs. I never connected it to Josef's escape, but *abba* saw the relationship immediately. I guess that is the difference between having lived through the experience and learning about it years later.

Hearing *abba's* explanation, Josef turned to his mother and embraced her, and the kissing and the tears started all over again until *eema* drew back, and without letting go of Josef s hands, said, "Please, go on, my sweet Yossi. What happened when you awoke the next morning?"

"Well, I was awakened by the sound of voices," Josef continued. "I looked up and there were two children, a boy a little older than me, a girl somewhat younger, and a man who I guessed was their father, standing and looking down at me. The man told the boy to go get his mother, who came from the house and was there in a minute. She was kind and told me to get up and come into the house for breakfast. You cannot imagine how hungry I was.

They all sat at the table with me while I ate fresh-baked bread with fresh eggs and drank fresh milk, things we had not seen for a long time. They asked me who I was and where I came from, and I told them the whole story starting with the ghetto, to the train, to the explosion, and finally my escape. I told them about Papa and Natan, and I remember asking them if they could help me find Papa. The father then asked me where was my Jewish star. I told him what I had done and where he could find it. He rose and went to the door and when he came back with it, he gave it to me and told me to keep it so that I would remember my parents and my little brother. After all, I didn't know where you were. I still have it in my desk at the church.

Hearing this *eema* started to weep copiously and kept repeating, "Oh my Yossi, my Peter, my Natan." I looked at *abba* and he had tears rolling down his cheeks and I wiped my eyes with my napkin. Josef put his arms around *eema* and rocked her until she regained her composure, and she said, "I am so sorry, Yossi. It is so many years. Please, darling, please tell us more."

"From that moment on, I became a member of their family," Josef continued. "I was out in the open when German soldiers came to take milk and eggs from them. I was just another Polish child, and since I spoke Polish, the Germans never questioned them."

"It took another year or year and a half and the war was over. Schools reopened full time and I went to Catholic school with the other children. In that Feurmann was not necessarily a Jewish name, they never asked me to change it. The story we told was that I was a cousin whose parents had been killed in the war. Catholicism was second nature to my new family and it became second nature to me. I went to church with them; I was a good student, and when I finished the equivalent of our Gymnasium, I was offered a scholarship to go to the seminary and given the opportunity to become a priest. It was an honor I could not turn down. My older, so-called cousin was already in the seminary, and it was only natural that I would follow him. I did well in the seminary, and I graduated with honors. Now, when I get together with my cousin, whose church is in Krakow, he calls me Jesus because Jesus was first a Jew."

Putting his arm around *eema* and looking into her eyes, Josef said, "Mama, I have never forgotten who I am or where I came from, but you must understand, this is where my life has taken me. I am very happy as a priest. I am beloved by my parishioners and I am well thought of by my superiors. To have found you, after all of these years, has given my life another dimension, but if you love me, and I know you do, then you must accept me for who I am."

Again, the tears and the kissing, and the words I'm sure Josef wanted to hear—that his mother did understand and did accept all that she had heard. And with that, another round of coffee was poured.

"So," asked *abba*, "is there the possibility of a trip to Israel in your future?"

"As a matter of fact, yes," replied Josef with great enthusiasm. "Next year, there is a conference scheduled in Jerusalem. I'll arrange to come a week earlier. Sholom told me about Tamar and her children, and about Ari. I want to visit the *kibbutz* and meet all of them. If you have room, I would love to stay with you for the week." Taking a pad out of his inside pocket, he called over the hostess and asked her for a pen or pencil. She brought over a pen immediately, with such a big smile that it seemed she would do most anything else he might ask. Thanking her for her kindness, Josef turned to Chaim and said, "May I have your address and telephone number? I'll stay in touch and give you more exact dates as we get closer to my visit, if that is all right with you."

"It would be our pleasure," said *eema*. "We have two empty bedrooms, since Sholom and Tamar moved out. You are welcome to stay as long as you wish.

Noting the address and phone number, Josef put the pad into his pocket and said to *eema*, "You may be sure, Mama that I did look for Papa and Natan after the war. I checked with all the agencies that dealt with survivors, but could find nothing. I had to assume they were murdered."

Eema again started to weep and said, "I, too, checked after the war. We have a good friend in Israel who is a member of the Prime Minister's cabinet, and he was unable to find anything. Chaim's family was also taken in one of the roundups when he was out of the ghetto. We could not find a trace of them, either."

"Oh, I am so sorry to hear that, Chaim," said Josef. "We have so much more to talk about. I would love to learn how you two met. Sholom told me about the Hotel Polski, but I am sure there are more stories to be told." Looking around the coffee shop, Josef said. "It looks like people are starting to come in for lunch. I am sure they need the table. Can we meet for dinner this evening at six? I have someone I would like to introduce you to. This will be my treat." Taking out his pad, he wrote down the name and address of a restaurant and handing it to Chaim, he said, "I know you will enjoy this restaurant. It is one of Warsaw's finest, and I only take special guests to it. Will that be good for you?"

"We look forward to it," said *eema*. As we all left the coffee shop, Chaim paid the bill and we walked Josef to the hotel entrance. With hugs and kisses all around, we confirmed our plans to meet at six for dinner. Going back into the lobby, *eema* said, "I can't believe what has happened. I'm still in shock. My head is spinning. He is so handsome. He looks just like Peter." Turning to me, she went on, "You know, Sholom, you could have driven right by and never noticed his name. Had the plaques been in another church, you would never have found him. This is all so hard to believe. It is truly a miracle."

"You are right," said *abba*. "But tell me, Anna, are you tired? Do you want to go up to the room and rest?"

"Oh, no," replied *eema*. "I was here not too long ago, but you have not been in Warsaw for more than twenty-five years. Where would you like to go and what would you like to see?" she asked Chaim.

Thinking for a minute, *abba* replied, "I would like to go through the ghetto and into the cemetery where we first met. The rest of the city doesn't really interest me. But I think we should be back at the hotel by four so we can rest before dinner." Turning to me, he asked, "Are you free to come with us?"

"I wish I had not sent Tomas away," I answered. "I took that tour two days ago, but I'll be happy to see it again through your eyes. I promise you, though; the one place we won't go is the Hotel Polski."

Walking out of the lobby into the sunlight, the first person I spotted was Tomas, leaning up against his taxi and smoking a cigarette.

Tomas, "I said."What are you doing here?"

"I know you need me. I bring people from airport to hotel and I see priest walk out, so I wait. I know you come out soon. Where we go?"

"Take us back to the ghetto and then to the cemetery, please. That is where my parents met. They would like to see it again after so many years. Then we'll go to the Israeli restaurant for some hummus, but we must be back at the hotel by four. Is that okay with you?"

"Is okay with me," replied Tomas. As we piled into the taxi, I told him that we would need him tonight at 5:30 and at 10:00 tomorrow to go to the airport, since we were all leaving Warsaw at about the same time.

Little was said during our ride through the ghetto. For me it was almost impossible to realize that this had been the ghetto or to imagine the horrors that took place so many years ago. For my parents…they lived through it. When we arrived at the cemetery, I stayed behind with Tomas as my parents wandered around and spoke quietly to each other. At one point, I saw them embrace, and when they returned to the car, they both had tears in their eyes.

A light lunch followed at the Israeli restaurant because we were still caught up in the emotions of the day and were more tired than hungry. When we got back to the hotel, we agreed to meet in the lobby at 5:15 so that we could talk quietly for a few minutes before Tomas came to pick us up.

Promptly at 5:30, he came into the lobby to look for us and out we went to the taxi. When I told him the name of the restaurant, he got a quizzical look on his face and shaking his head knowingly said, "Some fancy place." When we arrived at the restaurant, I asked Tomas to pick us up in two hours and take us back to the hotel.

The restaurant was indeed quite palatial. Looking around, *abba* said, "The church must have a good expense account to be able to afford a place like this."

When we mentioned Father Feurmann's name, we were immediately shown to a table for six. "I wonder who he is bringing?" said *eema*.

It was not long before Josef came in, accompanied by a little old Polish lady who looked like she was wearing her best Sunday go-to-church dress. We all rose as they approached the table, and speaking in Polish, Josef said, "This is my mother, Maria." Turning to me and speaking in English, he apologized and said, "I am sorry, Sholom, but my mother speaks only Polish, so much of tonight's conversation will have to be translated."

We all hugged with *eema* embracing her longest. She then turned to Josef and gave him a kiss on the cheek. Maria, who had obviously been told the whole story, stood and beamed with pride and tears in her eyes. When we sat, Josef ordered a bottle of wine as we looked over the menu.

Eema sat next to Maria, and they talked incessantly throughout the meal. I know it was all about Josef because I heard his name mentioned constantly. Josef sat next to *abba*, and the three of us talked, mostly in English. *Abba* told him where he met *eema* and how they had gone back to the cemetery earlier that afternoon.

The dinner was truly delicious. After coffee and dessert, Josef apologized for having to break up the party, but said he had an hour's ride to take Maria home, and then another hour to get back to the rectory. He paid the bill with a credit card, and we all walked out to the street. *Eema* hugged Maria, as they continued to talk in Polish. *Abba* hugged Josef, as did I, and we made him promise he would stay in touch and let us know when he was coming to Israel. He gave us his word and then turned to *eema*, who again started to cry. *Abba* gave Maria a hug and said something that made her laugh. I shook her hand and kissed her on the cheek, and Josef led her away to his car. Tomas was waiting for us and when we arrived back at the Hilton, we said good night to Tomas and reminded him to pick us up at ten o'clock tomorrow morning.

None of us was sleepy yet, so we decided to try the bar for a nightcap and to discuss tomorrow's plans. I knew where I was going, and my parents knew they were going home. Although I told them when I was still at home that I was going to Germany, my next stop, I felt, had to be announced with certain finesse.

Abba and I ordered drinks and *eema* ordered club soda. I knew what they were waiting to hear, so I told them exactly what had happened at the Polish archives and how I was disappointed. Despite the physical presence of the Hotel Polski, nobody knew anything about its role after the destruction of the ghetto. But on the other hand, it was at the archives that I learned of the plaques at St. Jacek's and that led to finding Josef. That was far more important than the history of the Hotel Polski. We all agreed to that.

I reminded my parents that from Warsaw I was going on to Ludwigsburg, Germany, where German archives were stored. I called them archives, knowing full well that was not so. I was not telling them the truth, but I had to do it my way. Ludwigsburg was the storage facility for transcripts of the trials of Nazi war criminals. I wanted to read the transcript of the trial of Colonel Hauptmann to see if there was any last minute information I might possibly learn about his days at the hotel. But of greater importance to me was the testimony of my mother. There was no question in my mind that she was obsessed with her days at the Polski. Her reaction every time it was mentioned was proof of that to me. I was sure that within her testimony or perhaps even the testimony of others, I would find some clue as to her behavior. Although I didn't care to admit it, even to myself, I suspected that her behavior could, in some way, be related to my paternity. Ludwigsburg, and perhaps one other stop after that, would be the end of my research.

I knew that my parents didn't know the transcripts were stored in Ludwigsburg, so they accepted my travel plans without comment. We finished our drinks, went up to our rooms, kissed each other good night, and planned to meet the next morning and then go to the airport. Their flight back to Tel Aviv was at 11:30, and my flight to Stuttgart was at 11:45. I had reservations at the Bahnhof Hotel in Stuttgart and had reserved a car for the morning following my arrival in Stuttgart.

Our plans went as scheduled. Tomas was on time as usual, and we said goodbye at the airport. My parents promised to take a day to visit Ari, and I promised I would be home within a week. I couldn't wait to see my son.

Chapter VII

My flight to Stuttgart was also uneventful. I took a taxi from the airport to the Bahnhof Hotel, registered, unpacked, and went down for a late lunch. The hotel was old but beautifully restored. It sat right next to the train station in downtown Stuttgart and was at the juncture of a number of streets with many shops and restaurants.

I spent the rest of the afternoon walking and found a huge toy store. I bought some toys for Ari and gifts for my nieces and for Pinky. I also found a china shop where I bought a beautiful piece of Rosenthal china for Moshe and Tamar. I felt compelled to express my gratitude for the care and concern they have shown for Ari. By this time, I had accumulated so many shopping bags; I looked for a luggage store where I could buy an inexpensive carry-on bag for all the gifts. Then back to the hotel, I went where I unloaded all of my purchases, re-packed them in my new carry-on, and headed down to the bar for a drink.

Sitting alone at a table in the bar, a young lady, whom I assumed was a prostitute, tried to convince me I needed company. I assured her I was quite alright on my own. I then went to the concierge to confirm my auto rental for the next morning. I inquired about the route to Ludwigsburg, and was promised a map when I picked up the car and asked for the name and location of a good restaurant for supper. The concierge suggested a *gasthaus*[16], or inn, which wasn't far and which I found without any difficulty. The menu was extensive and the waitress assured me that the chef would be happy to make anything that was not on the menu. A glass of German beer was a must and I ordered Dinkelaker, which was the local brew.

After a hearty dinner and a walk back to the hotel, I realized how tired I was and went up to bed. I turned on the television in the room, and there was "Hawaii 5-0" but this time it was dubbed in German. It didn't take long before I was out for the night.

By nine the next morning, I was up and out. The auto rental was just around the corner. They had my reservation and marked out the route to Ludwigsburg, as promised. It took about twenty minutes to get out of town, and then the Autobahn took me to the outskirts of Ludwigsburg. I stopped at a tourist information booth for final instructions to the Zentrale Stelle, where the material that I sought could be found.

A local street map got me to the Zentrale Stelle, and although Ludwigsburg is a well known tourist attraction with an old castle that looms over the city, I really had no interest in sightseeing. Being in Germany itself wasn't a thrill for me. I hoped I could find what I was looking for, do my work, and move on.

The Zentrale Stelle was an old building that looked more like a fortress than an archive. When I got there, I filled out the form that was given to me. The clerk then checked his card file to see if the transcript I requested was, in fact, in storage. He wrote a file number on a card and sent me to another room, some two flights up. I presented the card to the clerk on duty, and after a minute or two, was presented with the file.

I'd intended to just skim the transcript since I was quite sure that I knew what I was looking for. But when I started to read the testimony of the witnesses, I quickly realized I couldn't simply look

---

[16] Guest House

for what interested me. All of the testimony was fascinating. A number of witnesses had been rescued from Pawiak prison, others from Vittel in France. One witness, other than Shimon, who was referred to as Berl Rabinowitz in the transcript, had stayed for an extended period at the hotel during the tenure of Peter Hauptmann.

It was amazing, despite the fact that Colonel Hauptmann never testified on his own behalf, none of the other witnesses, including Shimon, could ever explain what the Nazis were attempting to accomplish.

I then came to my mother's testimony, which I read carefully. I was in a sweat when I finished. My mother's obsession with the Hotel Polski became quite clear. There was now also no doubt in my mind that Peter Hauptmann was my father. How this would alter my life, if at all, I hadn't yet thought out, nor did I have any particular reaction to the news. How she actually felt while she was in bed with Colonel Hauptmann was something I really didn't want to know. I assume my father, by which I mean Chaim, was aware of what was going on in those days, but these were issues that were between them. I'd have to think through all of this carefully and, above all, wondered if there was anyone with whom I could even discuss this. The one thing I didn't know at this time was what was said between *eema* and the Colonel when they were allowed to speak privately, but it was something I was determined to find out.

By the time I returned the file to the clerk, it was late in the afternoon and the only note that I made was the home address of the Colonel.

I headed back to Stuttgart, wondering all the while whether the address I had for Colonel Hauptmann was still valid. After all, it was fifteen or more years old. If it wasn't a good address, I had no idea how I would find him. For all I knew, he might have passed away in the years since I had seen him, but I knew I had to try. This would be the end of the road for me.

What kept going round and round in my head, though, was how I would deal with this information once I got home.

It occurred to me that the only one with whom I could readily discuss any of this would be Shimon. He must know the whole story. After all, he was there in the Polski with *eema* and had come to Palestine on the same boat. He must have known what was happening at the hotel and he must know when I was born. "Could I talk to *abba* bout this?" I wondered. How do you tell your father of close to thirty years that you know he is not your father? But he is my father. He is the man who raised me, loved me, and provided for me. And I love him. I let myself wonder if the Colonel loved *eema*, or if she loved him when they were together. It must have been so difficult for her. The Colonel in bed, on one hand, and Itzik waiting in the lobby on the other. It is no wonder she reacts as she does when we speak of the Hotel Polski. And what about Tamar? How can I tell her I am only a half-brother? I wonder if Avram and Feygl know. Of course, they must know, or at least Feygl must know. She went to Heidelberg with *eema* for the trial, and she was in the courtroom when *eema* testified. She must know.

My head was so full that I almost missed the exit off the Autobahn. It seemed as if a moment ago I was in Ludwigsburg, and the next moment I was back in Stuttgart. Parking the car in the hotel garage, I went to the auto rental office and told them I would be keeping the car for at least another two days, and would return it at the airport in Munich. It was no problem. I then went up to my room, washed my hands and splashed cold water on my face, and decided that I needed a big German beer. So, I went back to the *gasthaus* where I had dinner the previous night, ordered a stein of Dinkelaker, a schnitzel with kraut, which was the house specialty, and coffee and chocolate cake for dessert. Feeling full but still confused, I went back to the hotel, told them I would be leaving in the morning, and went up to bed.

I was in no hurry the next morning, so I had a leisurely breakfast in the hotel dining room, had the concierge mark the Autobahn to Munich on my map, checked out, and picked up the car.

Chapter VIII

When checking out of the hotel in Stuttgart, I asked the desk clerk if he could recommend a good hotel in Munich, and he suggested I try the Bayerischerhof. He wrote out the name, address, and phone number and with that information in hand, I felt confident I wouldn't have to waste time wandering about in a strange city.

It was a pleasant drive at about 90 kilometers per hour. The Germans have this way of pulling up behind you and then shooting out past you on the Autobahn. No matter how fast you are going, they will go faster.

At any rate, I got there in about two hours, found the hotel, garaged the car, and checked in with little difficulty. Compared to my room at the Polski, this was like being in a palace. Since I didn't know my way around, I decided that lunch in the hotel would be easiest, and then I would start my search for Colonel Hauptmann, or should I say, my father.

Approaching the concierge desk with the address I had copied from the trial transcript, I asked for a map of the city and whether the concierge was at all familiar with the address. The concierge took out a map, opened it, and marked the location of the hotel, and shaking his head, said, "Not in the city. I would guess this is in a farming community on the outskirts of Munich, or maybe even in another town."

Without telling him the source of my information, I insisted that the address was in Munich, but since he didn't know where it might be, he suggested that I speak to a gentleman who was sitting at a large desk off to his right that had brochures on it advertising tours.

"Herr Schmidt is a tour director and he may be more familiar with this area than I," he said, "Please accept my apologies."

I introduced myself to Herr Schmidt, showed him the address, and got a flicker of recognition. "How old is this address?" asked Herr Schmidt.

"Many years," I responded.

"I thought so," he answered. "There has been much municipal development over the last years in these rural areas. I am sure this was a farm at one time, but it may be a housing project today," he said with a smile.

"How can we find out?" I inquired. "I'm very interested in finding the gentleman who lived at this address."

"Let me see what I can do," said Herr Schmidt as he pulled out some smaller telephone books from his desk. "This area is in one of these books. Give me the name of the person and I'll see if we can find him."

For the first time in my life, I was hesitant to speak his name. I almost wanted to say Colonel, but I held back. "Peter Hauptmann," I replied.

Herr Schmidt found nothing in the first book. Although there were many Hauptmann's, there was no Peter. I thought to myself, if he listed his phone under his wife's name, I'll never find him. In the second phone book, there was a Peter Hauptmann at the address I had given him. Herr Schmidt wrote down the number for me and gave it to me with a smile, saying, "I'm glad I could be of help. These are old phone books, I hope you find him."

I thanked him and went up to my room. My hands were shaking. I couldn't believe I was betraying my mother! How could I ever justify what I was doing? After *eema* had returned from the reunion at the

Polski and I told her that the Colonel had come to see me, she was so angry that *abba* had to control her. I remember Avram saying that he was now out of our lives forever and here I am bringing him right back in. "By God, I have become my mother, an obsessed person." I could check out tomorrow, go home, tell them my research was complete, and never speak of Munich or Peter Hauptmann again. I owe it to my mother not to betray her "For God's sake, Sholom, what are you doing?"

It grew dark but I didn't turn the light on. I sat in the darkness and thought of Chava and Ari. I felt tears running down my cheeks. I thought of the discussions I'd overheard between my parents and between *eema* and Feygl about attending the reunion at the Polski. Nobody would go with her. Nobody cared to go. Everyone had been able to put the Polski behind them, but not *eema*. "Oh, *eema*, I understand you. Can you understand me? Please do not hate me for what I am about to do." Maybe he's dead and no one will answer the phone. That would be the solution, but in my heart, I know he is still alive. There is no easy way out.

Turning on the light over the desk, I dialed the number on the paper that Herr Schmidt had given me. It was picked up on the third ring. "*Grüss Got.*"[17]

"Peter Hauptmann?"

"*Ja*"

"This is Sholom Adler."

Dead silence. "Sholom, where are you? Why are you calling me?"

"I'm in Munich," I responded, "and was hoping we could meet."

"It would be my pleasure," was the answer. "I assume you are alone; your mother is not with you? Where are you staying?"

"I'm at the Bayerischerhof," I answered, "and I am quite alone. Will you join me for breakfast tomorrow morning?"

"Is nine too early for you? I assume we have much to talk about," he responded.

---

[17] Regards to God – a Bavarian Hello

"Nine would be fine," I answered. "I look forward to seeing you."

Hanging up the phone, I sighed deeply and to myself, "I have done it. Please, *eema*, forgive me."

In keeping with the German reputation for efficiency and punctuality, promptly at nine, through the revolving doors of the hotel, came Peter Hauptmann. His hair was white; he was clean-shaven and well dressed. In my mind, I calculated that he must be in his mid-seventies, perhaps close to eighty years of age. I rose to greet him, and he greeted me warmly. Another reunion in another coffee shop.

After ordering our breakfast, Peter said to me. "Let me tell you of a humorous statement made by Shimon Cohen who, as I am sure you know now, was the one who told me where to find you at the university. As I walked into his office, he said something to the effect that of all the people he didn't expect to see today, I was the first one on his list. I would have to say that the same is true for me, Sholom. So, tell me, why are you here and what do you wish of me?

We ate and we talked. I told him of my marriage and the birth of Ari for which he offered his congratulations. When I told him my wife had been killed in the war, a true sadness overcame him. I went on to tell him about leaving academia, working for Shimon and after the war deciding that my doctorate was necessary if I was going to get ahead in the government or the university. Hence, my visit to the Polski as the last piece of my research, and my discovery of Father Josef Feurmann. His eyes lit up with joy when I told him of my mother's coming to Warsaw to meet Josef, her oldest son, whom she thought had died in the war.

At this point, he interrupted my narrative to tell me that she had, on more than one occasion, blamed him for the loss of her husband, Peter, whose name he would never forget, and her two sons. He was sure that her joy was overwhelming when she learned that Josef was still alive, and must have been shocked to learn he had become a Catholic priest.

He then asked me to go on, and I told him about my visit to the Zentrale Stelle in Ludwigsburg. He had no idea what was kept there or why I would even go there, and he was quite shocked when I told him this is where the transcripts of the war crimes trials are stored. Learning of this, Peter became quiet while the waitress refilled our coffee cups. I could tell that he realized we were getting to the reason for my visit to Munich and I wasn't sure that he was pleased.

"I read the transcript, and although it shed no additional light on why the Germans engaged in the useless and murderous game they played at the Hotel Polski, it did convince me, beyond a doubt, that you are my father. The one piece of information lacking is what was said between you and my mother in the room at the conclusion of the trial?"

Peter didn't respond at once. He sat quietly, sipping his coffee and rocking slowly back and forth in his chair. Finally, he looked up and said, "I'll not take offense at your use of the words 'useless' and 'murderous.' I served my time for that. But I am hard pressed to betray a confidence."

I had come this far and I was not going to let him get away without answering me. "You chose to speak with her," I replied. "What did you have to say that was so important that her response could be deemed confidential?"

Shaking his head as if to say, I don't really know what to do, he said with a shrug of his shoulders, "It is so many years. What difference can it make? Sholom, you are putting me in a morally untenable position. Your mother warned me never to interfere in her life again, and Shimon threatened to kill me if I spoke out of turn. And now you come along and force me to interfere and reveal matters that were not to be spoken about."

"Tell me, Sholom, are you going to tell your mother that you saw me? Are you going to tell Itzik, what is his name now, that I am your father and not he?" Without waiting for an answer, he repeated, "What difference does it make? In those years, it was important to me. Now it is really of little consequence."

Sitting up straight and taking the last piece of toast from his plate and buttering it with precision, he said, "At the trial I learned, for the first time, that when your mother and Itzik left the Polski, she was pregnant. To me, there was no doubt in my mind that it was my child. In the little room, after the trial was over, I asked her to tell me about our child, to tell me about you. She refused, unwilling to admit that it was my child and she warned me never to interfere in her life again. As I recall, her reasoning was something to the effect that I had saved her life and now, with her testimony, she hoped she was saving mine. We were even and should never again have anything to do with each other. The judge gave us just five minutes to speak. Your mother was out of the room in three."

Again, shaking his head in a display of annoyance with me, he said, "Now that you know, what will you do about it? Send me a Father's Day card once a year?"

"Why are you so angry and annoyed with me?" I asked. "Just as you wanted to know about your son, however many years ago, why do I not have a right to know about my father?"

Relaxing a bit as the waitress poured a third cup of coffee for us, he apologized and said, "You are right. You have drawn a fair parallel. Just as your mother was overwhelmed with the discovery of her son whom she thought had died, I suppose that I, too, should be happy that my son has acknowledged me and come to visit me."

Looking at me with a smile, he went on. "Perhaps we should have Father Feurmann here since we are all in the confession mode. I believe he would be deemed to be your half-brother. And now, I have news for you, as well. You also have a half-sister. My daughter, Liese, is a professor of German history in Dusseldorf. We neither see each other nor have we spoken to each other for many, many years. She is considerably older than you and is still hung up over the fact that her mother was killed during a British raid over Cologne. She insists that with my rank, as an SS Colonel, I could have relocated her to a more protected area where she would not have been subject to the nightly bombings. Liese was in the country with my wife's sister, but my wife refused to go. I was in Berlin at that time and from what I learned, she chose not to go to a shelter when the alarm sounded and was killed by a direct hit. Liese was inconsolable when she learned of her mother's death. She screamed at me, and no matter how much I tried to talk to her, she would not listen. So, I gave up trying and I follow her success through other members of the family who are in touch with her. Would you like to meet her?"

"In a certain way, I would," I said with a smile, "but not on this trip. I have acquired a father, a half brother, and now a half sister. I think that is enough for a week away from home."

At that point, I realized that there was really little else for us to talk about. Peter insisted on paying the bill, and we walked out to the hotel entrance where Peter gave his ticket for his car to the valet. We said nothing to each other while we waited for the car to be delivered. When it came, I walked around to the driver's side with him, we shook hands and I thanked him for coming to see me.

He said, "If you tell your mother about our visit, please give her my best regards, and to your father, as well. My wife, whom your mother met at the trial, died a year or so ago, so I am now alone and think of your mother often. She was a wonderful woman when I knew her."

At this point, he actually embraced me, got into his car and drove off.

Again, my head was spinning. I had confirmed what I had suspected, but what would I do with the knowledge? I might as well go home tomorrow and head straight up to the *kibbutz* to see Ari. I'll let Tamar call *eema* and tell her that I'm back, and in the meantime it will give me some time to think everything out.

Back at the concierge desk in the hotel lobby, I took my airline ticket out of my pocket and asked the concierge to book me a flight the next day from Munich to Tel Aviv on Lufthansa. And so ended my week (or was it more) away from home.

Chapter IX

I had nothing to read on the plane except the airline magazine. I had no notes to review, so I began to think about how I would complete my dissertation. In truth, it was already pretty much completed but I was troubled by the fact that I had reached no conclusion as to the purpose or the rationale behind the Nazi operation at the Hotel Polski. I'd never heard of a dissertation without a conclusion, but I would have to paraphrase the questions and answers at the Colonel's trial as they pertained to the inexplicable pointlessness of what the Germans were doing or what they hoped to accomplish.

My mind wandered over the events of the past week. I had acquired a father and two half siblings—quite an accomplishment for one week's work! I thought of Chava. It was nearing three months since she had been killed and a Polish clerk tried to pick me up, as did a German prostitute. I must look desperate. I was desperate. I was desperate over the loss of Chava and I was desperate because I didn't know what to do with the information I had learned on this trip. And suddenly, it occurred to me, I had an immediate problem.

I didn't want to see my parents just yet. I needed time to think this through and discuss it with people who could, hopefully, give me some good advice. But since I was living with my parents, my car was parked in their garage. I wanted to go up to the *kibbutz* to see Ari, but if I went home and just got into the car and drove away, they would know I was back and would be angry with me for not stopping to see them. That would just add another layer to my already existing problem. I guessed I would have to kill an hour-and-a-half at the airport while I called Moshe and asked him to come pick me up and take me back to the *kibbutz*. After a day or two, they could call and tell *abba* that I was back. But I still wanted to speak to Shimon first. I didn't quite know how I would work all of this out.

When the plane landed, I called Moshe's office and, luckily, he picked up. "Sholom, are you home? Where are you? Is everything all right?"

"Moish, my best brother-in-law," I responded. "I have a favor to ask of you. But in answer to your questions, yes, I'm all right and I'm at the airport."

I then went on to tell him that I wanted a ride up to the *kibbutz* without going home to pick up my car because I didn't want to talk to my parents yet.

"You're a lucky boy," he replied. "After your mother came back from Warsaw, she was a nervous wreck from the excitement of having met Josef after all these years. She prevailed upon my parents to go down to Eilat, rest a little, gossip a lot, and sail away on a blackjack cruise. So, you can take a cab home, pick up your car, and be here in time for dinner tonight. How does that appeal to you? By the way," he went on, "why don't you want to see your parents?"

"Moish," I replied, "we have a lot to talk about. When I tell you the whole story you'll understand my problem. At any rate, thanks for the good news and I'll see you tonight."

What a relief. I went home, unpacked, showered, and changed my clothes and took out the gifts for the kids and for Moshe and Tamar. I then called Shimon and told him I was back and on my way up to see Ari, but would like to meet with him in a few days. He said he'd be in all week and would be happy to meet with me. I went down to the garage, picked up my car, and was at the *kibbutz* by late afternoon.

Seeing Ari made it all worthwhile. He jumped into my arms and gave me a big hug. I then gave him his toy, which he loved, as did Pinky and the girls when they saw the presents I had brought them.

Before dinner, I presented Moshe and Tamar with my gift from Stuttgart.

"Oh, no, you shouldn't."

"But I did"

"Oh, it's beautiful."

"Okay, let's eat."

Dinner was delicious since Tamar was an excellent cook. We didn't speak of my trip for two reasons. First of all, Tamar's girls were growing up and becoming young ladies and it was not something to talk about in their presence. But the second reason was more interesting. Tamar's second in command, with regard to the daytime care of the children, was a very attractive Yemenite woman by the name of Rena who was about Tamar's age. She fed Pinky and Ari first, and then dined with us. In conversation at the table, I learned that she had a Masters in child psychology, taught in the *kibbutz* elementary school in the mornings, and worked with Tamar in the afternoons. She had no family on the *kibbutz*, and although she had her own house, she took her dinner every night with Moshe and Tamar. She loved the little ones, enjoyed feeding them and getting them into bed, and would go back to her own house after the dishes were done. I could see that both boys loved her because they gave her hugs and kisses before she put them to bed. It was as if she were a member of the family.

When dinner was over and the girls had gone to bed, peace finally descended on the house. Rena said goodnight, kissing both Moshe and Tamar on the cheek and shaking hands with me.

"We are so lucky to have her, "said Tamar. "She is such a help to me, especially with the little ones."

Stretching out in the living room, Moshe asked, "Nu, my traveling scholar, why are you hiding? What is it that you don't want to tell your parents?"

"You know about Warsaw," I replied. "The discovery of Josef, a Catholic priest, was absolutely unbelievable. So now, my dear sister, we have a half-brother who, if all goes well, will be coming to visit next year. He knows about all of you and can't wait to meet you and the kids. He is quite handsome and *eema* says he looks just like her first husband."

"So far, no secrets," said Moshe. "What happened next?"

"Please promise me that what I tell you now remains between us," I answered. "I told the folks that I was going to Ludwigsburg to do some further research in the German archives, but what they didn't know is that Ludwigsburg is where the transcripts of the war crimes trials are stored. I went there to read the transcript of the trial of Peter Hauptmann, for two reasons."

"I don't think I'm going to like what I'm about to hear," said Tamar.

"You may not like it," I replied, "but you must understand, Tamar, that I had to learn the truth."

Turning to Tamar, Moshe said, "Don't be so quick to judge, Tamar, let Sholom finish." To me, he said, "What were your two reasons?"

"The first was to see if any of the witnesses at the trial had anything more to add to my knowledge of what happened at the Polski. I didn't know if the Colonel had testified and I wanted to see whether anything he said at his trial would contradict what he told me when I met him a couple of years ago. I learned nothing of relevance from the other witnesses, and the Colonel didn't testify on his own behalf, so that was a dead end."

"And the second reason?" asked Moshe.

I answered slowly because I knew that what I was about to say would cause a reaction, "Because I wanted to read *eema's* testimony." Without waiting for a comment, I went on. "I learned that after she finished testifying, the Colonel asked if he could speak privately with her and the court allowed it. What they said was not on record, but what was on record, the interrogation of *eema*, and her answers, told me what I wanted to know."

"And what was that?" asked Tamar in a breathless whisper.

I stood up, clenched my hands, heaved a sigh, and sat down on the couch between them; I put my arms around both of them, and said, "The Colonel is really my father."

"Oh, no," said Tamar. "What are you saying? What proof do you have?

Jumping up, Moshe turned to Tamar and put his arms around her as if to protect her from what he was about to say. "I am not surprised," he said to me. "Your mother's obsession with the Polski, her attitude toward you when you told her the Colonel had come to see you. I remember you saying something to the effect, "Is there something you're not telling me?" And then, with a sigh, he continued, "I guess there was."

Releasing herself from her husband's embrace and turning to him in anger, Tamar said, "Moshe, you're so quick to jump to conclusions," Then turning to me she said, "I ask you again, what proof do you have?"

"Tamar, is there any more coffee?" I asked. "I could use some right now."

"Me too," said Moshe. "Let me help you.

Bringing in two cups, one for me and one for herself, Tamar came back into the living room followed by Moshe, who held his cup and a pitcher of milk. "Okay," said Tamar. "We're listening."

"When the prosecutor told *eema*, who was on the witness stand, that before calling her she had been investigated and it was determined that when she left Poland she was two months pregnant, she broke down and admitted that she had been intimate with the Colonel. According to the stories that we have been told, I was born some seven months after they arrived in Palestine. Not only that, but I knew for a fact that was what the Colonel wanted to speak to her about in private. I'll tell you more about that later. So, my darling sister, I guess you now have two half- brothers."

There was a deadly silence. After about a minute with no sound other than the drinking of coffee, Tamar got up from the couch. For a moment, I didn't know if she was going to come over and hit me or hug me. But she took the cup out of my hands, sat down on my lap, put her arms around me, and said, "I don't care what you found out. We are still a family and I love you."

I was so relieved by her reaction that I hugged her and kissed her. "We are still a family," I said. "Nothing can change that."

Then my mother must have known all along," said Moshe. "But there is more to the story, isn't there?"

"Who are you," I replied with a laugh, "Sherlock Holmes?"

"I pay attention," said Moshe. "You said you had more to tell us later, and you said you know it for a fact. What do you know? °

"Listen and you shall learn," I replied. "But again, I ask, not a word to anyone."

"You went to Ludwigsburg and came home from Munich," said Moshe. "You went to see the Colonel. If your mother finds out, you are dead meat. Why did you have to do that?"

"There is more to that story than you can imagine, Sherlock," I replied. "Yes, I went to see the Colonel and, lo and behold, he is still alive and bought me breakfast."

"I don't believe you," said Tamar, shaking her head. "You are obsessed as *eema*. So what did the Colonel have to say?"

"I'll narrow it down as best I can. He had been married before the war; his wife was killed in a British air raid. They had a daughter who still blames him for her mother's death and doesn't speak to him. She is a professor of German history in Dusseldorf. So guess what? I have another half-sister."

"And what about the talk they had after the trial?" Moshe asked. "What is it you know as a fact?"

"The Colonel wanted to talk about me," I responded. "He told me this. He never knew that *eema* was pregnant when she left the Polski. She, on the other hand, refused to acknowledge that he was my father. He told me that the judge had given them five minutes to talk and *eema* was out of the room in three."

"This is too much for me for one night," said Tamar.

"It was a hell of a week for me, too," I responded. "But now do you see why I couldn't see the folks yet? I have to decide how to handle all of this. I called Shimon and told him that I'd like to see him by the end of this week. He is the only one I feel comfortable telling this to besides you two, of course. Do either of you have any suggestions?"

"You know," said Moshe. "Your mother spent most of her adult life trying to hide what she deemed to be her guilt over something over which she had no control and for which she had no reason to feel guilty. Over the course of all these years, I am sure your father knew, or imagined, what was going on at the hotel and my mother obviously knew since she was at the trial, and so, I assume my father knew. Shimon knew. So maybe when you tell her you know it will really make no difference. As Tamar said, we are still one family. What she had to do to stay alive saved many lives, and brought many new lives into being. I am willing to bet that she might be relieved it's over. The secret is out; it is no longer a secret and nobody has been hurt by it. How does that sound to you?"

Before I could answer, Tamar said, "Logically, it sounds right, but I am sure that emotionally it will be much more complicated. Listen, you guys, it is late and I have a full day tomorrow. Sholom, you can sleep a little later if you wish and then come to kindergarten, pick up Ari and spend some time with him. For now, though, let's call it a night. We all have a lot to sleep on."

And as we walked out and turned off the lights, Moshe said, "I wonder what Shimon will have to say? He's a man with a lot of insight."

Chapter X

I spent two more days at the *kibbutz*. I had Ari with me for the better part of the mornings and then I would take him back to the kindergarten for lunch. At that time, Rena came and helped Tamar serve the children. After lunch, the children would lie down for a nap. Tamar would leave Rena in charge so I sat and talked with her.

I admit, in a certain guilty way, that I was thinking of Rena as more than a friend and an aide to Tamar. My thoughts were confused. I knew I couldn't leave Ari at the *kibbutz* indefinitely although I also knew that my sister wouldn't have minded. But he was my son, and I wanted him with me. I wanted to be there as he grew up and not be just a visiting father. I didn't know if he had any recollection of Chava but I doubted it. He needed an *eema* and I couldn't help but notice how he had taken to Rena. I felt unfaithful to Chava thinking this way, but I was being unfair to Ari if I didn't.

Rena told me that she had not intended to spend more than a year at the *kibbutz*. She had ideas about her future none of which seemed to involve a man. I, too, spoke about my future and told her I was inclined to stay in academia once I got my doctorate. That would mean, to the best of my knowledge, I would remain in Tel Aviv. When I asked her if this is where she thought she might wind up she leaned over, kissed me on the cheek and said, "Who knows? It's a possibility."

Our routine remained the same for the next two days; however, on the second day, I called Shimon and made an appointment to see him the following day. That evening, after dinner, Rena asked me if I would care to walk her to her house. I was momentarily embarrassed, but both Moshe and Tamar encouraged me to do so.

We walked slowly, hand in hand, and talked about when we would see each other again. I promised her it would not be long and told her that I would miss our afternoon conversations. She said she, too, would miss them, and when we said goodnight, we kissed each other softly.

When I got back to Moshe and Tamar's house, they were waiting up for me.

"She's a very nice girl," Tamar said. "And she loves Ari."

"I know she is," I responded, "but I feel guilty even thinking about it. It is only four months since we buried Chava. It's much too soon to think about such things."

"But promise us that you will come back soon," said Moshe.

"I will, you know I will," I said, "But now tell me, have either of you any approach that I can discuss with Shimon tomorrow? I'll say goodbye to Ari in the morning and then I'm driving to Jerusalem to meet him for lunch."

"Let's do it the other way around," suggested Moshe "Tell him the story and see what Shimon has to say and when you get home, call us and we can compare notes. The folks will be home tomorrow evening, so they won't know anything about this."

"That sounds like a good idea," said Tamar.

"In other words," I said, with a laugh, "neither one of you has come up with anything. A big help you guys are."

"Well, who can have a half-brother with two fathers and two half-sisters all in one week and expect normal people like us to give him advice?" asked Tamar. "Let's go to bed and sleep on it for another night and see what tomorrow brings," she went on, as she came over and gave me a kiss on the cheek.

A quick kiss in the morning from Ari, because he could not be bothered with his father when his friends were waiting, goodbye to Moshe and Tamar, and I was off to Jerusalem.

Shimon was glad to see me, and we went to a fancy restaurant where many of the high profile government people ate lunch. Before we sat down, Shimon had to greet others who were there for lunch. After working the room and stroking those who needed to be stroked, he joined me at our table.

"Nu, so how long were you gone?" he asked.

"Eight or nine days," I responded. "But what I have to tell you is so unbelievable that we should order first so as not to be interrupted.

We gave our order to the waiter, and when he left the table, I started from the beginning. The Hotel Polski, St. Jacek's, my half brother, my parents' visit to Warsaw, Ludwigsburg, Munich, and ultimately Peter Hauptmann. Between Josef and Ludwigsburg, the waiter brought our food and I talked as we ate. Shimon kept sighing, shaking his head, and repeating, "I don't believe it. I don't believe it."

When I finished, the coffee came, and I now posed the question "How do I tell my parents?"

Without a moment's hesitation, he answered. "The same way you told me. There is nothing in this story that you don't have a right to know, and there is nothing in this story that you should hide from your parents. Your knowing what you know should finally give your mother the peace she has sought for close to thirty years. If she expresses anger over what you have learned, she will get over it. She must get over it and realize that she is guilty of nothing. If, at this point, she remains obsessed over her role in the Hotel Polski and her relationship with Colonel Hauptmann, then nothing, and I repeat, nothing will ever cure her. She must cure herself. Do you agree with me?"

With a big laugh, I responded, "You know what, Shimon? Moshe and Tamar feel the same way. So I ask you, how would you like to tell her?"

Signaling the waiter for the bill, Shimon turned to me, and with a big smile, said, "Don't ask me. I'm almost family, but not quite the one to get into the middle of this. You felt compelled to learn the truth, and now that you have learned it, use it to set your mother free. Frankly, I would like to be a fly on the wall when you tell your parents what you have uncovered, but, I think the reaction will be positive." Giving the waiter the check and his credit card, he turned to me and asked, "When do you think you will tell them?"

"My brother-in-law, Moshe, told me that they went, with his parents, to Eilat and are due back tonight. I'll have to see how tired they are and how late they want to sit up and talk," I replied.

As the waiter returned with the credit card and the bill, Shimon signed it and waved to some friends who were still eating. As we left the restaurant, I thanked him for lunch, we shook hands, and he said, "Call me and tell me what happens. Your mother listens to me. I'll jump in if there is a problem."

When I arrived back at the apartment in Tel Aviv, my parents were already there. As a result, I didn't have a chance to call Moshe and Tamar and tell them what Shimon said. With hugs and kisses, I asked them, "Well, did you get seasick and how much did you make at the black jack tables?"

How do you know where we were?" *abba* asked.

"I've been home for a few days," I answered. "When you weren't here I picked up my car and went up to spend some time with Ari. The kid loves the *kibbutz*. When I told him I was leaving, he gave me a kiss, said goodbye, and ran off with his cousins and friends. I am so indebted to Moshe and Tamar. They told me that you went with Avram and Feygl to Eliat, and I know *eema* likes to play blackjack."

"The tables were kind enough to us this time," *abba* said with a little laugh. Let us finish unpacking and then we'll go out for a bit of supper."

"No hurry," I responded. "I had a big lunch. I just came from Jerusalem where I met Shimon, and he bought me lunch in a fancy political restaurant."

"What is a political restaurant?" asked *eema*

"One where all the high profile government people go," I answered. "He had to shake hands with a dozen or more, some of whom he liked and some of whom, he told me, he didn't like."

What did you have to talk to him about?" asked *eema*.

"Finish your unpacking, and when we go out, I'll tell you all about it," I answered. "While you do your thing, I'm going to lie down for a bit. Call me when you're ready."

After arriving at the restaurant and ordering dinner, I. told them I had finished my research and was now going to organize it and submit my dissertation. When I receive my doctorate, I intended to have it published and would seek a full professorship. I asked whether they had any objection to my continuing to live at home for the immediate future and, of course, they didn't. When my life was settled, it was my intention to take my own place. We then spoke about Ari and what the future would hold for him. I told them about Rena, and they told me that they had not met her, as yet, but were glad that Tamar had competent help in the *kibbutz*. We then spoke of Josef and again acknowledged the wonderful and unbelievable miracle of my having found him. *Eema* told us that she had spoken with Maria at dinner, told her what Josef was like as a little boy, and also told her all about Natan. The question of his being a Catholic priest wasn't mentioned, although we all knew it hung in the air.

By the time dessert and coffee were served, we spoke of their little adventure to Eilat with Avram and Feygl. It was as if the question of the remainder of my trip was being specifically avoided, but I knew when we got home we would have to talk about it. And that is just how it happened. Once we got back to the apartment, *abba* asked me to tell them about the rest of my trip. I took a deep breath and said to myself, "As they say in England, in for a penny, in for a pound."

I reminded them that from Warsaw I had gone to Ludwigsburg because that is where the transcripts of war crimes trials were stored. I tried to soften it somewhat by insisting that I had to read the transcript to see if there was any more information that I could gather from the testimony, of the witnesses that would add to my knowledge of the Hotel Polski. *Eema* sat quietly and looked at me and I knew she didn't believe a word I was saying

"Did you read my testimony as well?" she asked.

"Yes, I did, *eema*," I answered "And it cleared up some very important things for me."

"And what were they?" she asked, rigid and white as a sheet.

Without a moment's hesitation, I answered, "The fact that Colonel Hauptmann is my father."

You could have heard a pin drop. *Eema* was squeezing *abba's* hand and rocking slowly back and forth.

"Nothing has changed," I said as I broke the silence. "You are my parents and there are no more secrets between us. Just as the people at the reunion considered you to be a heroine because you testified against Colonel Hauptmann at his trial, I consider you to be a heroine because you survived, you saved *abba's* life, and you raised a family here in Israel. What more could anyone ask?"

Without responding *eema* stood up, looked angrily at me, went into her bedroom and slammed the door behind her. *Abba* stood up as if to follow her, and I said, "Wait, there is more that I have to tell you."

"I am listening," said *abba*, sitting back down.

"Two days later, I had breakfast with Peter Hauptmann in Munich," I said, "and I learned that he has a daughter who is a professor in Dusseldorf. She does not speak to him and has not spoken to him since the death of her mother thirty years ago. So, I guess I have another half-sister."

"You really did this up right" responded *abba*. "Is there any more to this story that I should know, or may I now go in and try to comfort your mother?"

"Why are you angry with me," I asked. "Do I not have a right to know these things? Do you believe I think any less of *eema* because of her relationship with Hauptmann? You were prisoners. You did what you had to do to survive. So again, I say, nothing has changed. Let me tell you a funny bit. At one point, the Colonel got angry with me, and when I said he was my father, he asked, sarcastically, whether, from now on, I would start sending him a card on Father's Day. Isn't that a joke? You are my father. You raised me, you loved me, you taught me, and I am who I am today because of you."

"I went to see Shimon," I went on, "because I wanted to discuss this with him before I spoke to you. I wanted his opinion as to how I should handle this, and it was his advice to go at it straight from the shoulder. He made a very interesting remark. He said that with my knowledge of these facts, it should end *eema's* obsession with the Polski and her guilt over her relationship with the Colonel. It's now out in the open. You knew about it, Shimon knew about it, Feygl knew about it, and now I know about it, as do Tamar and Moshe. There are no more secrets. This should lift the burden from *eema's* shoulders. Please tell her this."

At this point, the door to the bedroom opened and *eema* came out. She looked as if she had been crying, but there was a slight smile upon her face. She walked over and sat down on the couch next to me. She put her arms around me and hugged me. Releasing me, she said, "If you read my testimony, you know I said that when General Seidl came to the Polski and I was sent to the bedroom, I left the door open just a bit so that I could hear what was being said. In this apartment, the doors and the walls are so thin that I didn't have to leave it open to hear you." With a bigger smile, she went on. "I hope that the Colonel paid for your breakfast. After all, that's what a father should do. And did he tell you that I refused to admit that you were his son? Well, you may be his son, but I am your mother and I refuse to admit that he is your father. That is my craziness and I am entitled to it."

Turning to *abba*, she embraced him, kissed him on both cheeks, and said to me, "Chaim is your father and, yes, you are correct. You had the right to know these things, and it changes nothing. We are still a family, and I can now say, with a certain sense of assurance, to hell with Colonel Hauptmann!"

The three of us embraced and I said, with love and devotion, "Oh, *eema*, I hope you mean it."

To which she replied, "I do. Now I can discuss it with greater ease. Let us get a good night's sleep and tomorrow you can tell us more about his daughter and his wife. Is she still alive?"

"No, she died a year ago. But let's talk about it in the morning."

Chapter XI

Eema stayed in touch with Josef by letter and by telephone. He was eager to come to Israel, and as it happens, he came at just the right time.

In the meantime, I completed and defended my dissertation and received my doctorate in Jewish history, and The Hebrew University in Jerusalem I offered me a full professorship. When I told my superiors at the University of Tel Aviv, they immediately matched the offer, which pleased me, because I really wanted to stay in Tel Aviv.

Once that was settled and I knew I would be economically secure, I purchased a large apartment, much too large just for me, near the university and moved out of my parents' home. Rena came down from the *kibbutz* on a number of occasions and helped me furnish it. Although it was unspoken, we both knew the apartment was for us and for Ari. My parents and Chava's parents met Rena when they went to the *kibbutz* to visit with Ari, but Rena and I kept our relationship to ourselves or so we thought. I'm sure that Moshe and Tamar knew we were seeing each other because I would get a *kibbitz* from Moshe after Rena would come back to the *kibbutz*. "I understand you had company?" he would say with a smirk. To which I would respond, "I don't know what you're talking about and besides it's none of your business."

More than a year had passed since Chava's death and I felt there was no reason to keep my relationship with Rena a secret any longer. If Moshe and Tamar knew about us, I'm sure my parents knew as well.

On her next visit to Tel Aviv, I asked Rena to marry me. I told her that I knew that Ari loved her and that I loved her both for myself and for the way she had shown her love for Ari. When I told her that if she'd marry me she would get two fellas at the same time, she opened her arms wide and asked how could she refuse such an offer …of course, she would marry me. She said we would need-time to make arrangements and it was time for me to meet her family, which I had never done.

Rena was dark haired and dark skinned and looked more like an Israeli than I. Her parents had come from Iran when Rena was young and were able to get out with considerable wealth. In the past, when she would come down and spend the day with me, she always spent the night at her parents' home. So, first I called *abba* and told him to have *eema* meet us at the store so we could all go out for lunch. I knew that my news would not come as a surprise. "It's about time," was all they could say, as they kissed and hugged us, and wished us *mazel tov*. They then told us that their first clue was when I insisted on such a big apartment. They knew that I was not taking in boarders; someone else in addition to Ari would be living there with me.

After lunch, Rena called her parents and told them she was bringing someone home for supper, and we would be there around six. As always, they were happy to hear from her and looked forward to meeting her "friend."

There was one more thing I had to do, and I asked Rena to accompany me. I called Chava's parents and asked if I could visit with them for an hour that afternoon. They immediately asked about Ari, and when I assured them that he was fine, they were glad to have me come over.

When they opened the door and saw me there with Rena, they knew why I had come. I told them of our plans, and they wished us well, but we all wept. I assured them that the door was always open for them to come and visit with Ari and that I wanted them to remain in his life. That was the right thing to say, but I don't know if either of us believed it. Again, with hugs, kisses, and best wishes, we left them, and as we did, we both looked at each other as if to say, "I know we did the right thing, but ..."

Rena's parents were wonderful, and their home was quite beautiful. Although I was not a Sephardi, I met most other qualifications. I was the right age for a husband. I was well educated, and I loved their daughter. My principal drawback was that I wasn't religious. They were terribly moved when they learned my parents were Holocaust survivors and looked forward to meeting them. I told them of the incident in Warsaw where I found Josef, and we all laughed at the fact that Rena would now have a Catholic priest as a brother-in-law. She had told them about Ari, and they were most anxious to meet their newest grandson. Rena's two older brothers were married so her parents already had a number of grandchildren. She also had one younger sister named Tsipurah who still lived at home. She joined in the festivities and appeared to be truly happy for Rena.

Before I left to go back to my apartment, for the night, we made plans to meet the following day, when I would drive Rena back to the *kibbutz* and tell Moshe and Tamar the news. I also wrote out the name and address of my parents and their telephone number, since Rena's mother wanted to call *eema*, and when I told them where *abba's* store was, they both said they knew it, they had purchased clothes and accessories there, and were sure they knew *abba*. That was really wonderful. Since I knew my parents would, in all probability, be home that evening, I offered to call them and when they answered, I put Rena's mother on the phone with *eema* and they chatted away. Without even asking us if we were available, they made a date for dinner after Shabbos ended. Both Rena and I breathed a sigh of relief over how well everything had gone.

Ari was close to three years of age at this time. He was a healthy, active child, spoke full sentences and could identify most pictures in a book if you could get him to sit still long enough. We decided rather than bring him down to meet Rena's parents; we would all go up to the *kibbutz* because it would be less of a disturbance in Ari's schedule. Our parents had gotten along well; not only had they gone to dinner together, but they had also visited one another's homes. Rena's parents met Avram and Feygl, and Rena's mother said Avram looked familiar. Although Avram still worked as a jewelry designer, he was one of the owners of the store and Rena's mother had seen him there on more than one occasion. This connection was confirmed when Avram took one look at a piece of jewelry she wore and laughed because he had designed it.

Rena's father had a station wagon that could accommodate six people, and on a Sunday a few weeks before the wedding, Rena and I and both sets of parents went up to visit the children and the grandchildren. When Rena introduced her parents to Ari, he took to them immediately, probably because they brought a gift with them he really liked. When they all left, he gave them both kisses. I looked at Rena and we both shrugged as if to say, "Another hurdle overcome."

Rena's parents expected our wedding to be held in the big banquet hall near their home. They were terribly disappointed when they learned that we wanted a small wedding to be held on the *kibbutz*. That's where our friends were and that is what was meaningful to us. We could not refuse them, however, when they asked that their Rabbi perform the ceremony. A date was set.

On Ari's third birthday, I went to his party at the nursery school. After the party, we told Ari that we were going to be married and Rena would be his *eema*. How much of it he understood, we will never know, but we felt it was the right thing to do. We decided to hold off with the news that he would be leaving the *kibbutz* and moving into the city. That would mean a new school and he would have to make new friends. It would have been a little too much for a three year old to absorb.

On the day of the wedding, there would be a surprise that my parents and I knew about but we kept secret. When he learned of the wedding date, Josef had rearranged his schedule. Instead of coming to Israel and staying with *eema* for a week before going to his conference, he would go first to the conference and then would come straight from Jerusalem to the *kibbutz* for the wedding.

It was a beautiful November day. There were so many people—more than we anticipated—and since the ceremony would be held outside and then the reception, the food and drink in the *shul*,[18] people could wander in and out and be relaxed. Almost the entire *kibbutz* was there, as was Rena's family—brothers, wives, and children, sister, aunts and uncles, cousins —it struck me that the Sephardim really took it to heart when the Bible said, "be fruitful and multiply." Avram and Feygl were there, as were Eitan and Miriam. Neither wore their uniforms and I wondered when we would be attending their wedding. Rena's sister and Tamar were both maids of honor, and Moshe was my best man. We had chosen the rings from a beautiful selection Avram had in his shop, and when all the chairs were set and we were about to begin the wedding, there was a collective gasp.

Down the aisle came this handsome Catholic priest, decked out in white with a big cross hanging from his neck, who was greeted by our family as if he was a king. After Josef was introduced to everyone, the Rabbi did what I thought was a wonderful thing. He asked Josef if he would like to participate in the ceremony and if he would stand next to him under the wedding canopy. Although *eema* would barely let go of Josef, she beamed when she heard the Rabbi's invitation, and as everyone settled down, the ceremony began. But the one thing that moved me beyond words was that, from the corner of my eye, I saw that the last two people to take their seats were Chava's parents. I pointed it out quietly to Rena and we both could have cried. They were such good people.

---

[18] Synagogue

The Sephardic wedding ceremony is somewhat longer than I was used to, but Rena had warned me beforehand and there was little that I could do. The crazy thing on my mind had been what part Josef would play? I had to assume that in a Catholic ceremony, there would be mention of Jesus. That would not have gone over big in the *kibbutz*. But just as I expected, Josef came through like the good brother, or should I say, Father, that he was. When called upon, he recited a psalm dealing with love and devotion, and after I broke the glass, he was the first one to hug me and wish me a *mazel tov*.

Josef is one hell of a guy, and, Catholic priest or not, *eema* has the right to be proud of him. I would never have found him if the clerk at the Polish Archives had not sent me to St. Jacek's to see the plaques and if I had not remembered his name from the stories that *eema* had told us years ago. I still shake my head in disbelief when I think about it.

After the ceremony, the kitchen staff set up the reception in the *shul* where people helped themselves to food and drink. It was a happy occasion, and to tell the truth, Josef was really the center of attention. I doubt he ever hugged and kissed so many relatives, or non-relatives, for that matter, in one setting.

Ultimately, the *kibbutz* people wished us well, gave us gifts, told Rena how much they would miss her, and wandered off to their own houses. Our relatives and friends headed back to the big cities, and we were left with the immediate family. Rena's parents made a date for dinner at their house with my parents, Josef, and Avram and Feygl. Chava's parents hung around long enough to be introduced to Rena's parents; and again tears were shed, particularly by Rena's mother when she learned who Chava's parents were. They had brought a gift for Ari and gave us a very handsome gift in honor of our wedding. Their being at the wedding was sweet and devoted, yet awkward, too, and when they left, I felt a great sadness for them.

My parents took Josef to their apartment, where he planned to spend a week before returning to Warsaw. Rena's sister went home with her parents. We went back to our apartment to finish packing because in the morning we were leaving on a one-week cruise of the Greek islands. We had arranged with Moshe and Tamar that when we returned, we would come up and start the process of weaning Ari off the *kibbutz*. We both felt that Rena's presence would be the comforting factor. Our plan was to enter him into a nursery school that had a good reputation and was not too far from our home. Prior to our marriage, Rena had already made some contacts with agencies in Tel Aviv with respect to a job, and I had to prepare to assume my professorial duties within the next thirty days. I had a lot of preparatory work to do. Above all, we wanted to spend time with Ari and help him through this transition because the last thing we wanted was for him to feel as if he had been abandoned.

We looked forward to our future and the new life, which had begun for us, as a family.

1975—Dusseldorf, Germany

Annaliese Gertrude Hauptmann

Chapter XII

She called herself Liese. She was in her early forties, pleasant looking with a slim figure, piercing blue eyes, and a blunt, bleached blond bob. She was bright, well educated, and a professor of German history. She lived in a university apartment complex for professors and visiting scholars who came to lecture at the university in Dusseldorf.

She was somewhat of an oddball in that her friends came and went. She would be close with people for a while but if, in the end, they disagreed with her philosophy, her backhanded approval of the Nazi regime, her anti-Semitism, and her waffling denial of the Holocaust, she would break up with them and move on looking for new people to call friends.

Her taste in lovers was not only bizarre, but short-lived and in some cases, tragic. She was once reprimanded by the administration and almost discharged after they discovered that she had taken one of her students to bed for a rather extended period. When she decided she had enough of him and chose to end the relationship abruptly, he killed himself. Rumor had it that between her various men, she also engaged in romantic interludes with occasional women she would meet on the campus or at bars she frequented. She drank, at times to excess, and had been seen staggering back to her apartment singing old German war songs

Her present boyfriend was a true enigma. The university had recently instituted a Jewish Studies Program and had hired an Israeli scholar by the name of Rafi Kremer to head the department. Liese met Rafi at a reception for professors and their wives. Rafi had no wife, and Liese had no husband or other involvement at the time, so she made a beeline for him. By chance, since he had no permanent address yet and was staying in an apartment reserved for visiting professors, which happened to be in her complex, she saw to it that she would escort him home after the party. As an Israeli, he was the exact kind of person, except for his good looks and the fact that he was at least five years younger than she, one would assume she'd have nothing to do with. But that was Liese.

Although they kissed rather passionately when saying good night, Rafi was wise enough to insist on going to his own apartment, and telling Liese that while taking her to bed on the night they first met would certainly be a delightful experience, it was just not his way. He needed more time and then, perhaps . . .

Liese, who had too much wine at the reception, apologized for being so forward and said she understood and hoped they could be friends. She went on to tell him that she wanted very much to discuss his syllabus for Jewish Studies with him as it might pertain to Jewish history, and since she was a history professor . . . He agreed and promised that they would get together soon.

And, they did get together and they did discuss his syllabus for Jewish Studies. Whether Liese really cared or not was not important. She turned on her charm and kept her anti-Semitism and her Holocaust denial ideas to herself. She was intent on getting Rafi into bed.

As he got to know other professors, Rafi learned of Liese's philosophies and prejudices, but in his discussions with them, he had to admit she had never expressed any of these unsavory concepts to him. Since it didn't take long for Liese to bed Rafi, and when, after a week or two of good sex he started to ask Liese some questions about herself, her family and other non-academic matters, she dropped her guard and her true beliefs started to emerge.

When in the midst of a romantic evening in Liese's apartment she let slip that her father had been an SS Colonel during the war, Rafi found himself unable to perform. When she questioned his reaction and he began to talk about the Holocaust, she got out of bed, put on a robe, and the debate began. Strangely enough, this didn't end their relationship. Rafi hung in, not for the sex, but due to his own intellectual curiosity. Whether they would have sex again was unimportant to him. This intelligent and attractive lady was delusional.

They went to some concerts on campus; went to the movies together; went to some excellent restaurants and to some bad bars, and when they were drunk enough they went to bed. As the weeks grew into months, Rafi learned that Liese never spoke to her father, was unaware whether he was still alive, and claimed she didn't care, which he sincerely doubted. She made it quite clear she wanted nothing from her father. As to the Holocaust, Rafi argued with her that, as an historian, she must be willing to accept German history from sources other than those that have long been discredited. She also knew, he insisted, whether she cared to admit it or not, the Holocaust was a fully documented event and that it could be proven that six million Jews were the victims.

The end came for Rafi when she partially acknowledged that the Holocaust might have happened, but it was really the Jews who brought it upon themselves. They were the enemies of Germany and if Germany was at war, it had the right to kill its enemies. When he asked why three million Polish Jews who lived in the *shtetl* were enemies of Germany, and she responded with the old canard about the worldwide Jewish conspiracy, he had had enough. In his own way, he felt sorry for Liese. How the university could keep a person with these ideas on its faculty was beyond him. Fortunately, she taught the history of Germany up to the start of the 20th century and he hoped she went no further than that in the classroom.

1975-77—Tel Aviv

Sholom

Chapter XIII

The two years that followed our wedding were really wonderful.

We returned from our honeymoon, picked up Ari and got him registered in nursery school. Being the adaptable kid that he is, he took to the new school with little trouble. And for his fourth birthday, he got the best present of all, a little sister. Rena's parents were overjoyed; my parents visited almost nightly. We called the baby Yehudit, and the gifts poured in from all sides. Rena and I were happy that I had the foresight to buy such a large apartment. At this point, we didn't have to move. Everyone had their own bedroom.

Eitan stayed in the army and was promoted to the rank of general. He was spoken of, according to Shimon, as a possible political candidate, with a chance to become a member of the Knesset. Miriam resigned her commission but stayed in the reserves, and they were married in a big ceremony with many military and political people present. I'm sure my mother thought they got married because she was pregnant, but this time, she was wrong. They went off to the United States for an extended honeymoon, and from what I heard, he went to the American War College while there, paid for by the Israeli government. Moshe's big brother now has a future. However, when they came home, Miriam was quite pregnant, and shortly thereafter they had a little girl whom they named Dorit after Eitan's mother whose name was Dvoira. At the naming ceremony in *shul*, Avram was beaming. This is what he had wanted for so long, a baby named for Dvoira who had simply vanished in an unexpected roundup by the Germans in the ghetto. When Avram was happy, Feygl was happy. Miriam's parents were the happiest of all, because Miriam was nearing forty years of age and they wondered if she would ever have a baby. It was truly a joyous occasion.

Josef came once a year for a visit, each visit a bit longer than the last. I don't know why, but discussions with him and the rest of the family made me think that he might be considering a lifestyle change. When he came to Israel he removed his clerical garb, collar and cross included, and if you saw him on the *kibbutz* playing with Tamar's girls or Pinky, or in discussion with the men, you would think that he was just another *kibbutznik*[19]. When I talked to Rena about my thoughts, she would laugh at me and say, "How can you tell what a priest thinks?"

Moshe and Tamar's *kibbutz* grew in size and prosperity. They built a rather impressive guest house and tours would come to the *kibbutz* by the busload. During the two-night stay, the tourists were shown the orchards, the crops, the canning factory, and volunteers were asked if they would like to get a feel for being a member of a *kibbutz* by working in the fields. In the evenings, there was entertainment, and the tourists left believing that they had really participated in the growth of the State. The *kibbutz* also attracted teenagers who came, stayed for their summer vacation, worked with the residents, and learned Hebrew. It was hoped that some of them would come back and be Israeli citizens. Not only was it a good plan, but on occasion it was even successful.

As far as I was concerned, things took a somewhat strange turn. From the moment I received my doctorate, the Hotel Polski was never again mentioned by the family. It was as if the name had become a museum piece; put on the shelf, never really to be looked at or

---

[19] A member of a kibbutz

discussed. A museum piece, not for display, but for storage or for research, should anyone else be interested.

I taught two courses, Jewish Biblical history and World Jewish history. Although the latter included the Holocaust, the Hotel Polski was such an insignificant part of the subject matter that it was never discussed in class. From the family's point of view, it was over and done with. It had been pushed, pulled and spoken about to such an extent that there was really very little else to say. *Eema* was happier than I have ever seen her. She loved her big family; she loved the grandchildren and she loved her husband. It appeared as though all was well with the world.

Rena and I couldn't have been happier. Ari loved his little sister, and when we had a chance, we would drive up to the *kibbutz*. His cousins and friends welcomed Ari as the big guy from the big city. Tamar's girls were too grown up to have much to say to us, but they did love to hold and play with Yehudit. Pinky was all over the place and making Tamar crazy. Her new assistant was good, but Tamar admitted, not as good as Rena. As the *kibbutz* grew, more children came and, as a joke, or maybe not as a joke, Tamar asked Rena if she would like to come back, knowing full well that it would not happen. Nevertheless, everyone was glad to see us, many of them having been at our wedding. Visiting the *kibbutz* was always a fun day for us and the kids slept in the car all the way home.

The mail was usually delivered late in the afternoon. Rena would pick up Ari at nursery school and then pick up the mail on her way to the apartment. It was on such an ordinary day that she found, in the mailbox, a large manila envelope, stamped with German postage and a return address indicating it had come from a law firm in Munich. She didn't open it but waited until I got home. We both looked at the envelope with no idea what it could possibly contain. "Let's open it and see," we both said at once.

Inside was a cover letter from a law firm, in Munich, along with a copy of a will written in German, and a bunch of forms, also in German. As Rena stood by impatiently, I read the letter twice to be sure I fully understood it.

"Nu," said Rena, "what is it all about?

Looking at her with a strange look on my face, I replied, "We have just inherited a very large sum of money."

"From whom?" she asked. "Who would leave us a large sum of money from Germany," she gasped, as she put her hand to her mouth.

At that point, I knew that she knew. "Yes," I said. "You're right. Peter Hauptmann has died and he left me his entire estate. I don't know what the exchange rate is between Deutschmarks and Shkolim[20], but it's one hell of a lot of money.

We both sat and looked at one another without saying a word, as which point Ari came out of his room, crawled up into my lap and asked me, "Everything all right, *abba?*"

I gave him a hug and a kiss, replying, "I just don't know, Ari. I just don't know."

Having had enough of this mysterious discussion with his father, Ari slipped off my lap, told Rena he was hungry, and went back into his room.

I looked at Rena and said, "I'm hungry, too, but let me tell you, this is going to create some scene with my mother." That would prove to be true, but beyond my wildest imagination.

There was a certain giddiness between Rena and me during dinner. It's not every day you learn you have inherited a sizeable estate, large enough to perhaps see both your children through university, and then some. After dinner, the children were put to bed and I decided to read the will itself, to be sure that I understood exactly what my "father" had in mind at the time it was written.

The first thing I noticed was that the will had been executed within a month or so of my visit some two years ago. Although trying

---

[20] Israeli money

to read German legalese was not easy, I was able to determine that Hauptmann had mentioned his daughter Annaliese Gertrude Hauptmann, and, to the best of my knowledge, went on to state that he had purposefully omitted her from the will because he had no familial ties with her. I wondered how seeing me twice in forty years was much of a familial tie, but then again, I thought, it is very possible that his relationship with *eema* played a strong role in his thinking. I could not imagine how *eema* would react to all of this. "Perhaps I ought to talk to *abba* first? I must discuss this with Rena. She will be a part of whatever happens here. Perhaps she will see things differently," I thought to myself.

The executors of the will were the lawyers who had prepared it, and the cover letter instructed me to return the forms enclosed by international courier, after having signed the forms in the presence of a notary. I didn't quite understand the significance of all of the forms, but the details didn't really concern me. On my way to work tomorrow, I'll stop off at the bank where we have our accounts and speak to the manager with regard to the exchange rate. I want to know as much as possible before I send the forms back and before I see my parents. I want to be sure I know what I'm talking about.

I can't say I wasn't pleased, excited, overwhelmed, and very nervous about this new development. There was no doubt in my mind that it would open up a lot of old wounds for *eema* and again bring up those issues she assumed had long been resolved. Maybe I was wrong. Maybe she would see this as justification for everything that she had gone through. It would be wonderful if she took it that way. But knowing her, I didn't think that would be the case. I need to hear what Rena has to say.

I told Rena that I would not sign anything or return any of the forms until I had discussed it with my parents. She, on the other hand, came up with an alternative plan: "Sign everything, send it back, get the money and then tell them."

If you are so sure your mother will be so upset by this," Rena reasoned, "then why upset her? She can't really do anything about it, one way or the other. We have no reason not to accept the money. Her reaction may be emotional, but it will not really change anything for us. So, if she knows nothing about it until after we have the money in the bank, then perhaps her reaction will not be as extreme as you anticipate.

Rena's idea made a lot of sense, but for some reason, I felt it was dishonest. When I expressed this to her, she responded by saying, "You went to Germany and never told them that you were going to read the transcript of the trial or that you were going to visit Hauptmann. You told them all of that after it was over. Why is this any different?"

"The transcript was one thing," I said. "It wasn't until I finished reading it that I decided to visit Hauptmann. What I learned from the transcript made visiting him important."

Taking my face in her hands, Rena answered quietly. "And the visit is what made us heirs to his estate. One thing follows the other. You don't think he would have bequeathed this money to you if you had not visited him, do you? His problems with his daughter were his problems. Anyone can disinherit a child and leave their estate to whomever they wish. I get the feeling that you are feeling guilty about this. Am I right?"

"No, I'm not feeling guilty," I responded. "I'm happy that we have received this bequest, virtually out of the blue. But I want to handle it correctly. My mother is the problem. For some reason, she will be hurt by what has happened. I don't know why, but she will say he has interfered in her life again, and I think I understand what she means. It's just not an easy problem to solve."

"Sholom, she is your mother; but we are your family. You handle it as you see fit, but you may be sure I am with you all the way. Whatever you choose to do, I'll support you."

Just hearing Rena say that made me feel better. It was worth a hug and a kiss, and when I let go, I said to her with a big smile, "So, what should we do?"

"Call your parents; have them come for dinner after Shabbos. They can see the kids before we put them to bed and, as I recall, your mother reads German fluently. Let her read the letter and the will. That way you won't actually have to tell her. She will learn it for herself. Your father will ask, "Tell me what you're reading?" She will explain it to him and I am willing to bet it won't be as bad as you think. How is that for a solution?" she asked, kissing me again.

I looked at Rena, waved my finger at her, and said, "That's why I married you. You're a smart kid. I'm going to call them now. Do you think it would be better if you called?" I asked timidly.

"I would never have married you if I'd known you were such a coward," said Rena, waving her finger back at me. "Give me the phone. I'll call them, Mr. Chicken."

Chapter XIV

My parents wouldn't dare walk into the apartment without gifts for the children. Ari runs to them with hugs and kisses, and when he gets his present, he races back to his room to tear off the wrapping paper and starts to play with the new game or toy. Yehudit, whom we call Hudi, is just as loveable. There is nothing she likes more than to crawl up onto her *Sabah's*[21] lap and have him look at a picture book with her.

When we have company, we usually feed the children first and put them to bed so that our evening is undisturbed. When the company is my parents, however, my mother loves to feed Hudi while Rena prepares Ari's dinner and then sees to it that he eats it. While the children are eating *abba* brings me up to date on what is happening in the store and I tell him what is happening at school. Then, when the house is quiet, we all have a glass of wine and sit down for dinner.

"Nu" said *eema*, "to what do we owe the honor of being invited to dinner?"

Not yet ready to get into the subject while we were eating, I replied, "I wasn't aware it was such an honor. I think I've seen you here once or twice before." And with a laugh and a joke, we spoke of other things. We learned that they had gone to a concert with Rena's parents but never told us. Rena was thrilled to know that our families

---

[21] Grandfather

were seeing each other and promised to give her mother a piece of her mind for not sharing the gossip.

When coffee and dessert were served, I finally admitted, "There is something we want to share with you."

"Aha," said eema, as she shook her finger at my father. "I knew there was something we didn't know." Turning to Rena, she asked, "You're not pregnant again, are you?"

With a big laugh, I responded. "No, *eema*. There are other things in life to talk about besides being pregnant."

To which she shot back, "What else is so important?"

"Let me tell you," I replied. I got up from the table, and as I was walking out of the room to get the envelope from Germany, I asked, "Are you still up on your German?"

Returning to the table, I heard *eema* ask, "Why, do I have to be?"

"Because I received a letter from some German lawyers I want to share with you and *abba* to tell me if I am missing anything."

Removing the letter from the envelope, I handed it to *abba* and he moved closer to *eema* so that they could read it together.

Abba was the first to react. "So, you are now an heir to a rather sizeable sum of money."

"I was quite sure that's what it said," I responded. "I also have a copy of the will that I would like you to look at. It's not very long."

As I handed him the will, *eema* looked up and said with suppressed anger, "Son of a bitch, it never ends, does it?"

I was shocked. I had never heard my mother curse or ever use an off-color expression. I knew she'd be upset, but I never expected this reaction.

Unsure of how to respond, I looked to Rena with a shrug as if to say," What should I say?

At which point, she reached out, took my mother's hand and said, "That is where you are wrong. This is where it ends. He is dead. He saved your life, he saved your husband's life, and now he has provided for his son. What more could a father do?"

"My God," I thought to myself, "I would never have thought of that answer. Not only is it brilliant, but it's true."

Rena then went on. "I suggested to Sholom that he fill out the forms, return them and get the money. Once it was in the bank here in Israel, we would tell you about it, because we did not intend to keep it a secret. But for his own reasons, Sholom thought that would be dishonest. He wanted you to know and he hoped that it would not upset you. Are you upset?"

Without giving her a chance to reply, *abba* interjected. "Your mother is always upset when there is any mention of Colonel Hauptmann. That is how she sees him. Not Peter Hauptmann, not Herr Hauptmann, but Colonel Hauptmann. We thank you, Rena, for not wanting to upset her, and we thank you, Sholom, for always sharing the truth with us." Putting his arm around *eema* and giving her a squeeze, he went on with a big smile. "Now we don't have to worry. In our old age, we know that we have someone who will take care of us."

Finally raising her eyes from the letter, *eema* said, "It's a lot of money, my children. Please use it wisely." Turning to *abba* she said "Come, Chaim, it is late. Let us go home."

With a hint of annoyance in my voice, I replied. "It's not so late, and you won't turn into a pumpkin at twelve o'clock. I want you to read the will. Please do it for me. It is, as you say, a lot of money and I want to be sure that I understand everything. Will you do that for me?"

"My sweet Sholom," said *eema* as she reached across the table and caressed my face. "You are becoming annoyed with me. 'My mother and her hang-ups.' Don't be annoyed. Of course, I will read the will."

Abba unfolded the will and they both read together. Not a word was spoken until they reached the sentence about the daughter. "I forgot all about her," *abba* said.

As they continued to read, Rena poured more coffee and I suddenly felt that maybe the storm was over. It would have been dishonest to have done anything without telling them.

When they finished reading, *eema* looked up, took a sip of the fresh cup of coffee and said, "There are no surprises. You are the only heir." Then turning to Rena, she went on. "I only hope, my darling Renatchke, that you are right. That now that he is dead, this is the end." Turning to *abba* she asked, "Did I miss anything?"

"Your German is much better than mine," he responded. "I give you credit that you could read a legal German document as well as you did. If you say there are no surprises, I cannot disagree." Turning to me with a big smile, he asked, "If I need a few bucks in my old age, will you lend it to me?"

"Without even charging you interest," I laughed. Going over to my mother and embracing her, I said, "I'm not annoyed with you. I could never be annoyed with you. I am just glad that all of this is out in the open and we can deal with it honestly and above board."

"You are right, and I thank you for that," said *eema* as she kissed me. "And now that the business part of the evening is over, I want another piece of cake with my coffee."

"Let me get it," I said heading into the kitchen only to be followed by Rena. Putting her arms around me, she said, "You were right. This was the way to do it."

"And you were right," I responded. "Your answer to my mother was brilliant. I'll never forget it. I only hope that she believes what you said and is not just saying it for our sake. Her obsession must end. Let us hope it has."

And with that, we carried the cake to the table, spoke about what we would do with the money and decided it would be wise to talk to Shimon. I'll tell him about the inheritance, and ask him for a referral to a good lawyer who could prepare trusts for the children and wills for us. With money comes obligations, and we must fulfill those obligations. Little did we know that it wasn't close to being over.

Liese

Chapter XV

Liese at her apartment in Dusseldorf received the same size manila envelope that Sholom received with the same return address. It also contained a cover letter, quite different in its content from that received by Sholom, a copy of the will of Peter Hauptmann, and only one form acknowledging receipt of the Notice of Probate to be signed and returned. As a distributee of the deceased, or a person entitled to inherit if there was no will, or if the will were not admitted to probate, Liese was entitled to notice of her father's death and what was to become of his estate.

Just as Sholom had no idea, originally, of whom these lawyers were or why they were writing to him, so, too, was Liese unaware of the lawyer's identity or why they would be contacting her. She was quite sober when she opened the envelope, and quite shocked when she became aware of its contents. She poured herself a good stiff drink before asking herself the obvious question: "Who the hell is Sholom Adler?"

The fact that an Israeli would be inheriting her father's estate defied her understanding. Her long-term antipathy towards her father softened somewhat when she stopped to estimate the size of his estate. Another stiff drink brought her to the conclusion that despite not having seen or spoken to her father for more than a quarter of a century, and despite the existence of the unknown Sholom Adler, she should be entitled to all of his money since she is the only surviving relative. Her father's brothers and sisters had all been killed in the war or had passed away; their kids, her cousins, had no claim. It should all be hers. So, who the hell is Sholom Adler?

She decided she had to find herself a lawyer in Dusseldorf, but first, she would have to renew her acquaintance with her old bedmate, Rafi Kremer. If she were to decide she needed a lawyer in Israel, perhaps Rafi could recommend someone.

Rafi's Jewish Studies program was quite successful and, he had since moved into his own apartment in the housing provided by the university. Taking out her faculty directory, Liese dialed Rafi's number. A young female voice answered the phone, immediately causing Liese some distress. The fact that she had some in and out visitors after her breakup with Rafi was fine for her, but the bastard couldn't wait to get a young thing into bed.

"Is Professor Kremer there?" she asked in her most professional voice. "This is Professor Hauptmann calling."

"Liese, my love," he said as he picked up the phone.

"Once you got rid of the old Nazi, you couldn't wait to fuck some young thing?" said Liese.

Completely ignoring her comment, Rafi replied, "Professor Hauptmann, what can I do for you?"

In a serious and sober vein, Liese responded, "I need some help with a personal matter that has to do with Israel. Can we meet and talk about it?"

"You sound serious and you sound troubled. Of course we can meet. But not in either of our apartments. How about lunch in the cafeteria tomorrow at one? Is that good for you?"

"I always knew you were a chickenshit guy," Liese answered. "Are you afraid you'll fall into bed with me? One tomorrow at the cafeteria is good for me. I'll see you there. And by the way, give my regards to the young thing. Is she as good as me in bed?"

Without answering, Rafi hung up the phone.

Leise's life continued to be full of surprises. When she and Rafi met at the cafeteria the following day and she told him the story about her father and the will and mentioned Sholom Adler. Rafi laughed and said, "Sholom? He's a good friend of mine. We've known each other for years from Tel Aviv University, where he is a full professor of Jewish history. What does he have to do with your father?"

"That's what I don't know," replied Liese. "Since you know him so well, could you call him and ask him?"

"Liese, I am hard pressed to do that," responded Rafi. "What would I say? I used to screw Annaliese Gertrude Hauptmann and she would like to know why you are inheriting her father's estate?"

"You know, Rafi, you are a shithead," responded Liese. "Why must you put it that way? You could say that we are both professors at the university and when I learned that Sholom Adler was the heir to my father's estate and was an Israeli; I came to you for advice. Unexpectedly, you told me that you knew him. Wouldn't that be a normal, polite way of asking the question?"

"Thank you for the compliment," said Rafi, "but I am not a shithead. I simply choose to respect someone's privacy. I have no reason to ask about his relationship with your father that caused him to inherit your father's estate. If you want to know the answer, then why don't you write him a letter and ask him yourself? I'm not saying you aren't entitled to know, but asking me to ask him is out of the question"

"All right, so you're not a shithead," responded Liese. "But tell me, how do I investigate this without contacting him directly? Do I hire a private investigator? Do I hire a lawyer here or in Israel? Tell me what I should do?"

"This is definitely weird," said Rafi. "Let me see if I remember the facts. Your father was a Colonel in the SS and went to jail for ten years as a war criminal. He must have done something terrible to warrant such a sentence. What connection could he have had to an

Israeli academic? I suppose the only way to discover how this came about is to try to trace your father's footsteps during the war years. Do you know anything about where he served or what his duties were? The reason I ask is that you really know nothing about him after the war, other than the fact that he remarried and lived in or around Munich. You got that from one of his sisters. Am I correct?"

"You've got an excellent memory," responded Liese. "That certainly shows that you have not forgotten me."

"Do you want my help or do you want to fuck around?" asked Rafi not bothering to hide his annoyance.

"You are a shithead," said Liese. "Why can't you just be nice to me? You know I like you. Of course I want your help; that's why I came to you."

Completely ignoring Liese, Rafi went on. "I've got to assume that after your father served his time and remarried he wouldn't have had anything to do with a boy who would have been, at best, a student. In all probability he wouldn't even have been born yet during the war years. So, how could your father have known him? It really is a mystery and the only accurate information that might exist regarding your father's activities would be found, I think in the transcript of his trial. Do you know where they are stored? I suppose we can find out. Are you willing to take the time to go and read the transcript?"

"I take it all back. You're not a shithead. You're a good friend. Your analysis and suggestions are valid. Yes, I'll take the time to find out where the transcripts are stored and read them but with one condition."

"And what is that?"

"If you come with me. I am sure they must be somewhere here in Germany. We could go, do what we have to and be back in a day or two at the most. Please come with me. I really need your help."

Two days later, Liese called Rafi. This time he answered the phone.

"The transcripts are stored in the Zentrale Stelle in Ludwigsburg. The timing is perfect. It is between semesters. We can catch an hour's flight to Stuttgart and then drive to Ludwigsburg. We can stay over one night and be back the next day. I will make all the arrangements. Please say you'll come."

"I'll come," said Rafi. "But can I bring my young thing?"

"Shithead," said Liese as she hung up the phone

Liese arranged for an early morning flight and made a reservation at a motel near the airport. At the auto rental, they mapped out the road to Ludwigsburg and they arrived there a little before noon. They followed the same procedure as Sholom had followed years earlier. They filled out the request slip, and were sent to the second floor where the clerk located the file, had them sign for it in his ledger, and let them sit at a long table in the room while he had his lunch.

Rafi's English was somewhat better than Liese's, and as a result, he read somewhat faster, telling her not to waste time on things that were not important. They were both shocked to learn of the sale of visas and exit permits at the Polski. Neither of them was at all familiar with what had taken place at the hotel, and neither made any comment as to Colonel Hauptmann's role as commandant.

After some three hours, they came to the final witness' testimony. Anna Adler, formerly known as Rosa Feurmann, was sworn in and they both paid very close attention to the part of the transcript where the prosecutor told the witness that she had been carefully investigated before being called. Despite the fact that the prosecutor told Anna that he knew that when she left the Polski she was two months pregnant, Anna testified that although her duties included living in the same suite with the Colonel her son Sholom was Chaim's son. Rafi looked at Liese and said, *"Mazel-tov,* you have a half brother."

"Mazel-tov, my ass," she responded. "What do I do now?"

"We return the file," answered Rafi matter-of-factly. "We now know what this is all about so we drive back and check in at the motel, find a good *gasthaus* where we can have a stiff drink and talk about it over some dinner." Putting the transcript back in the folder and handing it back to the clerk, Rafi asked, "Can you tell me who was the last person to request this file?"

Looking at his ledger and tracing back the index number, the clerk replied, "Sholom Adler."

"I'm not surprised," said Rafi. "When was that?"

"Some two years ago."

"Thanks for your help," said Rafi

They went to the motel and checked in. Liese gave Rafi a big smile when they entered the room with their overnight bags and she saw that the room had a king-sized bed. Rafi looked at her and said, "I'll sleep in the recliner," to which Liese put on a sad face. They took out the few things they each had brought for overnight and then went back to the desk to inquire about a good *gasthaus*. As Rafi had said earlier, a stiff drink, dinner, and some in-depth conversation was what the situation called for. What the rest of the night would bring was a later consideration.

They were shown to a quiet corner table in the *gasthaus*, ordered their drinks, and looked over the menu, which was some six pages long. The selection was unbelievable. With their drinks, they ordered *Russiche Eier*,[22] a kind of deviled eggs where the yolk is prepared with mustard and spices, served with thick black bread. They then ordered two different main courses promising to share. Neither said a word about what they had learned that afternoon. The ordering, eating, and drinking took up their complete attention.

When it was time for dessert, they ordered coffee and strudel. Finally, Liese looked up and said, "He's a bastard."

"Who's a bastard?"

"Sholom Adler. He's the child of my father and a Jewish woman prisoner, born out of wedlock. So he's a bastard."

---

[22] Russian eggs

"I hadn't thought of it that way," responded Rafi. "He's really a very nice guy. But I guess you're right. So what?"

"So, can a bastard inherit?" asked Liese.

"You can leave your estate to anyone you want. You can legally disinherit your children," answered Rafi. "It's not as if there is no will."

"That's your legal opinion. But what the hell do you know? You're a shithead. I need a real lawyer, maybe two. One in Germany and one in Israel. Do you know anyone?"

"Not offhand," replied Rafi. "But if you find a good German lawyer, he might have a contact in Israel or a book that lists lawyers and their specialties. How's that for a shithead answer?"

"I'm just kidding you, Rafi," said Liese. "You're a good guy. You came with me and your suggestion is a good one." Finishing her strudel and the whipped cream and taking the last sip of coffee, she went on. "I'm not finished with Sholom Adler. Come on, lover, let's go back to the room. It's been a long day, and I'm tired."

"I hope you mean that, about being tired," Rafi said as the waiter returned with Liese's credit card and they both stood up. "I could use a good night's sleep."

Fall 1977—Tel Aviv

Sholom

Chapter XVI

I followed the instructions set forth in the cover letter from the German lawyers. I had my signature notarized and returned the forms by courier so I would have a tracking number should they get lost or not be delivered. I enclosed a cover letter asking that receipt be confirmed and that I be advised as to when I could expect the funds. Since my German was too poor to write a grammatically correct letter, and I was sure that Hebrew would not be understood in Munich, I chose to write in English. If a translation was needed English would be easier.

Some two weeks later, I received a reply from the lawyers advising me that what I had previously sent had been received and it would take a couple of months, or perhaps even more, for the estate to be liquidated. Investments had to be sold and the proceeds collected; the real property was under contract, but title would not pass for at least sixty days and then taxes had to be paid.

The estimate that I received from my banker as to the value of the estate was tentative and became more so as time passed. I had no complaints, though; it would still be a vast sum of money.

More than ninety days went by, and when nothing was heard from the German lawyers, I began to grow anxious. I decided to call, and when the secretary heard my name, she put me right through.

We spoke in German, his being perfect while I stumbled along. I knew immediately there was a problem when he asked me if the name Annaliese Gertrude Hauptmann meant anything to me. When I acknowledged that it did, and I told him what I knew about her, he told me that she had obtained an Order of the German court enjoining the sale of the property and the transfer of any funds to me. He went on to tell me he intended to call me with these developments, and that within the next week I would be receiving a package containing a copy of the Order and the facts upon which it was based. He admitted it was quite unusual and suggested that I seek qualified legal counsel in Israel.

I told all of this to Rena and she had but one thing to say. "It's time to call Shimon."

I wholeheartedly agreed and told her that I would wait until I received the package so that I would have the documents to show him. Rena, on the other hand, suggested that I talk to him first and get his recommendation for a good lawyer. Since the documents that will be received will be both legal and in German, and although Shimon speaks perfect German, it is more important for an Israeli lawyer to analyze the issue.

Rena is a clear thinker and she is right. I called Shimon and made an appointment to see him in his office in two days. The one thing Rena and I both agreed on, was not to say a word to the family. I know for a fact that my mother would say, "Forget it, give her the money, you don't need it, just put an end to it." I was not about to do that. Should anyone ask, the answer is, it takes time to sell the property, taxes must be paid in Germany, and we have faith in the German lawyers. I hope that no one will ask.

Visiting Shimon was always a pleasure. Aside from the fact that there were still many people in his office whom I knew from when I worked there, Shimon was like an uncle to me. I saw him as family. We never met that he didn't ask about Rena and the children and send his regards.

This time we stayed in his office. I brought copies of the cover letter and the will, and when Shimon finished reading them, I was shocked by his reaction; it was the same as my mother's. He just sat, shook his head and said, "Will it never end?"

I told him my mother had said the same thing but went on to tell him what Rena had said, namely, that with the Colonel's death, it had ended. And now I told him the rest of the story about Annaliese Gertrude Hauptmann and the injunction she had gotten, and when I finished I admitted, even I had to agree, it looks like it will never end. I also told him I didn't know the basis of the daughter's claim and that I would be receiving the papers within a week. What I really needed from him was the name of a good estate lawyer, who spoke fluent German, hopefully whose office was in Tel Aviv.

"I have just the person for you," said Shimon. Going to his Rolodex, he looked up a number, dialed it and said to the person on the other end. "This is Shimon Cohen calling from Jerusalem. May I speak with Uri?"

It didn't take ten seconds and Uri was on the phone. The men joked around for a few minutes in Yiddish and then switched to Hebrew. Shimon told Uri the whole story, in brief, advising him that it was very confidential and, that the people involved were like *mishpocha* to him. He also warned Uri that this could get ugly. Shimon then introduced me to Uri and handed me the phone. I promised Uri that I would call him as soon as the papers arrived from Germany at which time we would set up an appointment. He was very kind and very reassuring on the phone, making me feel that I was in good hands, and that, above all I had done the right thing by seeking Shimon's advice.

Shimon wrote out Uri's name, address and phone number for me, and before I left, I promised him I would keep him informed as to what was happening. I made him promise, however, that should he run into my parents not a word about this be said. We shook hands, hugged one another, and I left his office. On the way home, I admitted to myself that I did feel better knowing the matter was in capable hands.

Arriving at home, I told Rena about my visit with Shimon, gave her his regards, and told her about Uri. She then told me that there was a message on the answering machine from Germany. "A man by the name of Rafi Kremer said he was a friend of yours and wanted to talk to you about something of great importance. He left his number and asked that you call him back this evening."

"Okay, madam detective," I said to Rena. "Let's see if you can figure this out. Rafi is the head of Jewish Studies at Dusseldorf. We know each other from here. He's a good guy and if he's calling from Dusseldorf where Hauptmann's daughter is also a professor, I bet he knows her and he knows something about this whole situation."

"Since you're the detective, you don't need me," responded Rena. "You figured it out by yourself. I guess I have no choice but to open my own detective agency," she laughed. "Here is the number. Call him."

I called and the phone was answered by a young woman. I asked for Professor Kremer telling her that Professor Adler was calling. Rafi got on the phone immediately, we kibitzed about his "secretary" who had answered the phone, and he assured me that she rendered excellent services.

When we got done with the small talk, he asked me if I could take time to come to Dusseldorf to give a lecture or two for his students in the Jewish Studies program. The university would pay all expenses and I could stay with him. He promised to get rid of his "secretary" but said there was someone else he wanted me to meet.

I concluded, the excuse for the call was the lecture invitation, but the real reason was the "someone else."

"Before I commit myself," I replied, "tell me about the someone else."

After a momentary pause, Rafi answered. "I believe that my friend, Professor Hauptmann is your half-sister. Wouldn't you like to meet her?"

The question took me back to my breakfast with Peter Hauptmann. He had asked the same question. Maybe I should have met her. Perhaps all of this could have been avoided?

"And how do you know all of this, Rafi?" I asked, with a slight sense of annoyance in that I felt that my privacy had been invaded.

Almost jokingly, he responded. "She received a copy of the will from the lawyers and showed it to me. Her one question was, 'Who the hell is Sholom Adler?' I told her he is a good friend of mine."

"You must be very close with Professor Hauptmann, I replied. "How come she came to you with her problems?"

"What are you, a detective?" he answered. "Let's say that when she saw you lived in Israel, and she knew I was Israeli, she took a chance. It was a wild coincidence that I knew you."

"I don't believe a word you're saying," I said with a laugh. "You were probably screwing her. But I'll have to pass on your invitation for another reason," I went on. "She is represented by counsel, and so am I. It would be improper for us to meet at this time. By the way, how do you know she is my half-sister?"

"That's a long story that we'll talk about when I see you," responded Rafi. "But as a friend, let me tell you some things that you might find interesting."

"Thank you, friend," I replied. "I'm listening."

"Liese, she calls herself Liese, is a bitter pill. She is an anti-Semite and I honestly don't know why the University keeps her on. She is a Holocaust denier, and for some reason I think that she got it all from her father. Beware of her," he went on. "She means to do you harm."

"But from what I know," I answered, "she had not seen her father for years, both during the war and after. He did ten years in Spandau. She never visited him. How could he have influenced her?

"A good question, my friend," said Rafi, "to which I don't really have an answer. All I know is that she is an angry lady. I assume that you will meet each other, in time, since, as you say, there is some sort of lawsuit pending."

"I guess we will," I answered. "But thanks for the heads up. And if you're serious about the lectures, I'll take you up on it when all of this is over. But now I have a question for you. If she's such a Jew hater and a Holocaust denier, why did she come to you?"

"That's a fair question," responded Rafi, "and it's another one to which I have no answer. For some reason, she attached herself to me on the night I got here. Yes, we screwed around a bit, but at first she kept her ideas to herself. When she let loose, I said goodbye. It was months later when she came back with the will and the other documents from the lawyer. She's a puzzle, but she's no fool. And, yes, I am serious about the lectures, but Sholom, take care and be careful with her. She'll do you harm, if she can," he repeated.

With that, we hung up the phone, and I related our conversation to Rena. Thinking clearly, as she always does, she told me to be sure to let the lawyer know about this conversation. The more he knows about Professor Hauptmann, the better it will be for us. I agreed.

Four days later, an envelope arrived by international courier. Rena signed for it leaving it for me to open when I got home. Inside I found a copy of the German Court's Order, a lengthy affidavit by Liese's lawyer, a short affidavit by Liese, and a Memorandum of Law. Needless to say, it was all in German and far beyond my knowledge of the language. The next morning, I called Uri and told him what I had received. He asked if I could have the documents delivered to his office so that he could read them and digest them before meeting with me. That seemed reasonable and I promised I would drop them off with his secretary on my way to the University. We then made an appointment for two days later and he insisted that I give him as much time as he deemed necessary. I told him that I would rearrange my schedule accordingly and that would be no problem.

I very much wanted Rena to go with me to Uri's office, but that would mean a babysitter. In the past, either my mother or her mother would be happy to come over, but since we didn't want either of them to know where we were going or why, she agreed to stay home making me promise to tell her everything that Uri said. She also reminded me to be sure to tell Uri about my conversation with Rafi.

I delivered the papers as I promised and could hardly wait for the two days to pass.

Chapter XVII

Although I had never been beyond the receptionist when I delivered the papers, Uri's outer office bespoke professionalism, competence, and security. I knew I was in good hands when I walked in and was directed by the receptionist to take a seat, while she called Uri's office to announce my arrival. She told me Uri's secretary would be out in a minute to escort me into his office.

It took but a minute and an attractive young lady came out of the inner offices, called my name, introduced herself, and asked that I follow her. From her accent, I got the sense that she was, perhaps, Russian. Many Russians who emigrated to Israel, when they were young, learned Hebrew rather quickly and went into service professions.

Uri's office was large and well furnished, as I expected. The thing that surprised me was Uri himself. He was small, fat, bald and much older than I expected him to be. His voice had sounded young on the phone when we spoke, and I simply visualized him differently. Nevertheless, his handshake was firm. He asked me to sit in a comfortable desk chair as he went around to an overly large judge's chair behind his desk. I saw the papers that I had previously delivered open before him. Casual family conversation ensued, and I got a kick out of the fact that he, too, knew *abba* from the store. Although I had never thought about it, I now realized that many of the well-dressed professional men must buy their clothes at *abba's* store.

As one must never lie to a doctor when describing the symptoms for which you seek his advice, I knew I wouldn't lie to Uri, or shade the truth in any way, when he asked me to describe the background of the case. Who was Annaliese Gertrude Hauptmann, what had she to do with me, and what had I to do with her father? Even as I spoke, I knew that much of what he was asking was set forth in the papers on his desk. I'm sure he wanted to hear how much I was willing to tell him, see what I omitted, and determine for himself, how much of it was relevant. It took me close to an hour to tell the story, starting with the Hotel Polski, Rosa and Itzik, the Colonel, passage to Palestine, the trial of the Colonel, his imprisonment, reading the transcript and concluding with my visit to Munich and breakfast with my "father." He never interrupted me but made intermittent notes of things that I assume he deemed important. When my story was completed, he thanked me for my honesty and, to my surprise, expressed regret that he had to put me through an emotional retelling of the history of the case. I thanked him for his concern and reassured him I was quite all right.

He went on to tell me that, in his opinion, the German lawyer who had prepared these papers may possibly be a Jew. When I asked him why he felt that way, he replied, "The complaint alleges two causes of action: The first, undue influence is rather standard, but the second is quite unique and shows some familiarity with the *Halachic*[23] law of inheritance. The German lawyer also requests that the German court having jurisdiction over the case apply the ancient Jewish law."

"What is he talking about?" I asked, "And is he right?"

"Whether he is right or not will require some research and perhaps a rabbinic consultation. What he is talking about is the Mosaic Law that says 'Should the estate of a deceased Gentile fall under the jurisdiction of a Jewish Court, it must be given to his Gentile kinsman.' Where this lawyer ever discovered that ruling is a

---

[23] Jewish law

mystery, unless he is a learned Jewish scholar or consulted one. I simply don't know. But I have enough time before I must respond to the German Court to have a rabbinic consultation, and to retain German counsel, since I, obviously will not be permitted to practice before the German Court. I am sorry to tell you, Sholom, this is very complicated, very time consuming, and will be very expensive. The only gratification is, if we win, or if we settle, there will be enough money to make the matter worthwhile. I'll send you a retainer statement and I would appreciate your remitting a check as soon as you receive it. In the meantime, I'll seek rabbinic counsel; I'll also speak to Frau Hauptmann's lawyer and seek counsel in Germany. Please, Sholom, do not be discouraged."

Pressing the intercom on his desk, he asked his secretary to come in with his calendar. When she did, we made an appointment for the following week. He promised to keep me informed by phone should he learn anything new.

When I left the office, I was suddenly feeling not as confident as I had been when I walked in. A German lawyer alleging a violation of Mosaic Law was an unbelievable concept, particularly when my own Israeli lawyer was unfamiliar with it. I'll discuss it with Rena and see what she has to say. If the truth be known, if *eema* were to say "give it to her, forget it," I might just do that. What do I need this for? And the expense. How much will this cost me? And what if we lose? All that money thrown out for nothing! Cool it, Sholom; let's see what Rena has to say.

The moment I walked through the door, Rena looked at me and asked, "What's the matter?"

I told her the entire story and expressed my feelings that perhaps, what we were putting ourselves through, was simply not worth it. We could get along very well without the inheritance. We never anticipated it, and what if we lose? We will have thrown out all of that money for nothing.

Rena understood my point of view and came up with an unusual answer.

"Since Uri says he has time, then we have time. Let's invest in the retainer and let's discuss the problem with Josef. He is a man who has spent his life listening to other people's problems and maybe he will see it in a different light. After all, he is a scholar of the Bible. I am sure he has studied the Old Testament as well as the New Testament. Maybe he will have some insight into the Mosaic Law issue.

As always Rena's reasoning made sense. Talking to Josef always has a calming effect. I liked the idea very much and agreed to call him after supper. With the time difference I was sure I would find him in his office.

As I expected, Josef picked up the phone on the first ring. He was delighted to hear from me, asked about the family, and was reassured when I told him everyone was well. When I told him I had a serious problem to discuss with him, he promised me he had all the time in the world to listen. I also told him Rena was on an extension. The two of them then *kibitzed* around for a bit and then I started to tell my story.

In that Josef knew all about the question of my parentage and my visit to Peter Hauptmann in Munich, I began with the will, the amount of the inheritance, Rafi Kremer, and his phone call to me. I then went on to tell him about the injunction by the German court brought by Hauptmann's daughter. The only comment he made after I told him about the allegation based upon the Mosaic Law was a low whistle followed by "Oh, boy."

After hearing the whole story he said, "I don't know enough law to know whether he has a right to ask a German court to apply ancient Mosaic Law to a modern situation. I doubt if this law is a statute that can be referred to, but it raises a hell of an issue. Will you two be home this evening? Let me think about all of this, and I'll call you in a couple of hours. That is not too late for you, is it?

I reassured him we would be awake and waiting for his call. When I hung up, Rena asked me, "Don't you feel better? I do."

I did feel better. I had the feeling that Josef would come up with a plan. We were both anxious to hear from him.

Our attempt to keep off the telephone was futile. First, Rena's mother called and they talked about the children, when they would visit, who went shopping to what stores and all sorts of other womanly things. Not five minutes later, my mother called wanting to know who had been on the phone so long; the line had been busy. She spoke to me briefly and then spent time schmoozing with Rena. We could not say anything because then she would want to know whose call we were expecting and that was something she didn't need to know.

We finally got rid of both mothers, and when the phone rang for the third time, we knew it had to be Josef. Once that was confirmed, we both picked up extensions so that we could listen and comment.

Out of curiosity, I asked. "Did you call earlier?"

"No, I didn't," he answered. "Why?"

I told him about the mothers and how we couldn't get them off the phone. He laughed and told us to be thankful that we had mothers. He then went on to describe his idea.

"I would like to meet Annaliese Gertrude Hauptmann," he said. "In order to do so, I need the help of your friend, Rafi Kremer. I have some free time and can fly over to Dusseldorf, but I need you to set the scene for me."

"How should I do that?" I asked.

"From what you have told me, Kremer pretty much knows the whole story. I also gather he knows Professor Hauptmann pretty well. You can tell him who I am, but at no time should he tell the lady that I am a priest. He can tell her that I am going to be a guest lecturer in the Jewish Studies Program dealing with the subject of Judeo-Christian relations and he thought, perhaps, she might be able to use me for her German history courses as well. Please understand, I don't really know where this will take me or how it will affect the pending litigation, but I wish to get to know her. Needless to say, I'll keep you informed as to what is taking place."

"You're absolutely right, Josef," I laughed. "I don't know what this has to do with the litigation, but if you want a little adventure on my account, all I can say is, why not. When will you be free to go?"

"As soon as you tell me that you have spoken with Kremer and that he is expecting me. At that time, you will give me his address and phone number. I'll see how many miles it is. Maybe I'll decide to drive. Once I am ready, I'll call Kremer and tell him I am coming. We have to be sure that she will be around when I am there; otherwise it will be a waste of time."

"I'll try and reach Kremer tomorrow," I responded. "I have both his home and his office numbers. But let me warn you, as far as Frau Hauptmann is concerned, she's a big drinker and likes both old and young men in her bed."

"You may be sure," Josef answered with a laugh "she will not get me to betray my vows. A drink, perhaps, but I gave up sex a long time ago."

At this point, Rena hung up the extension and came into the room giving me a very stern look just as she heard me say, "Listen, brother of mine, you don't know what you're missing."

To which he made the most unexpected retort. "Maybe someday I'll find out." He then went on. "Be in touch with me as soon as you can. I assume that time is of the essence."

"I'll get back to you as soon as I speak to Kremer, probably by tomorrow night. By the way, thanks, Josef, I don't know where all of this will lead, but I'm glad we're on the same team."

Another few words, goodbyes from both Rena and me, and I hung up the phone. I told Rena what Josef said about sex and asked her what she thought he meant when he said that maybe someday he'd find out. She thought it was a very strange remark, coming from a priest. We both agreed and we both questioned what Josef would accomplish by meeting Frau Hauptmann. If anything, we'd just have to wait and see.

But now it was time for bed. I looked at Rena, winked, and said, "Boy, am I glad I'm not a priest."

Winter 1978
Dusseldorf

Josef

Chapter XVIII

Sholom called me, gave me Rafi's address and phone number, and told me all arrangements had been made. Rafi knew who I was and was waiting for my call. Sholom also told me he had a young thing living with him but he promised to get rid of her during my visit so I could stay with him.

I called Rafi, and he asked me if I could book a flight that would arrive around four in the afternoon. He explained that he would be finished with class by that time and could pick me up at the airport. I arranged a flight that got me into Dusseldorf at 4:30. I called him back, gave him the flight number and the arrival time and was on my way only two days after my initial conversation with Sholom. Rafi assured me that Liese, as he told me she was called, had been told of my visit, she'd be around and was looking forward to meeting me.

Generally, priests travelling in a Catholic country are always beneficiaries of a respectful, religious attitude. I never knew, until this trip, that there was a clergy discount on air travel. (I wondered if they would give it to a rabbi?) The only places I had traveled previously were to Israel and Rome. Those trips had been arranged by the church, so I never had to pay for my own tickets. We were a large group and I paid no attention to the boarding procedure. But as a priest travelling alone, when you are ready to board the plane, you are permitted to board with people needing extra time, or in wheel chairs, mothers traveling with infants, or children who are unaccompanied by adults. Why getting on an airplane is deemed a priestly act of charity, I do not know, but perhaps it was thought that, as a man of God, the sooner I am on the plane, the safer the flight would be.

Since I was the only priest on the plane, Rafi had no trouble greeting me as I disembarked. I only had a carry-on, so we went directly to his car. I suggested that we go to his apartment first so that I could change into non-priestly garb. Should we run into Liese, by chance, I didn't want the secret revealed, as yet. I told him I knew about the young thing and if it was more convenient, I would be happy to stay at a hotel. He reassured me that she was at her own place and would come over only if we needed her to cook dinner for us. Aside from her other talents, she was also a good cook.

I thanked Rafi for the sacrifice he was making and told him that I planned to stay for no more than two days. He, on the other hand, suggested that if I could spend an extra day or two, he would very much appreciate it because in this way, I could deliver two lectures to his Jewish Studies students (all of whom were German both Protestant and Catholic) about Judeo-Christian dialogue. I would receive a stipend for my efforts that would cover the expenses of my trip. In Liese's eyes, my visit would be legitimate and exactly what Rafi had told her was the reason for my coming.

The idea of lecturing at a German university appealed to me and I agreed, subject to only one problem. I could speak enough German to be understood, but I certainly could not lecture in the language. Rafi's solution was, just as we were speaking English, since that was our common language, I could lecture in English. He would record the lectures and have them translated into German for those students who were not fluent in English.

By the time we arrived at his apartment, Rafi and I were not only friends, but colleagues as well. I hung up my priestly outfit, removed the cross and collar, dressed instead in slacks and a windbreaker, and we went out to a *gasthaus* for dinner. At this point, the only topic of conversation was Liese.

Rafi could offer no logical explanation for Liese's illogical way of thinking. He admitted that they had been bed partners until she let loose with her anti-Semitic nonsense. Strangely enough, she had the ability to hide it when she wanted to. It seemed that her beliefs were never directed at an individual. "She didn't dislike me personally because I was Jewish," he said, "She just dislikes Jews in general."

"Other than me," he went on, "I don't know if she even knew any Jews. She wavers on the Holocaust. As a professor, and please understand, she is not stupid," he said with emphasis, "she knows it is a documented event. The only thing that I can figure," he went on, "is she is so ashamed that it was perpetrated by the Germans, it is easier to deny that it ever happened."

"I don't know what your intentions are with respect to her," he continued. "What this will have to do with the lawsuit and her non-existent relationship with her father is beyond me. But I leave that to you."

"When are we scheduled to meet?" I asked.

"Tomorrow at lunch in the faculty dining room," Rafi replied. "She is very interested in meeting you. The first thing she asked how old you were and when I told her you were about my age, her eyes lit up. I am sure she will make a not too subtle attempt to get you into bed. I'd like to see her face when she learns you are a priest," he said with a laugh. "That will be a good one.

Continuing with the plans for tomorrow, Rafi said, "We will meet for lunch and after introducing you, I will excuse myself since I have a class at one o'clock. Liese is free until three, and I will pick you up at the dining room when she leaves. May I make a suggestion? If she wants to have dinner, put it off. Tell her that I have made other plans for us for the evening, but you don't know what they are. Let her be anxious, and believe me, she will be. She will assume we are going out drinking with some young women and that will piss her off. Suggest dinner the following night. She will suggest her apartment. Incidentally, she, too, is a good cook, and if you have dinner there, you will enjoy it. The rest I leave to you."

"It sounds like a good plan," I replied. "I really am not fond of deception, but in this case, I feel I have no choice. Now, tell me about the lectures. When and where?"

After dinner we went back to Rafi's apartment. I called Sholom before it got too late, told him I was with Rafi and would be meeting Liese tomorrow for lunch. I again promised that I would keep him advised as things progressed. I gave my regards to Rena and put Rafi on the phone for a brief minute. When he was finished, he hung up.

Stretching out on the couch, I said to Rafi. "This is crazy. I don't know where this is going, nor do I know how I can be of help to Sholom with regard to the litigation. I hope that Liese, by virtue of her anger or whatever moves her, opens the door for me. I cannot expect her to confess and ask me for absolution. I wonder when was the last time she was in a church?"

The faculty dining room was quite impressive, as was Annaliese Gertrude Hauptmann. We all arrived at the same time and were shown to a table by the hostess. Liese was attractive, well dressed and her hair and nails looked as if she had just come from the beauty salon. It made me wonder who she thought she was meeting and why. When the waiter came to take our order, Rafi excused himself telling Liese that he had a one o'clock class and reminded me, for Liese's benefit, that he would pick me up at three.

Our preliminary conversation was just that, chitchat. When lunch was served, Liese opened the door without a moment's hesitation by asking me, "So, what has Rafi told you about me?" Without waiting for an answer, she went on. "It probably wasn't very complimentary, and besides, why did you want to meet me?"

I was somewhat taken aback, because I never thought the question would be put to me so directly. A little white lie was now necessary. "To the best of my recollection, it was the other way around." Rafi told me that he told you I was coming to lecture, and you said you would love to meet me. Does either scenario trouble you?"

"Oh, not at all," she purred her response. "I'm always anxious to meet handsome men, but that is not quite the way I remember it.," she said with a big smile as she put her hand over mine. Wishing to get away from this conversation and where I imagined it was leading, I answered, "Nevertheless, it is my pleasure. But now, please tell me about yourself. Where are you from, and how long have you been teaching? You know that kind of stuff. Where were you during the war?"

"Aha," she said. "When you ask those kinds of questions, I know you've heard all kinds of stories from Rafi. Are you Jewish?"

"No. As a matter of fact, I am a Polish Catholic," I replied. "You are Catholic too, aren't you? What does that have to do with anything?"

"Actually, nothing," she responded, "and, yes, I am Catholic, but Rafi thinks I'm crazy and that I have crazy ideas. Since you're a Catholic, I feel I can talk more openly with you." Shrugging her shoulders, she smiled and said, "But who wants to talk about such boring things?"

With a little urging and after a second glass of wine, Liese shifted gears and began to answer my questions.

"My parents were Prussians. They had a certain snobbish attitude about them, and when the war came, my father was immediately appointed, by Himmler, who had been a family friend, to become a Colonel in the SS."

"I loved my parents and believed much of what I heard around the dinner table. After Germany invaded Poland and war was declared by the British, my parents insisted that I go live in the country with my mother's sister. Before the war, we lived in Cologne and never imagined that the British would bomb a city with such a famous cathedral. So, I went to the country, my mother stayed in Cologne, and my father was sent to Berlin. I stayed in touch with both of them, and when the bombings started, I begged my father to get my mother out of Cologne, and let her live in Berlin with him or come to the country with me. We were perfectly safe. From what I gathered my father did nothing, or perhaps my mother chose to do nothing. I never really knew. She was killed by a direct hit from a British bomber. From that day on, I never spoke to my father again. I insisted, in my own mind, that he was responsible."

"Do you know what became of him?" I asked.

"I heard from my aunt," she replied, "that for a time he was in Warsaw and then was sent to the eastern front. He survived, was tried as a war criminal, why I didn't know, but I learned why after reading the transcript of his trial. He did ten years in Spandau, got out, and became a farmer living near Munich. He remarried, the second wife died, and he passed away not long ago."

"Do you regret not having spoken to him?" I asked.

"I sure as hell do," she replied shaking her head and smiling. "I'm not sure I was justified in holding him responsible for my mother's death, but above all, when I saw the size of his estate and learned that he had left it to some Jew-boy in Israel, I was pissed. I don't know who the hell he is, but I have consulted a good lawyer and I'm going to give the Jew-boy a hell of a good fight."

I never thought we would get to the subject quite as quickly as we did. This was a good time to end the discussion and our lunch. We had been here close to two hours and I wanted out so I said, "I gather from your tone that you have strong anti-Semitic feelings, or is it just against this `Jew-boy, as you call him?"

"Yes, I have anti-Semitic feelings," she replied. "But I suppose you knew that from Rafi?"

Without answering directly, I said, "There is still so much we could talk about, but Rafi will be picking me up in a few minutes. I do not want to keep him waiting. Can we continue this at another time and place?"

"Absolutely," Liese replied with a big grin. "Come to me for dinner this evening and we'll have the whole night to talk."

"This evening is not good for me," I replied. "Rafi has made plans for us about which I know nothing. And tomorrow I must deliver two lectures to his classes so I must do some preparatory work. How about tomorrow night?"

"Rafi made plans?" she said with an ugly look on her face. "You'll probably meet his young thing and one of her friends. Take my word for it, you won't get much work done, tonight." With a brighter smile, she went on. "Okay, tomorrow night. Seven o'clock at my place. I am a good cook, you know. You bring the wine. Rafi knows where I live. It's not far from his apartment. I'll see you then. By the way," she said as she signed the bill, "lunch is on me. Only faculty members can pay the bill here. I hope you enjoyed it."

"I certainly did," I replied. "I enjoyed the lunch, I enjoyed meeting you, and I know we will both enjoy tomorrow evening. I thank you for this afternoon and, in advance, for tomorrow night." Taking her hands in mine as we rose from the table, I leaned over, kissed her on the cheek and escorted her out the door.

Rafi was waiting at the curb when we came out. She walked over to him and said, "Behave yourself tonight. Josef is a good guy. I can't imagine how he could be your friend. But tomorrow night he is mine." And with a wave, she was off, as I got into the car with a big grin on my face.

On the way back to his apartment, I told Rafi about my discussion with Liese and congratulated him on the fact that his evaluation of her was right on. Her lawsuit against Sholom was obviously motivated by two things. The first was the amount of money involved; the second was her resentment that her father chose a Jew over her. Which one was really first in her mind, neither Rafi nor I could decide.

When we returned to the apartment, I chose not to call Sholom deciding to wait until I had more to tell him. Rafi and I sat and talked about tomorrow's lectures, and at about seven in the evening, we went out for dinner.

I gave the lectures the following day, and it went well. The students were respectful, asked some intelligent questions, and Professor Kremer was pleased.

✦

I bought a good bottle of wine and by 6:30 was dressed in my priestly garb and ready to meet Liese. Her apartment was literally only a few blocks from Rafi's. He offered to drive, but I said I could use the walk, and with his instructions and her address in hand, off I went.

Arriving exactly at seven, I rang the bell and was greeted by Liese who looked lovely in her lounging pajamas. She invited me in with a strange look on her face: an incredulous, unbelievable, who-the-hell-are-you kind of look. When she finally spoke, she said, "If I knew this was to be a costume party, I would have worn my little French maid's outfit. That's a real stunner."

"Oh, this isn't a costume," I replied innocently. "My parishioners call me Father Josef. You may call me Father Josef, if you wish."

"Father Josef. Your parishioners. What the hell are you talking about?" she asked with a distinct tone of annoyance. "Who the hell are you?" she went on, "and why are you here?"

"Did you not invite me to dinner?" I responded. "Did you not tell me to bring the wine? So, I bought us a good bottle of wine," I replied as I handed her the bottle in the fancy bag with ribbons. "And I am truly a priest. I am the pastor of St. Jacek's in Warsaw. Why does that astonish you?"

Taking the bottle from me and turning away purposefully, standing with the light behind her so that I could clearly see she wore no undergarments, she said, "Yes, it does astonish me. I accept the fact that you are who you say you are, but then I have to ask, what the hell do you want with me? You may be Father Josef but you are not here to hear my confession. I must also assume that you are not here to get laid, although I have never screwed a priest. It might be different," she said in an offhand manner. Looking directly at me she went on, "So why are you here? Who are you?"

Looking her straight in the eye, I replied, "I am Sholom Adler's brother."

She stood motionless for a moment, then turned on her heel, walked over to an open bar in her living room, poured herself a stiff drink, offered me nothing and said, "Christ Almighty! This is too much for me. How in the hell can you be Sholom Adler's brother? What did he do, convert to Catholicism so he could inherit my father's estate?"

That remark stopped me dead in my tracks. Did she really know and understand the Mosaic Law that her lawyer had alleged in his pleadings? But I kept my cool and said, "You invited me for dinner. I am the same 'nice guy' that I was yesterday. We wouldn't want the food to go to waste, so why don't we sit down, open the wine, and have a drink? We can talk about lots of things over dinner?"

Shaking her head in disbelief over the entire situation, she said nothing, walked me over to the table and held the chair for me. She then walked over to the bar and got a corkscrew that she handed to me along with the bottle of wine, and finally said, "You do the honors while I bring dinner to the table." With that she walked into the kitchen and came out with salad and bread and butter calmly placing them on the table. She then walked back into the kitchen coming out with what smelled like a delicious stew still in the crock-pot in which it had been cooked. She then sat down across the table from me, and said, "Eat, drink, and talk. I'm waiting to hear this one."

I opened the bottle, poured wine into the goblets on the table, raised my glass and said, "To you, Liese, to a good dinner, to a good evening, and to lots of understanding." Sipping the wine, I continued.

"It's good wine." Liese almost emptied her glass in one swallow but said nothing.

I helped myself to salad and to bread and butter. When I asked Liese if I may serve her, she growled at me and said, "I'll help myself.

"As you wish," I replied as I started to eat while she refilled her wine glass.

"Aren't you going to eat?" I asked her. "The salad is delicious and the stew smells wonderful.

Helping herself to salad, she hissed at me and said, "Stop the crap and tell me why you're here.

Taking another sip of the wine and with a big smile, I responded. "I'm here to try and improve Judeo-Christian relations.

Are you here to try to talk me out of the lawsuit? Well, you don't stand a chance. If you had presented yourself honestly, I might be willing to listen to you. I have respect for a priest. But you come in as a swinger, as a friend of Rafi's and then. . ."

"And then what?"I interrupted with a sense of annoyance. "What are you so pissed off about? So, I didn't come here tonight to get laid. Does that mean that we can't talk and be civil to one another? And by the way, thanks for the compliment."

What compliment?" she asked. "I paid you no compliment."

"Oh, yes, you did," I replied with a grin. "Do you know how long it's been since someone called me a swinger?"

"Well, you're sure as hell not swinging tonight," replied Liese. "At least not with me you're not." Taking more than a sip of wine, she went on. "Well, are you going to tell me what this is all about and why you are here, or are you just going to stuff your face and walk out?"

"I'll tell you what this is all about," I responded, "if you promise me you will sit and listen. Do you promise?"

"I'll say yes because I am sufficiently curious," she answered.

Taking another helping from the crock-pot, I said, "This is really delicious. Rafi said you were a good cook." Liese sat and looked at me with a blank expression, so I went on and said, "It all starts with the Holocaust."

"Oh, shit, I knew it," she replied. "What the hell does the Holocaust have to do with you being here, bullshitting me yesterday while I paid for lunch, and coming over tonight dressed as a priest?"

You promised you would sit and listen, so please afford me that courtesy," I said quietly, "and I'll be happy to reimburse you for the delicious lunch, if that troubles you. But now I would like to continue if you will let your anger subside for a moment."

"All right," she said as she mopped up the gravy with a piece of bread. "I'll let my anger subside and you don't have to pay me back for yesterday's lunch. I promise I'll listen."

"My name is Josef Feurmann. I assumed my grandparents came from Germany, but I was born in Warsaw. My father was Professor Peter Feurmann and my father, my mother Rosa, and my little brother Natan and I were confined to the Warsaw ghetto. Until the Germans invaded Poland, we were a happy Jewish family with our Jewish friends and relatives.

"You were born Jewish?" said Liese incredulously as she finished the last of the wine. "But you're a Catholic priest!"

"You promised to listen," I responded, holding up a finger. She sat quiet as I went on. "My mother was out of the ghetto when the Germans rounded us up, and I was put on a train to a death camp with my father and my little brother."

I then went on to tell about how I escaped and how the blessed Polish family took me in, protected me, sent me to a Catholic school, and ultimately to the seminary.

At this point, Liese asked that I stop while she cleared the table, brought in coffee and cake for dessert, and then begged me to continue. Her attitude had changed. I had the feeling that for Liese, actually meeting someone who said that they lost part of their family in the Holocaust suddenly changed the subject from documented research to a living thing.

"You must have been so frightened, wandering in the woods by yourself. I don't know if I could have done it," she said with fear and concern in her voice. "And your parents and your little brother. Did you ever see them again?"

Smiling and reaching across the table, I patted her hand and continued. "My father and brother I never saw again, although I searched for them after the war. As to my mother, let me tell you, she survived, thanks to your father, and I was reunited with her some thirty years later."

"Oh, that is remarkable," said Liese shaking her head in disbelief. "How did that happen?"

"You read the transcript of your father's war crimes trial?"

She shook her head in the affirmative.

"Do you remember the details?"

She again shook her head in the affirmative.

My mother is Anna Adler, formerly Rosa Feurmann, and she is the mother of Sholom Adler who is both my half brother and your half brother." And with a smile, I went on. "Although we are really not related, I guess you can say we are quarter brother and sister. I know that's just a joke, but do you understand why I had to come and tell you this story?"

Ignoring my question, she said, quietly. "How did you find her after so many years?"

"Well, actually I didn't. I didn't know she survived. Sholom was in Warsaw doing research on the Hotel Polski, which was the subject of his doctorate, and he was told to go to St. Jacek's because of some plaques that we have on the walls of the church honoring the memory of members of the Polish underground. He saw my name. He knew it had been his mother's name before she emigrated to Palestine and by chance we met, talked, and I learned of the existence of family that I thought long to be deceased. Now here I am with you. Life certainly does come full circle."

She said nothing. She kept gathering the crumbs from the cake on her plate with her fork and then poured both of us another cup of coffee. And when she finally looked up at me she asked the question that I knew had to be asked. "But why the pretense? Was it for the drama? Were you trying to titillate me? Did you think I would not meet with you if you came to me as a priest?"

I was uncomfortable with the question but I knew I had to answer. She was entitled to an answer. "It is my fault," I replied. "I just didn't know how to approach you. Sholom made the contact with Rafi and I then choreographed the charade. I apologize if I hurt you. I didn't mean to do so. I told Rafi and I tell you. I hate deception, but I know I engaged in it. I hope you will forgive me."

With that, she rose from her chair, came around the table, took my face in her hands and kissed me on the cheek. "I forgive you, Father Josef," she said softly.

"But now where are we? I have a half brother who is a Jew and a quarter brother who is a Catholic. You must admit it is a very unusual family.

I helped her take the dishes from the table into the kitchen and when, in the kitchen, she looked at me with a smile and I gave her a hug. I did it to reassure myself that I had made my point and hopefully made Liese see things in a different and less belligerent light. Where this would take us, I still had no idea. But at least we could talk. No, not we. She had to be the one to carry on the rest of the conversation.

We left the kitchen, went into the living room where she poured schnapps for both of us, and we sat on the couch and looked at each other. I had nothing else to say. I waited for her.

"What do you want me to say?" she asked. "My head is spinning. When I feel this way, I usually go out and get drunk. If you were not a priest, I would take you to bed and have you make love to me. That would excite me, but yet, it would soothe me. It would allow me to think clearly. So, again, I ask you. What do you want me to say? What do you want me to do?"

"I have never read the transcript of your father's trial," I responded. "I only know what it said through Sholom's description of its contents. From what I learned, my mother was a prisoner at the Polski; your father was the commandant and took her as his companion. As a result, I am assuming a relationship developed, which I have never discussed with my mother, and that resulted in your father allowing my mother and her husband, Itzik, and others to emigrate to Palestine. Is that in essence, how you recall the testimony?"

"Yes, it is" she replied. "But regardless of the relationship, as you call it, she refused to acknowledge that Sholom is my father's child. If she refuses to acknowledge it, why should I?"

"Because we both know it is a fact," I replied. "You must understand, that which a Holocaust survivor wishes to acknowledge or wishes to recall, be it fact or not, is their defense against what took place. How they interpret what happened to them is how they overcome their guilt for having survived. For as much as she may love Sholom and her present husband, my mother lost her husband, I am speaking of my father, and little Natan, my baby brother. And just to bring you up to date, Sholom's first wife, with whom he had a child, was killed in the Yom Kippur War. He is now remarried and has a new baby. He also has a sister, Tamar, who has three kids. You are now a member of a large family, and may I say, a loving one."

I don't know why, but I suddenly got the feeling that what I had said angered Liese. She didn't respond, stood up, walked to the bar, and poured herself schnapps, without offering me any. Without sitting down, she looked at me and said, "Stop it! What am I supposed to do, feel all warm and fuzzy? I am not a member of your family, I never was and I never will be. You're a con artist. You're here to try to talk me out of my lawsuit against Sholom. As I said to Rafi when I read the transcript, 'He's a bastard.' He's the child of unmarried people. Of a roll in the hay. I don't know and you don't know if there was any relationship between them. It may have been plain outright fucking as a result of which Sholom was conceived. But Colonel Hauptmann was my father. He was married to my mother. I am the legitimate heir to his estate. So stop with your Jewish guilt. I'm unimpressed."

I sat and shook my head as she sat down on the couch next to me. "If that's the way you feel, then I guess there is nothing more to say," I replied. "Can I ask you to do one thing for me?"

"What's that?" she answered, coldly.

"I'll leave you my address and telephone number. Please don't throw it away. When the semester is over and you have some free time, call me, and you and I will go to Israel together. You can come just as a tourist, if you like, but I would like you to meet my mother. Wouldn't you like to know who your father was fucking, as you put it? Aren't you the least bit curious?"

With that, I took out a card from my wallet and handed it to her. She looked at it and said, "I won't throw it away." Then, looking at me with a smile, she went on. "You know, Josef, you should be a used car salesman. Your sermons must be worth listening to."

I thanked her for the compliment and promised if I left the priesthood I would definitely consider selling used cars. She walked me to the door. I leaned over and kissed her on the cheek and said, "Please stay in touch. Even if you just want to talk, I am always there for you."

She didn't reply, and as I left, we both waved to each other.

I walked back to Rafi's apartment not quite sure if I had accomplished anything or not. Liese's attitude annoyed me. She hadn't spoken to her father in thirty or more years but she suddenly became the devoted daughter when she learned of the size of his estate. Not a very honest position.

I opened the door with my key and found Rafi and someone who I supposed was the oft referred to young thing on the couch watching television. She looked up for a moment and then gave me a double take.

"He's a priest!" she said.

"So," Rafi replied, "do you think you're the only Gentile I know?" Turning off the TV he turned to me and said "Nu, how did it go?"

"It was very strange," I replied shaking my head. "I don't know if I did any good. She's angry, then she calms down and you think she understands, and then she gets angry again. I don't know, Rafi, I just don't know."

"Who are you talking about?" asked the young thing.

"You don't have to know," answered Rafi. Turning to me, he said, "You're not going to call Sholom now, are you? It's too late."

"No, I'll wait 'till tomorrow. I'll call him before I leave for the airport. My flight is at eleven. I have to be there by ten. Can you take me or shall I take a cab?"

"No, no I'll take you," said Rafi. "We can talk in the car."

"Good," I replied. "Go back to your TV. I'm going to pack and then I'll read a little and go to sleep." Turning to the young thing, I said. "It was good to meet you."

To which she replied, "Good to meet you, Father. Sleep well."

Winter 1978

Sholom

Chapter XIX

Josef called me after his return to Warsaw. He described his meetings with Liese but what I found most unusual was his invitation to Liese to accompany him, to Israel. We talked about this, and he justified it as a meaningful way to try to engage her. He felt that would be the best way for her to realize what it means to be member of a family. I told him that I really didn't care whether she was a member of a family let alone our family. His response was that just as he was my half brother, she was my half sister, whether I liked it or not, she was a member of the family. We talked a bit more and decided to let it go until we heard more from the lawyers and would then wait to see if we ever heard from her again.

After talking to Josef, I called Rafi and thanked him for his efforts on my behalf. He was most enthused when speaking about Josef and thought him one hell of a guy. He then added, as I expected, "Too bad he's a priest."

A number of months went by during which time I heard, with a degree of regularity, from Uri. One very interesting thing had been accomplished. Uri hired a lawyer in Dusseldorf who was recommended by a friend who practiced in Berlin. Our Dusseldorf lawyer knew Liese's lawyer rather well. Uri's plan was to try to get the two lawyers to agree that the case be transferred to the appropriate court in Israel since the thrust of the matter was an interpretation of Mosaic Law. This resulted in a lunch between the two lawyers where the issue was discussed, and from what Uri told me, Liese's lawyer was not at all against the idea. Needless to say, he would have to discuss it with his client. Although he found the case itself to be quite interesting, he didn't care for her as a person.

When told of the idea of transferring the case to an Israeli court, Liese became livid. She screamed at her lawyer, accusing him of selling out and asked him what she thought was a reasonable question, how could she expect justice from those Jew bastards? In reply, she was told that it would be costly to defend a motion opposing the removal of the case and she must keep in mind, they could lose and the case would be transferred whether she liked it or not. She insisted she would pay the fee to defend the motion but would not agree, voluntarily, to a change of venue.

While I got all of this third hand, I had to assume it was fairly accurate. But just as it would cost Liese, it was also costing me. I was responsible for the fee to the German lawyer, for the fee to Uri, and for the cost of Uri's flying to Dusseldorf on the return day of the motion for the change of venue. He insisted that he wanted to be there and go over the argument with our lawyer before he had to appear before the judge. What could I say? I wrote a check.

The rest of the family knew nothing about this. We had kept it a secret using the same old story about the time it takes to gather the assets. But that secret was given away, by accident, believe it or not, by Shimon. After his return from Dusseldorf, Uri reported to me that the argument went very well but he was sure it would take a couple of months before a decision was rendered. In the meantime, Uri, Shimon, my parents, Avram and Feygl, and Rena's parents went to a meeting of an organization in which they all had an interest. Before the meeting got started, Shimon came over to the table where my parents were sitting, accompanied by Uri, and introduced Uri to my parents and Rena's as Sholom's lawyer.

The unspoken reaction was, "Sholom's lawyer? Why does Sholom need a lawyer?"

At that point, Shimon knew he had blown it. He never realized that after all this time neither Rena nor I had ever said a word to our parents about the lawsuit.

Shimon told me the story the next day. I don't really know how he got out of the situation in which he found himself, but, not unexpectedly, we had company the next night. Both sets of parents brought cake and Rena made coffee.

"We met a friend of yours last night," my mother said sweetly. "Shimon introduced us to Uri, your lawyer. How come you never told us you needed a lawyer?"

At which point Rena's father said, "If you needed a lawyer, why didn't you go see Isaac? He's been my lawyer for years."

There was no point in pretending. I looked at Rena and shrugged my shoulders. "Shimon called us this morning and told us that he had introduced you to Uri last night. Shimon had referred him to us," I went on.

Rena interrupted and said to her father. "It's kind of an international issue and Isaac wouldn't have been the right lawyer."

At which point my mother looked at Rena's mother and, with a shake of her head, said, "I didn't know that we had such fancy children, that they had international issues."

Abba, who has no patience for this kind of patronizing dialogue, broke in and said to the women. "Enough already. Rena, Sholom, what is this all about? Is there anything that we can do to help you out? Does this have to do with the Colonel's will? Are you involved in litigation?"

At this point, both Rena and I, interrupting one another when necessary, told them the entire story, bringing them up to date with regard to the motion for a change of venue. And just as I predicted, my mother's reaction was, "What do you need it for? Give her the money. Why are you throwing away your money? Did you ever want for anything? Was there ever anything that *abba* and I could not give you or that Rena's parents wouldn't give her? Why can't you let things be? Why must you keep searching, for what I don't know?"

"Enough, Anna," said *abba*.

"Your mother is right," said Rena's mother. "Why are you pursuing this?"

As soon as my mother used the word "searching," I knew she was off the track and back to her old neuroses. Learning the truth about the Colonel, the truth about the Polski, was the one thing she fought her entire life, no matter how much she was accepted, and no matter how much she was loved.

As long as the issue is on the table, then my answer had to be honest and forthright. "I am pursing this," I said with particularity, "because my biological father left me his estate in his will. I am entitled to it. It will secure Rena, me, and our children for our entire lives. Yes, *eema*, this has to do with the Hotel Polski and you must be willing to accept it." At which point I went on and told them about Josef's involvement and his having invited Liese to Israel to meet the family.

My mother was beside herself with anger. When I finished, not a word was said by anyone. Suddenly, my mother got up, looked at my father and said, "Come, Chaim, take me home. Our son understands nothing. I do not feel welcome here. Everyone, even Josef, is against me."

"For God's sake, *eema*," I responded. "No one is against you. We didn't tell you because we knew that this would be your reaction. Josef tried to act as a mediator. We tried to see if he could resolve the matter amicably. I am still willing to do that but not everything happens just because you want it to happen in a certain way. Go, if you don't feel welcome here, but you are making a terrible mistake. When it comes to the Polski, you will never see anything other than your way. Go, *eema*, but remember that the war ended more than thirty years ago. It is time that you stopped fighting. You have no enemies."

The evening was too far gone. *Abba* took *eema's* arm and turned to look at me as if to say, we'll be back. Rena's parents said nothing, kissed us both and we promised to keep in touch.

When they left, Rena said to me that my answer to my mother was superb. We both knew they would be back.

Chapter XX

Abba and I spoke regularly over the next two weeks and I know my mother called Rena to ask about the kids. But she wouldn't talk to me. A few weeks after the encounter with my mother, Moshe called me. He told me that they were all coming to town for a Shabbos dinner at my parents' apartment and his parents would be there. I told him we had not, as yet, been invited. He told me he'd heard about the encounter, my mother had told Tamar all about it, and he reassured me that I'd hear from her and we would see each other on the weekend.

He was right. The invitation came through Rena and she accepted for both of us. The need to see the grandchildren outweighed all other considerations.

The others were there when we arrived. With all the hugs and kisses she was doling out, my mother just happened to miss me. We hadn't seen the girls in quite a while and they had really grown up in both looks and behavior. Ari and Pinky, aside from being cousins, took to each other like long lost friends. The girls, in the meantime, played with Hudi as if she were a doll. It was a wonderful reunion and nothing controversial was discussed as long as the kids were present. After dinner, however, when Hudi was napping and the others were watching television, I decided that the nonsense that prevailed had to be resolved. So I said to *eema* in everyone's presence, "You don't talk to me, you don't kiss me when I come to your home. You're happy to see Rena and the children, but as far as you and I go, we're finished. Right?"

"Don't talk like an idiot," she replied. "You are an educated person and you sound like a moron."

"But you didn't answer the question," I countered. "Am I right? You're never going to talk to me again?"

"Of course I'll talk to you," she answered. "And I'm sorry I didn't kiss you when you came in."

"That's probably because you didn't see me," I said with a laugh.

Everybody sat and watched as if this were a tennis match. The heads were going back and forth until Chaim broke in and said with a degree of annoyance.

"Okay, both of you. Stop the nonsense." Turning to *eema* he went on. "Anna, if you have something to say to Sholom, for God's sake, say it and let's get this over with."

Upset over the fact that Chaim had, in her mind, criticized her in front of the family, my mother replied, quite tartly. "Chaim, I didn't realize that you were the referee." Turning to me, she went on. "I'll be happy to talk to Sholom when he comes to the realization he can't keep going on with his life and keep stepping all over mine."

"Stepping all over yours? What are you talking about *eema?*" I responded.

Looking at me as if there were no one else in the room, she replied, "If I have an Achilles' heel or a sore spot, it is the Hotel Polski and anything connected with it. Your intellectual curiosity has never stopped digging into the Hotel Polski and this has affected me. Although I try not to show it, I know that you all are aware of it," she said looking at the others. "Now you've become the heir to Colonel Hauptmann's estate and, you are being challenged by his daughter, who, to my mind, has as much right to it as do you. If this matter goes to court, I know I'll be called to testify." Turning to Feygl, she said,

"Feygl, do you understand what I am talking about? Do you remember Heidelberg and what I went through when I had to testify at the War Crimes Trial?" And now, turning to the rest, she said, "And now I am going to have to go through it again so that my son can become a millionaire. At least in Germany no one knew who I was. Should I have to testify here in Israel and should the newspapers get hold of the story, after all, it's not a bad story . . . a Jewish woman has a child with an SS Colonel . . . I won't be able to walk in the street."

"Let me tell you something I'll never forget," she went on. "When the Colonel told me the very first night to go up and wait for him in his suite at the Polski, I encountered a Polish chambermaid who called me a whore. I'll never forget it. What I was told to do was completely beyond my control. I had nothing to say about it and could do nothing about it, and yet, in her eyes, I was a whore. What will I be called here in Tel Aviv?" she asked turning to me. "And what about you, Sholom? How will being the child of a Nazi officer affect your professional standing?"

"You wanted me to talk, now I have talked," she went on directly to me. "Now let me hear you talk." At this point, without waiting for an answer from me, she got up and went into the kitchen. I could hear her sobbing and Feygl jumped up and went into the kitchen behind her.

As Rena and Tamar were about to get up, *abba* put out his hand to restrain them and said, "She'll be all right. Feygl is with her." Turning to me, he went on, "Nu, boychik, what do you have to say?"

Sighing deeply, I replied. "Anything I have to say now would be the wrong thing. Let's not talk about it anymore. *Eema* had her say. I know how she feels, and whether I agree with her or not is not the issue, at this time. All I am going to say is, let's have some more coffee and cake and see what the future brings. Please, *abba*, accept that as my answer at this time."

Avram stood up, got the coffee pot, and said, "That's a good answer, Sholom. One should not reply out of heat or out of anger. I know you almost since the day you were born. You will make the right decision." And with that, he poured coffee for everyone while Tamar sliced more cake.

It didn't take long and in came Feygl, followed by *eema* who came over to me and gave me a big kiss on the cheek and looked around and said, "So, where is my coffee?"

The rest of the evening was pleasant and we all broke up when Moshe and Tamar had to drive back. Kisses all around and goodbyes. And when will we see you again and the kids saying, so let's go already, and home we went.

Two months after the Shabbos dinner, it was the end of February; the decision came down from the German court. The motion had been granted and the matter was transferred to an appropriate court in Israel. The decision was rather lengthy and Uri called me to his office when he received it and read it to me, translating that which I didn't quite get. We both agreed that the judge seemed to be saying that despite the fact that the issue was an interesting one, he really didn't want the job of making a decision based upon Mosaic Law. Since Liese's lawyer had raised the issue, the opinion went on to say that the judge was within his rights to transfer the matter to a country whose laws were, in part, based upon Mosaic Law. What he actually meant was in this way he wouldn't have to learn and then apply a law with which he was totally unfamiliar.

But now, Liese's lawyer had another problem. He had to find a lawyer in Israel who would take the case. This wouldn't be easy since we learned, third- hand, from Liese's lawyer to our lawyer in Germany, to Uri, that Liese went ballistic when she learned of the decision. She instructed her lawyer to take an appeal that he said was both a waste of time and money, so she fired him. She took the matter to two other lawyers, neither of whom would take the case, and she then went to a friend who was an Israeli (it must have been

Rafi) and asked him if he knew a good lawyer in Israel. He knew of no one so she went back to her original lawyer who now had to go to an international reference book in the law library and try to find the appropriate lawyer to handle the case in Israel. Needless to say, he did so.

The lawyer was an Orthodox Jew who, from what we learned later on, was quite excited to take a case that involved interpretation of Mosaic Law. Uri didn't know him, and in checking him out, learned that he was a scholar of both law and religion and was a serious practitioner of both.

It took a while for the Order of the court in Germany to be served upon Uri, and when it finally arrived at the beginning of March, he was impressed with the number of seals and ribbons that were affixed to it. In that Uri had not, as yet, heard from Liese's new lawyer, he filed the necessary papers in the Israeli court, served a copy of them upon Liese's German lawyer, and waited. When the time was about up and Uri said that he would move for a judgment by default on my behalf, he received an appearance from the Israeli lawyer. They met for lunch and Uri said he was quite impressed, so much so, that he had no choice but to seek a rabbinic authority with whom he could discuss the issue. Another month went by and Uri let me know that he'd received a notice from the court that counsel was to appear for a scheduling conference with the judge. It was not necessary for me to appear and he would keep me informed as to the outcome.

The judge told them that he had familiarized himself with the case, found it to be interesting, and asked Liese's lawyer how he intended to sustain the burden of proof based upon Mosaic Law. Before answering, the lawyer went into the issue of Sholom having exerted undue influence upon the deceased by virtue of his visit to the deceased some two months prior to the drawing of the will. When asked, by the judge, how he knew about that visit, the lawyer said he had spoken with the attorneys in Munich who were the executors and who had drawn the will. The deceased had told them about the visit.

At which point Uri told me that he chimed in, saying more as a joke than as a matter of law, that the deceased had also visited Sholom here in Israel a number of years before, in furtherance of Sholom's research about the Hotel Polski of which the deceased was the commandant. "Could it be that one could consider two visits over a period of some thirty years undue influence as opposed to no visits over thirty years?" When the judge inquired what Uri meant, Uri went on to say that Liese had never seen nor spoken to the deceased in the last thirty years. To which the judge looked at Liese's lawyer, shook his head, and said, "Let's get back to the Mosaic law."

Again evading the issue, Liese's lawyer went into a discussion of the rights of a "mamzer" or an illegitimate person, quoting Deuteronomy. He insisted that Sholom was, in fact, an illegitimate child and as such had no standing in the community "even to the tenth generation;" that he should not have been allowed to marry a Jewish woman, and that his children were also illegitimate. To which Uri replied, quoting Maimonides, that to prove kinship of an illegitimate birth, recognition by the ancestor who transmits the inheritance is sufficient. Therefore, the will was the dominant piece of evidence.

At this point, the judge became somewhat annoyed with both lawyers and, shaking his finger, said that he would not let this trial turn into a *"Bet Din"*. [24] This is a civil matter to be decided on the application if any, of Mosaic Law only as they apply to modern day statutes and precedents.

The judge then reminded them that the conference was really for scheduling dates for the exchanging of particulars and the taking of depositions.

Liese's lawyer said he was not sure his client would be willing to come to Israel, to which the judge said that that was her problem if she wished to pursue the case.

The next scheduling conference would be after Passover that was some three weeks away. At that time, the judge would see where the

---

[24] House of Law – Jewish Court

matter stood and would fix a trial date. His last words strongly suggested that we try to settle the matter since Uri, too, had the feeling that the judge didn't really want to get involved in Biblical history and interpretation of ancient law.

All in all, not a bad day.

Then the next most unexpected thing happened. *Eema* had been in touch with Josef who had promised to be in Israel and celebrate Passover with us. Some two weeks before Passover, he showed up. This was certainly an occasion for another dinner, and when the family was together, Josef greeted us all in slacks and a sport shirt wearing a *"Mogen David."*[25] I had a feeling as to what was coming and said it a long time ago to Rena. You could have heard a pin drop when Josef announced that he had left the church and was planning to stay with us in Israel.

When we finally caught our breath and *eema* stopped kissing him, we asked him for his rationale. "It was really very simple," he said. "It all comes down to family." Maria had died a number of months ago. She was his last connection to the family that raised him and to the church. Just as the church was his family for so many years, he now had a new family who loved him and whom he loved in return. It was time to spend the rest of his life with them. He had discussed this at Maria's funeral with his "cousin," the priest in Cracow with whom he grew up. His cousin said he understood, and when they parted, the two men exchanged hugs and kisses and promised to stay in touch with one another. Knowing Josef, I am sure he will. What a coup, to have Josef with us as a full-fledged Jewish member of the family. We wept, but it was for joy.

Eema insisted he could stay with them as long as he wished. He accepted only until he found gainful employment and could afford to

---

[25] Star of David

move out on his own. It was decided that since this year *eema* was making the *Seder*[26] and Shimon would be there, Josef should call him in advance, tell him that he is now here permanently, and ask Shimon to give a moment's thought as to where Josef could fit in today's Israeli society. I felt sure that something in the teaching field, in a university, might be just the thing. But let us hear what Shimon has to say.

---

[26] Passover Dinner

Chapter XXI

Unexpected things kept happening.

I received a call from Rafi who told me the following story: He received a call from Liese telling him that she had to go to Israel for a deposition, and she called Josef at the number on his card. She spoke to a priest at St. Jacek's who told her that Josef was no longer connected with the church. He had heard that Josef went to Israel, but he had no forwarding number. "So, what's happening?" he asked.

I told him that Josef had left the church and was now living in Israel with my parents. He cheered long and loud. He then asked where he could be reached and I told him that any call having to do with Liese is not one my parents should know about. I, therefore, suggested that he give me Liese's number. I'll tell Josef that she called so he can call her back without anyone else knowing about it. He thought that was a good idea, and gave me Liese's number. We then chatted for a while about his Jewish Studies program, what I was busy with, Rena and the kids, and we promised to stay in touch. It was good to hear from him.

I then called Josef at my parents' home and he answered the phone telling me that my parents were out for the evening. I told him that was good because we had to have a private conversation. I told him about Rafi's call and gave him Liese's number. He understood the need for privacy and promised to call her and let me know what was happening. He then told me he had spoken, on two occasions, with Shimon and that Shimon was looking into the chance of some position in a government agency dealing with Judeo-Christian relations. He went on to say that everyone thinks that because he had been a priest at one time in his life, he had expertise in the field. He lectured on the topic when he was in Dusseldorf, but that was in front of German students and he could bluff his way through. If this subject was going to become his future, then he had a lot of reading to do. We both had a good laugh; he sent his regards to Rena and promised to be in touch.

A couple of days later he called and asked whether we could have lunch at the cafeteria at the university. He made a big to-do over not having seen me or spoken to me for a long time. In that this was not true, I knew my parents were in the room while he was talking to me. It was understood that he had spoken to Liese.

We met the following afternoon at the cafeteria. "So," I asked, "what did the wicked witch have to say?"

"Be nice," said Josef. "She's not a bad person, just a little confused. I think we can straighten her out."

"Well, she sure as hell is confusing my bank account," I responded. "It has cost me a fortune in legal fees. I sincerely hope that I am successful just so that I can reimburse myself for the costs. The longer this drags on, the more I find myself agreeing with *eema*. What the hell did I need it for?"

"You needed it because you are right. You will be successful," he responded. "Now, let me tell you what she wanted."

"Rafi told me she had to come for a deposition, is that right?" I asked.

"You recall I told you that I promised her that if she would come to Israel on her own, I would accompany her," he replied. "Well, since she does have to come, not really on her own but for a deposition, she looked to me to keep my promise. After all, I was a priest at the time I made the promise and there is no way that I would go back on my word. At any rate, she will be coming next week. I said I would pick her up and take her to the bachelor faculty quarters at the university where she will be staying. I didn't know it but the university has some kind of corresponding relationship with the university in Dusseldorf."

"I did know that," I responded. "That is how they got Rafi to come to Dusseldorf. I wouldn't be surprised, if Liese wanted to, she could teach a short course here in Tel Aviv."

"I don't think she is so inclined," said Josef; "but I will mention it to her. It could cover her expenses."

"On second thought," I said, "I don't think that would work. She will be here right before Passover and that is spring break for the students. She'll be lonely on campus."

"Be that as it may, I have an idea of what I want to do with her when she's here," said Josef.

"Watch yourself, my brother," I said with a laugh. "Just because you're not a priest doesn't mean…"

"That's really not what I had in mind," Josef laughed. Looking at his watch he said, "Listen, you've got class and I have an interview for a job arranged by Shimon. I'll let you know what happens and we'll talk after she arrives."

We embraced; said goodbye and each went our own way.

Spring 1975
Dusseldorf to
Tel Aviv

Liese

Chapter XXII

My ticket was non-refundable. I knew when I was expected in Israel and I knew when I wanted to be back home. Although I felt that I was coming down with something on the day I left Germany, I imagined I'd be able to shake it in the warmer weather of Israel. Besides, my accommodations had been made. Josef was picking me up, and I had an appointment with my lawyer. I can't believe it; my lawyer, an Orthodox Jew.

Flying towards Israel my head was spinning with thoughts that I hadn't had for years, or perhaps ever had. Here I am doing exactly what I didn't want to do, and never thought I would have to do, all because of a man I had not seen in thirty years. Why do I feel like I'm being forced? I could have let the Jew-boy have the entire estate and let him choke on it.

As I sat and looked out of the plane window, I asked myself, why didn't I speak to my father in thirty years? He was a decent guy when I was a kid. A bit of a tight-ass. I assume he loved my mother, and she, him. I remember going to Tante Helga's when the war started and I recall their discussions. Helga begged Mama to come away from the city and come live with us in the country. We were certainly safe. There was nothing in the area to bomb, but Mama felt the same way about Cologne and the cathedral. It would never be bombed. She argued with Tante Helga about the paintings and the sculpture in the apartment. Who would take care of her collections? If she weren't there, the apartment would be looted. What the hell difference did it make? One bomb and it was all gone, the paintings, the sculpture, and Mama.

I don't recall my father's attitude in those years. Did he try to talk her into leaving Cologne? I recall her going to Berlin on various occasions to be with him, but then, when he was sent to Poland, I don't know if they spoke to each other again. After the bombing, he did come back from Poland for what passed as a funeral at Tante Helga's. I remember blaming him for Mama's death. I probably wasn't right then and I don't know if what I'm doing now is right. I think I'm developing a fever.

Josef was waiting for me at the baggage carousel. When he saw me, he gave me a big smile. I held my hands out and said no hugs or kisses. I'm coming down with something and I feel like shit. He offered to take me to an emergency room. "I declined and asked that he take me to my apartment where, hopefully, I would find a tea bag, and with some aspirin from my suitcase, and a good night's sleep, I insisted I would be better in the morning.

When we arrived, I barely had the strength to unpack. I took out a warm robe from my valise while Josef found a tea bag in the pantry and made me a cup of tea. I took two aspirin, made some stupid remark about this being the first time that I threw some guy out of my bedroom, and got into bed. He left his phone number on the nightstand, kissed my forehead and said that I was feverish, and made me promise to call him in the morning.

By six o'clock in the morning I thought I was burning up. Here I am, in a strange city, in a foreign country, and Josef is the only one I know. So, I called the number he had left by the telephone. The phone was answered in Hebrew by a lady, to which I replied *"Gruss Got"* and, continuing in German said, "May I speak with Josef?" I was so hoarse that my voice was barely audible. The answer came back in

German. "It is six o'clock in the morning. Where are you calling from and are you all right?"

"I know," I replied. "I am sorry to have awakened you. This is Professor Hauptmann. I am here at the university faculty apartments and I am not all right. I am really quite ill and I know no one in Tel Aviv other than Josef."

"Do you know the address and apartment number where you are staying?"

I answered and was told that the voice on the other end would be at my apartment in half an hour. I assumed I was talking to Josef's mother. At the moment it didn't occur to me that this was also Sholom Adler's mother.

I staggered out of bed, made myself another cup of tea, took two more aspirins, opened the lock on the door, lay down on the couch, and waited. In less than half an hour, there was a knock on the door and I croaked, "It's open."

In came a nice looking middle-aged woman. Since Josef bore no resemblance to her, I still was not sure who she was.

"Who are you?" I asked weakly.

"I am Josef's mother," she replied. "He told me you were here but he didn't tell me you were so sick."

"I just feel worse than I did last evening when he dropped me off. I am so sorry that I woke you this morning. I just didn't know who else to call."

Coming over to help me off the couch, she said, "You feel quite warm. Get back into bed and I'll call a doctor for you."

I had no will to resist, and when I got back into bed, I asked sheepishly, "What is your name?"

"I am Anna Adler," she said with a smile as she covered me up to my chin with the blanket. "You don't look anything like your father."

"How did you know my father?" I knew the answer, but I was curious to see what she would say.

Her answer stunned me. "I was his prisoner," she responded. "But we'll talk about that later. May I use your phone?"

And without waiting for an answer, she picked up the phone and dialed a number. Hearing only one side of the conversation, I heard her say, "Yossie, I am with Liese. She is quite ill. Go into the kitchen and look in the telephone book on the counter and give me the number of Dr. Elie Goldschmidt." She waited a few moments and then picked up a pencil and started to write. I then heard her say, "Yes, I'll let you know. No, you don't have to come over now. I'll tell you when you can come over."

"You call him Yossi? I said with a smile.

"That was his name when he was a little boy," hesitating a moment she went on, "We had a friend in Warsaw, a prominent lawyer whose name was also Josef and we called him Yossie, as well. My children used to play with his children. But them, one day, in the ghetto, the Nazis came up and swept up Yossie and his family and my Yossie and my family. That was a long time ago."

"My God," said Liese to herself. "I keep asking myself the same question, what am I doing here? These people will drown me with their Holocaust stories."

Please let me speak to Dr. Elie. It is an emergency." Obviously, the doctor got right on the phone and I heard, "Elie, I am with a guest of Josef's who is at the faculty apartments at the university. She is quite ill and I would be most thankful if you could come over and see her. If you can get away now, I'll wait here." She then gave him the address and the apartment number.

For as strange as it may seem, just knowing that there was somebody with me and that a doctor was coming over, I started to feel a bit better. It had been a long time since anyone ever showed this much concern for me, and to think they were Jewish people, people against whom I carried a long-time, prejudice. I was totally confused.

Turning to me, Mrs. Adler said, "I'll wait for the doctor. He should be here in half an hour and then I will go to the market and get you some food. I know you haven't eaten anything in probably a day. You just stay in bed and rest and I'll wait in the other room. Try and get some sleep.

I actually did fall asleep, and the next thing I knew, the doctor was there. He took my temperature, examined me, listened to my heart and my lungs, told me I had a severe case of the flu and should plan to stay in bed for at least three days, and I should take it easy. He then called the university pharmacy for a prescription, and before he left, he turned to me and asked the only question for which I was not prepared. "By the way, why are you here?"

Looking at Mrs. Adler who had a smile on her face when she heard the question, I responded, feebly, "I have an appointment with a lawyer. I guess I'll have to cancel it for a week."

"A week won't do it," said the doctor. "Next week is Passover and I am sure the lawyer won't be in his office. I know I am taking off, except for emergencies."

"Liese doesn't have to worry," said Mrs. Adler to the doctor. "We'll take good care of her while she's here. I'm sure her lawyer will be happy to see her a week later."

And with thanks from both me and Mrs. Adler, the doctor left, leaving us alone. Taking out Israeli money with which I was unfamiliar and handing it to me, Mrs. Adler said, "I am going shopping. If the pharmacy delivers the medicine, pay for it and take it as the doctor prescribed. I will be back within the hour. We will have breakfast together."

"I thank you, Mrs. Adler," I said. "I don't know why you are doing this for me. You know who I am and yet you are so kind. It is as if I were a member of your family. I am not a poor woman, Mrs. Adler. I'll pay you back for the medicine and the doctor and the food. Please do not worry."

"Oh, I am not worried," she responded. "I know you will pay me back. And besides, aren't you family. You're Sholom's half sister. Isn't that right?"

I didn't know if she was being sarcastic or not, but before I could answer, and really not knowing what to say, she was out the door. I closed my eyes and tried to get some sleep before the pharmacy would deliver the medicine. I did drop off and the next thing I heard was someone in my kitchen. In came Mrs. Adler with a bowl of hot oatmeal, and another cup of tea with honey and lemon. The money still lay on the night table, so I guessed that the pharmacy had not come. I hope I didn't sleep through the delivery. I needed the medicine.

In the midst of breakfast, there was someone at the door. Mrs. Adler took the money from the night table, saying, "It must be the pharmacy," and went to the door. She came back with the medicine, and taking out two capsules from the bottle, she told me to take them with a sip of tea, which I did. During breakfast, we both sat together, but little was said. I did ask her to tell me about my father, and her answer was, "He was a nice man."

As soon as I finished eating, she told me it was time to sleep. She cleaned up the dishes and said she would be back later and would bring food for a couple of days. "Nothing beats chicken soup," she said, and again I didn't know whether she was being sarcastic. Once the immediate emergency was over, her attitude towards me seemed to change. It was as if she was doing all of this for me with a chip on her shoulder. Maybe I was just reading too much into it. After all, I did awaken her at six in the morning and she was right over. Perhaps, although it wasn't yet ten o'clock, she was tired. Whatever it is, I am thankful. I've had something to eat, I've had my medicine, and now let me rest.

I must have slept for some three to four hours, and when I awoke, I felt somewhat stronger. At about two in the afternoon, Mrs. Adler returned with two full shopping bags. I got out of bed and sat in the living room while she put things away in the refrigerator. She brought not only chicken soup, but the chicken as well, noodle pudding, salad fixings, and bread and butter. I thanked her repeatedly and again expressed my desire to take the time and talk with her. She again rebuffed me saying something to the effect, not now, maybe later. She heated up a cup of soup for me, and with some bread and butter, I had my lunch. She reminded me to take my medicine as the doctor prescribed and told me that tomorrow Josef would look in on me. If I needed anything, he could get it for me. When she came close to me while I was eating the soup, I stopped and took her hand and said, "Please don't be angry with me," to which she replied in a rather offhand manner, as she took her hand from mine, "I am not angry with you, but now I must go. Eat, drink tea, take your medicine and rest, and you'll feel better," she said with a smile as she left the apartment. For some reason, I felt very much alone.

During the course of the week, Josef kept me company and nursed me back to health. As my strength returned, we walked around the campus. He asked me if I would like to meet Sholom Adler and I declined. When he told me that I would be meeting him in a couple of days since he was taking me to the Passover *Seder*, I backed off. I told him that I felt quite strongly that that was one place that I didn't belong. He, however, was quite insistent. Under the circumstances, I asked him to tell me what I was going to be witnessing and he said it would all be explained during the *Seder* itself. The only thing he would tell me is that the word "*Seder*" meant "order" in Hebrew. It was an historic retelling of the Exodus.

The fateful day came and Josef told me he would pick me up at two in the afternoon. As always, he was right on time and had an unexpected gift for me. I opened it and found a *Haggadah*[27] in Hebrew and German. He explained to me that this was the "script" that would be used for the *Seder*, and since it would be conducted in Hebrew, I could follow it in German. He found the *Haggadah* at the university bookstore and I was pleased that he thought about making me as comfortable as possible in a situation he knew I didn't want to be in.

He then told me there was an inscription in the front of the *Haggadah*. I opened it as one would open a book in German but saw

---

[27] Story of Passover

no writing. I looked questionably at Josef who smiled and said, "Liese, it is a Hebrew book. It is read from right to left. Somewhat embarrassed, I muttered, "I knew that" and turned the book over. When I opened it there was the inscription, "Welcome to the family" and signed, "Your quarter brother, Josef."

I thanked him, kissed him on the cheek and with no knowledge of what I was getting myself into, I said, "I guess we should get going."

When we got to his mother's apartment, I was literally shaking with fear. I don't know how I allowed myself to be caught in a situation such as this. Family and friends were there when we arrived, and I realized that Anna was the only one I knew. She greeted me in a friendly yet cold manner, and between her and Josef, I was introduced to the others. I did recognize the name Shimon Cohen when I was introduced to him. He had been a witness at my father's trial and I remembered his name from reading the transcript. When I was introduced to Sholom, he simply nodded but didn't say a word to me.

While the eating, drinking and socializing was going on, I stuck close to Josef. Unexpectedly, the doorbell rang and when Anna opened it, a ditzy looking woman came in, announced that she was Anat Stern from *Ha'aretz*, a popular Israeli newspaper, and that she had an appointment with Josef. Josef greeted her and introduced me and told me he had made an appointment with Ms. Stern for an interview before the *Seder* was to start. It would only take about a half hour and he invited me to accompany them into a nearby bedroom where we would be away from the crowd. Again, I didn't know what this was all about, but I went where I was invited.

Ms. Stern took out a tape recorder and put it on a table between two chairs where she and Josef sat. I sat on the edge of the bed and listened while the interview took place. Josef told her his whole story, which I had heard before, starting with the ghetto in Warsaw and ending with his giving up the priesthood and coming to Israel. When it was over, she thanked him, they shook hands, she shook hands with me, repeated my name as if she wanted to remember it, and when she went out, Anna asked if she would like to stay for the *Seder*. She thanked her and said she was on her way to her parents who lived nearby. When she left, everyone was called to the table and the *Seder* began.

Silently, I thanked Josef for the German translation. The youngest child, I do not really recall whose child it was, asked the four questions. Josef had told me in advance that since his parents were not religious people, they would skip over many pages, which I didn't mind at all. One thing that was not in the Hebrew/German *Haggadah* was a prayer in commemoration of the six million Jews killed in the Holocaust. Josef translated it for me and while it was being recited. I felt terribly vulnerable at that moment, as if everyone were looking at me.

When they opened the door for *Eliahu Ha'navi*, Elijah, the prophet, Josef explained that he visits all Jewish homes during the *Seder* and at each home there is a glass of wine set aside for him. In my own mind I thought of Santa Claus visiting the homes of all Christian families on Christmas eve. No wine, just cookies. A piece of *matzoh* was hidden and the four glasses of wine were drunk. Then the meal was served.

The dinner was delicious. My appetite had returned and I really enjoyed it although there were many dishes with which I was unfamiliar. I didn't quite understand when, after the dinner, all the kids left the table to search for the hidden piece of matzoh, but then, when it was found, Anna's husband gave all the kids, not only the one who found it, a reward. I was told that the hidden matzoh is called *afikoman*. Strange, I thought to myself, a Greek word.

The *Seder* then went on for a bit with more prayers, more wine, some singing, and ended with "Next Year in Jerusalem", This I absolutely did not understand, since Jerusalem was only a few miles away. Why not go there this year? The kids left the table, the little ones were put to sleep and the older ones went to watch television. When we were only adults at the table, Anna asked Josef, with a smile on her face, "Nu, Yossie, how long has it been since you attended a *Seder?*

Josef knotted his brows and his eyes filled with tears. "The last *Seder* I attended, he said softly, "my little brother Natan asked the four questions and we were in the ghetto."

Realizing how inappropriate the question was, Anna gasped, her eyes filled with tears and she grabbed her husband's hand.

"Oh, Yossie," she said, "I didn't realize what I was asking."

Catching his breath, Josef replied, "That's okay, mama. It's a good question. If I were still a priest, it would be a lead-in to a sermon. But since I am no longer a priest, and Liese is a guest in our home and unfamiliar with our holidays and our customs, let me say something to her.

I was sitting next to him and he took my hand in his, looked at me and then looked away, smiled at the others, and went on. "Some Jewish holidays are called for in the Bible and some are not. But they all represent an important event in Jewish life. Passover celebrates the Exodus from Egypt, *Rosh Hashonah*[28], the New Year." And turning to me, he went on. "Each year we read the five books of Moses and we celebrate the end of the reading and the beginning of the rereading. We celebrate the Torah. I don't know if you ever heard of *Chanukah?*[29] That is the holiday that falls around Christmas-time. It doesn't come from the Bible but celebrates a military victory commemorated by lighting eight candles. But Passover is the most important holiday of all because, if you read the Bible, you will see that God constantly speaks to the Jewish people, particularly when they deviate from the path He has chosen for them, by telling them to recall that He brought them forth from Egypt with a strong hand and an

---

[28] Jewish New Year
[29] Festival of Lights

outstretched arm. Regardless of which holiday it is, God plays a role in all of them."

"But yet, the most revered of all the holidays does not commemorate a special event in Jewish history. It is *Yom Kippur*, the Day of Atonement. On that day, God drops the severe attitude and gives us a break. He turns around the entire relationship between himself and his people. It is on that day that the prayer book says: 'For transgressions against God, the Day of Atonement atones; but for transgressions of one human being against another, the Day of Atonement does not atone until they have made peace with one another.'"

"Isn't that strange" he said, as he looked at me and shook his head. "The more I learn about Judaism, the more I see how much Catholicism took from it." At that point he poured himself some more wine from the bottle that was still on the table and said, "Enough theology for one day." And looking at me he asked, "Well, what do you say, Liese? Was it interesting? Was it different?"

He had backed me into a corner. I was growing increasingly angry because I had the feeling that this was all a put-up job. "Day of Atonement; make peace with one another; God's relationship with man." It was now my turn to talk. It was expected, so let me get something out of all of this aside from a good dinner.

Looking as relaxed and unconcerned as I could, I said, "When I first met Yossie (I had never called him that and I am sure it made his mother furious), he came to see me in Dusseldorf. I didn't know why and I am not sure he knew why. I think it had to do with the difference of opinion between Sholom and me. I am talking about my half-brother, Sholom. It appears that without being aware of it our father caused a conflict between us."

At this point I could see that Anna was seething. I thought she would cause blood to come from Chaim's hand, the way she dug her nails in. But I calmly continued. "Yossie told me his whole life story and it was a painful one, and yet, a joyous one. He had found his mother. And as we sat and talked, I in my lounging pajamas and he in his priestly garb, I told him that if he ever left the priesthood he should become a used car salesman. He had the gift of gab." Turning to Josef, I said with a big smile. "Remember that, Yossie?" And each time I called him Yossie, Anna looked more and more like a volcano about to erupt. "His gift of gab was great. He was trying to sell me something but wouldn't reveal the product. He left me his card and said that he would travel with me to Israel, but when I called him to tell him I was ready to travel, he was gone. He had already left the priesthood, left Warsaw and come to Israel. Nevertheless, when I got here, I was ill, and Anna took good care of me, as did Yossie and I am indebted to them for that. As far as Sholom goes, he hasn't said a word to me. Not very brotherly."

Continuing in the same cool and relaxed way, I went on. "Being here with all of you today is a very unique experience for me for more than one reason. It is obvious that I have never been to a *Seder* and I have to thank Yossie for finding a *Haggadah* in both Hebrew and German so I could follow what was being said, but what is even more important to me is who you are."

There was a dead silence. Finally, Anna growled at me and said, "Who we are? What do you mean by that?"

"I have never met as many people in one room who knew my father, as are gathered here today. It is some thirty years since I last saw him. Would those of you who knew him be kind enough to tell me about him?"

Again, a dead silence. Everyone was looking to the other and wondering who would be the first to speak. Unbelievably, it was Eitan who said, "He scared the hell out of me. I remember him as a tall good looking guy with the shiniest black boots I ever saw. I recall wondering, who polished them for him. I never spoke to him, I was just a kid, but I remember he sat next to us in the dining room one morning when we had breakfast." Turning to Moshe, he asked, "Do you remember him at all, Moshe?"

And with a laugh, Moshe replied, "Not me. I barely remember the Hotel Polski.

At which point Avram said, "I, too, remember his black, shiny boots, but I never spoke to him. I spoke only to Shimon. But the one thing I'll never forget was when I came to the hotel my name was Shloime Katz, the boys were Ernst and Moishele, and Feygl was Rivka Bronstein. When we left the hotel, we became the Grossman family courtesy of your father. We were there for a short period when Anna and Chaim were there but we didn't know each other at that time. I never heard your father raise his voice to anyone, but in my heart I don't know who it was that sent us to Pawiak prison, and then on to Vittel in France. But that is a story for another time."

Picking up as Avram finished, Shimon said, "I suppose that I knew your father best. He came to the Polski a week or so after I did. We had lengthy conversations about what we were doing and whether there was any logic to it."

"By the way," he interrupted himself," my name was Berl Rabinowitz and it was through the good graces of your father that I became Shimon Cohen." Going on, he told how he had been a representative of a Jewish organization which had gotten word of the Nazi's plan and been assigned to help implement that plan first at the Hotel Royal and then at the Polski. "At the risk of my life and the life of my family, you can believe I was scared to death."

Turning to me, he said, "Your father was a calm and well organized man. I never heard him holler or scream at anyone. He gave orders and they were obeyed. Whether it was his orders that resulted in people being taken to Pawiak prison and shot, I cannot say. It was not my place to question what took place outside the very limited sphere of my duties. We took the travel documents of dead Jewish families, had them re-validated and put together new families from the survivors of the Jewish population of Warsaw. Most of the visas we were able to obtain were from South American countries, all of which were on the side of the Germans. They had no German internees to barter for the Jews and on more than one occasion, I spoke at length with your father about what we were doing. We were literally sending these people to their deaths. I remember those discussions so well. He shook his head helplessly, said quietly that he assumed I was right, but we went on doing what was expected of us." Looking over at Avram and Feygl, he said with a smile, "I remember when I gave you your travel documents, you looked at them and were about to tell me the picture looked nothing like the two of you. I hadn't thought of that for years." Then turning to me, he went on. "But it made no difference. This was all some sort of a game. Those of us around this table and perhaps a few others were the only winners."

"I also recall that he was quite unhappy in his job at the Polski. I knew, after the visit by General Seidl, he would be leaving. I didn't know what would become of my family and me until he told us we were being sent to Palestine for Germans interned in Turkey. For that, I thank not only him, but Anna, as well. She knows what I mean."

"Oh, one other thing," he continued. "He came to see me in Jerusalem after he got out of Spandau. He asked to meet Sholom. We spoke for a brief moment and I told him where he could find him. I know that he did visit him. Other than that, I never saw him again."

Turning to Sholom, I asked, "What did he want from you?"

Before answering, Sholom asked his mother if there was any more coffee. Not saying a word, she stood up, went into the kitchen and came out with a fresh pot. It was passed around the table, cups were refilled, and then Sholom looked at me and said, "He came to visit me at the university. I was unaware of my relationship to him at the time, but since I was writing my doctoral dissertation on the Hotel Polski, when he introduced himself to me I knew who he was. He appeared to me to be a kindly old gentleman and I found it hard to believe that he had been an SS Colonel. We spoke of his role as commandant of the hotel and of the … and I don't know what to call it … project, plan, scheme… and I must say that even then, more than close to thirty years after leaving the Polski, he couldn't give a clear or convincing answer as to what he was supposed to accomplish."

"Nevertheless, I appreciated his input. I could never have gotten it from anyone else."

"But you did see him again?" I asked.

Although he spoke openly, Sholom's tone was never friendly. He responded, "Sometime later, after finding Yossie, as you call him, in Warsaw, I went to Ludwigsburg, read the transcript, realized who he was, what his relationship was to me, and went to see him in Munich. He bought me breakfast and asked me it if I would now send him a Father's Day card each year. I did not know him as all the others knew him. I found him to be a pleasant man. All the others knew him in a different time and in a different place."

At this point, I looked up to the head of the table. Chaim and Anna sat next to each other but neither said a word. So, finally, I said, "Mr. Adler, you were at the hotel for many months. You must have had some contact with my father. What can you tell me?"

"To be honest, Professor Hauptmann," he responded, "your father scared the hell out of me. I don't recall ever saying a word to him in all the time I was there. But I will say, he kept his word. Once he decided that Rosa—that was Anna's name at the time—was to be his companion, he said he would protect me, and he did. Incidentally, my name at that time was Itzik Grynshpan. Your father gave us the names Chaim and Anna Adler so that our new names would correspond to the exit visas. We had nothing to offer for our freedom. I had false papers, as did most of the people in the Hotel. Anna had no papers at all. At any time she could have been sent to Pawiak and executed, but your father protected us, as he promised. Needless to say, for that I am thankful. But I suppose Rosa…that is how your father knew him…She knew him best of all."

Again, not a word was said. Everyone looked to Anna. She was the only one left who had known Colonel Hauptmann and who had not spoken. Unexpectedly, she got up and left the table and went into the kitchen. No one knew quite what to do, and as Chaim stood up, Feygl motioned him to sit down and she went into the kitchen. We could hear voices but could not quite distinguish what was being said. It took another minute or two and Anna came out followed by Feygl who went back to her seat. Anna didn't sit down but stood center stage.

"So, now let me ask you a question, Leise," she said to me. "What is it that you want me to tell you about your father?" And without giving me a chance to reply, she went on. "You want me to tell you that I accused him of killing my husband Peter and my two little boys? Do you want me to tell you that he asked me to call him Peter and I said I would never do that because my husband's name was Peter? Then he told me that he had a nickname since he was a child. Do you know his nickname, Liese?"

"Yes, I do," I answered quietly, shaking my head. "I hadn't thought of it in a hundred years, but I remember as a child he told me that his nickname was Googy. Is that what he told you?"

"Yes, that is what he told me," she answered. "But I was never allowed to call him that in public, only when we were together." Pulling out her chair, she sat down and went on. "And we were together quite a lot. Many dinners and many nights in his suite.

Anna was growing tense. "Shall I go on?" she asked. "Do you want the details?

I had not foreseen the consequence, of my original question. I didn't know if I wanted her to go on. Am I being unfair? There are people in the room who may not know the intimate details of her relationship with my father. It is really not their business. How do I answer her?

"Only if you want to tell them to me. Not just to me, but to all of your guests," I responded. "I do not wish to force you to say anything that you don't want to say or to reveal anything that you don't want to reveal. I didn't ask the question to embarrass anyone or to be a troublemaker. I may have been wrong in my behavior towards my father and now it is too late for me to do anything about it. Here I am at a Passover *Seder*, in Israel, a place I never thought I would be, with the greatest number of people who knew my father. All I was seeking was some insight into a subject about which I know very little."

"I don't believe you," Anna shot back. She was wound up and nothing I could say was going to stop her. "You came here to make trouble for my family and now you are trying to get out of it with this daughterly attitude that you never had during your father's life."

There was no point to my responding. Turning to Josef, I said, "Josef, I obviously wasn't welcome here to begin with and it was a mistake to bring me. Please take me back to the apartment."

As I stood up and took Josef's hand, Anna screamed, "You sit down. I'm not finished with you or with your father. There is a lot more to tell. Why do I have to carry the burden by myself?"

I sat down, and as I did, Chaim got up and tried to put his arm around his wife to calm her, but she shook him off and said to him, "You, too, Chaim. It is time that you knew the truth."

At that moment, Shimon spoke up and said, "Anna, you have told me on numerous occasions that I am your oldest friend here in Israel. So listen to your oldest friend. You owe no one any explanation of what took place during those years. The problems between Sholom and Liese can be argued out at another time and at another place. This is Passover. It is not the time for recriminations."

At which point Anna sat down quietly and said to everyone, "May I go on?" No one answered since no one could stop her from going on, and she said, "It is my belief, Liese, that your father was well aware and probably ordered the executions of hundreds of people at Pawiak prison." A deep sigh went out around the room. "The reason I say this," she went on, "is because I recall an incident when a package of clothing from Pawiak arrived in the Colonel's suite. I opened it and on top was a very pretty designer dress with bullet holes in it. Incidentally, all the dresses I wore had to have the bullet holes sewn up. When I looked at the dress, I told the Colonel that just yesterday, a woman here in the hotel, had worn that dress. He insisted that there had to be more than one such dress in all of Poland, and when I insisted, he grew angry and had the package and the dress removed. He was very angry with me for a number of days and that frightened me. I knew that if I angered him, both Itzik and I could be on the next transport to Pawiak." Then, with a laugh, she said, "I recall him telling me I was the best cared for Jewish woman in Poland."

Avram interrupted and said, "Don't forget, we spent more than ten weeks at Pawiak before we were shipped to Vittel. I can tell you there were executions going on all the time. When we were allowed out into the yard, you could see the blood up against the wall."

"Thank you, Avram," said Anna. "I knew I was right. Even when my relationship became more comfortable and less hostile, I always feared the Colonel's authority for both myself and Itzik." Going on, in a somewhat calmer tone, she said, "I think I was with the Colonel for about three months, perhaps a week more or less." She paused. "He didn't take me to bed until after the first or second week."

Again there was a collective sigh and Chaim said, "Please, Anna, you do not have to relive this. It is over. The Colonel is dead."

In an almost dreamlike way, she responded. "Liese, your father was a wonderful lover. When he wasn't absorbed with his military duties and when he wasn't troubled by events of the day, and we were together at night, he was my Googy. He loved me. I know he did and I loved him." Her voice now rose out of her dreamlike state and she said, with emphasis. "But I loved Itzik. Itzik was always waiting for me; he was always there. How could I tell him what I was doing upstairs with the Colonel?" And her voice dropped. "Yes, perhaps I was a whore." And in a plea for understanding, she said, "I was a prisoner. I could not walk out of the hotel. If I left, I would be shot in the street and Itzik would be sent to Pawiak. So, I fell in love with my jailer. He made me feel like a woman, an excited and sexy woman. He could do that and I responded and Sholom was the result."

"So, now, Liese", she asked. "What else do you want to know about your father? Everyone feared him, as did I, but I loved him. When he told me that he was setting us free, I said to him, 'Perhaps after the war ...', and his answer was something to the effect that he could not look so far into the future. And yet, when the authorities arrested him, he was attempting to board an El Al flight to Israel. Who do you think he was coming to see?

Speaking quietly, I responded. "I assume he was coming to find you. I don't know if he was married at that time or not. But I must tell you, I cannot put myself in your place. I have never loved nor was I ever loved by anyone as you described. But I must ask you one last question. Why did you deny the fact that Sholom was his son? I cannot believe, in my heart, that when you spoke to him, after you testified, there was any other subject other than his son. He learned it for the first time at the trial and yet, you denied him. Why did you do that?"

She didn't answer at once. She sat and folded her napkin. No one said a word. I wasn't sure the others were even breathing. Finally, she looked up at me and said, "Because denying that Sholom was his child was my only link to sanity. People who met me here in Israel for the first time used to look at Sholom as a baby and say, 'Oh, he looks just like Chaim.' I would smile and thank them and say to myself, How wrong you are.' Raising her voice, she went on. "My life here is one of order, of love, of devotion, of a new family, of a husband who fought in the War of Independence for this country. I had no choice. Your father had to become a bad dream, a nightmare that I had to overcome and forget."

And with more anger than before, she said, "If the damned fool had not continued to use the name Peter Hauptmann and had not bought a ticket to Israel on El Al, he would never have been apprehended. There would have been no trial and my whoreish behavior would not have become a matter of record. Can you not see that he brought all of this upon himself? He may have been Sholom's father but Sholom was never to become his son."

She then exploded, and lashing out particularly at Sholom, she screamed. "But no one would leave it alone. The Hotel Polski was my obsession. Your father was my personal, gut wrenching guilt, and instead of trying to help me, the research, the trial, the questions . . . the endless questions . . . , my son Sholom, with his half brother and half sister. I feel that I am crazier now than I was when I was a prisoner in Colonel Hauptmann's bed." And with that, she broke down in hysteria.

Again Feygl jumped up, but as she did, Moshe and Tamar's girls came into the room and stood as if paralyzed with fear when they saw Anna crying. Finally, the older one asked, "*Safta*,[30] why are you crying? Don't you feel well?"

Anna quickly dried her eyes with her napkin and rushed over to the girls. Embracing them both she said to them. "I am crying because I am so happy to have such beautiful granddaughters who come to my house for Passover. Come to the table. Would you like some more macaroons?"

The girls coming in gave everyone the break that they needed. I asked Josef to please take me home. It had been quite an afternoon. Rena's parents were talking to Rena and Sholom, Avram got up and was talking to Eitan and Miriam, Feygl was hugging Anna, while Shimon and his wife just sat and watched. I hoped that in the confusion, we could get out unnoticed, but as we were trying to leave, I heard Anna call my name. I turned to look at her and she came over to me, put her arms around me and said, "Liese, I'm so glad you're feeling better and that you could spend Passover with us."

I thanked her and I said, "I am sorry that I upset you so." But not letting me finish, Anna replied, "Oh, no. You did wonders for me. I owe you a debt of gratitude."

I looked at Josef as if to say, "What in the hell is she talking about," but I certainly didn't want to get into another discussion with her at this moment. I wanted to go home. So, I replied, "I am not sure what you mean, but you must excuse me, I really must go now.

To which she said, in the most patronizing way, "Yes, dear, I

---

[30] Grandmother

understand." She kissed me on the cheek and said to Josef, "Take good care of our guest, will you Yossie?" And with that, we left the apartment.

Neither of us spoke for the first ten minutes of the ride. Finally, Josef asked me, "When are you supposed to see your lawyer?"

"After the weekend," I replied.

"Good. Then I'll see you tomorrow. Do you want me to come up now so we can talk?"

"No," I answered. "I have enough leftovers to make something for supper and I'd just as soon be alone tonight. Thanks, anyway." And with that we arrived at the apartment, I leaned over and kissed him on the cheek, and got out of the car without another word being said.

When I got upstairs, I made two telephone calls. The first was to Lufthansa. I rearranged my ticket home and got on the first flight out in the morning. I had no desire to remain in Israel for another day. The second was to my lawyer. I knew he would not be in but I would leave a message on his answering machine. I told him that I was withdrawing my claim; I was leaving Israel, and would not be keeping my appointment. I instructed him to send me his bill for his services to my address in Dusseldorf. I thanked him for his concern and said goodbye.

I spent the rest of the evening packing, eating whatever was still in my refrigerator, watching some television with English subtitles, and went to sleep. In the morning, I took my keys down to the caretaker, thanked him for his courtesy, asked him to call a taxi for me, and gave him a tip. My Israeli odyssey came to an end.

Josef

Chapter XXIII

Chaim and Anna, Avram and Feygl, and Sholom and Rena were all invited to Rena's parents for the following night. I was also invited but declined, saying I had to look after Liese and I doubted that she would want to come. So, the next morning, when I went over to Liese's apartment and knocked on the door, I could not understand why no one answered. She could be out taking a walk but she really didn't know her way around.

Going down to the caretaker's office, I inquired whether he knew the whereabouts of Professor Hauptmann, and in response, the caretaker held up the keys to her unit, telling me that she had left early in the morning and would not be returning. He then said, "I've seen you here before. Are you Josef?" I acknowledged that I was and he handed me a bag and said, "She asked me to give this to you. She knew you would be here."

I looked in the bag and found the *Haggadah* I had given her and a note which read, "Thanks for the *Haggadah* but I guess I am really not a member of the family. Liese."

I was stunned. This is not what I had expected. I never had the chance to talk to her about last night, but I just didn't anticipate her running away.

A week later, there appeared in *Ha'aretz* a lovely article about me written by Anat Stem. It told how I escaped from the train taking me to the death camp, how I grew up in the care of a Polish family who sent me to Catholic school and the Seminary, how Sholom discovered me, by chance, in Warsaw, as a priest in St. Jaeck's, and how I chose to ultimately return to my own family in Israel. A real human-interest story. But then, as a postscript, the reporter told how she had interviewed me prior to the Passover *Seder* and present, among the family members, at the interview, was Professor Liese Hauptmann from the university in Dusseldorf. The article went on to say that the reporter found Liese's presence strange and somewhat out of place, as a result of which she chose to do a little bit of research.

Liese's father was a Colonel in the SS during the war, was in Warsaw at the time of the destruction of the ghetto and for some time thereafter, and was ultimately convicted as a war criminal. Even more unusual was the fact that he was apprehended by Israeli authorities at the El Al counter in Munich attempting to board a plane to Israel. The article concluded by asking, "What is Liese Hauptmann to this family and why was she celebrating Passover with them?" She ended her column by saying, "I bet that is also a good story."

The End

Epilogue

After the *Seder* the family grew further apart. The truth might have set Anna free but it did little for Chaim. Despite all the years that they had been together, what Anna revealed at the *Seder* was something that Chaim knew, as long as it remained unspoken. On many occasions he repeated to Anna, to himself, and to others that he was thankful to Anna for saving their lives. At no time did he ever require any explanation or description of her relationship with the Colonel. They were both prisoners, and prisoners, if they want to stay alive, do what they are told. Ultimately, however, hearing Anna express her feelings for the Colonel was more than he could bear. What he thought he knew and what he thought he could accept was better left unsaid.

Nevertheless, they stayed together because of their love for the family, for the grandchildren, and, in a strange way their love for each other. They never spoke of the Hotel Polski or of Colonel Hauptmann again, but it was never the same.

Sholom was the one most affected by his mother's reply to Liese. It caused him to see his mother as two different people. He anticipated that when the truth would emerge, if ever, his mother would have been the victim, the prisoner of the harsh, evil SS Colonel. This, in turn, caused him to see his "father" as two different people. The first being the kindly gentleman who visited him some years ago at the university, and who more recently bought him breakfast in Munich; the second as the stereotypic Nazi, Jew hater, the harsh, evil, SS Colonel. However, once his mother admitted her feelings for the stereotypic Nazi, Jew hater everything changed. Although she was a prisoner, she was never the victim. He could not conceive of what would have happened to her if she refused the Colonel's request. However, she didn't. Sholom had no choice but to acknowledge that he was the product of the love relationship between the prisoner and her jailer and this was just something that he could not accept.

Sholom remained close with Chaim and would have lunch with him at least once a week. Other than inquire as to her health, Sholom would never speak of his mother nor would either of them ever mention her outburst at the *Seder*. He did attend and participate in family *simchas*[31] but he and his mother managed to stay away from each other.

Liese withdrew her claim and Sholom ultimately received the entire inheritance from the estate of Peter Hauptmann. Some two years thereafter Sholom was offered a position as head of a Jewish Studies Program at a prestigious university in the United States. He accepted, and at a farewell dinner he and his mother kissed with obviously little affection and she wished him well. That is as far as it went.

Ari received his *Bar-Mitzvah* training in the United States but for the ceremony itself, the family returned to Israel and stayed with Rena's parents. The services were held at the Sephardic Temple and Anna and Chaim as well as the rest of the family were invited. Both sets of grandparents were given *aliyahs*[32] and on the whole, it was a

---

[31] Festive occasions

[32] The honor of being called to the Torah

very happy occasion. For the ten days that Sholom, Rena and the kids were in Israel, the *Bar-Mitzvah* and the reception that followed were the only times that Sholom saw his mother.

Chava's parents were also invited. They sent a beautiful gift to Ari, but didn't come to the services.

Nothing was ever the same again.

Anna clung to Josef who ultimately married a women whom he met in the agency in which he worked. She was lovely and gave Anna the respect that she deserved. Since both Josef and his wife were too old to have children, they were happy to be together, to be part of the family, and to partake of the joy provided by their nieces and nephews. Josef and his wife stayed in touch with Sholom and Rena and visited them in the United States.

The one person with whom Anna remained close was Feygl. After all, no one knew her like Feygl and no one had kept her secret like Feygl. Aside from the women remaining close, they also remained close as couples. Both Avram and Feygl were aware of the rift between Anna and Chaim and were, of course, terribly unhappy about it. Although Feygl talked to Anna and asked her to try and reconcile with Chaim, Anna refused. She insisted to Feygl that it was not her fault that Chaim could not face that which he claimed to know for so many years. She loved him but she would not take his burden upon herself. She had carried the weight of her guilt for her behavior at the Polski for all these years and she was finally free. She had rid herself of her guilt and refused to replace it with Chaim's inability to face the truth.

Moshe and Tamar remained close to the family. They ultimately left the *kibbutz* and moved into the city where Moshe became head of a large food cooperative and Tamar became principal of a nursery school. They stayed in touch with and visited Sholom and Rena, but could do nothing to try and heal the rift between Sholom and his mother.

And so, to a great extent, the family fell apart, and to a lesser extent it stayed together. If you look for a reason why these things happened to this family, and if you went back far enough you could blame it on the Holocaust; you could blame it on Peter Hauptmann; you could blame it on Sholom's dogged insistence on learning the truth; you could blame it on Liese Hauptmann; you could blame it on Anna's guilt for having survived when so many others didn't; or you could blame it on the human frailties which we all possess and which are too numerous to mention.

THE
FINAL AFFAIR

CHAPTER ONE

The list has six names on it. If I add my name it makes seven. Always an odd number so that I can vote and break a tie. Next to each of the names is a plus or minus sign. Five pluses and one minus. Ed will be against it. If it's new, he's against it. Sometimes he makes a valid argument and sometimes he just likes to hear himself talk. Let's see what the others have to say.

Fr. Joe Gregory, President, Head Chaplain, and Dean of Capernaum Catholic University, brought his work home so he could look over the list for the third or possibly fourth time. Sighing, he put the list into his folder, the folder into his briefcase, put the briefcase on his desk, and decided it was enough for tonight.

Notice of the meeting was given a week ago, by mail, with a copy of the agenda attached. Although, during the intervening week, he had seen all of the people that had been invited and were expected to attend, no one had mentioned it or the subject matter. Maybe his pluses and minuses are wrong. What he is attempting to do is unique for the university and is generally unheard of, for a Catholic institution.

"Oh, to hell with it," he said to himself, as he turned off the desk light and headed for the kitchen and his nightly glass of warm milk before bedtime. "Let's see what tomorrow brings."

The small conference room adjoining Joe Gregory's office was sufficient for today's meeting. Pads and ballpoint pens were laid out at each seat; glasses and pitchers of ice water were on trays in the center of the table and on the dresser, at the side of the room, were pitchers of orange juice, donuts, and bagels with cream cheese. Since Fr. Gregory called this a "morning meeting," bagels and cream cheese were a required and expected staple.

Fr. Gregory kept the door between his office and the conference open so he could see when people arrived. Fr. Robert Smith, Provost and Executive VP, accompanied by Jack Robbins, the CFO, were the first to amble in. Taking his briefcase from his desk, Fr. Gregory joined them, and as good mornings were exchanged, coffee was poured and bagels were shmeared.

"I smelled the coffee coming down the hall," Fr. Edward McGuire, VP for Administration, bellowed as he held the door open for General Counsel, Marie Robinson. Before the door could close they were followed by Fr. Juan Carlos, VP for Academic Personnel, and Fr. Leo Gentile, VP for Student Affairs and head of the History Department. Briefcases were placed on their chairs as they all partook of the morning refreshment, chatted with one another, with no mention being made of the subject matter of the meeting. Despite the fact that they all worked at the same institution, their particular specialties kept them apart and the opportunity for a "morning meeting" was somewhat of a reunion.

"Ok, guys, let's get to it," said Fr. Gregory as he tapped his water glass with his pen. Seating himself at the head of the table, he took his folder from his briefcase, put the case on the floor by his seat, and opened the folder. As the others were sitting down, the door to the room opened and students, who worked for the university in various capacities, came into the room, cleared away the dirty dishes and silverware, brought in fresh carafes of coffee and pitchers of ice water, where necessary.

Fr. Gregory thanked the students and waited for them to leave. He then nodded to everyone and again wished them a good morning. Without looking at the file in front of him he said to the group, "You all know that there is but one subject on today's agenda. I trust that you looked over the material I sent you and look forward to hearing your comments." Not a word was said by anyone, as they each looked to the other.

"Hey, guys," said Fr. Gregory. "You are the heads of this institution. If what I propose comes to fruition, I could say you are the 'gantze makhers' of this school. Get yourself a Yiddish dictionary and look it up. You won't talk; okay, so I'll talk."

"A Jewish Studies Program at a Catholic university is somewhat of a novelty. So when it was proposed to me by some wealthy Jewish friends, who said that it would be fully underwritten," at which point he grinned at Jack Robbins, the Chief Financial Officer, "I had to give it some serious thought, and I did." Standing up and walking behind his chair, Fr. Gregory went on. "We have over twenty thousand students in three campuses in this city. Roughly three percent of those students are Jewish. In our Law School, considerably more than three percent are Jewish. So, let's think like academics. A new program, a new course of study, fully funded; a new concept for a Catholic university expressing our expanding view of education. I have checked with other schools that have Jewish Studies programs and, believe it or not, all of the students who take the courses are not Jewish. Please realize that there is something unique about Jewish Studies. These people existed before we did and they outlived some of the world's greatest powers. Is there anyone in this room who can say that there is nothing to be learned from all of this?"

At which point Fr. McGuire, head of Administration, spoke up. "C'mon, Joe, how many black students do we have? What'll be next? Swahili Studies and then remedial Swahili? There are lots of interesting subjects that colleges can teach but there has got to be a limit. We are a Catholic university. There are those who say that we have overstepped our bounds already with some of the stuff that we teach. And what about..."

"Excuse me, Ed," said Fr. Gentile, Head of Student Affairs. "I must ask, who will do the teaching, and what will be taught? Where will he or she live? Is that included in the funding by your friends?"

Before anyone else could speak, Fr. Gregory opened his file, looked at his list of pluses and minuses, saw the minus next to Fr. McGuire's name, shook his head, knowingly, and said, "In answer to both of you, who will teach and what will be taught is for the next meeting. I have pursued these questions and will have more to report at that time. As to where he or she will live, that is included in the funding. And as to remedial Swahili, please Ed, let's stick to the subject."

Raising his hand as if to ask for permission to speak, Fr. Rob Smith, the Provost, asked, "Joe, have you brought this up before the Board of Overseers?"

"Absolutely not," answered Fr. Gregory. "I will not go to them until I have approval from the academic heads of the institution and I am hoping that I will have complete unanimity."

"I have a problem or what I see might be a problem," said Fr. Gentile. "With a Jewish Studies Department I expect there will, ultimately, be a request for a Hillel chapter on campus and frankly, my greater fear is a possible outbreak of anti-Semitism, rallies in support of or against Israel; issues that we have not had to confront, as of yet. So far we have lived in peace."

"And if I can finish my thought," said Fr. McGuire with a scowl, picking up where he left off, "you know that the Catholic Church does not come off looking so good when it comes to Jewish history. The Crusades, the pogroms, the Inquisition; what the hell do we need all of that for?"

"Hey, Ed," responded Fr. Gentile. "If that's a part of Jewish history, it is, whether we teach it or not. I'm more concerned with today's political issues than with stuff we can't do anything about."

"I never thought you guys were such a bunch of old ladies, pardon me Marie," said Fr. Gregory with a nod to Marie Robinson. "Ed, if we teach American history don't we concern ourselves with how we treated American Indians? It's a sad part of the culture, but it's part of the history. Consider what is being suggested. A whole new department; a whole new course of study that will give the university positive publicity. New students, all fully funded. All of the issues that have been raised are possible problems, and maybe or maybe not a bit too premature, but as I said before, I want unanimity. If I can have that I will come to the next meeting as well as to the Board of Overseers with a budget, a commitment for funding, a possible curriculum, subject to the input of whoever will teach, and the CVs of some adjuncts who have been recommended for the position. This will be nothing more than an add on to the history department and it will be under their jurisdiction. You won't be able to major in it; you won't be able to minor in it, and you certainly won't be able to get a degree in it. So, are we in agreement? What say you, Ed?"

"I guess so," said Fr. McGuire, grudgingly, "but I wish those kids hadn't taken the bagels away so quickly."

With a laugh and with handshaking, everyone stood up as Fr. Gregory said, "Marie and Jack, will you give me another minute?"

When the room cleared out, fresh coffee was poured and all three huddled around the front of the table. Turning first to Marie, Fr. Gregory said, "There's a lot of legal work to do. I suggest you go back in the files and check the last new program that we introduced and use that as a model. To be honest, I don't even remember what it was or if you were even counsel. But it must be in the files. Then I need an employment contract, no names, for the new professor. I know I used the word adjunct but he will be a full professor, no tenure, necessary publishing, three years, six months' notice."

"I notice you said 'he,'" responded Marie. "Have you chosen someone?"

"I have, but it's not for publication. When I was approached by my Jewish friends, months and months ago, I thought long and hard about the idea. You know that we have a collaboration of sorts with the University in Dusseldorf and they have had a Jewish Studies Department for a few years. So I called my friend, the Chancellor, and we had a long talk, more about politics than about education. What motivated a German institution to install such a program and he asked me what motivated a Catholic institution to even consider it. It was an interesting conversation; two institutions with historically anti-Jewish backgrounds talking about Jewish studies. He had his Jewish studies professor call me, an Israeli, and we spoke at length about what courses were being taught, the number of students, the reaction of German students to Jewish students, etc. When I asked him if he knew anyone that he could recommend, he recommended another Israeli that I contacted and met in Rome some six weeks ago."

"Prior to that I had Fr. Juan Carlos form a secret search committee who found some very capable candidates in the US, some of whom I interviewed here, but my choice is the Israeli. You notice that Juan said nothing during the meeting. He knows what this is all about. So everything we say in this room is between us."

"Lawyer-client confidentiality," said Marie with a laugh. "I'll get right to work."

Turning to Jack, "As far as funding goes, Jack, I will call in my friends and we will sit down with them. Have a budget prepared, be sure to cover all bases, and check, as quietly as you can, about housing. This guy has a wife and two kids that will be coming with him so he'll need a good-size apartment or house. Line some stuff up, check with Fr. Carlos since he knows what's going on. Get an idea of cost. It all has to be included in the package."

Holding his hands out to both of them, Fr. Gregory went on. "This is a big gamble. I don't want to end up with egg on my face or bring disrepute to the university. Tell me when you are ready to meet with the financial people; I will get them in and let us try and get this done and on my desk within the next week to ten days. I will then take it to the Overseers and back to the board. Good luck to you both."

All three rose, shook hands, Marie and Jack left, and Fr. Gregory picked up his briefcase and went back to his office.

"Not as bad as I expected," he said to himself.

CHAPTER TWO

Hitler's rise to power created fear in Jewish communities throughout Europe, however, the Polish government reassured its citizens that they would be protected and their army was ready to fight. All of this gave minimal confidence to the vast number of Jews then living in Poland and elsewhere as German laws against Jews were being enforced in Germany.

During the last days of August 1939, Irving and Fannie Adler were married in Warsaw, Poland and left for England on their honeymoon. The Adler family were well to do people. Irving's father, Chaim, having started out as a tailor, worked himself up to a manufacturer of expensive men's suits and coats. Irving, after graduating university, had gone into his father's business and his sister, although younger than Irving, was already head of bookkeeping and accounting.

Irving's mother, Anna, had been a school teacher and worked for a number of years after she and Chaim were married. When Irving was born, Fannie's mother, Sarah, came over to care for the baby for the first year or two, but when business improved, Anna stopped teaching and stayed home with Irving and then with his sister.

On September 1, 1939, it all changed. As the German army pushed toward Warsaw, Chaim Adler called his son in England and told him that under no condition was he to return to Poland. Chaim sent a sizeable sum of money to the hotel where his son was staying, telling him to find a place to live, giving him the name of some people whom he knew in the business and to stay in touch.

Irving did as his father wished. They stayed in touch for over a year by an occasional phone call, but mostly by letter, and by the end of 1940 Irving learned that his parents and his sister were forced out of their home, and their business and all their assets were confiscated. They ended up in the Warsaw ghetto. An occasional piece of mail followed, but then, nothing.

As World War II was ending, the Americans and the British were involved in mopping up operations in the West and Russia was heading toward Berlin from the East. The destruction made parts of Europe unrecognizable and as the concentration camps were liberated, refugees wandered from country to country in an attempt to get home and find if any of their families had survived.

A degree of organization started to appear with the displaced person's camps where the refugees were taken in, fed nourishing food, given necessary medical treatment and some semblance of normalcy was being reestablished.

Irving and Fannie lived out the war in London and by the end of the war they had a son whom they named Charles, in memory of Irving's father, Chaim, who they were sure had not survived.

The years went by. They had a daughter, Sara, named for Fannie's mother, who perished in Auschwitz. They lived in an upscale Jewish section of London. Chaim's initial contacts in the garment trade proved to be wonderful people who took Irving into the business in which he was now a partner.

And then, one day, something very unusual happened. Fannie brought in the mail with a strange look on her face. "Irving," she said, "this is very peculiar," as she handed him a letter with an April, 1943 postmark. They both recognized the handwriting. With trembling hands Irving opened the letter, a letter from his father, a letter from the ghetto. It was brief and simply said that the ghetto will soon be destroyed and he doubts if he will ever be able to write again. He ended with love from mama and signed it, Papa.

Irving and Fannie embraced each other and wept like babies. How could this happen? This letter is twenty or more years old. Where has it been all this time?

At this moment Charlie came home from university and, seeing his parents in such a sad state, asked what had happened. They showed him the letter. He then suggested to his father that tomorrow, first thing in the morning, they go to the post office and inquire as to where the letter had been all these years. It was decided that would be the plan, but they also agreed that, although she is a teenager, Sara should be shown the letter. After all, this is a family tragedy and she is old enough to understand.

At dinner that evening, after seeing the letter, Sara insisted that she, too, wanted to go to the post office with her father and brother. And then Sara came up with a thought that overwhelmed them all. "Is it possible that they are still alive?" And she then went on to tell them about a girl in her class in school whose parents had hired one of these investigating agencies who try to locate survivors. She did not know how successful they were but after a number of years, and, she assumed, quite a bit of money, they did locate a missing brother who had survived.

Irving jumped up from the table and gave Sara a big kiss. "That's my 'meidel'[33]," he said. "I would never have thought of it." Returning to his seat, he went on, "My parents have to be people in their late seventies, or more, at this time. But is it possible? No, it's not. If they were alive papa would have tried to contact me. Who knows?" Turning to Sara he said, "Ask your friend if she could give you the name of the agency. Are they here in London?"

"Ok, Papa," said Sara. "Tomorrow we'll go to the post office and Monday I'll ask my friend."

The explanation at the post office proved reasonable. This particular branch was being renovated and during the reconstruction a

---

[33] Girl

closed room was found with many old mail bags and hundreds of undelivered letters. They were asked to understand that the war was on, most of the men were in the armed services, London was being bombed, and these things just happened. They had nothing to do but accept the explanation and be thankful that the letter had ultimately been delivered.

After school on Monday, Sara came home saying that her friend would get the name and address of the agency that her parents had used. It took another two days but she finally got it and Irving called and made an appointment.

Their offices were in an old building in the financial section of London. There did not appear to be more than a half dozen people working and Irving wondered how they were ever able to produce any results. The head of the office and an associate told him that they had branches throughout the world, had been in business since the end of the war when people in the DP camps were seeking information about their families and had, in fact, reunited many survivors with their relatives in the United States, Britain, and elsewhere.

Irving gave them the background as best as he could recall and showed them the letter they had just received. They recorded the session, made copies of the letter, negotiated a fee, which was paid on the spot, and told Irving that they would be in touch, but warned him it might take months and maybe years before anything was uncovered, so please be patient.

That evening, at dinner, Irving reported to the family about the day's activities but admitted that he did not feel very confident.

CHAPTER THREE

It was at least six weeks before the Passover Seder that Sholom told Chaim that he was going to Rome to be interviewed for a job at a university in the United States. It was at the Seder that he told Chaim that he had gotten the job and would be leaving Israel with Rena and the children within the next three months. He asked Chaim not to say anything to Anna; he would tell her when he thought the time was right.

Chaim did not wait for Sholom to tell his mother he was leaving and ultimately told Anna himself. She was beside herself. It became even worse when she learned that Rena's parents, Sholom's in-laws, had known about it for some time. When she learned of Sholom's imminent departure she sat and wept. Chaim tried to soothe her and explain that it was a wonderful opportunity for Sholom, the children would receive an American education, and it would give them a reason to travel to the States.

Anna just could not accept it. "The children, when will I see them again? This is all my fault. Why can no one understand it; understand me?" she pleaded, as Chaim took her in his arms, something he had not done in quite a while, and tried to comfort her.

When she quieted down she looked at Chaim and asked, "How long have you known about this?"

"For a number of months, but Sholom asked me not to say anything. He only learned that he had been accepted for the position a day before the Seder."

Shaking her head in acceptance, she said, "I don't know how many times I spoke to Rena and she never said a word. Am I such a terrible mother?"

"No, of course not," answered Chaim. They will be here for a number of weeks before they have to leave. Their apartment is on the market and that must be attended to. I will call Sholom and tell him that I told you and you can then make arrangements with Rena to see the children whenever you wish. Is that all right with you?"

"Thank you, Chaim. You know I will do anything for the family." Turning away from Chaim, she said aloud, "When will I ever have peace?"

CHAPTER FOUR

Sholom, Rena, and the children, Ari and Hudi, were given a lovely old house on the Capernaum campus. Sholom was accepted warmly by the other faculty members and both he and Rena attended many social affairs sponsored by the university. Although it didn't bother Sholom particularly, Rena was troubled by the obvious Catholic atmosphere that surrounded almost every activity on the campus. Since the children were now in full-time public school and went to after school classes at the nearby Temple, she got a job teaching Hebrew at the Temple. They were glad to have her and she saw the children every day when they came to class. Although the children absorbed the English language like sponges, Rena would speak Hebrew to them and get angry when they would respond in English.

Fr. Gregory was pleased with his choice. Sholom was a good teacher, chose his courses, with thought and logic, and with consideration of that which would be best for the new program. After two years, the program had enough students to necessitate the engaging of an adjunct to teach additional courses as they were added to the curriculum. Sholom also started an adult lecture series on matters that had never before been discussed or considered at Capernaum. The university paid for the advertising for these lectures and at first there were more priests in the audience than Jews. One of the local rabbis came to him and suggested that the lectures would attract more people if they were given in a Temple because Jews felt uncomfortable on the campus with crosses in every room. But Sholom was insistent, the university did good publicity, and soon more people came, without hesitation.

***

During the course of his professorship, Sholom published an interesting paper dealing with the church and the Holocaust and was awarded a new contract, without question. His academic tenure at the university was secure and all appeared to be going well.

CHAPTER FIVE

During the years that passed, Irving received regular, discouraging reports from the agency. He was not surprised and, little by little, the issue lost its importance. Charlie graduated from the university and joined Irving in the business, which continued to be profitable. Sara was in her third year at the university. Life was quiet except for Charlie, who met Sandra on a blind date. They got along well. They were both bright people, loved the movies, the theater, an occasional concert, avoided the ballet, had mutual friends, all of whom loved good food. Above all Sandra was Jewish.

Charlie met Sandra's parents when he would pick her up at her house and they liked him. On a family occasion Charlie brought Sandra along. She fit right in and Irving and Fannie thought she was lovely. She had graduated from the same university that Sara was attending and the two girls talked about classes, teachers, boyfriends, and got along famously. After a year, or so, it was an exclusive relationship, the parents met, and it was time to talk about serious stuff. When should they get married? Where should it be held? How big an affair? The parents took over and arrangements were made. Charlie insisted on choosing the ring and Sandra was overjoyed with his choice. The honeymoon was, as yet, undecided.

❧

Life has its way of intervening and something unusual and unexpected occurred. Irving got a call from the agency asking him to come to their office. Of course, he went without hesitation and was told that the agency had located two people in Tel Aviv with the names of his parents, Chaim and Anna Adler, their passport had the correct home address in Warsaw that Irving had given them, the age, although there was no direct evidence of it, appeared to be right, early eighties. All things being equal, it should be his parents.

Irving was overwhelmed. He came home and was ecstatic. At dinner that night, Sandra was there, and Irving told Sandra and Charlie that he would pay for their honeymoon (which he had intended to do, anyhow) and they would go to Israel and look up Charlie's grandparents. If these were the right people, Charlie would call, and Irving, Fannie, and Sara would be on the next plane. Charlie and Sandra loved the idea. The next day Irving called his travel agent, arranged the trip for the day after the wedding, and arranged a hotel for them for a two-week stay. Hugs and kisses all around.

The one thing they never considered, nor did it even cross their minds, what happens if these are not Charlie's grandparents?

❧

Charlie and Sandra flew El-Al non-stop from Heathrow to Ben-Gurion. They were overwhelmed at how easy the flight had been and how quickly they had passed through Israeli customs and immigration. A car had been reserved for them at the airport and they were given a map and specific instructions how to get their hotel in Tel-Aviv. Under ordinary circumstances a trip like this, their first visit to Israel, would have been booked through a tour group, but it had been decided back home, since there was family business to attend to, and should they be successful, the touring would come later. Talking quietly to Sandra, Charlie expressed the thought that if they were not successful the touring would come a lot sooner than expected.

Having a confirmed reservation, check-in was easy and when they looked out of the picture window in their room all they saw was sky, beach, and water. It was magnificent. Although the flight had not been that long they were both tired, so they unpacked, and since this was their honeymoon, they decided that a bit of rest and relaxation would be in order.

At dinner in the hotel they were both happy to be married, to be in Israel, to be together, but the real purpose of the trip caused them to be nervous. For as anxious as Sandra was to get the family portion of the trip over with as soon as possible, Charlie was hesitant. "Let's take a day and relax," he suggested. "Then we can ask them at the hotel to mark out the route to the house and we can do a dry run, see where they live, what kind of neighborhood, decide if we should bring them anything. I don't want to just go barging in."

And that is just what they did. They spent the day at the pool, walked on the beach, had lunch in a nice restaurant recommended by the concierge at the hotel, looked in the store windows at the high fashion, and came back to the hotel for more rest and relaxation before dinner. Without it being said, they both knew that they were killing time. The honeymoon aside, they were there for a reason, so before dinner they took their map to the concierge, gave him Chaim and Anna's address, had him mark out the route, learned that it was an upscale neighborhood, and after dinner took the car for a dry run, with the understanding that they would visit the following evening.

The next morning they picked up a tour at the hotel of a magnificent museum in Tel-Aviv where models had been built of many of the synagogues in Poland destroyed by the Nazis during the war. After lunch, the pool, rest and relaxation, dress for dinner and after dinner, as was agreed, they were off to visit Chaim and Anna. But before they left, Sandra decided that the right thing to do, when you go visit someone that you really don't know, is to bring flowers. Fortunately, there was a florist in the hotel lobby and they chose an attractive bouquet, had it wrapped in colorful tissue with ribbons, and were off.

It took some twenty minutes to get from the hotel up to Herzliya, a suburb just north of Tel-Aviv. It was a community of high rises and hotels and expensive restaurants right on the beach. They found the house, parked in visitor parking, and met with the concierge who asked their names and inquired as to the tenant they were going visit. The fact that he asked them in English meant that he recognized that they were obviously not Israelis. "Chaim and Anna Adler," responded Charlie.

"Relatives?" asked the concierge, with a smile.

"Perhaps," said Sandra, as the concierge called and spoke Hebrew with whoever answered. A brief conversation ensued and when the concierge hung up, he gave them the apartment number and told them which elevator to use.

When the elevator door opened they headed toward the apartment and saw Chaim standing in the open door. When they got to the door, Anna appeared with a big smile at which point Charlie said, "I am assuming you are Chaim and Anna Adler. I am Charles Adler and this is my wife Sandra."

"You assume correctly," said Chaim with a grin. "Are we related?" But before Charlie could answer Anna said, "Please, we don't have to stand in the hall. Come in and let us be comfortable. I can tell by your accent that you come from England."

Walking into the foyer of the apartment, Sandra said, "What a magnificent apartment." And handing Anna the flowers, she went on, "These are for you. We thought they were lovely."

"Yes, they are," replied Anna. "Let me put them in a vase and we can have coffee and you can tell us why you are here."

Leading them into the breakfast room that was always set for company (no conversation could be had without coffee and babka or strudel), Anna got down a vase, filled it with water, and set the flowers in the middle of the table. A lot of smiles but not a word was said except to compliment Anna on her ability to put flowers in a vase. How lovely they looked. Sandra offered to help Anna with the cake and coffee and appeared to be more at ease than was Charlie. You got the feeling that he knew he was in the wrong place.

With the coffee poured and the cake on the table, Chaim said, "Now tell us why you are here."

Charlie sat stone faced, played with his napkin, and almost looked as if he were going to cry. "Charlie," Sandra said, "Chaim asked you a question."

Looking up, Charlie blurted out, "You are not my grandparents."

There was a moment of silence. Finally, Anna said, "No, we're not. Why would you think we were?"

In desperation and with tears running down his face, Charlie replied, "It all worked out. The names, the addresses, the ages, it had to be you."

Reaching across the table and putting her hand over Charlie's, Sandra said, "Charlie, start from the beginning. The Adlers cannot possibly know what you are talking about."

Regaining his composure and wiping his eyes with the napkin, Charlie apologized and explained that his father, Irving Adler, the son of Chaim and Anna Adler, had left for England on his honeymoon prior to the German invasion of Poland in 1939. He was then told by his father and mother never to return to Poland, survived the war in England, and a number of years ago hired an agency to try and track down his parents. "Your names, the address on your travel documents, your ages all corresponded. You should be people in your eighties but you're not. The coincidences are so overwhelming; what will I tell my father?"

Chaim and Anna looked at one another in shock. Without saying it they both knew; the Hotel Polski. Getting up from her chair, Anna went over to Charlie and taking his hand in one of hers and Sandra's hand in the other, she said, "Children, drink your coffee and eat your cake. We have a long story to tell you."

Not quite knowing how to begin and with a look on his face that said "What do I need this for?" Chaim said in a quiet and troubled way, "My real name was Itzik Grynshpan and Anna's name was Rosa Feurmann. We were partisans. Anna lived in the woods after her family was taken and she taught the partisans how to make explosives that slowed down the trains to the camps. I lived in the Jewish cemetery on the outskirts of Warsaw after the animals took my family while I was out of the ghetto on a work detail. Anna came to the cemetery and that is where we met, and where we learned about the Hotel Polski."

He then went on to tell them about the Hotel Polski, the sale of exit visas taken from the bodies of Jews who had perished in the Warsaw ghetto, at which point Anna continued. "The strange thing was that those who paid for exit papers did not survive, for the most part, but we, who had nothing, were sent to Palestine in exchange for some Germans interned in Turkey. To this day, no one has been able to figure out what was the purpose of the entire operation."

"Chaim and Anna Adler were the names given to us when we left the Hotel Polski for Palestine," continued Chaim. "We have used them ever since we were given our freedom. We never intended to defraud anyone, nor did we ever think that there would be family who would search for them."

"What a sad and strange story," said Sandra as she wiped tears from her eyes. "Do you have any children?"

"Of course," replied Anna. "We have a son, Sholom, who is a professor in the United States and by coincidence wrote his doctoral dissertation on the Hotel Polski, and we have a daughter, Tamar, who lives here in Israel. We have grandchildren; a rather large family."

"I don't know anyone who ever heard of the Hotel Polski," said Charlie. "Do you know what happened to it? Is it still there?"

"We know it is still there," said Anna, shaking her head knowingly, "and we know that the commandant was sent to prison as a war criminal. That is enough for us. More than that we don't know nor do we try and think about it."

"Then there is no question that my grandparents are dead," said Charlie, with an air of finality. "I will tell your story to my parents when I speak to them tomorrow."

"May I make a suggestion?" interrupted Chaim. "Since I am sure they would have been on the next plane if your grandparents were alive, how about asking them to visit Israel and we can all get together? It would be our pleasure."

"That sounds like a wonderful idea," said Sandra. "What do you think, Charlie?"

"I'll suggest it," responded Charlie, somewhat skeptically. Getting up from his chair and holding his hand out to Sandra, he went on, "I guess our mission is finished and we can start to see Israel. I think it is time to go." Turning to Chaim and Anna, "I thank you for your kindness, your hospitality, and for sharing your story with us. You have been very kind."

And with that they all headed out toward the front door. With handshakes by the men and hugs and kisses by the women, and with the hope that they would see each other again, knowing full well that they wouldn't, Charlie and Sandra headed for the elevator.

Going back to the breakfast room to put the dishes in the dishwasher, Chaim said, "You know Anna, these kids presented a problem. What if there are other Adler relatives who could make a claim against us? I don't know for what and if it turns out that we are not legally married, that could be another complication. Maybe it's time we got married?"

"Maybe it is, Chaim, maybe it is. And maybe then the Hotel Polski will stop haunting us."

CHAPTER SIX

Even though there was a faculty advisor for the school newspaper, it was agreed that unless something was, in his opinion, scurrilous or capable of causing an uproar on campus, he would give the editors free reign over what they published and the opinions that were expressed. Over the years the faculty advisor had to intercede on two prior occasions and in both occasions the matter was resolved amicably.

It was a week before the next issue was due to be published and distributed and for the first time in the history of the university, the faculty advisor called Fr. Gregory and asked for an immediate appointment and it was immediately granted.

As a result of that meeting, Fr. Gregory convened a secret session consisting of Fr. Robert Smith, the Provost, Fr. Juan Carlos, VP for Academic Personnel, and Marie Robinson, General Counsel. This was no breakfast meeting; no coffee, no bagels, no cream cheese.

All three arrived almost simultaneously and found a rather worried looking Fr. Gregory pacing behind his desk. "What's up, Joe?" asked Fr. Smith. "Is someone ill? Has someone died?"

"Please sit and let me tell you what's happened," replied Fr. Gregory. As they all sat down with worried looks on their faces, Fr. Gregory went on. "Sometimes the students in this school give me a pain in the ass. Where they get their information from defies me."

"What are you talking about?" asked Marie. "Why are you so upset?"

"Yesterday I received an emergency call from the faculty advisor of the school newspaper. He had to see me at once. This is the first time this has happened in all the years I have been here. Of course, I told him to come right over, which he did and he told me about the feature story in next week's edition."

Rolling back from his desk, Fr. Gregory stood up and asked, "What do any of you know about Sholom Adler, head of Jewish Studies?"

"A good man," said Fr. Carlos. "I know him well. We've spent many hours together. I have met his wife on a few occasions. She teaches Hebrew at the local Temple and if we ever give the course, maybe she could teach here. Did you know that Hebrew was the first course taught in Harvard?"

"No, I didn't know that," said Marie. "I met Sholom only once at the reception and he seemed like a very nice guy."

"I've spoken with him on a few occasions," said Fr. Smith, the Provost. "I think he's done a remarkable job here at Capernaum. He has nothing to be ashamed of. But what does this meeting have to do with Professor Adler?"

"According to the faculty advisor," replied Fr. Gregory, "the students have uncovered and are prepared to feature the fact that Sholom Adler's father was a Nazi SS Colonel who was convicted of war crimes and did time as a war criminal. Where they got it from, I don't know; can they prove it, I don't know. To me it is an impossibility. I read his doctoral dissertation about some weird hotel in Warsaw where the Germans were selling exit visas. I, personally, interviewed him and I know that Juan here vetted him. I assumed he was born in Palestine, his parents were Holocaust survivors, his father fought in the Israeli War of Independence. How the hell could he be the child of a Nazi war criminal? What a story! The child of a Nazi war criminal heads our Jewish Studies Department. Now you know. I need some good advice." And with that he took his seat.

Not a word was said, as they all looked at one another waiting for someone to speak. Finally, "Can we stop the story?" asked Fr. Smith. "Call the faculty advisor and have him bring in the kids that found out this information, assuming it is true. Adler has a family. Can you imagine what it will be like for his kids if others learn that their father is the child of a Nazi war criminal?"

"And if it's not true," said Marie, "the libel suit to which the university will be subject will be astronomical. Fr. Smith is right. The story must be stopped, right or wrong."

Without a moment's hesitation, Fr. Gregory opened a folder on his desk, found the telephone number he was looking for and made a call. "Roy, this is Joe Gregory. I'm at a meeting dealing with the problem we discussed and I must see the editor of the paper and the kid who wrote the article. By the way, who is the editor this year?....Sidney Kaplan, Jesus Christ, a Jewish kid?....Well anyway, find them, pull them out of class if you have to, and get them over here in the next fifteen minutes. We've got to kill this story, but you don't say anything. Just coming to this office should scare the shit out of them, I hope....Okay, I'll see you soon, and don't forget to bring copies of the article."

Hanging up the phone and turning to the others and shaking his head, Fr. Gregory said, "You know, this is a problem for me from more than one point of view. I am sure there are teachers in colleges and high schools all over the world, and particularly in Germany, who are the children of people who were active Nazis during the war. But we have one who is head of Jewish Studies. However, if properly handled...."

"That is just what I was going to say," interrupted Fr. Carlos. "If properly handled this could be a good human interest story."

"What bothers me most," said Fr. Smith "is Adler's kids. The idea that the world would know that their grandfather was a convicted Nazi war criminal...."

"But isn't that the case with most kids in Germany today?" chimed in Marie.

"But the difference is," replied Fr. Smith, "that's in Germany. There isn't any choice. Some of those children and grandchildren will grow up to be scholars or scientists or artists and the world wouldn't care. But this is different. We must see the article and see the spin that they put on it. Will it bring discredit to the school?"

"We are all assuming that this is true," said Fr. Gregory, "and how it got past us also bothers me. Adler is still the most qualified candidate, wouldn't you say, Juan?"

As Fr. Carlos was about to respond there was a knock on the door, the door opened, and in came Roy Black, the faculty advisor and professor of English literature, followed by Sidney Kaplan, the editor of the paper, and Lauren Tyler, a cute little co-ed, the author of the article, whose skirt was a little too short for a meeting with Fr. Gregory.

Rising from his chair, Fr. Gregory welcomed them, Roy introduced the students to the others, chairs were moved around to make room for everybody, and when everybody was seated Fr. Gregory, speaking to the students, said "I am sorry if Professor Black had to take you out of class, but we have a problem that we have to talk about and resolve at once." Without a moment's hesitation, he went right on, "My office has been informed of the content of the lead article in this month's school paper about Professor Adler. Before we even read the article, which I am assuming someone has brought with them, I want you to know that in all my years as head of this institution I have never interfered with the publication of a single article, but this is different. You are treading on thin ice. If anything in this article is not true or is subject to interpretation, this school may face a mighty lawsuit, which, need I tell you, we do not need. That is why Ms. Robinson, General Counsel for the school, is here. And there is also the social implications, the family implications, and the implications to the school that have to be considered. May we see the article?"

Professor Black distributed copies to the others and there was silence as they all sat and read. Sidney and Lauren looked around the room and then at each other, both shrugging their shoulders and grimacing as if to say, "Boy, we are in for it."

As each one finished reading, they handed the article back to Professor Black who put them into a folder in his briefcase. Keeping his copy on his desk and turning his attention to the students, Fr. Gregory asked, "Where did this information come from?"

"It started off with me," said Sidney. "When I was a freshman, I thought it kind of strange that a Catholic institution should have a Jewish Studies Department. But what do I know?" he said with a shrug. "I took some courses with Professor Adler over the years and in conversation he let it be known that his family were Holocaust survivors and mentioned that his dissertation was on the Hotel Polski. I have an uncle who is a Holocaust survivor and I always had an interest in the subject. I became active in the school paper and this year, my senior year, I became the editor. So, I went on the internet and when I looked up Hotel Polski I learned that there were hundreds of them in Poland because all it means is Polish hotel. I narrowed my search and finally got to what he was talking about, and since his dissertation was published, I was able to read it."

"The business about selling false ID's by the Germans got to me and it occurred to me that if his family got out of the Polski then their names must be false. So, I gave Lauren here an assignment to see what she could dig up. She came up with this info about Colonel Hauptmann's trial and Professor Adler's mother being called to testify and then one thing led to another. Hey, Fr. Gregory, Sholom is a good guy. I don't want to cause him any trouble, but you have to admit, it is a hell of a story."

"And there's even more," said Lauren. "Do you know that Professor Adler has a half sister who is a professor at the university in Dusseldorf and that he inherited the colonel's estate? She got nothing."

Pushing his glasses down to the end of his nose and looking over them at Lauren, Fr. Gregory responded with a long drawn out "Noooo, we didn't know that." Turning to Fr. Carlos he said, "Juan,

I think we ought to let these kids do our vetting in the future. They obviously do a hell of a lot better job than we do."

"It appears that you're right, Joe," said Fr. Carlos with a grin. "But what do you want to do?"

Looking directly at the students and Professor Black, and with a wave of his finger, he replied, "I do not want this information to come out until I authorize it. I have never interfered with the school paper or what it published even though I did not always agree with what I read, but this is different, this is special, this is personal. To be honest with you, I don't know how this will resolve itself but it must do so without any negative publicity against the school or Professor Adler. I will speak with him and give the matter thought. I will then get back to you. Find another lead article for this month's paper."

Roy Black got up from his seat, as did Lauren, but Sidney Kaplan did not move.

"Father Gregory," he said. "This is an honest piece of news. Lauren did a lot of work in uncovering this information. Why are you blackballing it?"

Seeing that this discussion was going to go on, Professor Black and Lauren sat down again as Fr. Gregory took off his glasses and with a look of annoyance at the fact that his instructions were not being followed but with a sense of admiration for this young man who stuck to his guns. He looked at Sidney and asked, "Mr. Kaplan, what does your father do for a living?"

"He's head of a large accounting firm here in the city and, as a matter of fact, he asked me to ask you, if I ever had the chance, that if you were thinking of changing accounting firms he would like to be considered."

"Mind your manners, young man," growled Professor Black. "Do you think this is a joke?"

"That's okay, Joe," said Fr. Gregory, with a laugh. "Who knows when we'll need a new accountant?" Turning to Sidney, he went on, "Tell your father I appreciate his offer and will take it under consideration, but now I have to ask you a question. Before engaging your father or his firm do you not think it would be proper to investigate the people to whom I would be entrusting private or confidential information?"

"I guess so," replied Sidney.

"And guess what vetting your father turned up?" asked Fr. Gregory. Without waiting for any further reply, he went on, "Do you know what Murder Incorporated was?"

Shaking his head no, Fr. Gregory looked at Lauren who was also shaking her head no.

"It was the Jewish Mafia, closely associated with the Italian Mafia. They were in the business of murder, bootlegging, prostitution, money lending, etc. Our investigation showed that your father's tuition in college and graduate school was paid by Murder Incorporated where he was accused of having killed at least two people and, as a collector for usurious loans, was also a knee breaker. This report was somehow leaked to a local newspaper and it made the headlines. You're an adult and you may think this is cool, as you young people say, but how about your younger siblings? Do you think they would have any friends or be invited to anyone's house if their parents knew what your father had done? So, Mr. Kaplan, draw a parallel. What would your investigation do to Professor Adler's children? I am a great respecter of freedom of the press, but to make a lousy metaphor, your right to swing your fist has to stop where my nose begins. Do you get it?

Getting up from his chair, Sidney said, "Yes sir, I get it. I'm not quite sure it is the same, but you're the boss. Deem the story killed."

"Thank you, Mr. Kaplan," said Fr. Gregory as Professor Black and Lauren got up from their chairs. "And young lady," he went on with a smile, "in the future, while on campus, the skirt could be a bit longer. Your legs will be just as pretty."

"Oh, yes sir," said Lauren with an embarrassed laugh. "I would not have worn this if I knew I was going to see you today. I apologize."

And without letting anything more be said, Joe Black opened the door to the office and waving goodbye to the others, issued the kids out.

After they left no one said a word. Finally Fr. Smith, the Provost, spoke up, "We should have called in the head of the drama department. This would make a helluva play."

"Good theater or bad," said Marie, "what are you going to do?"

Frowning, Fr. Gregory said, "The kid with the short skirt bugged me when she said that Adler has a half sister teaching at Dusseldorf. I spoke to the head of Jewish Studies there; he recommended Adler. I wonder if he knows the half sister and what else he knows that he didn't tell me. I have to talk to him again."

Relaxing and with a sigh, he went on, "Okay guys, enough drama for one morning. You may be sure that no resolution will be made without consultation. I will be in touch. Now, back to work."

CHAPTER SEVEN

Charlie and Sandra returned home and with great sadness repeated the result of their visit with the Adlers. Shaking his head, knowingly, Irving said, "It's what I expected."

The following evening, Sandra's parents insisted on dinner at their home and with the whole family together Charlie and Sandra told them all about Israel, their sightseeing, floating in the Dead Sea, and finally got around to the story of their visit with the Adlers.

After listening attentively, Sandra's father Jack said, "There is something that doesn't make sense."

"What did I miss?" asked Irving. "I've heard the story twice."

Looking around and shaking his head, Jack replied, "Reparations." Turning to Irving he went on. "Irv, you told me that your parents had been wealthy, you had art and antiques in your home, your father owned a factory and employed lots of people. Am I right?"

"Yeah, you're right. So where are you going with this?"

"I'm no expert," continued Sandra's father, "but I know there are lawyers that specialize in this field. The German government is paying reparations for property taken and stolen from Jews in occupied countries. Now follow me. If you, Irv, were to make a claim for property in Warsaw you would tell them that your parents' names were Chaim and Anna Adler. They would investigate and tell you that Chaim and

Anna Adler are alive and well, living in Israel. They could make the claim on their own behalf. But we know that your parents are dead and these people got their identities through this Hotel Polski business. I'm not sure I understand it and I am quite sure that these people have no idea as to the identity of the people whose names they were given, but there must be a way to work this out."

"Hey, Jack," said Irving. "You're one smart fella. None of this would have occurred to me. Do any of the lawyers in your office have any knowledge about this subject? Because from what you say it is more than just an application for reparations. In some manner or means these people have to be forced to give up their names, would you not say?"

"Now I'm just talking without any real knowledge. I will check with some of the other solicitors in my office and see if they can refer me to someone. But I'm thinking about a lawsuit against the German government."

"Are you kidding?" Charlie chimed in. "The German government? On what basis?"

"The Adlers in Israel got their identities through an ill-conceived wartime plan of the German government. To learn more about that I have to ask Sara for a favor." Turning to her, "You are still at the university, are you not?"

Without saying a word and looking questionably at Charlie's father-in-law, she nodded her head in agreement.

Now turning to Sandra, he asked, "Did the Adlers in Israel not tell you that their son was named Sholom, and he was a professor at a university in the United States and he wrote his doctoral dissertation on the Hotel Polski?"

"That's what they told us," she replied.

Turning back to Sara, "Please find time to go to the library and see if they can help you find a copy of his dissertation. I am assuming it was published since that would have been necessary for him to get a professorship in America. His dissertation would be the most informative piece of information that we could find about the Hotel and what went on there."

"Okay," said Charlie, hesitantly. "What's next?"

"What's next is something that I have to do," answered Jack. Looking around at everyone, he said, "I have to find out where the records of war crime trials are stored." Turning specifically to Charlie he went on, "You said that the Adlers told you that the commandant of the hotel was tried as a war criminal. If so, I want to read the judges' decision that resulted in his imprisonment. Their decision will review what took place at the Hotel and from that we can conclude that the German government was responsible for his war crimes. That could be the basis for an action against the German government."

"Dad," replied Charlie. "You're the lawyer, not me, but would you not have to go to Germany or Poland to get jurisdiction?"

"Maybe," responded Jack. "But I think we can get jurisdiction here in England."

"Okay, King Solomon," said Irving with a laugh. "How would that be possible?"

"I'm willing to bet that one of the judges at the war crimes trial was an Englishman," answered Jack. "I think that might do it."

At which point Sandra got up from her chair and with a very determined look said, "Let's just stop this. Reparations or not, you're all getting carried away with yourselves."

"Uh-oh," said Charlie. "Something's not right. When Sandra gets that look on her face we're in for it."

"Don't make jokes," said Sandra. "Stop and think of what you're doing. If you sue the government you have to name Chaim and Anna Adler. After all, you want them to give up their identities of the last 30 or more years, as well. Isn't that right, Dad?"

"I assume so," said Jack.

"And if you do," Sandra went on. "You are going to make these people relive the horrors of the Holocaust, the destruction of the Warsaw ghetto, their imprisonment in the Polski, as well as their salvation under an assumed identity so that you can get money for some artwork or factory in Poland. Dad," she said, looking at Irving, "I don't mean to disrespect your parents, or you, for that matter, but is that something you would do? After all, they didn't choose their new names. It was part of the awful plan that the Nazis were engaged in." Turning to her father, she went on, "Come up with another idea, Pop. This one will never happen."

Having sat quietly, never saying a word or expressing an opinion, Fannie, Charlie's mother, looked at Sandra and said, "Sandra, darling, you know why I love you, because you are a mentsch, a person with feeling for others." Turning to Jack and to Irving, "Forget it, my dears. We are not going to create any more hardship for these people. They have been through enough. I'm not saying I would not like to get reparations from the German government. After all, my parents were killed by those bastards, as well. Jack, do your research and perhaps you can talk to others who are more familiar with the entire subject and see if they could come up with a better idea. But suing the Adlers is just not going to happen."

At which point Sandra and her mother applauded Fannie's little speech. Turning to Irving, Jack said with a laugh, "Irv, are you going to let your wife talk to you that way?"

Getting up from his chair and hugging Fannie, he replied, "She's been doing it for more than forty years. How can I stop her?" Turning to the others he said, "Jack, Sylvia, it's always wonderful being with you. It's late and it's time to go. If everyone will do their homework, maybe the next time we get together we will have a better answer."

And with hugs and kisses the evening ended.

CHAPTER EIGHT

Over the course of time Sholom and Rena had visitors from Israel and they always made it a practice to introduce them to Fr. Gregory. The first ones to come were Rena's parents and although they treated Fr. Gregory with the utmost respect, they were quite perturbed by their grandchildren living in such a Catholic atmosphere.

The next visitors were Sholom's sister Tamar and her husband Moshe. They kidded Sholom and Rena about the crosses in every classroom, even the ones in which he taught Jewish Studies. Fr. Gregory, on the other hand, found their visit to be very informative. Since Moshe and Tamar had lived a good part of their life on a kibbutz* and after leaving the kibbutz Moshe was now a representative of large farming cooperative, Fr. Gregory was quite fascinated by kibbutz living and farming in general, subjects about which he knew very little.

It was a big event when Sholom's half brother, Yossie, and his wife came to visit. It was a quiet morning for Fr. Gregory as he sat at his desk, drank his coffee, and read the local newspaper. Sholom had asked if he could bring over some of his family for a visit and Fr. Gregory was more than polite and expected them about 11.

Punctual as always, Sholom showed up at exactly 11 accompanied by two others who he introduced as Fr. Josef Feurmann, his brother,

---

* Collective farm

and his brother's wife, Professor Sheva Feurmann. With a warm handshake to both and a big grin Fr. Gregory asked, "Sholom, what are you a wise guy? Fr. Feurmann and his wife? Oh, I see. Your brother is a Protestant minister?"

As all the others stood with big grins on their faces, Fr. Gregory waved his finger at Sholom and said, "I'll get to you later. Is this one of your Israeli jokes?" Then turning to Sheva he went on, "but first let me talk to Professor Feurmann. Please, let us sit down; we have so much to talk about."

And as they all took their seats Fr. Gregory turned his attention to Sheva and said, "Sheva, I am unfamiliar with the name. Also, what is your teaching specialty?"

"Fr. Gregory," replied Sheva, "we have heard so much about you. It is so good to finally meet you. As to the second question, I teach Jewish Biblical History at the same university as Fr. Feurmann. As to where we met, we both worked at a social service agency and at a conference where we both spoke, the program had our degrees listed, mine in history, as well as Fr. Feurmann's background. After our talk we were approached by a gentleman who asked us if we would like to teach at the university level. So, we left the agency and became professors. Not full professors, at first, but we worked our way up" And with that she gave her husband a pat on his arm. "Sheva is short for Bathsheva. Remember David and Bathsheva? Well, he didn't pluck me off a rooftop, but he did win my heart."

"Of course, I did not make the association." Turning his attention to Sholom, he said, "Okay, my learned scholar, who is this guy?" he asked, turning to Yossie.

At which point Sholom got up from his chair and going to the back of his brother's chair, he put his arms around his brother and replied, "You remember I told you I had a brother Yossie? Well, this is Yossie."

With a grim look, Fr. Gregory asked, "So, what's with the Fr. Feurmann business?"

Getting up from her chair, Sheva said, "With all due respect, Fr. Gregory, I know where this is going. I've heard it a hundred times. Sholom promised to show us around the campus and this is the time to leave you two guys alone. Will you excuse us?"

"Of course," said Fr. Gregory, "but let's have lunch at the school cafeteria. Sholom, call Rena and tell her to join us, if she can, at let's say, twelve-thirty." And as an afterthought he went on, "I love Rena. Her knowledge of Sephardic customs is fascinating."

Sheva walked over to Yossie and gave him a peck on the cheek as he stood up, and he and Fr. Gregory escorted Sholom and Sheva to the door and shook hands with them as Fr. Gregory said to his secretary, "Call the cafeteria and tell them to have a table for six for me in a quiet corner at twelve-thirty and bring in a pot of coffee for my guest and myself."

Yossie returned to his chair while Fr. Gregory pulled up a chair alongside of him and said, "Okay, Yossie, what's this all about?"

With a serious look on his face Yossie asked, "Father, have you ever been to Warsaw?"

"Many, many years ago. Maybe fifteen or twenty. There was a convocation of educators in Rome at which I spoke and then we all went in different directions. I and a few others went to Warsaw. But before we go any further," he went on as his secretary brought in the coffee and a cup for Yossie, "your name is Josef and my name is Joseph. So, if you're Yossie, why can't I be Yossie?"

"Why not?" said Yossie as he accepted a cup of coffee from the secretary, with thanks. "But now think back. When you were in Warsaw did you ever have occasion to go to St. Jacek's?"

"Yes, I did. It was a most beautiful church. And it had plaques of Polish partisans. I remember it well."

"Do you remember the pastor?"

With that Fr. Gregory put down his cup and went to a book case at the side of the room. "I keep a diary of all my travels. Let me find it." Searching for a few minutes he looked up and said, "I found it, and yes, here it is. St. Jacek's. The pastor was…" looking over at Yossie and shaking his head in disbelief he said, "Fr. Josef Feurmann. Yossie, it was you?"

"Yes, Yossie, it was me. I thought you looked familiar when I came into the room. I didn't recall from where, but now I do."

"Okay, from one Yossie to another. Now you must tell me the story."

And with that Yossie launched into the story of his escape from the Nazis, his having been taken in by a lovely Polish family, of being educated in Catholic school, being sent to the Seminary, and ultimately becoming the second in command at St. Jacek's and upon the death of the priest taking responsibility for the running of the church. The story went on with Sholom doing research on the Hotel Polski and being sent to the church because of the plaques of the partisans, finding him strictly by chance and remembering that his mother's name had been Feurmann, asking some very deliberate questions until they both agreed that they were, indeed, half brothers.

He went on to relate that his mother and Chaim were on the next plane to Warsaw and you can imagine her reaction when she saw him. "My father, and my baby brother, were killed by the Nazis. Believe it or not, I came to Israel for Sholom's wedding to Rena and showed up in my priestly whites and blessed them under the canopy. You can't believe the reaction when a priest shows up at a Jewish wedding. Later on I met his half sister in Dusseldorf and then in Israel after her father, the Nazi colonel, died. She was a piece of work. She tried to get me into bed and the only way I got out of it was to show up in priestly garb and assure her it was not a costume."

During the entire telling of the story, Fr. Gregory sat shaking his head in disbelief. And then he asked, "So, when did you decide to give it up?"

Pouring fresh coffee for himself, Yossie went on, "Fr. Gregory, Yossie, this is the closest that I've come to a confession in many years. I need not say, Forgive me Father for I have sinned, because I have not sinned, but not a day went by in my life as a Catholic and as a priest

that I did not think of myself as a little Jewish boy who went to cheder.*
I never got to bar mitzvah, the Germans saw to that, and by the time
I was thirteen I was in Catholic school. It was not like a stone in my
shoe but just a few grains of sand. The reminder of who I was was always there. But Yossie, you know and you can understand, as a priest
I was alone. I had a Polish brother with whom I had been brought up
who is also a priest and when I told him I was leaving the priesthood I
was shocked at how well he took it. How he understood me. Now I
had a mother, a family, people who loved me for me. The joy on their
faces when I would come to Israel for a visit was indescribable. This
was life, this was love, this was family. I came to the conclusion that
the itinerant Jewish rabbi that was crucified didn't offer me any of that.
So, I gave up a wonderful congregation, I gave up the priesthood,
moved to be with my family, and now I'm surrounded with all the
things that are meaningful to me, including a wife.

Coffee was sipped and nothing more was said. Finally, Fr. Gregory spoke up. "Yossie, I know what you mean and I don't know what
you mean. Probably because if I left the priesthood I wouldn't know
where to go or what to do. I suppose I could teach. I have family here
and there but we are not very close. Loving, but not very close. The
thing that gets me is that I don't feel overly religious anymore. Yes, I
go to services on Sunday and then watch football in the afternoon. I
am now a businessman who wears a clerical collar. Running this institution is a big responsibility; big staff, big payroll, lots of students,
but very little Catholicism. Yossie, you've given me a lot to think about
but will you do one thing for me? I would love for you to speak to the
faculty. Your story is so unbelievable. It must be shared."

"But it is not a story that furthers the church. What I didn't have
and what, perhaps, others do not have caused me to renounce the
faith. No one will let me stop the story without asking what happened
and why am I not still a priest. I will, of course, do what you ask, but
please think about it. Would it have the effect that you want?"

---

* Jewish religious school

"Yes, I see your point. Let me think about it but let us get together again before you leave. Now a brisk walk to the cafeteria and some lunch. This has been quite a morning for me."

But think about it he did and Fr. Gregory again asked Yossie to speak to which Yossie agreed. There was quite a crowd both of priests and lay teachers. Yossie was wise enough to stress the early years leading up to his return to his family in Israel and the audience was most sympathetic to the story of a little Jewish boy on his way to the gas chamber who escaped the Nazis and grew up to be the priest in charge of a major church is Warsaw.

But, needless to say, when the questions and answers came the issue of his leaving the priesthood was one that had to be answered. Yossie handled it admirable. He spoke of the duality of the person, not only in body but in soul. Although the small flame of his Jewishness burned in him when he was a priest, his comfort and ease at being a speaker at the Catholic institution like Capernaum brought him back to his Catholic upbringing.

The audience accepted his answer and greeted him with love and affection during the social part of the evening following his talk. Sholom, Rena and Sheva were proud of him and Sholom commented that Yossie would make a good politician. Fr. Gregory couldn't stop thanking him and basked in the flow of the congratulations he received for having obtained the services of such an interesting speaker.

Although Sholom stayed in touch with Chaim both by mail and by phone, and Rena sent pictures of the children to both sets of grandparents, Chaim and Anna never visited.

CHAPTER NINE

The message light flashed anxiously on Fr. Gregory's telephone. He got into his office at the usual time and looking at the flashing light said to himself, "For God's sake, it is only eight o'clock in the morning. Who the hell would call me in the middle of the night?"

His secretary would not be in for another half hour; she made the coffee and brought in breakfast from the school cafeteria. "So, whatever it is, they can wait," said Fr. Gregory to himself, as he sat down at his desk and looked at his schedule for the day. The flashing light, however, was relentless and with great annoyance as expressed in two words, "Oh, shit," he picked up the phone.

"Joe, it's Roy Black. The Sholom story has been leaked. Not by the kids that were in your office. They swear that it wasn't them. Others knew the story and for all I know they may have sold the story because it has appeared internationally. I don't know who picked it up but it might have been one of the wire services. Please call me and tell me what you want done."

Hanging up the phone Fr. Gregory sat and stared off into space thinking, "I hope she brings a bagel and cream cheese with my coffee." Shaking his head in both anger and annoyance, he went to his files and searched for the Sholom Adler file. Finding it, he sat down at his desk, thumbed through it until he came to the name Rafi Kremer, University of Dusseldof, Germany and a telephone number. Thinking to himself, "It should be in the middle of the afternoon in Germany", he dialed the number and after three rings it was answered by in German, by a woman.

"Professor Bernshtien, Jewish studies."

"Professor Bernshtein, where is Professor Kremer?" inquired Fr. Gregory.

"Who is calling?", asked the woman.

"This is Father Gregory from Capernaum Catholic University in the United States."

"Ach, ja", answered the woman. "Father Gregory. I recall speaking with you. But Professor Kremer is no longer here. He has taken a position with another university some many months ago.

"Do you know where I can reach him?"

"I do, but I cannot give out that information. If you will give me your number I will try and reach him and tell him you have called. He can then reach you. Is there, perhaps anything I can do to help you?"

With a sense of frustration, Fr. Gregory shook his head and asked, "Did you know Sholom Adler?"

"I did not know him, but I know that he and Professor Kremer spoke on a number of occasions. Is there a problem with Professor Adler?"

"Did you know that his father was a Nazi Colonel and did time in prison for war crimes?"

"No, I did not know that, but does that make a difference?"

"I would like to know why Professor Kremer did not tell me that? It might not make a difference in Germany but in America it might make a big difference."

"I am sorry I can not help you, but Father, many of the teachers and professors here in Germany had fathers or grandfathers who were members of the Nazi party. If he is a good teacher, what difference does it make? I, too, am a Catholic and, if I may, may I tell you a story in confidence which you may find relevant?"

"Yes, of course, my dear, please", responded Fr, Gregory with growing frustration.

"My father was killed in the war and I now live with my mother." And with a giggle she went on, "I hope to be married soon and to move out, but that is not my story. I have been with Jewish Studies since the program began and when I told my mother that I was the secretary to the professor of Jewish Studies she became angry and screamed at me, "Your father died fighting the Jews and now you work for them?"

"And I asked, "Fighting the Jews?", her answer was "That is that the war was all about." So you see Father, I am not sure that I know why I told you this story, but in my mind I see some sort of relationship between your story and my story." And with a sigh, "Perhaps not."

"Perhaps there is", said Fr, Gregory, in a calmer state of mind. Perhaps there is. Let me think about it. And by the way, what is your name, my dear?"

"Ursula."

"Well, Ursula, I thank you for this little chat and please tell Professor Kremer, when you speak to him, that I called. It is not necessary for him to call back."

"It was my pleasure to speak to you," responded Ursula and with that they hung up.

The next call was to Sholom, at home. For as unnerved as Fr. Gregory was, that's how calm Sholom was when he was told that Fr. Gregory wanted to see him in his office as soon as possible. They agreed to meet at 9:30.

With a sigh of great relief, Fr. Gregory heard the door open and knew it was his secretary and coffee would soon be at hand. She greeted him happily, and was praised for bringing in a bagel and a shmear, but was told before making coffee, call Fr. Juan Carlos and Marie Robinson and see if they can be here at 9:30.

They all showed up on time and greeted each other without knowledge of what was coming. When everybody was seated and had their coffee, Fr. Gregory started the meeting by addressing Sholom.

"Sholom", he said. "Did you know that Rafi Kremer is no longer in Dusseldorf?"

"No, I didn't. How did you find out?"

"I called to speak to him and have a long talk with his secretary. She wouldn't tell me where he'd gone."

"Maybe if I called she'd tell me. Is there a problem?"

And with that, the meeting really began. The issue was raised, they spoke of the students who had uncovered the issue, and the discussion that took place was only between Sholom and Fr. Gregory. The others sat as if they were watching a tennis match.

In that Sholom found no problem in acknowledging the identify of his biological father, Fr. Gregory started to feel that maybe this was, in fact, a tempest in a teapot.

"One last question," said Fr. Gregory. "Sholom, what do you want me to tell Roy Black with regard to the story?"

Without hesitation, Sholom replied. "It is my hope that you can kill the story. Not because I am ashamed of my parentage or anything like that. It's my kids. I don't want them subjected to any misunderstanding. I assume the time will come when I have to tell them that their grandparents were prisoners, that their grandmother had a relationship with the commandant, but they're too young. I have avoided it up till now and I would like to keep avoiding it. Does that make sense?"

Everyone understood and agreed. Goodbyes were said and all that was left was for Fr. Gregory to call Roy Black, which he did when the others left the room.

"Roy, Fr. Gregory. Do not publish the story. Thank the kids for their investigative journalism and since they know that the story was leaked, the general consensus of opinion is that it will be forgotten by tomorrow. Sholom wants it killed on behalf of his children and I can't say I blame him."

After some small talk it was agreed. Fr. Gregory hung up the phone with a shrug, as if to say, "Maybe I don't understand what is going on in the world today, but, after all, who am I?"

CHAPTER TEN

Sholom headed straight back to his house. Both his and Rena's classes were in the afternoon and he knew that she would still be home. When he walked in Rena took one look at him and knew something was wrong.

"What was the meeting about and why are you so upset?" she asked.

"You won't believe it," he replied. "Somewhere during my lectures I mentioned that my dissertation was on the Hotel Polski and I assume I told them what went on there. I've spoken about it many times and never thought anymore about it. Well one of these nosey kids decided to investigate not only the Hotel Polski but me as well and was about to publish an article in the school newspaper that my father was a Nazi SS Colonel. Roy Black, an English professor, I don't think you know him, who is the faculty advisor to the newspaper called Fr. Gregory, who asked Roy to call in the kids who wrote the article and they all met, and it was agreed that they would kill the story. Fr. Gregory also called Rafi Kremer in Dusseldorf and was obviously pissed that Rafi didn't tell him about all of this and about Liese, to which Fr. Gregory told me that Rafi's answer was that half the professors in Germany have fathers who were Nazi officers. To make matters worse, just today it was learned that the story was leaked to some world-wide press service and now I'm a celebrity. I understand Rafi's answer but Germany isn't the US. Can you believe it? Fr. Gregory already met with counsel and was preparing to defend a lawsuit. I don't know who he thought was going to sue him," he shrugged in disgust. "Maybe me."

"Do you know if anybody else has seen the story?"

"I don't know anything more than I've told you. We must protect the kids. They are too young to learn who their safta* was screwing while she was a prisoner, but I guess…"

"Sholom, stop that!" Rena interrupted. "Yes, the children have to be protected, but it's time you quit your irrational thinking. You weren't there and if Chaim can live with it then you can live with it."

Waving off Rena's remark, Sholom continued, "What I was going to say is that I will have to call my father and tell him what is happening. It is too late now; he will be home. I'll call him in the morning at the store and we can talk without my mother walking in on the conversation." Throwing his arms in the air and with great annoyance, he turned from Rena and said to no one in particular, "When will this ever come to an end?" Turning back to Rena he shook his head as if in agreement. "That is the only thing in which I sympathize with my mother. This damn thing never seems to end."

In a quiet and comforting voice, with a smile on her face, Rena said, "Listen, celebrity, I know what makes you feel better. Since I'm not dressed yet and we still have an hour let's go upstairs and then you can take me to breakfast."

With a look of deep admiration on his face, Sholom replied, "You are such a wise woman, Rena." And off they went.

The next morning Sholom called his father in the store and, as always, was greeted with love and loads of questions about the children, Rena, what's happening at school, are Jewish Studies successful, you're not

---

*Grandmother

becoming a Catholic in that environment are you, and on and on. Sholom was used to the questions and he answered everything in good humor. As far as his conversion was concerned he said, "Wouldn't that be a thing. Yossi, a Catholic priest becoming a Jew and me, a Jewish kid becoming a Catholic. The world is crazy enough as is."

Turning serious, Chaim asked, "So what's up? Is there a problem?"

"Let's hope not." And with that Sholom went through the entire story and explained that it was possible that there might be some mention, as a human interest story, in the papers in Israel. He was sorry that he had to put the burden on Chaim, but he thought it was only right that Chaim break it to eema* as gently as possible. "Try and make as little of it as you can," Sholom said. "We know how eema gets when this subject is brought up."

Chaim acknowledged the problem and thanked Sholom for giving him a heads up. Again, with love and long distance kisses, they said goodbye and promised to be in touch.

---

*Mother

CHAPTER ELEVEN

Nothing more was said about the Adlers or the Hotel Polski until about two weeks after the dinner at which they had all been together and Sandra made her big speech.

Jack called Irving at his office saying he didn't want to bring up the subject at the upcoming Shabbos dinner, but he had learned where the transcripts of the Colonel's trial were stored. "I doubt if I can get to it, though," said Jack. "You need a reason and clearance to be entitled to read it and you would have to go to a small town in Germany. It cannot be copied or allowed to leave the premises, so I guess we will have to rely on the doctoral dissertation, if Sara was able to get it."

"I don't know," replied Irving. "She never mentioned it again. I wonder why. Should I ask her?"

"If you do, do it quietly. I don't want to make a fuss and I don't want any family arguments. This Friday it's at our house. We can talk privately."

And with a few more "How's this one, and how's that one," and the latest Jewish joke, they hung up.

Irving asked Sara and was told that she had gotten the dissertation, had read it, thought it quite unusual in describing what went on at the Hotel Polski, but did not bring it up because if the matter was to go away, why talk about it. Irving kissed her for being insightful and asked if he could read it before they went to Jack and Sylvia's on Friday night. He promised not to say anything, and asked if it was okay to share the material with Jack, to which she gave her consent.

Keeping a copy for himself, Irving had a messenger deliver the original to Jack and called him to tell him it was coming. Irving again indicated he had no idea where any of this was going but would wait until Friday and then the two of them would sneak away into Jack's den before they lit the candles.

And that's just what they did. It was Jack's suggestion that he try and get the name of the best lawyers in town, who were specializing in the field of reparations, and he would make an appointment. "We'll take the dissertation to the lawyer, explain the entire situation as best as we understand it, see if the lawyer has any knowledge of the Hotel Polski and what went on there, and see what suggestion the lawyer can make as to how to solve the problem." Jack also suggested that Irving have a list of property including not only the real estate but the artwork and the antiques, as best as he could remember. In this way, if the lawyer saw that there was serious money to be gotten if he pursued the matter, his interest would be that much greater.

Irving agreed and understood that this might cost a pound or two for the consultation, and expressed his willingness to follow Jack's advice. Hearing their names called by the wives and knowing it was time for Shabbos dinner the men nodded to one another in agreement, promised to be in touch, shook hands, and wished each other a "Gut Shabbos" and went out to join the family.

CHAPTER TWELVE

Jack found the one firm in London that represented people who were entitled to reparations, made an appointment claiming that he had a client in a very unusual situation, and he and Irving met with counsel in his chambers. Neither Jack nor Irving said a word to anyone else, in either family, that they were pursuing this.

Counsel's chambers were impressive as was Lord Mayer Greenspan, chief counsel. When Irving heard his name he commented to counsel that in the story that he was about to tell him there was a very important player whose name was originally Grynshpan and he came from Warsaw.

"I, too, came from Warsaw as a child. My parents got out in August of '39, just before the invasion. But then again, Grynshpan was not an unusual name."

Before starting, Jack and Irving were offered tea or a soft drink, which they both declined. And now Irving started the story, taking his facts from that which he had heard from Charlie and Sandra and making reference to Sholom's dissertation, which he had brought with him. Asking that he be allowed to make a copy of the dissertation, Lord Greenspan admitted that he had never heard of the Hotel Polski, knew nothing about the sale of visas, and acknowledged that this entire story was, indeed, strange and provoking. Without asking, Lord

Greenspan now ordered tea and soft drinks be brought for everyone, told his secretary not to disturb him, and said he would be with these gentlemen for another hour or so.

He then inquired of Irving as to the source of his knowledge about the Adlers living in Israel. Irving told him about having hired a firm to try and locate any survivors. It took a couple of years and they came up with the Adlers. I then sent Charlie and Sandra to Israel with the hope that they may have been my parents and Charlie's grandparents. If so, we would be on the next plane. All the statistics fit, but the people were not nearly the right age and when they learned why the kids had come to see them, the Adlers told them the whole story about the Hotel, the sale of visas, and where they got their names. Sholom is their son and the facts contained in the dissertation line up perfectly with what the kids were told.

Jack then told Lord Greenspan that Sholom was a professor of Jewish Studies at a Catholic University in the United States and also told him about the court martial and where the transcript was kept. Lord Greenspan acknowledged that he knew of the storage of the transcripts in Ludwigsburg and agreed that although the transcript might be the icing on the cake, it was not really necessary as long as the Adlers were alive, and perhaps others who could testify as to what went on at the Hotel.

Before going any further, Irving then told Lord Greenspan that Jack wasn't just his attorney but that Jack's daughter was married to his son and that she was strongly protesting any further involvement in this matter. She felt that the Adlers had gone through enough, living through the war and surviving the Warsaw ghetto uprising, and we should not put them through a repetition of those years for a few pounds.

"I must assume that you disagree with her or else why would you be here?" asked Lord Greenspan. "Am I correct?"

Both Irving and Jack heaved a sign and shook their heads as Irving said, "I agree with her but the question is, for which I am aware that

I have to pay for your time, is there any other way to do this? I agree that I cannot imagine what these people lived through, but by the same token, I am not comfortable with people living with the name of my parents. If they did some research could they not make a claim for reparations in the name of my parents? Please, Lord Greenspan, I am sure they would never do this. All they want is to live their life out in peace and quiet in Israel. The gentleman, Chaim Adler, whose name was Itzik Grynshpan, is a very successful haberdasher in Tel Aviv, they have other children and grandchildren. I am terribly confused. We have not told any members of our families that we are here. What are your thoughts?"

With a smile, Lord Greenspan relied, "That's a coincidence. My family was in the clothing and haberdashery business in Warsaw." Then rising, as if to say the meeting is over, Lord Greenspan went on, "Let me think about this and confer with my colleagues. The entire matter is intriguing and I must see whether any of the other fellows have heard of the Hotel Polski." Turning to Jack, he said, "I will be in touch with you in a few days and we will get together again. I am not prepared to walk away from this."

Shaking hands with Irving and Jack, Lord Greenspan opened the door to his office and accompanied the men to the office waiting room. Again, with handshakes and we'll be in touch, they left the office.

CHAPTER THIRTEEN

Although they wouldn't admit it, Charlie and Sandra's visit caused Anna and Chaim concern. The questions they asked and the issues they raised had never occurred to them. Itzik Grynshpan and Rosa Feurmann, were living, to the best of their knowledge, under names of people who had died in the Holocaust. No one had ever made an issue about it.

When they, and Shimon and his wife, and the others, were released from the Polski and ended up in Palestine in exchange for some Germans that had been imprisoned by the Turks, their lives were saved, and they were forever to be known as Chaim and Anna Adler. Who could expect this?

And how about Shimon Cohen? After all, he was now a high-ranking government official, a friend of the Prime Minister, and was still using the name that Col. Hauptmann had given him when he left the Hotel. What a shock it would be if someone came along and called him Berel Rabinowitz, his original name. But, as has been the case in the past, when what appeared to be a problem with no immediate solution, they decided to call Shimon.

As always, Shimon was happy to see them and welcomed them into his office. They laughed, they reminisced, they inquired of one another's families and their mutual friends while drinking coffee and eating babka, until Shimon said, "So tell me, what is the problem?"

Shimon was quite surprised when Chaim told him it is a problem that can affect him as well. They then related the story of Charlie's and Sandra's visit, who they were, that they came from England, why they came, and how Charlie wept when he realized that we were not his grandparents. Their visit brought up a second problem. "I doubt if you remember but my name is Itzik Grynshpan," Chaim said with a laugh. "And Anna is Rosa Feurmann."

"Oh, my God," said Shimon. "I remember the first names, but I have no recollection of the last names. But I do see how it might affect me." For the moment no one said a word.

With a deep sigh Shimon went on, "I can't say that this problem is one that never occurred to me. But it is one that affects all of the group who came from the Polski."

Interrupting him, Chaim said, "I recall that Avram's name was originally Shloime," and turning to Anna he inquired, "do you know Feygl's original name?"

"I don't know if I ever did," Anna replied, "but think about the children and the grandchildren. Avram's son Eitan is a general in the Israeli Army under a false name, and their Moshe and our Tamar and the girls are living under assumed names given to us so we could get out of Poland. And what about Sholom? Here's one I'm sure you never heard."

"Not more trouble, I hope?" asked Shimon.

"Let us hope not," replied Anna. "But this is why I don't sleep at night. Sholom called Chaim and told him that the college newspaper that is published at the college where he teaches could not let well enough alone, so some students did an investigation into Sholom's background and discovered that he was the child of a Nazi war criminal."

"Oh, my God," replied Shimon.

"But that wasn't enough. The head 'macher' at the school killed the story but someone leaked it to a wire service. It obviously isn't that much of a story since it has never gotten over here, nor anywhere, as far as I know, but can you imagine what I will have to go through if that story ever is published in Israel?" asked Anna.

Shaking his head in agreement, Shimon responded, "It has not been easy for you, Anna, I do admit. But for now things are quiet. Let us hope they stay that way."

"At least you were married to your wife when you were at the Polski," Chaim went on. "So, when you were given a new name you could still claim you were married. We never married. My wife had been killed as had Anna's husband. We met as partisans in the cemetery and stayed together ever since. Sholom's last name is Adler but it should really be Hauptmann, as you well know. These kids created all sorts of questions for us. Our children are all illegitimate. What should we do, at this point in our lives, to get this straightened out?"

With a shake of his head, Shimon replied, "It is not an easy question but I am going to give you an easy answer. Do nothing. No one is bothering you. I can understand how these kids upset you. Without knowing them, they upset me, looking for their grandparents while we know that they are long gone. If you never hear from the 'British' branch of your family again, what difference will it make? Sholom will remain Adler as will the two of you and let us all live and be well."

"Both Chaim and I felt the same way," said Anna. "But yet it bothered us. What if we do hear from these people again? After all, we are living under their family name. Here's a good one. Can we inherit from them or they from us? You know, Shimon, we are not people who look for trouble but even now, so many years from the Hotel Polski, problems still come up." With tears in her eyes, Anna got up from her chair and embraced Shimon and said, "I wish I had never heard of that place. I survived but haven't had a moment's peace." Turning to Chaim, "Come, Chaim, we must let Shimon work. Let Mr. and Mrs. Adler go home."

With hugs and kisses and when will we get together and good fellowship, they thanked Shimon for his time and his always good advice, and off they went. But they knew, the problem had not been solved.

CHAPTER FOURTEEN

All was quiet at Capernaum Catholic University. The kids were getting bigger. Ari was looking at girls. Sholom's classes were growing and there were talks about the University giving a minor in Jewish Studies The one new thing was, since Jewish Studies was under the History Department, the head of the Department called and asked if Rena could come in to see him. Her first thought was that Sholom had gotten himself into trouble, she hoped, not with a student and was shocked when she learned that the University was offering her a position as an instructor in Hebrew.

She was told that it would be a course to be taught under Jewish Studies and had a big laugh with the head of the Department when he told her that Sholom would be her boss. To which she replied, "So, what else is new?"

Needless to say she accepted the offer and when she told Sholom he, too, laughed and said now we will have two Professor Adlers in the same family. They were both overjoyed with the offer but now Rena had to rearrange her teaching schedule at the Temple. Sholom and Rena, by their presence, by their teaching, by his lectures, had brought a lot of new interest and strength to the local Jewish community and all problems were easily solved and worked out to everyone's satisfaction.

Still, things happened. Coming home from teaching one day Rena picked up the mail and found a letter from a law firm in London addressed to Sholom. When he got home she presented it to him with the question, "What on earth is this? Have you inherited someone else's estate?"

To which Sholom replied with a big smile, "Who knows; after all, I am a celebrity. Let us open it up and see what riches await."

Slicing open the envelope Sholom read aloud to Rena, that a Lord Greenspan, Queen's Counsel, is coming to visit and would like me to be available for a meeting at a specific date and time next week.

"That's nervy," said Rena. "Who the hell is he and what does he want with you?"

"All he says is that it has to do with a family matter."

"I hope this isn't something that is going to upset your mother."

"I do, too, and I will call my father tomorrow morning and see if he has any idea what this is all about. I wonder if this has anything to do with Chaim?"

"Why do you ask that?"

"Because to the best of my recollection Chaim's original name was Greenspan only with a Polish spelling."

"Well then, maybe he inherited someone's estate."

"That would be nice," said Sholom.

علم

Chaim was glad to hear from Sholom and when he learned that the lawyer was English, he told Sholom the whole story about the visit from Charlie and Sandra and said that he felt that this had something to do with it. "Your mother and I were somewhat upset by the visit because we saw that it could present a problem. What type of problem we weren't sure." He also told Sholom about their visit with Shimon where they discussed the problem, as it could affect Shimon and Avram and Feygl, and what about Eitan, as Israeli general using an assumed name. So, we decided to take Shimon's advice and do nothing. They joked about the name Greenspan and Chaim insisted that he always knew that he was related to British nobility. Sholom promised he would let Chaim know about the visit and they would speak next week.

Lord Greenspan came to Capernaum Catholic University, located Sholom's house and, with Rena present, they met. When he started to tell them about Charlie's and Sandra's visit, Sholom told him that Chaim had told him all about it, but asked what did all of this have to do with him or his family in Israel?

Lord Greenspan hoped that what he was going to tell them would come as a surprise and that he would, perhaps, then have the upper hand in the discussion. So, he was somewhat deflated when he learned that what he had come to say was not really news and that both Sholom and Rena were cool about the whole thing. He decided to shift gears and went into a long discussion of his firm's work in the fields of reparations and how Chaim and Anna Adler, by use of the names given to them at the Hotel Polski, were, in fact, perpetrating a fraud on Irving and Fannie Adler, Irving being the natural born son of Chaim and Anna.

"Please understand," Lord Greenspan went on, "when I say fraud I do not mean any purposeful or malevolent action by them. Professor Adler, I read your doctoral dissertation and I understand or tried to understand what went on at the Hotel Polski. Chaim and Anna Adler, your parents, were victims and this was their means of escape. I do not hold them responsible for their use of the name. The original Chaim Adler was a wealthy clothing manufacturer in Warsaw, had a large factory, employed many people, had a home with art and antiques, and your parents, by use of their name, are depriving Irving Adler of a rightful claim for reparations."

"So why did you come see me?" asked Sholom. "What is it that I can do?"

"I am asking you to act as an intermediary," replied Lord Greenspan. "I want to discuss the problem with them and see what kind of a resolution is possible. Again, I beg you, this is not a threat. I imagine that I could start a lawsuit but that would be nasty and unforgivable. The Adlers in England have forbidden me from doing that. The problems that the Holocaust has created are so immense that they defy description. Permit me a personal note. My investigation has shown that you are not the son of Chaim Adler and for as devoted as you may be to your mother and to Chaim as well, your intervention in this matter will not benefit you, financially, in any way. Please, Professor, please work with me. You may call me at any time and I will be happy to speak with you."

Rising from his seat, Sholom said, "Okay, Lord Greenspan, I understand the problem. I have no idea as to how to solve the problem but I will speak to Chaim tomorrow and then get back to you. But before you go, I must ask you, is it possible that you are related to Chaim because his original name was Greenspan, with a Polish spelling?"

Rising from his seat and extending his hand, Lord Greenspan replied, "It is a possibility. I, too, came from Warsaw as an infant and Greenspan had a Polish spelling. I understand that Chaim is a haberdasher and my family were in the clothing business in Warsaw and then in London. So, who knows, Sholom, we may be distant cousins."

With warm handshakes, discussions went on for another minute as to when the Lord was going home, did he have family here in the States, and with a promise to be in touch, the visit was over.

"What do you think about this?" asked Sholom.

"It will affect your mother," said Rena shaking her head, knowingly.

CHAPTER FIFTEEN

Irving and Jack met with Lord Greenspan upon his return from America.

"So, how did it go?" asked Irving.

"I'm not sure," replied Lord Greenspan. "They were very nice, charming as a matter of fact. We kidded around about the fact that Chaim Adler's real name was Greenspan with a Polish spelling as was mine, and said that perhaps Chaim and I are cousins. But the best I could get, and I really didn't expect more, was that he would speak to his parents and get back to me. So far, no word."

"Irving," said Jack, "don't look so disappointed. What else could you expect? This must have come as quite a shock to them."

"Not at all," said Lord Greenspan. "I was disappointed in that. They knew all about your children having visited. The only thing of which they were completely unaware was the issue of reparations. It is about that that I am waiting to hear."

"So, I guess there is nothing else to say at this time," said Irving, as he and Jack got up from their seats, shook hands, and were reassured that as soon as he had any word, Lord Greenspan would get them back.

Sholom did not call Chaim immediately. He was not sure why but he and Rena agreed that they had to think about it and decide how to approach the situation. Looking for their grandparents was one thing, but reparations was another. They both felt that there was something ominous about this.

It took a week but ultimately he had to call. Again, so as not to upset his mother, he called Chaim at the store.

"I'm surprised I didn't hear from you before this," said Chaim. "The lawyer came, didn't he?"

"Yes, he came," replied Sholom. "But now there's a new player in the game."

"A new player? Tell me."

"It is no longer a problem of their disappointment in that you are not their parents or grandparents. It is a problem of reparations. Chaim Adler, you are sitting on what might be a big pile of money to which the heirs of the original Chaim Adler may be entitled. He wanted me to act as an intervenor, but I have no idea what to say or do."

"In other words, since the original Chaim Adler was a wealthy man in Warsaw before the war, I am keeping them from making a claim?"

"As long as Chaim and Anna Adler are alive, I'm talking about you and eema, and even though we all know the original ones are not, their heirs cannot claim reparations from the German government. I can understand their point, but I have no solution to the problem."

"Let me speak to your mother about this," said Chaim with a tinge of anger in his voice, "and perhaps I will have to talk to Shimon and even Avram as well. This is an issue that could affect all of them, too. Give me a few days, I'll get back to you."

And with love and regards and kisses to the children, the call came to an end.

It took three days for Chaim to call back. He called in the evening when the children were at home and they each had to talk to their saba[*] and asked for everyone at their second home. It took fifteen minutes before Sholom could get the phone away from them.

"So now you've heard all the news from America," laughed Sholom. "What's new?"

"Needless to say, your mother is upset. This is all Col. Hauptmann's fault. Give them what they want. We don't need more trouble…the usual. I've thought about it, spoken to Shimon, who had no real answer to the problem, and decided that you should tell them that there is nothing I can do. This is not of my making. Let them sue the German government. I will be happy to testify as to how I got the name and the identity, as a result of which I assume their parents are deceased. More than that," he repeated, "there is nothing I can do. For them this has to do with money. I lost more than money in the war. And above all, I don't want your mother involved."

"I think that is a fair answer," replied Sholom. "I'll call England tomorrow and let you know what your cousin, Lord Greenspan, has to say."

And again with hugs and kisses the call came to an end.

Lord Greenspan was happy to receive Sholom's call but was less happy to hear Chaim's response to the issue. He thanked Sholom for getting back to him and said they would be in touch.

---

[*]Grandfather

CHAPTER SIXTEEN

Fr. Gregory could not have been happier. Things were going well at the university. The students had found a new lead article for the paper in place of the Sholom Adler story and the leak of the story did not seem to have any repercussions.

Fr. Gregory got to know Rena not only as Sholom's wife, but as a professor since she was now teaching Hebrew and they had gotten together at one or more faculty functions where he spoke with her about life in the Levant before coming to Israel. He also had occasion to meet Ari and Hudi, and the children, knowing who Fr. Gregory was, were on their best behavior.

So it was quite a shock when his secretary came in one morning and told him that there were two gentlemen to see him and showed him their credentials as officers from the US State Department, Immigration and Naturalization. Needless to say, he did not keep them waiting and offered them coffee, which they declined.

The gentlemen's names were Bob Crane and Christian Perez. They were both dressed in black suits, white shirts, and red neckties; they could have been twins but for Perez's Hispanic complexion. They both carried briefcases and did not appear to be overly comfortable in the extreme Catholic setting of Fr. Gregory's office. Fr. Gregory assumed that both men were Christian and Perez was a Catholic. So, why the discomfort?

As soon as the subject was announced, Fr. Gregory understood their problem. The topic under discussion was Sholom Adler, a professor at the university who, it appears, entered the United States under an assumed name. As soon as they mentioned Sholom's name they apologized and made it clear that this had nothing to do with anti-Semitism or the fact that he was an Israeli and a child of Holocaust survivors. The State Department has the greatest respect, etc., etc.

"Do you know Professor Adler?" asked Crane.

"Of course I do," replied Fr. Gregory. "I know all of my professors. But what is this all about? Professor Adler has been here for years. He was thoroughly vetted before he was hired. His wife now teaches here as well. Is she also involved in this? What brought this about?"

"His whole family may be involved," answered Perez, taking a folder out of his briefcase. "What brought this about is a story that our office heard about the fact that Professor Adler is the child of a Nazi officer and Adler isn't his real name."

Thumbing through the folder, he went on. "His father's name is…Hauptmann, and his mother's name is…Feurmann. So, where did Adler come from?"

Before replying, Fr. Gregory picked up the phone and, on the intercom, told his secretary to bring Sholom Adler's doctoral dissertation from the file. Not a word was said until she came in with the folder and handed it to Fr. Gregory, who was now standing behind his desk. Handing it back to her he said, "Make two copies for these gentlemen and bring them right in."

Sitting back down and with a tinge of anger in his voice, Fr. Gregory finally replied. "Do you guys know anything at all about the Holocaust?" Without waiting for an answer, he went on. "Professor Adler's parents were prisoners of the Nazis. Did you ever hear of the Hotel Polski? I'm sure you didn't. When you read what my secretary is printing you'll understand that names mean nothing. What the hell difference does it make what name he used? He's an Israeli citizen in this country with the right to work as a Professor of Jewish Studies."

But before he could go on the door opened and his secretary came in, giving each of the agents a copy of the dissertation. Without looking at it, Perez said, "Hold on, Father. You know if you vetted him as you said you did, that Professor Adler's father was a Nazi officer, so how can you say that his parents were in prison?"

With great annoyance, Fr. Gregory interrupted Perez and said, "Listen to me, Mr. Perez. I didn't say they were in prison. I said they were prisoners. Do you have any knowledge at all of what happened to the Jews in Poland under the Nazis?"

At which point Crane, noting Fr. Gregory's annoyance, interrupted, and said, "And did you know that the people that he claims are his parents were never married? We would like to speak to him and perhaps his wife, as well."

Shutting his eyes for the minute in the realization of what was happening, Fr. Gregory finally stood up and said, "Okay, guys, let's make a deal. I don't know how many days you have here but I will produce Sholom Adler after you have read his dissertation and have contacted Washington and discussed its contents and then come back to me and tell me that there is still a problem. That's fair, isn't it?"

With a sense of annoyance, Perez said, "Fr. Gregory, we're not social workers. We didn't come here to be lectured about the Holocaust. What does his dissertation have to do with anything?"

With a smile on his face and a casual wave of his hand, Fr. Gregory replied, "You're annoyed, Mr. Perez?" And wiping the smile off his face, he went on. "Well so am I. You don't just come in and disturb the peace and quiet of my campus with your know-nothing allegations. You're a Catholic, Mr. Perez? Well, I'm your priest. Do you think I would do anything to hinder your investigation? I'm not lecturing you; I'm giving you information in furtherance of your investigation. Take it for what it's worth and then come back and tell me if you still have a problem. Put it in your briefcases and that's that for today."

And with that he walked to the door and opened it. Seeing that there was nothing more to say the agents put away the dissertation, rose from their chairs, and Crane said, "I'm sorry Father, we did not mean to make you angry. We're just doing our jobs. By the way, I'm a Catholic, too."

"Bless you my son," said Fr. Gregory as he shook hands with both men. "Bless both of you and if you're around I look forward to seeing you at services."

CHAPTER SEVENTEEN

It took two weeks for Fr. Gregory to hear back from Immigration. He received a letter and was most relieved when he learned that the US Government was no longer going to pursue Sholom. Under the circumstances he felt that it was time to let Sholom in on what had happened and he would give him a copy of the letter should there be any future conflict with regard to his status.

Getting home from class, Rena told Sholom that there had been a message on their answering machine from Fr. Gregory's secretary saying that Fr. Gregory would like to see him first thing tomorrow morning. With a big smile she asked Sholom, "So what's with you and Fr. Gregory? Has he caught you fooling around with the coeds?"

To which Sholom replied, "What do I need the coeds for when I have an old lady like you at home?"

"Old lady," said Rena. "Wait until tonight. I'll show you what an old lady can do."

"I can't wait," said Sholom with a leer as he picked up the phone and called Fr. Gregory's office, confirmed the appointment, and promised to bring the bagels and cream cheese.

Arriving with his bag full of goodies and getting a big smile from the secretary, Sholom was ushered into Fr. Gregory's office. Settling in with coffee and a bagel with a shmear, Sholom asked, "So what's up?"

"If I didn't like you and if you didn't know where to get the best bagels, I would have to say, Sholom, that you are a pain in my ass," said Fr. Gregory.

"What did I do now?"

At which point Fr. Gregory related the whole story of the visit from Immigration and Naturalization and put the question to him just as the agents had asked it, "If your father was colonel, what's his name, and your mother's name was Feurmann, I remember that because of your brother, what a swell guy, then where in the hell did Adler come from. So I gave them a copy of your dissertation and told them that the answer was to be found in the writing of the history of the Hotel Polski. Needless to say they didn't know what in the hell I was talking about, but with that I got rid of them and yesterday I received this letter from them. The copy is for you."

Scanning the letter quickly, Sholom thanked Fr. Gregory, and then, shaking his head and with a worried look, "Did you ask them how they learned any of this?"

"I did, and their answer was that they heard but wouldn't say from where. I am assuming from the story of a month or so ago."

"So then let me tell you not only a story, but a big problem," said Sholom, "and I don't know how to resolve it." With that he launched into the story of the Adler family in England, the visit of the Adler children to his parents, and the visit from Lord Greenspan.

"Jesus Christ, Father, sorry, I don't mean to be disrespectful, but this is becoming a maze. I don't know how to get out of it. I see their point of view but I certainly see and understand my parents' point of view."

Shmearing the cream cheese on the second half of his bagel, Fr. Gregory shook his head and said, "You know what, Sholom, you are a pain in the ass. I don't know what to tell you or what advice to give you, but please know that I am here for you and definitely want to be kept in the loop." Taking a sip of his coffee, he went on, "This is a strange one but there must be an answer. Let me think about it."

Wiping his mouth with his napkin, Sholom said, "Thank you, Father, for your concern. I will keep you in the loop and if you have a heavenly thought, please get back to me." With that he rose from his chair and shaking hands with Fr. Gregory said, "Have to get to class," and left the office.

By this time Sholom knew the time difference between the US and Israel. He didn't have a class but wanted to reach Chaim in the store so he went home, gave Rena, who was on her way out, a brief overview of his meeting, and showed her the letter and then called Tel Aviv. Chaim was in, and listened patiently as Sholom told him the whole story. After he was done, all Chaim could say was, "This is getting to be a real problem."

CHAPTER EIGHTEEN

Unbeknownst to Irving or the rest of the Adler family, Jack, Sandra's father, was so fascinated by the problem of the use of the name Adler by the family in Israel and the question of reparations that he met secretly with Lord Greenspan where they discussed the possibility of an action against the German government. Jack was honest enough to tell Lord Greenspan for the second time that the Adler family had spoken against such a plan since they did not feel it right to put the Adlers in Israel in a position where they had to relive the horrors that they had gone through.

Lord Greenspan understood and also asked how Jack thought that jurisdiction could be gotten in England against the German government. Jack again suggested that if one of the judges at the trial of the colonel had been English and since the trial was designated as a war crimes trial, that perhaps England might have jurisdiction. Lord Greenspan shrugged at the idea but it was decided that he would call Sholom again and since Sholom knew his parentage by having read the transcript of the trial, he would know if one of the judges was English. With that knowledge, he would then talk to others about what he deemed to be the remote possibility that jurisdiction could be obtained.

Lord Greenspan made the call and the conversation was less than friendly since he refused to tell Sholom why he wanted the information that he sought. The idea of suing the German government was never mentioned and it never occurred to Sholom. Lord Greenspan knew that the question that he asked would go back to the family in Israel, but could not imagine that anyone would have any idea as to why the question was even asked.

That is exactly what happened. Believe it or not, it was Chaim who saw the question to be one which would relate to a possible lawsuit, but he saw it as one having to do with the British government. A British judge could give England jurisdiction, perhaps, but why and over what? What relief could a British court give against people who were Polish by birth and were now Israeli citizens? So it was again decided that Chaim would go to Shimon and see if he had any idea of what this was all about or if he had a judge or a lawyer with whom he could discuss the problem.

Lord Greenspan did not get back to Jack for some ten days. When he did he told Jack that he had spoken to Sholom, one of the judges was British and none of his colleagues or other counsel who were experts in reparations thought that the British judge at the war crimes trail would confer jurisdiction to a British court over a lawsuit against a foreign country. To which Jack's response was, "But the Adlers in Israel don't know that. Suppose we use it as a threat?"

Lord Greenspan did not like that idea either, and was somewhat annoyed with Jack for thinking the way he did. He did not practice law by threatening people with threats that had no legal basis. Jack backed off immediately and came up with an alternate suggestion, namely, that they invite everyone to London, assuming Irving will be willing to pay for it, and if we get them all in one room, perhaps a solution to the problem can be worked out. Lord Greenspan thought that was reasonable but would speak to no one until Jack spoke to the Adler family, got their consent, and made it clear to Irving that this would be a big number.

And that's how it was left.

CHAPTER NINETEEN

It was Shabbos at the Adlers' in London and Jack and Sylvia had been invited, unbeknownst to them, for a special announcement. The talk was spirited and happy and as the families sat down Charlie rapped his fork against his glass and stood up. "Before the matzoh ball soup, let's all wish a mazl-tov to Sandra." Standing next to Sandra, he went on, "Sandra is pregnant and you, 'alte kokkers,' are going to be grandparents."

The screaming, the kvetching, the hugging, the kissing, the "how could you not tell me," "what month are you in?" "are you seeing Dr. Margolin, he delivered you" went on for half an hour until Fannie announced that the soup was getting cold and we could talk while we ate.

While the excitement continued Irving and Jack looked at one another as if to say how can we talk about anything else? Their looks did not go unnoticed and at a break in conversation Sandra asked, "Why are you two guys looking at each other like you've got a secret? Do you have something to tell us?"

Although Jack had been more involved than Irving, it was really an Adler matter and Jack deferred to Irving. "Please," Irving said. "I don't want anyone to get upset, especially on such a happy occasion, but certain things have happened that you should be aware of." Everyone stopped eating but not a word was said, so Irving went on. "Jack and I have been in touch with a fancy lawyer. As a matter of fact, he is a Jewish Lord, but he is also an expert in the field of reparations. As a matter of fact he went to America on our behalf and met with the professor, the son of the Adlers in Israel, and discussed the issue with him."

Before he could say another word, Fannie interrupted, "I thought we said we were going to forget about this and you are spending this kind of money, sending a solicitor to America, without even telling me about it? Have you lost your mind?"

In an attempt to get Irving out of trouble, Jack spoke up. "Fannie, don't be angry with him. This is my doing, as well. As a lawyer, I was fascinated with the subject of people having the same name and how it came to pass and I, kind of, talked Irving into this."

"How far have you gotten?" asked Charlie. "Has the Lord come up with a solution to the problem?"

"No, not really," answered Jack. "But we have an idea that we thought we might try out on all of you."

"My two aristocrats," said Fannie, "associating with a Lord. How much is this going to cost me?"

With a sheepish look on his face as if he had been caught with his hand in the cookie jar, Irving said, "It might cost quite a bit, but if we can get the matter resolved we'll make it back and a lot more."

"If a lawsuit is involved, then I don't even want to hear it," said Sandra. "We all agreed that we were not going to go down that road."

"No, no lawsuit," responded Irving. "We thought if we could convince the Adlers, the ones that you met in Israel and their son, the professor, to come to London and to meet in Lord Greenspan's chambers, he could explain the problem and," turning to Charlie he went on, "you said they were nice people," and turning back to the others, "and see if we can come to a meeting of the minds and get the issue resolved. I grant you it will cost a couple of pounds, I can't ask them to do this at their expense, but we thought that like this we could all get to know one another, they could be made to see our side of the issue and then a solution could be reached."

"A couple of pounds?" said Fannie. "You know, Irving, you've become a crazy man. And if you get back all of these 'tschotchkes' that you're talking about, is our life going to be any different?"

"Fannie," he replied with an angry tone. "I've never denied you anything from the day we left Warsaw, but these are my parents and these are people who are using my parents' name. I want answers to these questions and I want this problem resolved."

"But, Pop," said Sara, "did you read Sholom Adler's dissertation? He explains what was going on at the Hotel Polski and how people were given exit visas and papers with the names of others who had been killed. What more is there to know?"

With a low growl, Irving looked at Sara and said, "I want them to stop using your grand-parents' names. Those names are holy to me. You may not have known them, but they were my parents and they gave up their lives for your mother and me, so don't tell me that I can find the answers in a dissertation."

At this point Jack took over the conversation and addressing himself to Irving he said, "Enough, Irving. Please, no anger. Everyone has a right to their opinion. Let us discuss this with Lord Greenspan and see if he even thinks this is a good idea. Please, everyone, it is Shabbos, Sandra is going to be a mother, we are going to be grandparents; we have so much to be happy for."

Fannie got up and walked to Jack's chair and gave him a kiss. "You are right and that is why we love you, even though you are a trouble maker." And with that everyone laughed, went back to their dinner and while walking back to her chair, Fannie gave Irving a scowl and said quietly, "Fancy, schmancy, Lord Greenspan."

CHAPTER TWENTY

Lord Greenspan met with Irving and Jack in his chambers and they budgeted out the approximate cost of flying Chaim and Anna from Israel, Sholom and Rena from the United States, two hotel rooms for three days and a food allowance, and it came to a number that would have made Fannie scream. Irving hesitated. This was a fortune to spend on a plan with no assurance of success and with no real alternative if the plan did not work.

The meeting then evolved into a discussion about the lawsuit against the German government with Jack pushing the idea and Lord Greenspan pushing back. Although the promise to the family was that no lawsuit would even be considered, it was decided that if Irving would fund the budget, the concept of a lawsuit would only be discussed to see how the others felt about it. This made Irving feel a bit better because they could, at least, talk about the issue with the people that would be involved and then they would see the reasonableness of the suggestions that had been made so as to avoid the lawsuit. What those suggestions might be was not at all clear to Irving, but without contacting Fannie, he told Lord Greenspan it was a go. To himself he was saying this did not include Lord Greenspan's fee. Business better be good this year.

The meeting broke up with the understanding that Lord Greenspan would make the arrangements. Sholom would be the first to be called since he had a teaching schedule and could only be available during a holiday break. Once that date had been fixed, at least a month or more in advance, he would write to the Adlers in Israel, but was quite sure that they would already know since Sholom would call them.

And so, the following morning Sholom got a call from Lord Greenspan inviting him and Rena to London for a paid, three-day holiday for the purpose of trying to resolve the issue of the use of the Adler name. Needless to say his parents would also be invited so it would be a family reunion. That was not something that Sholom really wanted and he turned down the invitation, initially, for two reasons. The first being that he did not think there was anything to talk about and the second being that he had no one with whom he could leave his children. This was the way he felt and if Lord Greenspan had any other suggestion to make, please call him back.

Rena was home during the call and stood with a puzzled look on her face, hearing only one side of the conversation and Sholom told her the entire conversation as soon as he hung up. What was there to talk about? As far as the children were concerned, Rena said we would take them with us. What a great way to spend a couple of days in London, show the kids the changing of the guard, and have them spend some time with their grandparents, whom they have not seen in quite a while. All of this at someone else's expense? Why not?

To which Sholom replied, "Before you get yourself all excited and go out on a super Sephardic shopping spree, let me call my father and tell him what's up. If he wants to go, of course, we will go. It will be the first time I've seen my mother since Ari's bar mitzvah."

"Such fancy alliteration," responded Rena. "But as to your mother, how long are you going to keep up this hostility? Don't you think the kids are aware of it? It's time you made peace with her."

"Let's not get into that. Let me call my father. I can get him in the store. But Rena," he said with a troubled look, "this creates a new problem that we've never discussed."

"Like what?"

"The kids are old enough to know where babies come from. I don't know whether you've ever had that talk with them. I know I haven't. But it will then become evident that their safta was screwing, sorry, had a relationship with the colonel as a result of which their father came upon this earth. But that would mean that Chaim is not really their grandfather."

With a sense of annoyance, Rena responded, "What are you saying? Colonel Hauptmann is their grandfather? Come on, Sholom, don't be ridiculous. Firstly, he is dead. Secondly, they never knew him, although they have heard plenty about him, and thirdly Chaim is their saba. He is the only one that they know. They love him and I question whether they will even think about it."

With a sense of relief, Sholom kissed Rena and said, "Okay, you wisest of wives and mothers. I hope you are right."

Unexpectedly, Chaim took a positive attitude toward the trip. He had never been to London, nor had Anna, and, as he told Sholom, this whole thing has been on his mind and if there is a chance to get it resolved it would pay to take the trip. Besides, if they bring Ari and Hudi, they'll all go sightseeing together.

༄

As anticipated, Lord Greenspan called back the following day. Sholom told him that his parents were willing to sit down and listen, a date was set, but the only hitch was that they needed two more plane tickets for the children and a second hotel room for them. If it was in the budget, then it was a go. Lord Greenspan, without talking to Irving, said it was a go and when he told Irving about the additional expense, Irving groaned loudly, but since he agreed to the plan to begin with, what could he say? Arrangements were made, hotels were booked, and plane tickets were sent. "Oh I forgot, you'll need cars at the airports to pick them up and take them back. Gevald!"

CHAPTER TWENTY-ONE

Since he promised to keep Fr. Gregory in the loop, Sholom stopped off at the office without an appointment, early in the day, before class.

"You come at this hour without bringing bagels, then there is something afoot," said Fr. Gregory, warily, but with a big smile.

"No, there is nothing ahand or afoot. And sorry about the bagels. You wanted to be kept in the loop and I'm doing just that. Got a minute?"

"Aha, then something is afoot? Sit." Then calling out to his secretary, "Coffee for Professor Adler and myself."

"We have been invited to London for three days, with the kids, all expenses paid, at the end of the semester."

"Why?"

"The way the lawyer presented it, he is inviting my parents, and they hope that with all of us together in one room some solution to the problem can be reached. Frankly, I didn't want to go. I don't see what the solution can be, but Rena got all excited. A free trip to London with the kids, they'll see their grandparents, and if there is no resolution then the English Adlers will have spent a lot of money for nothing."

In came the coffee and while the same was being poured nothing was said until the secretary left the room.

"Well doesn't the idea of seeing your parents excite you? I don't think they have been here since you came to the school."

"Got an extra minute?" sighed Sholom.

"Adler, why do you have so many problems? What is it? Please tell me. I'll pretend you're a Catholic and this is confession."

"You know, Father, you can always make someone feel good," said Sholom with a laugh. But then taking a sip of coffee he went on. "Although you know my father was the Nazi colonel you never asked about my mother. Well, something happened years ago that caused my mother to explode and reveal her feelings about my 'father,' and I put the word in quotes, and that resulted in my changing my feelings and my relationship with my mother. When she expressed positive feelings for that Nazi bastard, my thinking changed and I have never overcome it. I could see her as a victim, but not beyond that. Although I speak often with my father in Israel, I choose not to speak with my mother and haven't done so since we went back to Israel for Ari's bar mitzvah. So the idea of seeing her in London does not thrill me despite the fact that Rena keeps telling me that it is time I got over it."

Fr. Gregory sipped his coffee in silence. Finally, looking Sholom straight in the eye he said, "You should have started off this story with the words, 'Forgive me, Father, for I have sinned.'" And going on in a firm voice, "Because you have sinned. Honor your father and your mother. It says so in the stones of Judaism. You honored your 'father,' and I quote, you went to see him in Germany, you inherited his estate, but your mother, who gave birth to you and nurtured you, who lived through horrors that you could not imagine and who, in fact, was saved by that Nazi bastard, you refuse to honor her? What is wrong with you? Have you ever discussed this with your brother Yossie? I bet you haven't. He would tell you exactly what I am telling you. When you see your mother, hug her, kiss her, love her. She is your mother, and you should say 'kaddish*' for her when she dies. Go to London. Have a great time and solve this problem before you solve the other."

---

* Prayer for the dead

"One other problem," said Sholom rather sheepishly, "that has caused a minor disagreement between Rena and myself." And without waiting for a word from Fr. Gregory, he went on. "The kids. If they know anything about my parentage, they have never said a word. We have kept it from them, as you well know. Going to England with no real explanation as to why we are taking such a long trip for only three days could easily result in questions. After all, Ari is getting ready for college and Hudi is in high school. Rena feels it is time to talk about it but that means we will admit that Chaim, their grandfather, is not really their grandfather. I said that we can say the trip is for resolving the names of their grandparents arising out of the Hotel Polski business and they know lots about that."

Shaking his head in understanding, Fr. Gregory replied, "News flash, Sholom. The story of your parentage is on the wire. The fact that the kids have never heard it or read it does not mean that they don't know despite what you think. But if they don't then the time has come that they should be informed. Better from you and their mother than from a strange source. And as far as Chaim goes, he will always remain their grandfather. You know it and who better is there to reassure them than the two of you."

Finishing his coffee, Sholom stood up and said, "You know what, Father, you would make a good rabbi." And with that they shook hands, embraced, and Fr. Gregory said, "Come see me when you get back. I'll bet you'll have good things to tell me."

The children were excited about the trip to London with the extra added attraction that they would be seeing their grandparents. Neither of them asked why they were going and that evening, when they were supposed to be doing their homework, Hudi came into Ari's room with a troubled look upon her face.

Hudi was a beautiful teen-ager with a dark complexion, much like her mother, and an active social life, which troubled her mother. Ari, on the other hand was a tall, Germanic looking guy bearing a true resemblance to his grandfather, Colonel Hauptmann and was a good student and a good son. The kids were close to one another and on more than one occasion would talk to each other if they had problems that they did not care to discuss with their parents.

So when Hudi came into his room, Ari said, "I can see by the look on your face that there is a problem. What's up?"

"You know more about this than I do. Why are we flying to England, business class for three days? It doesn't make sense. And saba and safta are coming. What's going on?"

"From what I can gather," Ari replied, "and I get this from overhearing conversations, that the Adler name, which they got from the Polski…you know what that's all about…belongs to someone else and they're trying to straighten this out."

"Well, then, I don't understand the problem. We've heard the story, more than once, that saba and safta were given the names by the colonel and that is how they got out of Poland and went to Palestine. So, obviously, it was someone else's name. But there's more to it than that. You know as well as I that abba does not speak to safta, they have never come to visit while the rest of the family has, and now we will all be together in London…How is that going to work itself out?"

"Let's go ask them. Enough with the secrets. It's time we knew what was going on."

CHAPTER TWENTY-TWO

Although Ari and Hudi had flown back and forth to Israel on a number of occasions, British Air to London, Business Class, was different. They each had their own TV, they could stretch out when they were tired and had their meals served to them as if they were adults. Even Rena chuckled to herself that this was kind of swell, while Sholom sat deep in thought.

"This is truly a conflict," he said to himself. "These people are entitled to the names of their parents but how can my parents be expected to give up their identity at this late date? I don't see a solution but maybe the solicitor has something in mind." Figuratively shrugging his shoulders, he ordered another scotch from the flight attendant, despite the dirty look given to him by Rena, drank it and ate the peanuts that accompanied it and then, taking Rena's hand in his, closed his eyes and slept until dinner was served.

Their luggage came off pretty quickly and they went through customs and immigration without a delay. They got a laugh when they exited immigration and saw a driver in livery holding a sign with their name who took their luggage and led them to a limousine and drove them to the Mayfair Hotel, a lovely old London hotel overlooking the park. Two rooms had been reserved for them. One with a king-sized bed for Sholom and Rena and one with two queen-sized beds for the kids. There was an adjoining door between the rooms so it was considered a suite. They were told that breakfasts had been paid for, as had the rooms, of course, as well as any other expenses incurred in the hotel, but after that they were on their own. Inquiring whether Chaim and Anna Adler had checked in, Sholom was told that they were expected later in the afternoon.

Rena insisted that they all rest and wait until saba and safta come and then it will be like a party and we will all go for dinner. Despite the luxury of the flight, with the time change and all, everyone said they could use the rest. The kids were told to unpack their valises and not to fight. As soon as they got into their room Ari figured out how to use the remote, it was different than his at home, and they each jumped onto their own bed to watch British TV. Sholom went down to the lobby to look around and buy a newspaper while Rena unpacked their valise and when he returned to the room she was fast asleep.

Some two hours later the phone rang in Ari's room and when he answered he heard his saba's voice, "Ari, is that you? I thought I was calling your parent's room. We are here."

"Saba, how are you? How is safta? We are going to have dinner together."

In the meantime, Hudi went to the adjoining door and knocked calling out to her parents, who were fast asleep, "Saba is on the phone. Do you want to speak to him?"

"I'm coming," said Sholom, as he staggered off the bed and opened the door to the kids room and took the phone from Ari. "We've been waiting for you. Are you guys okay? Do you want to rest or should we meet in the lobby in 30 minutes?"

"Let us unpack. Make it an hour. There is lots to talk about."

Returning to his room, Rena was awake and inquired as to the schedule. "We have an hour," Sholom told her, going into the bathroom to wash his face and comb his hair.

"Good," said Rena. "That will give me a chance to put on fresh makeup. Go in to the kids' room and see that they have unpacked and have them wash their hands and faces before we go down. But before we go, behave yourself in front of your mother. Enough is enough."

"I got the same lecture from Fr. Gregory," said Sholom with a laugh, as he went back into the kids' room.

۔لم

Ari and Hudi went down to the lobby long before the hour was up and sat facing the elevators waiting to see their grandparents get off. Sholom and Rena came down next and they all waited together. It did not take long and Chaim and Anna came down and when the elevator doors opened the kids ran to them for hugs and kisses. Others in the lobby smiled at the scene because there is nothing nicer than seeing kids with their grandparents who love them.

Rena went to them first and again the hugs and kisses and how are you? Sholom waited until Rena was finished and he approached Chaim with a big hug while Anna stood and waited. When he finished he looked at his mother and with a smile said, "Don't I get a hug?" Anna was overcome. She had waited for years for this moment. She came to Sholom with open arms, with tears in her eyes, and would barely let him go.

Rena, Chaim, and the children went into the bar followed by Sholom and Anna, arm in arm. The kids had Cokes and the others ordered drinks and the discussion dealt with sightseeing after the morning meeting. It was understood that Rena and the children would visit some of the high spots of London and they would all meet back at the hotel for lunch. By then the issues to be discussed at the meeting would, hopefully, be resolved, and if not their schedules would be known and other plans could be made. It was decided that dinner this evening would be in the hotel dining room and after dinner the kids would go into their rooms and the adults would get together in Sholom and Rena's room and talk about tomorrow.

CHAPTER TWENTY-THREE

After breakfast the following morning, Rena went to the concierge desk of the hotel and booked a morning tour of London for herself and the children. She was told that it was conducted in a double-decker bus and they could sit on the upper deck, something none of them had ever done before. They were told to wait and someone would pick them up and take them to the starting point of the tour, but be sure to have an umbrella. In London you never know.

Meanwhile, after hugs and kisses, Sholom and his parents, with address in hand, took a waiting taxi to Lord Greenspan's office. Upon arriving, Irving, Fannie, and Sandra were already there, Charlie had to go to work, and after a moment's pause Sandra went to Chaim and Anna and they all embraced. With a big smile Sandra said to her in-laws, "These are the Adlers from Israel and I assume," turning to Sholom, "that this is Professor Adler."

"You see, Sandra," said Anna, "I told you we would see each other again. I didn't think it would be in a lawyer's office, but who knows."

Despite Sandra's enthusiasm, everyone felt the awkwardness of the moment. Finally Sholom stepped forward and said, "The young lady has it right," and extending his hand to Irving he introduced himself and his parents. Shaking hands with Irving, Chaim simply said, "Chaim Adler" and turning to Anna, "my wife, Anna Adler."

Replying quietly, Irving responded, "Irving Adler, my wife Fannie Adler. Sandra you know." Hands were shaken all around and then each side went to a neutral corner of the reception area waiting to be called into Lord Greenspan's chambers.

They did not have to wait long. Lord Greenspan himself came out to welcome them. He greeted Sholom with a warm handshake as if they were old friends and Sholom introduced Lord Greenspan to his parents. When the introductions and the handshaking was over, they then followed Lord Greenspan into the law library where there were seats for all, coffee, tea, and ice water on the table, for those who may care to have some, as well as a pad and pen in front of each seat for note taking. The big surprise was that Jack was waiting for them and when Sandra saw him she exclaimed, "Daddy, what are you doing here?"

In a somewhat embarrassed voice he answered, "Well, you know that we all talked about this problem and Lord Greenspan did not object to my sitting in."

In reply, Sandra said, "This is my father," and pointing to Chaim, Anna, and Sholom, she went on, "the Adlers from Israel and Professor Adler from America." Everyone nodded to each other but not a word was said.

No one quite knew how to start. Not a word was spoken and while one poured ice water, the other took coffee, and others started to doodle on the pads. Finally with a sense of frustration Irving blurted out, "So now we're here. But where do we go from here? Lord Greenspan, why don't you get the meeting started?"

Lord Greenspan took a very direct approach. Rather than go over the facts he said, simply, "You know the issues. How do we resolve them?"

To which Chaim replied, "Why must they be resolved? I am aware that we bear the names of Irving's parents. How it came about is set forth in Sholom's dissertation dealing with the Hotel Polski. Irving seeks reparations for the loss of his father's assets. I seek reparations for the loss of my wife, and children, as does Anna for the loss of her husband and son." For the purpose of the drama he went on, "One of her sons survived and became a Catholic priest. We have all sustained losses. I thank Irving for bringing us together and for giving me a chance to see my grandchildren. What else is there in this world other than happiness with your grandchildren?"

Unexpectedly, Fannie spoke up, looking directly at Anna and said, "My, God, how did you find him? A Catholic priest. What a shock that must have been."

To which Anna replied with a smile on her face, "Yes it was a shock, but he now lives with us in Israel and is no longer a Catholic priest. How we found him is a story for another time."

Hoping that the dialogue between the two women might be to his advantage, Lord Greenspan said, "I'm sure that would be a fascinating story and," addressing himself to Anna directly, and in the most conciliatory of voices, asked, "do you see any way of resolving the issues of the use of the name?"

Looking around the room, and in a skeptical tone of voice, she replied, "I am sure there are ways, but I'll stick to my husband's response. My children and grandchildren are all Adlers. I can't expect them all to go to court and spend tons of money for a new name…I don't know what it might be." And turning to Lord Greenspan she said, "It might even be Greenspan."

With a laugh, he replied, "I'd be honored," and looking over at Chaim, he went on, "Sholom told me your name was originally Grynshpan and that's how my parents spelled it. Perhaps we are related?"

Before Chaim could reply, Jack, who was sitting nervously at the edge of his chair felt that the conversation was getting away from the topic, interjected, "We had discussed the remote possibility of a lawsuit against the German government for the implementation of the plan that took place at the Hotel Polski. After all, that's how the Adlers got their name."

Hearing this, Sandra got up from her seat and said, with anger, "Daddy, we agreed that this would not be a possibility and we would not talk about it."

To which Jack replied, defensively, "We are looking for a solution. We are not springing this upon anyone. Lord Greenspan doesn't think very much of the idea so all I'm doing is putting it out for discussion. Everyone who is involved is here. Maybe someone has another idea...."

But before he could finish his thought, Sholom spoke up and said very seriously, "If you would sue the German government, I would testify on their behalf."

On hearing Sholom's statement there was a collective gasp, and momentarily not a word was said. Then not believing what he had heard and with a shake of his head, Lord Greenspan said, "Wow, that is some statement Sholom. Why would you testify on behalf of the German government?"

Looking around the room and opening his arms as if to embrace everyone he replied, simply, "Because we are here. We are alive. We were not killed, as were so many others who participated in their evil plan. If the heirs of those who died wish to sue, that's their right, but that evil plan kept us alive, for which I thank my mother and Chaim, for looking after her. I grant you it was all fortuitous; my mother and Chaim were partisans and coming to the Hotel Polski was for information gathering purposes only. But that very plan for which you would choose to sue is the plan that kept us alive and kept a number of our friends in Israel and elsewhere alive. Despite the fact that to this day no one can explain why the Germans thought that "saving," and I put those words in quotes, Jewish lives would result in repatriating Germans, is without understanding, it was, for us, a good plan. So, what would be the basis of your action?" Shaking his head in a negative way, he went on, "Suing the German government for saving our lives is not much of a plan."

With a big smile on his face Chaim said, "So you see, Lord Greenspan, that's why he's a professor and why I'm a haberdasher. What more is there to say?"

With a tinge of anger in his voice Irving spoke up and said, "So that's it? There is no solution? This has all been a waste of time?" And rising up from his chair and turning to Fannie, "Come Fannie, let's go home." Turning to Lord Greenspan he went on, "You obviously have nothing to add or to suggest. Not only has this been a waste of time but a waste of money as well. Please send me your bill." And turning to Chaim, "Have a good visit with your grandchildren. We are leaving."

To which Chaim responded, "Irving, sit down. Lord Greenspan won't charge you any more and tell us what do you want us to do? Can we give up the name Adler? That is the name by which we became Israeli citizens."

"I do have a suggestion," said Lord Greenspan, as Irving took his seat. "Leave the rest of your family out of it. Let them all remain Adlers. Their identity is no problem for Irving. How about you and Anna go to court in Israel and change your name back to Grynshpan and…I believe it was Feurmann, am I right, Anna? Then take Israeli names like so many other Europeans have done. And I know I am speaking out of turn, but investigation has shown that you are not married. With your new names you could then become newly married Israeli citizens. This will free up the names of Chaim Adler and Anna Adler and allow Irving to pursue his claim for reparations. Is that something worth thinking about?"

"Oh, what an idea," said Irving, looking pleadingly at Chaim. "If you agree, I will cover any expense you might have in connection with the change of name. At least tell us if you will think about it."

Shaking his head in agreement, Chaim answered, "Yes, we will think about it. We will be here for two more days and you will have our answer before we leave. Irving, I understand your problem and I promise to do what I can to help you solve it. And I sincerely hope that we see you and your family again before we leave."

With that, everyone got up and hands were shaken, Anna and Fannie embraced, Jack shook hands with Chaim and with Sholom, Sandra again embraced Chaim and Anna, Lord Greenspan stood at the door and shook everyone's hand as they left the room and the meeting was over.

CHAPTER TWENTY-FOUR

The afternoon following the meeting and all of the next day was spent in holiday fashion, sightseeing, antiquing, and other tourist activities. Late in the afternoon of that day Chaim called Lord Greenspan and asked if he could come in for a brief meeting with Irving; just the three of them. Everyone was scheduled to leave on the following day and Lord Greenspan made the unusual request of asking Chaim to come in a half hour earlier so they could talk about family and see if there was any possibility that they were related. An appointment was set for ten AM for Chaim and ten-thirty for Irving.

This time the meeting was held in Lord Greenspan's private chambers. Coffee was served and the two men traced their families back as far as they could, concluding that maybe they shared a great-grandfather. Chaim invited Lord Greenspan to come to Israel with the understanding that now he had "mishpocha*" there.

At ten-thirty, promptly, Irving arrived and Chaim reassured him that he was taking Lord Greenspan's suggestion very seriously, promised to work to resolve the issue, and explained to them both that the problem, although personal to Irving, affected more than one family. Telling them in confidence that Shimon, who was a Jewish organizational worker who worked on behalf of a Jewish social service agency

---

* Family

with the Germans in their scheme of selling visas and exit permits and was sent to Palestine with the original group, was now a minister in the government. Nevertheless, he continued to use the assumed name that was given to him by Colonel Hauptmann. He also told them about their best friend Avram, whose original name he had forgotten, but who came to the Polski with his two sons, his wife had been killed by the Germans. He was matched up with Feygl to make a family to correspond to the exit papers and their younger son married his daughter and their older son was a general in the Israeli Defense Forces, also under the assumed name given by the colonel. There were others as well, and they must realize the implications that the name change could have. And to bolster his argument he also told them about the visit of US Immigration accusing Sholom of coming to America under a false name.

They both said they understood the problem and would wait to hear from him. Lord Greenspan walked them to the door of the office where both Chaim and Irving embraced each other and Irving said, "When I embrace you as Chaim Adler, I feel that I am embracing my father but you are just a few years older than me."

To which Chaim replied, "Yes, you were married in '39 and I was married in '35. But we are brothers. We may not have had the same parents, but we are brothers and I look forward to seeing you and Fannie at our home in Israel."

"It would be our pleasure," said Irving with a smile. "Don't be shocked if we come knocking at your door."

Turning to Lord Greenspan, Chaim said with a laugh, "Lord Grynshpan, I expect you, too. Don't disappoint me. After all, there are not too many Israelis who can say they are related to an English lord."

And with a laugh and warm handshakes and pats on the back the meeting ended with each one going their own way and each one thinking, has anything been resolved?

When Chaim returned to the hotel Ari and Hudi were waiting for him in the lobby. Delighted to see them, he asked, "Are you waiting for me? Are you all packed?"

"Yes, Saba, we were waiting for you. Can we talk to you for a few minutes before you go upstairs?" asked Ari.

"Of course, children. Why so serious? Is everything alright?" asked Chaim as they went to a corner of the lobby and sat down.

"Ari and I," said Hudi, "did not understand why we were all coming to England for so short a time and why someone else was paying for it and why you and safta never came to visit us. It has been many years. Everyone else came but not you. We knew that abba did not get along with safta but we never knew why. Now, it appears, they have reconciled and we are happy. But before we came we asked abba and eema what this was about and they told us."

"We now know," continued Ari, "that you are not really our saba, but we decided that we had to tell you that we knew it. To us it makes no difference. We love both you and safta just the same and to us you will always be our grandparents. We just wanted you to know."

With tears rolling down his cheeks, Chaim took both children in his arms and reassured them that he loved them and will always be their grandfather and reassured them that the next trip that he takes will be to America to see them. Drying his eyes and with his arms around both of them they walked to the elevators and Chaim said, "Let this be our secret." Kissing each one as the elevator door opened, he said, with a big smile, "Let's see if everyone is packed. It really is time to go home."

By twelve noon the Adlers checked out of the hotel and all went to the airport, Sholom and Rena and the kids back to America and Chaim and Anna back to Israel. The one great result of the visit was the warm farewell between Sholom and his mother and the promise that their next trip would be to America. Sholom assured them that Fr. Gregory would be happy to see them. The idea of the Catholic environment in which they lived caused Chaim and Anna to sigh.

CHAPTER TWENTY-FIVE

Quietly opening the door to the outer office, Sholom poked his head in and asked the secretary if Fr. Gregory could spare a few minutes. "Good to see you, Professor Adler," she responded, motioning for Sholom to come in while she picked up the phone and asked Fr. Gregory whether he had a few minutes for Professor Adler.

"He'll be right out," she said, with a big smile as the door to Fr. Gregory's office opened and out he came.

"Back already?" he asked. "How did it go?"

Shaking hands and following him into his office, Sholom responded, "Well, I followed your advice and made peace with my mother. That was a good thing."

"And as to the rest of it?" As they seated themselves opposite one another in front of Fr. Gregory's desk.

"The lawyer suggested that my parents go to the court and simply change their names to Israeli names, as many Europeans had done. Forget about the rest of us. I will remain an Adler as will my wife and children and then the English Adlers can do what they wish."

"Not a bad suggestion but totally unnecessary. My solution is better."

"You have a solution?" asked Sholom in amazement. "This I have to hear."

"Oh, I've thought about the problem since you called it to my attention. By the way, how was London? Did Rena and the kids enjoy themselves?"

"We had a great time. Irving Adler must have spent a fortune. But, come on, Fr. Gregory, let me hear your solution."

"You know what, Sholom, we've known each other long enough that you can call me Joe. Yossie. That's it, you can call me Yossie."

"Okay, Joe or Yossie, or whatever you want to be called. Stop the games. What is your solution or are you just kidding me?"

"No, I'm not kidding, but let's have coffee first." Calling out to his secretary he asked for two cups of coffee, which were brought in immediately on a silver tray with a pitcher of cream and various sweeteners. Settling back with his coffee, Fr. Gregory was about to speak, but Sholom interrupted him.

"Before you give me your solution, let me tell you about the other problem that needed resolving." And with a big smile he went on. "I know it will make you happy to learn that my mother and I have resolved our difficulties. You lectured me, Rena lectured me, and you both were right. It was time. And as to the kids, I must admire them. They are nervy. Before we left they came to us and asked us what was going on. Why were we going for only three days on such a long trip and one thing led to another. We took your advice and we told them the whole story and on the way home Ari told me that he promised his grandfather that he wouldn't say anything, but he wanted me to know that both kids spoke to Chaim and with tears and hugs and kisses, that too was resolved."

"So now, let's hear from you."

"Oh, Sholom, that's the best news I could have heard. All of those problems resolved; the family back on track. What could be better? Now my resolution to the other problem is as follows: You Sholom are the solution."

"Me, how am I the solution? I wasn't even born when they were given the name Adler."

"I know that. But you are the product. Who is your father? There are no longer any secrets. The British lawyer knows all the facts as does Irving Adler, his client. So why not use the facts to your advantage? You sit down with my attorney. She is a lovely lady and knows what is going on. I think you met her once or twice at college functions. Let her put the facts into an affidavit that will read, to the effect, I, Sholom Adler, being duly sworn, depose and say: I am the son of Colonel what's his name and whatever your mother's name was. He was the commandant of the Hotel Polski located, etc., etc. and she was a prisoner confined therein. Then go on with the story of what was taking place at the hotel and end up with the fact that the names that were given were those of deceased persons who died in the Warsaw ghetto. You say, under oath, that this information is true based upon the reading of the transcript of the war crimes trial, your own conversations with your father, the colonel, after he served his time as a Nazi war criminal, your research of the role played by the Nazi's in the administration of the Hotel Polski as set forth in your dissertation, and the history of Chaim and Anna Adler, presently residing in Israel. How can anyone then doubt that the identity of Chaim and Anna Adler is the one given to them by, and I quote, 'your father,' which saved their lives, and that as such, they, Chaim and Anna Adler residing in Israel, bear no relationship to Irving Adler, the son of the pre-deceased, Chaim and Anna Adler. Give this affidavit to the British lawyer, let him use it to pursue his client's claim, your parents in Israel need do nothing, and everyone can remain with the name Adler."

Looking up with a beaming smile, Fr. Gregory went on, "Pretty good, huh kid? What say you?"

Having finished his coffee during Fr. Gregory's solution, Sholom put the cup down and with raised eyebrows said, "Yeah, that's pretty good. I think I told you that the English Lord was a Jew and there was a chance that he was distantly related to Chaim. When I give him this solution and tell him that it came from a Catholic priest, I'm sure his Lordship will look askance. Joe, that's a hell of a solution. I don't know why it can't work. Let me digest it, get it to my parents and then to his Lordship, and I'll get back to you." Shaking his head in admiration, Sholom smiled and repeated, "That's a hell of a solution."

CHAPTER TWENTY-SIX

The letter from the ghetto dated 1943, and delivered close to thirty years later, was indeed the last time that Irving heard from his father or his mother. The world watched and held its breath as the ghetto uprising began. History tells us that its success was short-lived. When the Germans decided that they could not be made to look like fools and brought in heavy artillery, within two weeks the ghetto was destroyed and for all intent and purpose Warsaw was now free of Jews. The only building left standing was Pawiak prison.

Chaim, Irving's father, foresaw the future very clearly, but fate played a role that he could never have foreseen. A day or two before the revolt began a Nazi officer came to their room in a half-destroyed building where they lived, inquired as to their names, checked their papers to verify they were telling the truth and then ordered Chaim to follow him to Gestapo headquarters. Chaim refused unless he could take his wife, Anna, with him. With a show of annoyance at Chaim's refusal to follow an order, the officer agreed and Chaim and Anna left the ghetto, unknown to them for the last time, and proceeded to Gestapo headquarters.

Knowledge of the death camps had reached the ghetto; the trains were taking people away each day and Chaim and Anna, feeling that death was imminent, could not imagine what they had done to be summoned to Gestapo headquarters. Speaking quietly to each other in Polish, knowing that the officer did not understand, they promised to be brave and expressed their love for each other, should this be the last time that they would be together.

Arriving at Gestapo headquarters, they were taken to the office of a Major who asked the following questions:

"You are the Chaim Adler who owned and ran a clothing manufacturing plant outside of the ghetto?"

"I am."

"Who is running it now?"

"I have no idea. It was taken from me some two years ago and I doubt if it is still operating."

"If the German government were to supply you with fabric and other necessary material as well as with labor, could you reestablish the factory?"

"Who would buy the finished product?"

Somewhat annoyed as to Chaim's question, the Major growled, "You are a nervy Jew. Who would buy it? No one would buy it. You would be making uniforms for the German army. And," he went on with a leer, "it might even save your life. What do you think of that?"

"Of course, Major. That was a silly question, but since the factory is outside of the ghetto, where would we live?"

"You, your wife, and a German officer who will oversee your activities will all live on the third floor of the factory. There are rooms there that can be adapted and turned into sleeping quarters. You will not leave the premises, everything, including what little food we have to live on will be brought to you."

Shrugging his shoulders as if in recognition, Chaim replied, "The third floor? Yes, I know the third floor. And the workers? Who are they and where will they come from? Will they have any experience?"

"Where they come from is not your concern and if they have no experience you will teach them. I assume you accept this life-saving offer and if you have no other questions an officer will take you to the factory, you are to examine its condition, what machinery is needed, make a list and give it to the officer. We will see what is available for you to get the factory up and running, but I warn you, such a life-saving event will not come again. Do not think of leaving the factory and do not betray my trust."

With no idea of what this was all about or why it was happening, Chaim shook his head and said, "Yes, Major. We thank you and you can trust us."

Sitting in the back of the car and holding Anna's hand, Chaim thought back and realized it was more than two years since he had seen the factory. The car was being driven by a German soldier and next to him was a young lieutenant, who, Chaim assumed, would be their watchdog. Not a word was spoken during the trip. Looking at the Warsaw that they remembered, both Chaim and Anna sighed, continued to squeeze one another's hands, but did not make a sound.

Chaim deemed what was happening to be some sort of Nazi trick that he could not understand. They could have been put on the train for "resettlement," as it was called. Who knew about me and about the factory? None of this made any sense. And to be put in the hands of this young officer. Does he know anything about running a tailor shop? Struggling inwardly, shaking his head and sighing he looked at Anna and could not imagine what she was thinking as she watched the streets, that she knew so well, go by.

It took fifteen minutes and they were there. The building was still standing; the windows had been blown out; the front door stood open, hanging by one of the hinges, and some of the neighboring buildings had been destroyed. Getting out of the car Chaim, who understood some German, heard the soldier ask the lieutenant, "What the hell are we doing here?" to which the lieutenant replied, with a shrug, "I just follow orders."

CHAPTER TWENTY-SEVEN

It took two weeks before they could start working on the first uniform. During that time German soldiers cleaned up the building, restored electricity and water, installed a boiler so that Chaim could have steam needed to press the uniforms, brought in beds from their warehouse of stolen furniture, and set up a small kitchen. The front door was rehung and the windows were boarded up. All of this was done under the supervision of the young lieutenant who would leave the premises, on occasion, to shop for what little food was available in the stores. He was a rather pleasant young man, did not seem to be particularly anti-Semitic, and the three of them would eat their meals together and talk about their families and where they came from.

    The one thing that remained in the building was the cutting table. It took some ten days before two sewing machines were brought in along with fabric for uniforms as well as other military decorations and insignias. Chaim needed no patterns. He knew how to cut a man's suit and could alter what had to be altered to make it a uniform. As to the military decorations and insignias, he asked the lieutenant. After two weeks two Polish tailors were brought in and work began. It went very slowly and after a week the Major from Gestapo headquarters appeared and chastised Chaim for the lack of progress. With nerve that he did not believe he had, Chaim spoke up and told the Major that if he had more machines and more labor there would be more progress. Despite the fact that the Major resented being spoken to in this manner, within the next few days more machines appeared as did more workers and the pace of work was picked up. Uniforms were cut and sewn, but not finished, until the officer appeared who needed the uniform. Then it would be fitted to the officer's satisfaction. This went on for some two months and Chaim and Anna felt as if they were almost back in business.

In that the lieutenant was friendly to them, Chaim inquired as to whether he could correspond with his son who lived in London. "Absolutely not," was the response. "Just as you are not permitted out of the building you are permitted no contact with the outside world. And besides, there is very little postal service in Poland and none whatsoever to England."

"May I ask you one other question, something that has been on my mind?" said Chaim. And without waiting for the lieutenant to respond he went on. "How come all the workers that have been brought in are Poles? Are there no Jews that can be gotten? I knew many of them who were excellent tailors."

With a laugh, the lieutenant responded. "Chaim, you and Anna are nice people, but you are very naïve. Consider yourselves lucky. You are the only two Jews alive in Warsaw. The ghetto has been destroyed. There may be some still living in hiding, but at this point you are the last. So be happy you are alive. Keep working and don't ask questions."

And so, without knowing why they had been chosen to remain alive, Chaim and Anna continued to exist in his old factory and although they were not permitted to leave the building, the two soldiers who were stationed at the front door never objected when they came out to sit on the steps and get a breath of fresh air.

CHAPTER TWENTY-EIGHT

Nothing about this made any sense. Work went on for a number of months during which Chaim and Anna were bored with their existence but thankful for being alive. Winter was approaching and rather than uniforms, material was brought in for warm coats. From conversations overheard, Chaim learned that many of the soldiers were being shipped to the Russian front and the lieutenant, with whom they had gotten friendly, was promoted to captain and sent off to the East. He was replaced by an older and more irritable sergeant who resented acting like a watchman and an errand boy but was thankful that he was not being sent to fight.

Toward the end of the year the Gestapo major came to be fitted for a new winter coat and brought with him a man dressed in civilian clothes who was introduced as Colonel Schenk. The colonel needed a new uniform and a winter coat and was told it would take a bit of time for both to be ready. He claimed to understand and said he would return when necessary. The major, in the meantime, was fitted in two sessions, was pleased with his new coat but acted nervous and irritable and told Chaim that he would not be seeing him again. Chaim understood that to mean that he, too, was being sent to the East. When leaving Chaim tried to be polite and wish him well to which the Major replied, "Lucky Jews."

It took three fittings for Colonel Schenk's uniform and winter coat to be ready and when he appeared for the second time, there was no one else present other than Chaim and Anna. The workers were in a separate room, the sergeant was upstairs eating lunch, and Anna was helping Chaim with the finishing touches. There was no heat in the building and all the occupants would go into the pressing room whenever they could to enjoy the little heat that came from the pressing machine. It was difficult working all bundled up but there was no alternative.

So when Colonel Schenk was asked to try on the uniform, he said to them, in Yiddish, "How can you work under these conditions?"

Anna dropped the scissors she was holding and Chaim stopped dead in his tracks. Staring at the colonel, Chaim replied, "We are alive. That is better than most Jews in Poland can say. But who are you? How do you know Yiddish?"

Looking about to be sure no one else was present and speaking softly, the colonel said, "My name is Lev Rosenshtein, I am a partisan and have worked undercover with the German army using forged credentials. I have been instructed by the partisans to see to it that this factory be closed and that the two of you be transported out of Poland to a neutral country."

Without batting an eyelash Chaim responded, "I do not believe you. This is some trick. You are a Nazi sent to…"

But before he could finish, Lev interrupted him and said, "I understand your hesitation but tell me, Chaim, do the Nazis have to use trickery to kill the Jews? You could have simply been taken from here, someone else put in your place, and sent to a concentration camp and been murdered."

Looking at Chaim, Anna replied, "Chaim, darling, he is right. If we can get out of here we will be able to find Irving and his family. We will be saved. Listen to him. He has come to save us."

Not waiting for a reply, Lev said, "I have watched the routine. I know when the sergeant goes shopping. I will come back for the final fitting for my coat and when I leave through the front door, I will occupy the attention of the soldiers. The two of you will have packed as little as you can and will leave the building by the basement entrance. There will be a German staff car waiting for you. It will be driven by what looks like a German soldier who is also a partisan. I will come around the corner and get in next to the driver and we will be off. If anyone stops us, I will be in full uniform and claim you are my prisoners. One very important thing, leave all identification with your name, your passports or whatever you have been given by the German government. You will be given new, forged documentation, which will be your identification from now on. Are you clear?"

Hesitantly he agreed. "When will you be back?" Chaim asked.

"When the time will be right. I must go now." Looking at himself in the mirror, Lev said, "You do good work. This is a beautiful uniform." And out he went.

It took two weeks before Lev showed up again. By this time, Chaim and Anna thought that it had all been a dream or that Lev had been caught and they would never see him again. They had put together their meager possessions in a battered suitcase and had hidden it under their bed waiting Lev's return. Everything was in order and went as anticipated. He picked up his new coat, went out to the front door while Chaim went up to the third floor and got the suitcase, and they both went down to the basement and out the back door. Not a soul saw them leave and when they opened the door of the staff car and got in the back, the "German" soldier turned to them and said, "Shalom." Within another half minute Lev was in the car and they were headed out of Warsaw.

When the sergeant returned from his shopping he went to the fitting room to tell them that he was back and found no on there. Checking with the workers they claimed not to have seen Chaim or Anna. Going back to the fitting room he found their passports and other identification on the table and for the minute was not quite sure what to make of it. So he took his groceries up to the third floor and figured they must be in their bedroom. Needless to say, they were not there and it dawned on him that they were gone. He had no choice but to call Gestapo headquarters and report what had happened. They would charge him and God knows what would happen to him.

It was as he expected. An officer from Gestapo headquarters came to the factory, was furious when told of the escape of the "prisoners" and gave the sergeant one last assignment. Take the passports and other documentation to the Hotel Polski and give them to Colonel Hauptmann. He will know what to do with them and then report to Gestapo headquarters.

CHAPTER TWENTY-NINE

Not a word was spoken during the first ten minutes of the trip. Chaim held Anna's hand tightly feeling both the joy of being freed and the fear of being captured. They rode through the destruction of the city that they had known so well and finally Chaim spoke up and said to Lev, "What is this all about? Why have you chosen us and where are we going? We have no identification and if we are stopped…"

At which point Lev interrupted him and said, "I have new papers for you, a new passport, and will answer all of your questions. Let us get out of the city first and lessen the chance of our being stopped and having to answer someone else's questions."

After another fifteen minutes they left the city, drove through farming country, and ultimately stopped at an inn outside of a little rural village. When the patrons of the inn saw the German staff car and a colonel in full uniform with a driver, they thought it best to disappear and when they entered the inn it was quite deserted except for the bar maid and the owner. Lev requested a private room, ordered a meager lunch because that was all that was being offered and a pitcher of beer. They all used the facilities and when the lunch was brought and the door was closed they sat around the table and ate. Consuming the meager lunch and a glass of beer did not take long, at which point Lev took his briefcase, opened it, and handed Chaim and Anna travel documents and new passports in the name of Lilly Kostuchko and Gregor Kostuchko, Polish nationals, from a city far distant from Warsaw. "I am assuming," Lev asked, "that you both speak Polish because that and what little German you may know will be the only languages that you will speak from now on to anyone that you may meet. Is that understood?"

"Yes, we understand," responded Anna while both she and Chaim shook their heads in agreement, "but why and where are we going?"

"Although it is believed," said Lev, "there are still a few thousand Jews living in Warsaw, in hiding, on the Aryan side of the city the two of you are the only ones that are out of the ghetto and running a servicing business for the Germans. In order to stop the business from functioning, incidentally it will be destroyed in the next few days, we had to get you out, which we have accomplished. We are heading toward a small Polish seaport where you will be taken, with some others, hopefully, to neutral Sweden, to live out the rest of the war."

"Hopefully," asked Chaim. "What do you mean by hopefully?"

"After we drop you in Ustka, some three hundred miles from here, you will be in the hands of others who have, to date, been successful in their efforts. It is a dangerous trip, but the rewards are great. There will be no 'Nazi Colonel' to protect you. You will follow the orders of the people who will be transporting you and now that you know the whole story it is time to move on. We cannot spend too much time in any one place. I am estimating that we should reach our destination by tomorrow night," and with a smile, he added, "hopefully."

It took another day and a half. Sleeping was done in the car. The driving was done by the three men in rotation while the others slept. It took convincing for Chaim to put on the German army helmet when he was the driver so there would be no question that he was a soldier with the colonel beside him. Gasoline was confiscated from Nazi outposts along the way at the demand of the colonel and food was taken at rural inns and guest houses in the most remote of possible locations.

Late on the second day they reached Ustka and were taken to a boat shed on the waterfront. They were greeted by a soldier in a German army uniform who was also a partisan who welcomed them into the shed where there were eight other people. After taking their valise out of the trunk and reassuring Lev that they had their new identification papers and passports, they said goodbye to him and the driver with hugs and good wishes for all.

The partisan in the German army uniform gave everyone some soup and bread and told them to hurry it up because they would be leaving as soon as they finished. They were then given life jackets and instructed that they must wear them until they reached Sweden. They were told that they would only travel at night since there were German patrol boats going back and forth in the Baltic Sea, which they were going to cross to the Danish island of Bornholm. Although the Germans had occupied Denmark they had no troops on the island and it was used as a daytime rest stop by those refugees who were on the way to Sweden.

The captain of their boat knew the German patrol schedule and was able to elude the patrol boats getting the group to Bornholm without incident. There they were met by a Danish partisan who took them into a boat shed that had cots and told them to rest and wait for food to be brought to them

Since nobody really knew or trusted anyone else there was little conversation between the people. Could one of them be a Nazi spy? They all understood that they had to wait until the sun went down and, as a result, it was the longest day of their lives. But finally they were told to be ready and taken aboard another, smaller boat for the final leg of their trip to Simrishamn, Sweden.

It was a dark night and the distance they had to travel was not that great. Everything seemed to be going well and people started to talk to one another. Suddenly a bright light went on and through a loud speaker the captain was told, in German, to stop moving and prepare to be boarded. The captain was a Dane and spoke some German. He tried to explain to his passengers that he was near Swedish waters and if he could get there and out of international waters the Germans would never dare to come aboard the boat. Changing course to get out of the light he accelerated only to hear a cannon shot fired from the German patrol boat. It missed but the second shot was a direct hit, the boat blew up and all the passengers were thrown into the Baltic Sea. The searchlight then turned on the people in the water and a machine gun started to fire. Fortunately, Chaim and Anna had been hurled behind a large portion of the wrecked boat, were unconscious because of the blast, but were not hit by any bullets.

The Germans, assuming they had completed their mission soon stopped firing and pulled away leaving what was left of the boat to sink into the water. It did not appear anyone was moving but when the sun came up the fisherman of Simrishamn found Chaim, Anna, and another person alive on the beach.

CHAPTER THIRTY

The morning mail was always delivered promptly at eleven o'clock and dropped on the desk of Fr. Gregory's secretary. The daily procedure was for her to go through it, discard the "junk" mail, open what was left, and attempt to take care of those items that did not need Fr. Gregory's personal attention. The balance was brought in to him with her comments, if necessary, and a refill for his coffee cup.

On a regular day the procedure was followed with one exception. With the mail in one hand and the coffee in the other she struggled to open the door and said, "Here's a weird one. Do you know anyone in Simrishamn, Sweden or are you planning to retire, or maybe you're trying to get rid of me?" she asked with a laugh.

"None of the above, but if it looks like a good deal, perhaps. Would you like to run away with me to Sweden?"

"Sure it would be just my luck. I would run away with a Catholic priest to a country that has free love."

"Free love, oh, it's not free?"

Putting the coffee on Fr. Gregory's desk along with the open mail for him to look at, she went on, "I didn't open this one. It was marked 'PERSONAL,' addressed to the head of the university with no name, and if it had pictures of Swedish girls in bikinis, I didn't think you would want me to know."

"You're right, I wouldn't, but since you're here and I know you wouldn't rat on me, let's open it and see what it's all about." Taking a sip of coffee and reaching for the letter opener on the desk he examined the envelope carefully. "It comes from a sanitarium in a town I've never heard of. Perhaps it is some priest trying to get in touch with me." Turning to his secretary he asked, "Get me the atlas from the bookcase. I want to find this town and see if it will give me a clue. Maybe it is just an advertisement suggesting that I do retire to this lovely place."

Going to the bookcase and coming back with the atlas she said, "Joe, you're such a ball buster. Why don't you just open it? Maybe it is an ad and you'll just throw it away."

Shaking his finger at her and with a leer, he responded, "Have you no sense of mystery? When is the last time we received a letter from…" and looking at the return address, "Simrishamn with a silent 'n' at the end?" Then opening the atlas to the index he found the listing, went to the page, found the town and looking up in bewilderment, he said, "Doesn't mean a damn thing to me and that also has a silent 'n' at the end."

"To hell with the 'n's'," his secretary said in frustration. "Will you please just open the letter?"

Without another word being said, he opened it. It was two pages long and as he started to read it he said, "Oh, my God." Hearing this, his secretary, not being able to wait, got up and went around to his side of the desk and read along with him, and as they read they both said, "Oh, my God."

When they finished reading he asked, "Where is Sholom Adler?"

"Wait, let me finish," she said. Taking another few seconds, she went on, "on vacation, but I have no idea where. I think they took the kids on a cruise to Hawaii. That's what I heard."

"Okay, then do what I tell you. Get the overseas operator in London and find me all the Lord Greenspans that are listed. Ask her to limit herself to lawyers, solicitors, barristers, or whatever the hell they call themselves over there. When you get the right one, ask the operator what time it is in London. If it is normal business time, call him, and put me on the phone." Picking up the letter, he said, "This is unbelievable."

It took about fifteen minutes but then she buzzed Fr. Gregory who picked up the phone and heard his secretary say, "Lord Greenspan, this is Fr. Joseph Gregory of Capernaum Catholic University in America," and knowing that Fr. Gregory was on the phone, she hung up.

"Capernaum Catholic, isn't that where Sholom Adler is a professor?" asked Lord Greenspan.

Knowing that he had the right party on the line, Fr. Gregory responded, "That's right, and I know I am speaking to the right Lord Greenspan."

"Yes, you are, Father. Sholom has spoken of you. Your solution to his family's problem was a sound one, but in the last analysis it would still have resulted in two families with the same name. The Israeli Adlers chose to change their name to Nesher, which is the Hebrew word for eagle. Adler when translated is the German/Yiddish word for eagle. I believe they may have even gotten married under their new name, so all is well with them. What can I do for you? I assume Sholom and his family are alright?"

"Oh, they're fine. I believe they are away on holiday, but I have some remarkable news for you. By the way, do you still represent Irving Adler?"

"Yes, in his claim for reparations, but what is the news? Please tell me."

"I hope you have time, because this is most unusual."

"All the time in the world, Father. I love mysteries."

With a deep sigh, he went on. "I received a letter from a sanitarium in a little town on the Swedish coast called Simrishamn. It tells the following story. During World War II, a German patrol boat blew up a small ship in the Baltic Sea carrying, what they presumed to be,

Jewish refugees from Poland. Three people survived and were found on the beach the next morning. A couple and a single man. The single man could not be saved but the couple were brought to the sanitarium where they lay in a coma for a couple of weeks, the wife recovering first. They had water-soaked Polish identification on them, barely legible, and nothing indicated that they were Jewish. When the man opened his eyes he recognized his wife but neither of them had any knowledge of where they were or how they got there, nor were they able to speak coherently. Under the circumstances there was no place the sanitarium could send them, since they really didn't know who they were or where they came from, despite the identification that they carried. It was assumed it was false, in any case. And so they remained patients from the end of the war till today. The Swedish government paid for their care and they did recover to some degree. Speech was difficult and if they spoke, they spoke only Polish. She recalled he was a tailor. Fortunately, there was a nurse who was Polish on the staff and she could understand her. He rarely spoke. They had no recollection of where they came from but were obviously bright people because over the years an instructor started to teach them Swedish and little by little they learned to read it to some degree but could not speak it. The letter goes on to say that one day he picked up a Swedish magazine and read a little story about an Israeli professor of Jewish Studies, Sholom Adler, who taught at Capernaum whose father was a Nazi colonel. They weren't quite sure what Israel was but became excited when they read that the people that the professor considered his parents were Chaim and Anna Adler. Suddenly the dam broke. He got so excited that he almost choked. They rushed to find the Polish nurse, and with the article in hand, they dragged her down to the administrator's office and the nurse told the administrator that they claimed that was their real name. The wife's speech was somewhat better and she informed the administrator that they had a son in England named Irving. They were quite agitated and had to be sedated and hence the letter to me since there was no other way to contact Sholom. What do you think of that? Chaim and Anna Adler are still alive. They must be in their eighties."

"That is the most exciting news I've heard since I don't know when. Let me give you my fax number. Please fax the letter to me and as soon as I receive it I will contact Irving. I assume he will go to Sweden and bring his parents back to England."

"This is exciting to me for another reason," replied Fr. Gregory. "Let me go back a few years. The story that they read in the magazine came from unwanted research that some students did for an article that was to appear in the college newspaper. I killed the article because neither Sholom nor I wanted it published, but someone leaked it to a wire service. We never heard about it until today. What a coincidence. What an unbelievable story."

CHAPTER THIRTY-ONE

And so it ended. Irving and the rest of the family flew to Simrishamn and brought home his parents and installed them in an expensive rehabilitation facility where they would receive not only physical care but psychological and emotional care in an attempt to bring back as much of their memory as they could. It was interesting that Irving's mother recognized Irving immediately, but his father did not. Chaim took Anna's word for who Irving was, but the other unusual thing that happened was when they saw Irving, the limited amount of speech that was available to them was no longer Polish, but converted instantly to Yiddish.

When Sholom came back from holiday he was told of the news and immediately notified his parents who were overjoyed to learn that Irving's parents were still alive.

During the course of his last contract term with Capernaum, Sholom was contacted by a prestigious university in Israel, which offered him the position of head of the history department and both Rena and he were excited when he accepted the offer. The funny thing was that both Ari and Hudi were unhappy at the thought of leaving. They had become completely Americanized and had their American friends, although they continued to speak Hebrew at their mother's insistence. Ari was preparing to go to an American college and even considered going to Capernaum, which Rena did not want. A compromise was reached when they told him that he could apply to American colleges if he came back to Israel, served his year in the military, and then made his decision.

Fr. Gregory was devastated when Sholom told him he was leaving and going back home. They had become very close over the years and truly loved and respected one another. But Fr. Gregory understood that the time had come and made peace with it.

Back in Israel, Chaim and Anna Nesher had become great-grandparents. Moshe and Tamar's girls married over the years and had children, and Anna had little ones to love. Since Moshe was Avram and Feygl's son, they too became great-grandparents and were even closer to Chaim and Anna than before. Chaim sold the store to his employees who continued to provide him with an income and he decided, in his retirement, to take up painting and enrolled in art school.

Yossie continued to teach Holocaust studies, but in addition, he, without any effort on his part, got involved in the motion picture business. A script writer learned of his story, interviewed him, and wrote a script based on his escape from the Nazis, his Christian upbringing, the Seminary, becoming a priest, and then discovering his Israeli family and returning home. The film was a successful human interest story and was shown at Jewish film festivals all over the world, and Yossie and his wife were asked to appear and talk about his life and the film.

Shimon retired from the government. He organized a society of people who had been confined to the Hotel Polski and asked them to write about their recollections and had a book published that sold quite a few copies. Anna did not participate.

Anna, what about Anna? Time healed the rift between Anna and Chaim. After Sholom, Rena, and the children returned, a family gathering needed not only the dining room but bridge tables for Moshe and Tamar, their girls and their husbands, and the little ones as well as Avram and Feygl. On one such occasion, Yossie and his wife came back from a film festival and told the family that after the film had been shown and he had answered the audiences' questions he was approached by a patron who addressed him as Fr. Feurmann and told him that he was one of his parishioners.

"Frankly, I didn't remember him, but shook my head knowingly and learned that although he was obviously not Jewish, he heard about the film and remembered me and when he learned that I would be there he had to come. It was nice being remembered, but I assured him I was no longer Fr. Feurmann. Just plain Yossie Feurmann."

At which point Sholom spoke up and said, "Here's an old story that I don't know if I told all of you. I think I told Abba. When I was teaching at Capernaum, Fr. Gregory called me in," and turning to Yossie, he went on, "You remember him, don't you Yossie," to which Yossie nodded, with a big smile, "I was told that two agents of US Immigration came to see Fr. Gregory about not only me but Rena, as well, claiming we were in the United States under false pretenses with false names. My last name should have been Hauptmann since he was my father, and using Adler was a crime."

"We never heard that one," said Tamar. "So, what happened?"

"Well Fr. Gregory gave the agents my doctoral dissertation about the Hotel Polski and who Hauptmann was and how the name Adler came about and within a couple of weeks he got a letter from Immigration saying the matter was being dropped."

While Sholom was finishing his story, Tamar's oldest crawled up into Anna's lap and when Sholom finished he looked at Anna and asked, "Who is Hauptmann?"

Giving the little one a hug and a kiss she replied, "Oh, someone I once knew. I don't even remember him anymore. Not very important." And looking him straight in the eye, she said, "You know, you're a little monkey."

THE END

Leon H. Gildin – Author

Leon H. Gildin is an attorney who has represented writers, composers and actors. He has acted as both an attorney and a principal in the development of properties for television and motion pictures. He has also produced both on and off-Broadway.

In the midst of his legal practice Mr. Gildin authored a short story which became a play entitled, ***APPEAR AND SHOW CAUSE***, which opened the season at the Cleveland Playhouse and was awarded the Audelco Award in New York for its off-Broadway production. Mr. Gildin also wrote, ***YOU CAN'T DO BUSINESS (OR MOST ANYTHING ELSE) WITHOUT YIDDISH***, published by Hippocrene Books, New York, which sold out and is still available on Amazon.com.

He has recently published, ***THE POEMS OF H. LEIVICK AND OTHERS – YIDDISH POETRY IN TRANSLATION***, Finishing Line Press, Georgetown, KY.

The first novel of the Trilogy, ***THE POLSKI AFFAIR***, tells of a little known event that took place during the Nazi occupation of Poland at the Hotel Polski in Warsaw following the destruction of the Warsaw ghetto in 1943. The book was awarded the 2010 International Book Award for historical fiction and explores the moral struggle of those who survived and the fortuitous nature of that survival. The balance of the Trilogy continues the story of the survivors and their children and the ghosts that haunted them for the many decades that followed.

Mr. Gildin now resides in Scottsdale, AZ with his wife, Gloria.

CPSIA information can be obtained
at www.ICGtesting.com
Printed in the USA
LVHW03s1737050618
579660LV00010B/731/P